Praise for Minerva Spencer & S.M. LaViolette's THE ACADEMY OF LOVE series:

"[A] pitch perfect Regency .... Readers will be hooked." (THE MUSIC OF LOVE)
★*Publishers Weekly STARRED REVIEW*

"An offbeat story that offers unexpected twists on a familiar setup." (A FIGURE OF LOVE)
Kirkus

"[A] consistently entertaining read." (A FIGURE OF LOVE)
Kirkus

Praise for Minerva Spencer's THE OUTCASTS:

"Minerva Spencer's writing is sophisticated and wickedly witty. Dangerous is a delight from start to finish with swashbuckling action, scorching love scenes, and a coolly arrogant hero to die for. Spencer is my new auto-buy!"
-NYT Bestselling Author **Elizabeth Hoyt**

"Fans of Amanda Quick's early historicals will find much to savor."
★*Booklist STARRED REVIEW*

"Sexy, witty, and fiercely entertaining."
★*Kirkus STARRED REVIEW*

More books by S.M. LaViolette & Minerva Spencer:

THE ACADEMY OF LOVE

The Music of Love
A Figure of Love
A Portrait of Love*
The Language of Love*

THE OUTCASTS

Dangerous
Barbarous
Scandalous

THE REBELS OF THE *TON*

Notorious*
Outrageous*
Infamous*

THE MASQUERADERS

The Footman
The Postilion*
The Bastard*

THE SEDUCERS

Melissa and The Vicar
Joss and The Countess
Hugo and The Maiden*

VICTORIAN DECADENCE

His Harlot
His Valet
His Countess

ANTHOLOGIES:

Bachelors of BondStreet
The Arrangement

*upcoming books

His Countess

S.M. LAVIOLETTE

Crooked
Sixpence
CS
P
Press

Chapter One

London

Gideon pulled almost all the way out, teasing Marissa's tight entrance with the thick head of his cock before slamming into her, hilting himself balls deep, glorying in her wet heat.

Marissa absorbed his savage thrusts while her skilled mouth and tongue worked the beautiful young woman spread out before her.

Gideon loved this arrangement more than any other when it came to bed sport and he'd rarely encountered such accomplished and responsive whores as Marissa and Delia.

So why was it that even with so much female beauty arrayed before him, Gideon couldn't help feeling a trifle . . . bored?

But it would scarcely be gentlemanly to exhibit such ennui while both ladies were laboring so hard to please him, so he resumed his thrusting.

"Lovely, *very* lovely," he murmured, his eyes riveted on the prone woman's face as her body stiffened with exquisite tension that ratcheted her slim form tighter and tighter, until she cried out and shuddered, her narrow hips bucking violently.

Beneath him, Marissa gasped for breath and Gideon smiled as he thought about her jaws and clever tongue and how much both must ache. Well, all part of the ultimate pleasure.

Delia's breasts were heavy and full for her delicate ribcage and they trembled fetchingly while she fought to catch her breath.

Gideon gave her a moment to rest before saying, "Again."

Delia squirmed, her relaxed body tensing at his command. "Oh, please. I can't, Mr. Banks, please, I have nothing left—"

"Shhh," he murmured. "You can, Delia. Come for me just one more time, darling."

Gideon knew he'd been saying something to that effect all night, but her explosive orgasms were turning out to be the best part of this evening. It was his opinion that the only thing in the world *almost* as good as climaxing oneself was watching—or giving—another person an orgasm.

Which reminded him . . .

"How are you doing, Marissa?" He lowered his body, resting his chest on her slick back and then reached beneath her, thumbing her stiff peek with expert flicks. "Such a good, patient girl," he whispered. "Do you need release, sweetheart?"

She whimpered, her sheath tightening around him. "Yes, please, Mr. Banks."

Gideon stroked her toward climax while he pumped. He'd been fucking her for close to an hour and hadn't allowed her to come. The poor thing must have been clinging to the last vestiges of self-control, because she began contracting and shaking before the last word left his mouth.

"That's right," he urged as her cunt contracted hard enough to snap his prick in half.

Gideon took great pleasure in exercising control over his lover's bodies—especially when it came to the granting and withholding of sexual satisfaction. On a normal night he might have made Marissa wait longer, perhaps not allowing her to orgasm at all while he and Delia indulged endlessly.

But he was not feeling like his normal self tonight. Indeed, he'd not felt like himself for quite a while.

Gideon shrugged the annoying thought away and finessed a second, less intense, climax from Marissa. He then used her body's juices to massage her back hole, lightly probing her with his thumb. Should he take her anally—would that give him satisfaction? Release?

His cock experienced a mild twinge of interest at the notion, but not enough to make him bother.

Besides, it was past time to let the women rest, even though it seemed *wrong* to finish the night the way things stood. Namely: without him experiencing even a single orgasm. But, lately, orgasms had

2

become increasingly elusive. He could stay hard for hours—all night—but had difficulty reaching his own pleasure. It had started to become ...boring.

"Mr. Banks? Is aught amiss, sir?"

Gideon realized he'd stopped moving. Delia was staring up at him, her eyes shadowed with concern and something else—exhaustion, he supposed.

His cock, still inside Marissa, began to soften.

She twisted her head to look at him. "Sir? Did I do something wrong?"

Gideon pulled out of her without answering and stepped from the bed, his knees aching and popping. He'd paid for the women in advance—taking them for the entire evening—so he didn't need to engage in the tiresome business of post-coital commerce.

"I'm done, you may leave," he said over his shoulder as he strode naked and flaccid toward his bath chamber and shut the door behind him.

Once he was alone inside the room, he sagged against the door and closed his eyes.

"Bloody *hell*." He was tired and his body felt so very, very heavy. When was the last time he'd slept? Why couldn't he simply come home after a day of work, eat a meal, and go to sleep in his own bed? By himself?

Yes, that was what he wanted: to crawl into his bed and sleep for days. Not the bed in the room he'd just left, but the narrow single bed that only Gideon ever used, the one in the small, plain room connected to the *other* side of this bathing chamber. Even sleeping through one bloody night would be good.

Unfortunately, that wasn't possible now.

It was almost morning and he had a meeting with his business partners in less than three hours.

Why did he seem to be getting worse with every day that passed? His business partners—Fanshawe, Chatham, and Smith—were men who never caviled to pursue their sexual needs, but even they looked askance at his excesses. Increasingly they treated him as if he were sex-crazed and insane when it came to his excessive whoring, not to

3

mention the number of mistresses he kept mounted—three at the moment.

Christ.

He'd not even fucked two of the women for well over a month.

What the hell was wrong with him?

Gideon groaned at the question—one he couldn't answer—and then slid down the door until his arse hit the cold marble floor. He hugged his knees to his chest and dropped his heavy head onto his arms and closed his eyes.

God, he was so bloody, bloody tired.

Taunton, England

"I don't understand? How can this be?" Alys demanded, even as a part of her brain reminded her that this was the third time she'd said those exact same words.

"I'm terribly sorry, my lady, I know it's a shock."

Alys could only stare at Beekman, her dead husband's solicitor. Well, he was the new earl's solicitor now, she supposed.

"Are you certain he is the one?" she asked, and then grimaced at her own stupidity. Of course he was certain: after all, the search had gone on for over a year.

"Yes, my lady, quite certain." Beekman hesitated and then said, "There *is* something to be said for Gideon Banks: he is exceedingly wealthy." Beekman's cheeks and even the tips of his ears turned a cherry red.

Alys knew what the older man meant; Alys's dead husband had left matters at Foxrun—his family's ancestral estate—in dire condition. It was a miracle that Alys still had a roof over her head after what Sebastian had done to the once majestic country home.

Although the Taunton Earldom wasn't the only destitute house in Britain, Alys's departed husband, the fifth Earl—had done more than most to run through what little rents the much-depleted estate produced.

"I don't understand the nature of Mr. Banks's, er, I mean the new earl's, family connection—would you mind explaining it to me?" Alys asked, as if she might be able to expose some flaw in what had,

4

undoubtedly, been a thorough and expensive examination of the Taunton lineage.

"Of course, my lady. The Sixth Earl is the only grandson of your late husband's grandfather's youngest brother, Geoffrey Dornan. I'm afraid all connection was severed two generations ago, immediately upon his marriage to a woman in the, er, theatrical field."

Alys bit back a groan.

"The issue of *that* union was one son, a Mr. Alexander Dornan, who married Judith Banks, the daughter of a rather successful tailor—"

"Good Lord—a tailor?" The man was no better than a servant!

Mr. Beekman continued. "The couple had two sons: Lloyd and Gideon. Their mother died when Gideon was six years of age and the boys' father—never a favorite with Mr. Banks, his father-in-law—disappeared with his two sons. It wasn't until Gideon was eleven that his grandfather was able to locate him in an orphanage in East London."

Alys shook her head "Why would a father rather his sons go to an orphanage than a grandparent?"

Beekman looked equally perplexed. "It seems Mr. Dornan was a rather, er, spiteful and selfish man. In any case, the elder brother had died by then of some sort of fever. I'm afraid I don't know the details. It seems young Gideon was a precocious child and his grandfather paid to send him to the Colchester Royal Grammar School, a small but highly respected establishment. A year or so after his grandfather took him in, Gideon took Banks as his surname, which is why he was so hard to find. Gideon took top honors at Colchester and won a place at Wadham College."

Alys sat up. Well, this was heartening.

"He was ejected from Oxford only three months after entering."

"For what?" she forced herself to ask.

He cleared his throat, his eyes on his hands rather than Alys. "For matters of, er, *lrshrshy.*"

"I'm sorry, I didn't catch that last bit?"

Beekman's prominent Adam's apple bobbed. "That would be lechery, my lady."

She briefly closed her eyes and shook her head.

"I daresay he has grown out of such youthful frolics, my lady. After all, that was when he was two years shy of twenty and he is now eight-and-thirty."

"He might be better," she said, "Or he might be a good deal worse."

Mr. Beekman had nothing to say to that.

"Is he married?"

"No, my lady."

Alys couldn't decide whether that was good or bad. On the one hand, a wife might be able to hold the man in check. On the other, a wife might be a vulgar mushroom who'd have charge of the house over which Alys was long accustomed to being mistress. Of course *that* would soon change, no matter what his marital status.

"I know you'd not planned to go up to London this Season, my lady. But with this new development, you might wish to consider it. I'm meeting with Mr. Banks next week and anticipate I'll send out the request to the Lord Chancellor not long after. I don't see there being an issue with proving his provenance and I daresay he'll have his hands full once he receives his writ for the upcoming session." He sighed. "That's all to say that I'm not sure when he will have time to make a trip to Foxrun."

Alys considered Beekman's suggestion without dismissing it out of hand. Although she was out of mourning, she certainly hadn't intended to go to Town—ever.

Not only was her jointure barely enough to afford her much entertainment, but the days when she might have enjoyed a London Season were long past. Besides, she knew absolutely no one in London. Her brother, the Marquess of Bolt, was a deeply religious man who only went for his duties in Lords, leaving his wife and ever-increasing brood in the country.

"It pains me to recommend such a thing," Beekman began, and then stopped when she met his embarrassed gaze.

Alys sighed. "Yes, I know what you are trying, very subtly, to say: without the new earl's kindness, I shall be without a roof over my head."

"Er, well, not quite, perhaps. But certainly you could be in an uncomfortable position."

That was understating matters. She could go live with her brother and his loathsome wife—which would be the equivalent of entering a nunnery but with maiden aunt duties regarding the children—or she could find some other distant relative and beg for a menial position. She supposed most women in her position would consider re-marrying the only true choice, but after eight years of tolerating Sebastian's whims and follies, she had no intention of submitting to such humiliation again. At least the first two options did not include giving a man legal power over her person.

"There is your life estate in the Dower House, of course, but in its current state it is ... well ...."

Again, she knew what he was trying to say. "I understand, Mr. Beekman—the new earl is legally compelled to allow me to live there, but he has no duty to make the house habitable."

It wasn't a question, but he nodded.

"So you recommend I go to London to petition the new earl?"

"I think it cannot hurt, my lady. Also, once he learns of his new position there will be many calls on his—well, on his generosity. It would be better for you to approach him as soon after he learns of his new position as possible."

Alys smiled. "Ah, you want me to take him by ambush."

Mr. Beekman's pale face darkened and Alys felt a twinge of shame for teasing him; he was only trying to help her.

"I take your meaning, sir, and agree. Tell me, when are you planning to inform him of his change in status?"

"Next week. I was only waiting on one more document, and I found that in the family records here."

Yes, that was why he'd come—at least his official reason—to secure whatever was needed to confirm the new earl. Unofficially, he'd come because he'd always been kind to her.

Alys inhaled deeply, and then let her breath out slowly. So, she would have to go on bended knee to the cit who now controlled the house she'd called her own for almost a decade. Life, it appeared, would continue being an exercise in humiliation.

"I shall do what I can to make him see the wisdom of repairing the Dower House, my lady. And I shall also emphasize his responsibility to provide a safe haven for his predecessor's countess. I daresay he will not make any immediate plans to commence repairs on his rural properties, but a word from you might cause him to make the Dower property a priority."

Alys smiled again, even though she didn't feel like it. "Thank you—I am not unaware of your efforts on my behalf."

His expression became one of discomfort. "I only wish I could do more." His jaw worked, as if he might say something, but, instead, he pressed his lips together.

"Very well," she said, "I suppose I shall begin packing for London."

Chapter Two

Gideon knew laughter was not the correct response, but he couldn't help himself. "An earl?" he repeated. "I'm a fucking *earl?*"

The chap across from him, Gideon thought his name was Beakham or some such, flinched at his vulgar response. Well, too bloody bad. He'd better get used to the fact that Lord Gideon Banks, the new Earl of Taunton, did and said whatever the hell he pleased.

"Yes, my lord. The Sixth Earl of Taunton."

"Good God," he muttered. "Me, Gideon Banks—a bloody earl."

The other man cleared his throat.

"Why are you looking at me like that?" Gideon demanded.

"I wanted to apprise you of the fact that the family name is actually Dornan."

Gideon shrugged. "You can call me Marie Bloody Antoinette if you like, but for the purposes of my *significant* business interests I will remain Gideon Banks."

The solicitor swallowed and nodded, his gaze shifting nervously.

Good, Gideon liked to keep his subordinates on their toes. Hell, he liked keeping *everyone* he dealt with on his or her toes. Well, that wasn't quite true; he actually enjoyed several other positions a great deal more.

The older man cleared his throat. "When it comes to your new duties, if you need assistance with, er, issues of deportment or —"

"I don't need assistance with a damned thing and I'm plenty familiar with how nobs *deport* themselves."

Gideon had briefly rubbed shoulders with titled toffs at Oxford. Indeed, he'd quite liked several of them, until his arse had been tossed out for fucking the bagwig's daughter. It wasn't that he didn't *deserve* getting tossed out because he most certainly *had* fucked her. But he'd been fucking her along with two others—a lord this and an honorable that—neither of whom had received so much as a slap on their delicate wrists for shoving their cocks into the little tart.

He shrugged off the ancient gripe; that was the way of the world.

Gideon saw the other man was waiting, his eyes assessing him in a way that spoke as loudly as words. He was thinking, Gideon suspected, that the new earl *looked* like a lord—or at least he greatly resembled the storybook princes one often saw in picture books.

Gideon *did* look like those princes; fair-haired, blue-eyed, tall, and well formed, but he knew that he fairly reeked of dissipation. Still, that was yet another characteristic so many aristocrats possessed.

"So," Gideon said, leaning back in his chair and resting his expensively booted ankle on his knee. "What moldering pile did I inherit along with this fancy new moniker, Mr., er, what was your name again?"

"William Beekman, my lord. I was his lordship's man of business as were my father and grandfather."

"His lordship must have had a lot of business to need all three of you."

Beekman looked pained. "I meant—"

Gideon grinned. "I know what you meant Beeky—may I call you Beeky? You meant that it is a tradition of longstanding in your family to serve the Earls of Taunton. I'm all for tradition, old thing. And I must say I am honored to now have you serving *this* earl. So, Beeky," he said briskly, "What else have you got in that leather satchel you keep fondling?"

The other man's entire body—perhaps even his brushy eyebrows—were stiff with mortification as he opened his satchel. Gideon knew he shouldn't tease the poor old fellow—he'd seen immediately that old Beeky had no sense of humor—but the man had better know sooner, rather than later, what his new lordship was like. And if he didn't like Gideon's irreverent humor he could bugger off and find another master to serve.

"There are two properties, my lord. The house on Berkeley Square and the family seat, Foxrun, in Somerset." He extracted two thick portfolio's and set them on Gideon's immense ebony desk, exactly where Gideon had fucked his chambermaid—or at least the woman he *paid* to pretend to be a chambermaid—not ten minutes before Beeky's visit. His lips twitched at the thought of what the staid man-of-business would say to know his new employer's ballocks had recently rested just where his hand lay?

"—and I'm afraid the farms have not produced to capacity since well before his lordship's time." He was looking at Gideon and Gideon realized he must have missed the man's maunderings while he'd been amusing himself.

Gideon pulled the heavy stacks of paper toward him, opening the one on top and flicking pages quickly.

"I daresay your lordship will require some time to—"

Gideon kept turning pages, ignoring Beeky's wittering. Only his closest associates knew he was able to absorb information this fast and faster from a page. It was, he supposed, a valuable skill although he'd long ago stopped feeling any pride in his ability. He didn't need to look through many pages to see the state of affairs. Roof leaks, foundation cracks, rotten wood, some sort of disgusting house-eating beetle—Gideon shivered at that—and myriad other disasters awaited him, or, more likely, *his money,* at Berkeley Square. He closed the folder and slid it aside to look at the one beneath.

"I took the liberty of putting the information for the Dower House on the top of the file as Lady Taunton is—"

Gideon's head whipped up. "Lady Taunton?" He smirked. "Did I inherit a wife along with these two decaying piles? How convenient."

Beeky's already red face reddened even more and he sat up as if somebody had just jammed a barge pole up his arse. "Lady Alys Taunton is your predecessor's widow, my lord."

Gideon gave the older man a smile he hoped was soothing. "There, there—no need to fly into a pucker, Beeky. I'm afraid you'll need to get used to my sense of humor—*if* you wish to work for me. Cit though I might be, I gathered her ladyship was likely the last earl's wife or mother. So," he said, flicking through a few more pages. "She gets to live out the rest of her days on the estate, does she? And I'm to hose and house her?"

"Not at all, my lord. Lady Taunton has her own jointure. It is merely the matter of the Dower House that requires your attention."

Gideon's eyebrows descended. "Did you say *requires?*"

11

Beeky recoiled. "I'm sorry, my lord. Perhaps that was not the correct word."

"Perhaps not," Gideon agreed, looking at the few documents pertaining to the ancient cottage. Yes, it was in even worse condition than the country and London houses.

"At my urging Lady Taunton has come to London. She arrived yesterday, my lord, and is staying at the house on Berkeley Square."

Gideon looked up at that. "I see," he said, sitting back in his oversized leather chair, his eyes narrowing. "She is staying in *my* house. And this is something she does every year?"

Beeky swallowed hard enough to crack a walnut. "Er, not in general, my lord. The last earl was in the habit of spending the Season here—certainly while the session was in—but her ladyship spent most of her time at Foxrun."

"I see," he said again, but softer this time. So, she'd come to town to beg—or demand, more likely—and had commenced her begging/demanding by commandeering his bloody house.

"I assured her ladyship you would not begrudge her the use of Taunton House while she was in town."

Gideon frowned. If the house was his, then it was his—wasn't it? He didn't appreciate people making free with his possessions; he never had. No doubt that came from not actually *having* anything for the first twelve years of his life, but his attitude hadn't changed now that he was swimming in lard. What was his, was his.

"If we are to get on, Mr. Beekman," Gideon paused, allowing his changed tone to sink in—allowing the other man to understand there was the jolly, friendly earl, and there was *this* earl. "You'd better consult me in the future before making free with my belongings—the same goes for my new relative. Are we clear, sir?"

Beekman nodded vigorously. "Of course, my lord. I did not mean to make free. Indeed, Lady Taunton tried to demur, but I convinced her it would not be amiss. This once. So *I* am the one you should blame for taking such liberties."

Gideon let him swing on his gibbet for a long moment before grinning. "*Of course* it's fine, Beeky. I'm quite looking forward to meeting my new relative—how *are* we related? Some sort of cousin-in-law, twice-removed, and so forth?"

"Er, not quite."

Gideon shrugged and gave a dismissive wave. "Well, I shall call her cousin to make life easier."

"Of course, sir."

Gideon examined the man. Beeky was not nearly so superior as he'd been when he'd entered the room. That was good. People tended to believe Gideon's light-hearted, casual attitude indicated a lack of seriousness or intelligence. But most people—especially someone like Beeky, a man who was essentially his servant—learned to extend the proper respect sooner rather than later.

Was Gideon prickly about receiving respect? Perhaps, but then he'd earned the right to be prickly. He'd gone from a despised son of a drunken, ignorant, over-proud gambler to something lower than a rent boy, to one of the wealthiest men in Britain. So yes, he could be as prickly as he liked.

"Lady Taunton is otherwise occupied today, I take it?"

Beeky blinked. "My lord?"

"I was just wondering why *she* is not here to advocate on her own behalf."

Beeky's horrified expression was priceless. "But she is a *lady,* er, my lord. Ladies do not call upon gentlemen they've not been introduced to—not even, er, cousins."

"Is that so?" Gideon asked, keeping his tone mild. "I did not know that. I daresay there are many such, er, rules of gentlemanly behavior I don't know. Luckily I shall have you to guide me through those treacherous shoals."

Beeky met Gideon's hard smile and looked as if he might be ill. "I never meant to imply—"

"Tell me, when *should* I call upon a lady?"

"Any time, my lord. I'm sure her ladyship would be pleased to receive you any time."

"In my house."

"Er, yes, sir. In your house."

Gideon was suddenly tired of baiting such easy prey. "Tell her I shall be around tomorrow—two-ish if that suits. Now," he said, briskly. "You may leave this paperwork here. I shall summon you later in the week once I've gone through it. Go ahead and do whatever it is you need to do to secure my seat in Lords." He grinned at the thought of telling his partners *this* particular little gem. "Let me know if there is any trouble or anything I can do to facilitate—well, whatever."

"I don't anticipate any trouble."

"Excellent, that pleases me." Gideon leaned across his desk, the abrupt movement causing the other man to flinch. "You please me, Beeky. If you continue to do so, I daresay we shall get on swimmingly. Now, you may go."

Beeky shot to his feet. "Very good, my lord. Thank you, my lord. Er, I look forward to serving you."

"I look forward to *being* served, Beeky." Gideon then turned to the schematic he'd been drafting before the solicitor arrived, his action clearly signifying dismissal.

But as soon as the door closed Gideon sat back, his lips curving slowly into a grin.

"Great, bloody hell," he whispered, his heart pounding. "I'm a fucking earl."

❤

Alys had only been in town three days and had already learned enough about the new head of the family to make her want to run screaming. Unfortunately, she had nowhere to run *to,* at least nowhere that Lord Taunton didn't own.

The second day after her arrival she'd received her first ever morning call. You could have knocked her down with a feather when she read the card Bingle brought to her: Lady Amelia St. James, the sister of Alys's brother's wife. Two more different women, Alys could hardly imagine.

"I know you've not put up the knocker and we've never actually *met*," Lady Amelia said when Alys greeted her and the two friends who'd accompanied her. "But we are family, after all."

"I'm very pleased you called," Alys told her, not sure if that was really true as she took in the *extremely* stylish woman and her equally stylish friends. But what else could she do but welcome them?

While her sister-in-law was a plump, colorless, and excessively devout woman whom her brother kept constantly pregnant, Lady Amelia was like a brightly plumed bird. A *red* bird, with matching red lips. Alys didn't think she'd ever seen a woman wearing face paint before.

Alys had barely sat down with the women when Amelia made it clear why they'd come. She laid a red kid gloved hand over Alys's. "We've just heard, my dear."

Alys frowned, wondering how Lady Amelia could have missed word of Sebastian's death for over a year. But then it occurred to her. "Oh, you mean about the new earl."

"My *dear, darling* Lady Taunton!" Lady Amelia had a laugh rather like a peacock's screech and Alys jumped. "He is simply a *savage*."

"And an exceedingly gorgeous savage at that," Mrs. Jane Norbert-Simpson told Alys as they sipped weak, almost cold tea in the drafty, moldy-smelling sitting room: the best of the four sitting rooms the house had to offer.

"He is a part of the *Bohemian* set— and very much aware of his attractions," Lady Amelia added.

"I know Letitia Fullerton made a fool out of herself over him," Mrs. Norbert-Simpson said, causing the other two women to titter.

"Oh, yes, indeed." Lady Amelia leaned forward, her expression avid. "I understand she presented poor old Henry with a blond-haired, blue-eyed daughter."

All three women cackled, bringing to mind Shakespeare's infamous trio of witches.

"She tried to end it all," Amelia said in a whisper that was actually louder than her normal, ringing, tone.

"This poor woman tried to *kill* herself?" Alys asked, appalled when all three of her guests snickered.

"Mmm hmmm. She'd started showing up on Gideon's doorstep, begging him to take her after Fullerton filed for divorce."

Alys swallowed hard. "And G—Lord Taunton, did *nothing?*"

"Oh, he did plenty—just not with *her*," Delphine Moreau, the third woman said.

"I understand he keeps *prostitutes* at his house, posing as servants," Amelia hissed like a giant, red-lipped snake.

"Not only that, but he also keeps *three* mistresses," Mrs. Moreau added.

The women spent several minutes sharing speculations while Alys's head whirled with thoughts of the new Earl of Taunton. So, Gideon Banks—or Dornan, rather—was the sort of man to drive women to kill themselves?

Alys had often thought of killing Sebastian, but never herself.

"Mr. Norbert-Simpson says Gideon is *obscenely* wealthy," Mrs. Norbert-Simpson said nibbling the one biscuit she'd taken, making a moue of distaste, and setting it delicately back down on her plate.

"Yes, I'd heard that. He's part of some group of cits who've made great heaping piles of money. I believe one of the men is Edward Fanshawe." Amelia clucked her tongue. "Poor Blandon's daughter."

"Fanshawe," Alys murmured. Even in faraway Somerset people knew of Catherine Fanshawe and her notorious divorce, which her husband had sought on the grounds of marital infidelity, but which had also left Lady Catherine—the daughter of the Marquess of Blandon— an extremely wealthy woman. There were tales of debauchery and impropriety, but Alys had never credited them. Now, however . . ..

"Fanshawe married Natalie Hartwicke not long ago," Delphine Moreau said.

The other two women chuckled.

"Yes, but the Hartwicke creature had Fanshawe all along, didn't she?" Amelia retorted.

Alys refused to ask what they were talking about.

Indeed, she'd turned the conversation away from gossip after that and the women had soon left. It had been clear they'd only come for one purpose: to spread tales about the new earl.

Not long after Lady Amelia's call there had been the visit from Beekman, warning Alys that his lordship would pay a call on her today.

"The new earl is," Beekman's brow furrowed as he hunted for some word. "Well, he is unusual. It is best not to, er, underestimate him. Although he is essentially a product of the stews, he is not, by any means, unintelligent."

So, that was what Alys was waiting for: a gorgeous cunning whoremonger.

Alys glanced around the grim sitting room as she awaited his arrival, wondering what he would make of his new inheritance. Wondering what he would make of *her*. She cut a quick glance at herself in the age-

16

spotted mirror that hung across from her. Her reflection showed her what she already knew: a woman past her prime. At almost twenty-six she was practically in her dotage and would certainly be viewed as such by a man who no doubt considered himself a connoisseur of women.

Three mistresses? *Three* mistresses!

Fortunately Sebastian, a man who'd been a profligate spender, had never kept a mistress—or not as far as Alys knew. Not that she'd ever looked too closely. Alys had always been perfectly satisfied that Sebastian was leaving her alone. In truth, she hadn't cared how many women he'd gone to after she'd learned the truth about him: that his charm was but a thin veneer over his selfish, debauched, drunken core.

Alys wasn't sure which of them had been stupider: her foolish, romantic, sixteen year-old self, who'd been so impressed by a handsome face and charming manner, or Sebastian, so lazy that he'd married Alys for her rather middling dowry when he should have been on the hunt for one of these American heiresses that seemed to be falling from the trees like overripe fruit.

Because the truth—as she'd learned after their marriage—was that only a fortune could save poor Foxrun.

There was a soft knock and Alys looked up. The door opened and Bingle stood on the threshold, his eyes a bit wild. "Lord Taunton to see you, my lady."

"Thank you, Bingle. Please show h—"

An angel appeared beside the staid old butler and Alys gawked. Good Lord! Had Amelia and the other women merely said he was *gorgeous*? He was . . . heavenly.

"My lady, thank you so much for receiving me today." Even his voice—while not of her class—was a beautiful and only lightly accented baritone. He strode toward her with the grace of a cat, his coat and trousers were closely tailored—immodestly so, in Alys's limited experience—and displayed his broad shouldered and narrow-hipped physique to stunning advantage.

"It's my pleasure, my lord. I was just about to order tea, would you care for some?" she asked as he bowed over her hand.

His full, dark pink lips curved in a smile that was so wicked her body heated. "I should *adore* some tea."

17

Alys nodded to the hovering Bingle, who shut the door while wearing an openly worried frown.

"I do hope you'll forgive me for coming up to London without your invitation, my lord, but I hoped to meet you before the Season went into full roar."

His heavy lids lowered over eyes that were celestial blue, in keeping with his heavenly appearance. The expression in those eyes, however, was the farthest thing from angelic that she could imagine.

"I'm so pleased you took the time and made the effort, my lady." He glanced around the room with a slight curl of his lip. "I feel I should offer an apology for the state of my hospitality." His sneer shifted into a grin. "Although I suppose I can hardly be held responsible as you arrived before I could do much to make any changes."

His gentle admonishment was enough to leave Alys in no doubt as to whether his beautiful mouth held fangs.

She felt her neck and face heat. "I shall not trespass long upon your hospitality," she said stiffly.

He chuckled. "Oh do forgive me if I gave you the impression you were not welcome. I daresay I shan't commence repairs until I've had time to thoroughly investigate the state of affairs here. So you shan't be in anyone's way."

Alys could see by the amused twinkle in his eyes that he knew exactly how offensive he was being. What a loathsome, odious, mushroom.

"I have no desire to remain in London," she said truthfully. "I came regarding my imminent occupation of the Dower House."

"Yes, I seem to recall reading that. In rather a bad way, is it?"

"Yes, my lord. It was last occupied in my husband's grandfather's lifetime by one of his sisters, a spinster who remained there until her death."

"And this is what you propose to do?"

Alys blinked. "I beg your pardon?"

"You wish to remain in this cottage until *your* death?"

Alys could scarcely believe the man. "That is my right, my lord."

He held up both hands, the smirky smile she was already coming to dislike curving his full, shapely lips. "Please, I meant no offence; I'm merely concerned with your future."

A disbelieving laugh slipped out of her before she could check it. "Oh? How kind of you."

He appeared not to notice her sarcasm and smiled. "You're welcome, my lady. You see, I count your care as one of the duties I've inherited. Think of me as standing in the way of brother to you—" he paused at her unladylike snort. "I can see that notion amuses you."

It actually revolted her, but that would be impolitic and unwise to point out.

"Or perhaps you prefer to think of me as a . . . cousin?" he said when she didn't respond.

Alys didn't want to think about him *at all*, but she had little choice. "A cousin? Yes, well, that is stretching matters, but is not an entirely unbelievable fiction."

"I'm so glad we can agree on something." His lips seemed to thin slightly and Alys realized she needed to be very, very careful with this man.

"In any event," he continued. "What I was trying to say—not very successfully, it appears—is that you may inhabit the house—Foxrun, is it?—for as long as you wish. I will doubtless begin evaluating the properties for repairs at some point, but my initial examination gives me reason to believe the tenant dwellings are what require my immediate attention."

Alys's eyebrows lifted.

"I can see that such a practical assessment surprises you."

She opened her mouth to deny it—to say what surprised her was that a man like *him* would even consider such mundane matters—but he answered his own question.

"I'm shocked at the neglect these people—now my dependents—have suffered, my lady. I'm determined to improve as many of their, er, hovels as possible before the beginning of winter."

Alys had to bite her tongue. She agreed with him entirely, but she couldn't help feeling as if he were blaming *her* for the wretched state of affairs at Foxrun.

The door opened and Bingle himself arrived with the tea.

19

"Thank you, Bingle," she said after he set the tray down on the table.

Alys felt the weight of Lord Taunton's eyes on her as she prepared the tea, her movements clumsy and stilted. That was, she suspected, his intention.

"How do you take it, my lord?"

When he didn't immediately answer, she looked up to find him wearing that unsettling smile. "Any way I can get it, my lady."

Alys stared, and he laughed.

"Black and strong," he amended.

The glint in his sky-blue eyes made her shiver. It would be good, she decided, to take herself back to Foxrun—to *run* back to Somerset—at the earliest opportunity.

— ❤ —

Gideon shifted on the luxurious leather of his carriage seat as he considered the woman he'd just left behind. Lord, what a superior bitch! For all that she'd been sitting in *his* bloody house—uninvited, by the way—she'd certainly had no problem looking at him as if he were a pile of shit she'd stepped in.

So, this was his predecessor's wife? Gideon had met her type times beyond counting when he'd worked as a bank clerk for three dreadful years. Well, now he didn't have to lick her slippers or take whatever abuse she felt like dishing out. Not that he'd ever been particularly good about toad-eating those who'd attempted to show him his place. His place? Ha! His place was that bloody falling down pile she'd been resting her precious arse in without his permission. Gideon smirked as he recalled her stunned reaction to his own brand of haughtiness.

Gideon considered himself an expert in two areas of life: machinery and sex. And the prissy countess had found him about as sexually arousing as a piece of agricultural equipment. That, in addition to her cool, condemning stare, had pushed him toward incivility faster than he would have liked. But she'd asked for it, and he'd given her what she feared: the boorish behavior of an insufferable cit. So at least now she had good reason to loathe him.

Gideon was accustomed to women staring at him, but not with such open condemnation. Still, as much as she'd disliked him he'd still felt her eyes roaming his toggery: a gray suit that fit like a second skin, the fabric tight over his chest, shoulders, and crotch—all magnificent parts of his body he enjoyed putting on display.

For all that she'd frowned as if she'd just eaten something unspeakably sour, Gideon found her quite pleasant looking. Perhaps a bit thin by his standards, but he'd liked her tiny little waist and tightly corseted bosom. Yes, at first appearance Lady Taunton had exactly what appealed to him: a thick, glossy auburn rope of hair she'd coiled around her head like a crown and eyes the color of coal dust ringed with an unexpected white gold.

Her mouth was overlarge for her heart-shaped face and her plump lips were just the sort he liked to kiss and fuck. That upper lip—a true bow-shape—paired with a plump little pillow of a lower lip was pouting and wicked. With her rather adorable snub nose—and *without* her sour expression—she was a sensual beauty with a sweet body that even her hideous mourning dress could not hide.

And that was another thing—why was she still in mourning? Beeky said the last earl died over a year ago? Had she been so in love with her dead husband that she would sequester herself in her Dower House and dry up?

Gideon hadn't met many aristocrats since leaving Oxford, although he'd fucked plenty of their wives: bored women who gave money away to artists and *causes* and looked for something or somebody to make their tedious existences worthwhile.

He felt a self-mocking smile twist his lips at the thought—those women weren't really so different from Gideon in that regard.

Although he hadn't known Taunton, he'd seen the man at a debauch a few years ago. It was one of those Roman bacchanals so many bored peeresses like to throw. The parties were masked—or at least they started off that way—so the women could invite riffraff like Gideon without their husbands finding out.

He'd gone to the bash with his business partner, Smith—back when Smith was still fun. Gideon had found the party a bit flat and had gone looking for Smith after a few hours. He'd found him balls-deep in the Earl of Taunton's arse.

The earl had looked terrified at being caught, but Smith being Smith—which was to say utterly unpredictable and out of control—had smirked, not pausing his savage pumping for even a second while he invited Gideon to join them and avail himself of the earl's mouth.

Gideon had demurred. Not because he had anything against fucking men—he rather enjoyed it, in fact—but the pale, bloated Taunton had not appealed to him.

So, that had been his only meeting with Taunton.

Gideon knew that having sex with other men didn't mean a man didn't also enjoy women. So he supposed it was possible that Taunton had gone home to his castle in the country from time to time and swived his prim little wife silly.

But something in the woman's face and posture made him doubt that. No, if he'd ever seen a woman who needed a proper fucking, it was the Countess of Taunton.

Not that he would be the one supplying her with that service—as much as he wouldn't mind. But even if she didn't already loathe him, it was unlikely they'd see each other again for a long, long while. In fact, he'd wager a hundred pounds on her going back to Somerset before the month was out, once she realized he wasn't going to pour money into the Berkeley Square house just for her comfort.

He smirked. No doubt she'd hoped for a town respite from tatty old Foxrun.

Foxrun. Good God, what a stupid name. Perhaps he'd change it to something less idiotic. Gideon's Folly? He snorted.

In any case, he'd not leave the pretty young countess cold and homeless. Gideon wasn't a complete arse, just a partial one. He'd make sure enough money was spent on Foxrun to keep the place from falling down around her ears, but he certainly wouldn't make any effort to fix up her little widow's roost until he'd seen to more important matters.

He'd not been taunting her when he'd said he'd repair or rebuild or replace—whatever the hell was necessary—to get the farms back in working order. It wasn't that he believed they'd ever earn enough to pay for the bloody place, but it was a matter of pride that his farmers not live in squalor.

But all that was something he could think about some other time; Gideon found he was throbbing for some feminine company. He rapped on the roof of his carriage and the panel opened swiftly.

"Yes, my lord?"

Gideon couldn't help grinning at the title. Would he ever get accustomed to hearing it without getting an erection?

"I've changed my mind about going to Number 14," the club he owned with his partners, and where he'd planned to do some boasting. "Take me to Miss Victoria's."

"Yes, my lord." The panel slid shut and Gideon adjusted his cock, which had become half hard not at his title, but at the thought of Victoria.

She was his newest mistress and he'd not paid a call on her in weeks. But something about the haughty Lady Taunton suddenly made him want the nubile brunette fiercely.

He didn't know why that was, because the two women looked nothing like each other—aside from them both being dark haired. While the countess barely came up to his shoulder Victoria was a strapping wench not much shorter than Gideon.

And unlike Lady Taunton's dainty curves, Victoria was voluptuous. Lastly, Victoria was extremely submissive—a characteristic he demanded from his women—while Lady Taunton had silently blazed and chaffed at his pointed reminders of her dependence on him.

Gideon was smirking at the memory of his countess-baiting when he remembered that his young, long-legged mistress wouldn't know she now belonged to an earl. He grinned; she'd be tickled.

At barely twenty she was the youngest and most recent of the three women he maintained. He'd all but given up on finding another mistress when he'd seen her at the Birch Palace—a whorehouse that catered to peculiar tastes, most of which Gideon possessed.

If you liked to whip or be whipped or watch or be watched—it didn't matter, you could find whatever you desired and likely discover some entirely new vice at the Birch Palace.

Although Gideon had to admit he was finding it increasingly challenging to come up with a sexual act that he'd not already tried at least once. He experienced an odd pang at the thought that life no longer held the limitless possibilities it once had.

Thinking about the Birch Palace inevitably made him think of his partner, Edward Fanshawe, the only man Gideon knew who even came close to being as big a whoremonger as himself. But even Edward had slowed down now that he'd married. Not because his wife made him slow down. No, indeed. The new Mrs. Fanshawe—an up and coming painter—was a woman who embraced her husband's tastes and desires as much, if not more, than he did.

Indeed, the last time Gideon had seen Nora had been at the Birch Palace, where Edward had—surprisingly—invited him to participate in his birthday gift to Nora.

Gideon stiffened—in the best way—at the memory of that evening. The new Mrs. Fanshawe was no great beauty but she had a potent sexuality and a submissive nature that made Gideon hard just looking at her—and that was with her clothing on.

It turned out that Nora's fantasy—being tandem fucked by two men in public—had, ultimately, been Gideon's responsibility because he'd been the one who'd taken Edward to a favorite brothel of his in Glasgow when the two men had last been there on business.

It had been plain to see how much the public fucking had aroused Edward that first night so Gideon hadn't been surprised when Edward had gone back the next night, and the next.

But it hadn't been until Edward invited Gideon to the Birch Palace that he'd learned what *else* Edward had liked so much in Glasgow.

Gideon still couldn't decide what stunned him more: that Edward had invited Gideon to fuck his wife while he watched—and *God* had *that* been divine—or that Edward had had his cock pierced in Glasgow.

Gideon shivered just thinking of how painful such a thing must be. Still, he had to admit he admired the look of the big silver bar in Edward's thick crown. He also suspected it offered superlative stimulation for one's lover. It was tempting to visualize his own, more than respectable, prick sporting similar jewelry, but he would never be able to do it, not even if he had a woman like Nora to use it on.

Gideon spread his thighs on the soft leather seat, gently massaging his balls as he thought about that night. He'd not wanted to ask Edward why he'd chosen Gideon to share in such an erotic intimacy, but he'd been unable to resist.

Edward had shrugged, but his eyes had been hard and jealous. "Nora wants you." His mouth had twitched into a grudging smile that had never reached his eyes. "She says you're pretty."

For the first time in decades, Gideon had blushed. To tell the truth, he found Nora Fanshawe a bit unnerving with her confident sexuality and utter devotion to Edward's pleasure. But he'd been as flattered as hell that she'd chosen Gideon.

"We're here, my lord."

Gideon had been stroking himself without considering the results and the front of his trousers were damp and wrinkled. He grinned as he hopped out of the carriage. His pants would soon be puddled on Victoria's bedchamber floor, so it hardly mattered what a mess they were.

Gideon was halfway up the steps of her smart townhouse when the front door opened and Gordon Loring, the husband half of the couple he'd hired for Victoria's comfort, stood in the entryway.

"Mr. Banks," he said, his eyes flickering nervously.

"What is it?" Gideon demanded, suspicion blooming in his chest. "Is she gone out?"

"Er, no, sir, not gone. That is, well, she has company."

Gideon pushed past him and took the stairs two at a time. He heard them before he saw them because Victoria hadn't bothered to close the door to her—*no*—*their* bedchamber.

"Oh, yes, please! Harder, Harold! Harder!"

Gideon crossed his arms over his chest and leaned against the doorframe as he watched a naked hairy arse pumping into his soon to be ex-mistress. The man—Harold, apparently—still wore his shoes and trousers. Hell, he still wore his coat. Only his hat and cane lay over a chair beside the door.

His thrusts were jerky and artless and it was clear to Gideon he was fucking for his own release rather than his lover's pleasure. Victoria was carrying on in a theatrical manner and making—Gideon realized with some irritation—the same noises she made when *he* was plowing her.

Well, there was a humbling thought for you.

It was less than a minute before Harold thrust into Victoria one last time and grunted, his buttocks spasming as he jerked, filling Gideon's erstwhile mistress with his spend.

Gideon began clapping.

Both actors yelled and scrambled to get off the bed, their limbs tangling so completely they slid to the floor with a crash.

Gideon tilted his head to see around the bed to where they lay thrashing on the floor.

"Goodness, that looked like it hurt," he observed.

Victoria was the first to her feet, her beautiful face a mask of horror, pushing down her diaphanous skirts but forgetting her bodice was still shoved beneath her full, lovely breasts.

"Oh—oh, Gideon! I didn't expect you—"

He threw back his head and laughed. "No," he said, shaking his head. "I should think you didn't, darling. And who do I have the honor of hosting in my house—in my bedroom? Harold, I know that much. Harold who?"

Harold—an extremely young fellow, Gideon now saw—fumbled with his trouser buttons, his cheeks—the ones on his face—a dangerous shade of red. "Just what the hell—"

Gideon lifted a staying hand. "Now, now, Harold—such language in the presence of a lady."

The other man's jaw dropped.

"If you are quite finished here, perhaps you might give me a moment with Victoria?" Gideon asked, earning an even more stupefied look.

"Get *out*, Harold!" Victoria's sharp, hard eyes never left Gideon's face. They both waited while Harold moved with clumsy haste, neither of them speaking until they heard his feet clattering down the stairs.

"Ladies first, sweetheart."

Victoria blinked her huge brown eyes and took a hesitant step toward him.

"No," he said raising his hand. "I think you'd best answer me from there. I'm not sure I could behave like a gentleman if you came within arm's reach." It amused Gideon greatly that she'd not pulled up her bodice—a temptress to the end. Well, he had no objection to eying what he'd already paid a great deal for.

"You left me here, Gideon." Her long dark lashes fluttered and her eyes began to glisten. "I was so lonely—and bored. What was I supposed to do?"

"Read a book? Stitch a cushion cover?"

Her plump, kiss-bruised lips parted. "But—"

Gideon smiled. "You're right, my darling, of course you couldn't do those things."

She brightened, her full mouth curving, hope tinging her alabaster skin a fetching shade of pink.

"I see now I should never have taken you from your happy position at the Birch Palace. Never fear, when I leave here today, I shall speak to Madam Dumas about taking you ba—"

She rushed at him and grabbed his upper arms, tears sliding down her cheeks, her eyes imploring. "But I thought you *liked* seeing me with other men."

He stroked her sweet, rounded jaw with the back of his fingers. "Yes, darling, but *I* like to pick the men and I also like to make sure I've been invited."

"Please don't send me back, Gideon. I promise—I shan't do this again. Really. I just—"

Gideon removed her hands from his arms and set her at a distance. "Have your maid pack a few things, Victoria. I'll have Mrs. Loring send along the rest of your belongings tomorrow."

Her hand moved like a flash, but Gideon was faster and caught her wrist in a viselike grasp. "Now, now, sweetheart. Let's not become ugly."

She spat at him and then stepped back, her eyes wide at what she'd done.

Gideon chuckled as he took his handkerchief from his pocket, smiling at her while he wiped spittle from his chin, mouth, and cheek.

His mild reaction seemed to incite her and she sneered at him. "This house is *mine* and I shan't let you take it from me. Everyone knows you give houses to your mistresses like other men bestow bonnets. If you believe I'll allow—"

"You might wish to read the agreement you signed, Victoria." He carefully refolded his handkerchief. Now," he said, tucking the white square back into his pocket. "I'm off. I'll send my coach around this evening at six. Do be ready for it, my dear, or you'll have to engage your own transportation." Gideon turned and strode from the room.

"I always hated you! Did you know that? I only pretended to enjoy your vile, disgusting touches." Her voice rose the farther away he got. "There's something dreadfully wrong with you—some part of you is warped or missing. You might be attractive on the outside, but inside you're ugly and twisted." She was screaming, now. "Every moment your hands were on me was a misery—and I'm not the only one. It's just your money women crave, Gideon, nothing but your *money!*"

He paused at the head of the stairs, his anger beginning to slip from its tight moorings as he listed to her rant.

"I'm *glad* I shan't have to tolerate your loathsome prick any longer! If you didn't have so much bloody money, you'd always be alone."

Gideon opened his mouth to say something pettish and cutting, but then closed it and began to descend the stairs.

Victoria was saying everything she could think of to hurt him, but that didn't make it any less the true: it *was* his money that brought women flocking to him. For all his handsome looks, he knew few women would tolerate his abrasive, selfish personality for long without the money.

He smiled grimly as he took his hat and cane from Loring. Well, he was bloody lucky then, wasn't he? Because he had *piles* of money. More than he could spend, in fact; enough to buy all the affection he would ever need or want.

Chapter Three

Alys saw no reason to prolong her visit to London or to Lord Taunton's uncomfortable house. With his assurance—no matter how grudgingly given—that she was welcome to remain at Foxrun for the foreseeable future, she was eager to get home.

Before she left, however, it seemed only proper to strip the house of personal effects. There was nothing of hers, of course, but Sebastian had been quite a clothes horse.

Alys instructed her maid, Thursby, to give every last stitch away to an orphanage or workhouse—wherever there might be boys old enough to wear any of it.

"And I shall be very displeased if you sell it, Thursby," Alys told the habitually frowning woman, her grumbling making Alys realize that was exactly what the older woman had planned to do.

Alys spent one full day going through the library, selecting a trunk of books to take along with her. Why not? She wasn't stealing them as they would only be going from the earl's London home to his country estate. She'd read everything worth reading in the Foxrun library twice over. Besides, she didn't get the impression that the new earl was a great reader.

In addition to the packing, she'd supervised an overall cleaning of the house so that it would be ready for his next inspection. The last thing she wanted him to think was that she was the sort of woman who wasn't grateful.

The cleaning took longer than she'd expected with the stripped-down staff, so it wasn't until ten days later that she was standing on the platform at Paddington Station.

All she had was one trunk, her portmanteau, and a smaller bag containing daily essentials. She'd purchased first class tickets for both herself and Thursby, not liking the notion of the older woman being jostled in the crowded third class car, even though that meant Alys had to spend the trip sitting next to her bitter, gin-smelling servant.

Thursby was loudly directing the porter *exactly* how to stow Alys's baggage when somebody behind them said, "Well, what a surprise! And a pleasant one, at that."

Alys recognized his voice, but it was still a shock to turn and see the gloriously handsome Earl of Taunton. He wore navy today, a color which contrasted flatteringly with his fair hair, hyacinth eyes, and pale skin.

"Good morning, my lord," Alys said in a tone that was cool but not unfriendly; she had no desire to make him her enemy, but she could not force herself to say she was *glad* to see him.

His lips pulled into a mocking smile and she knew he was fully aware of her omission.

"I have to admit it was not such a surprise," he said. "I had it from Bingle that you were leaving today."

"Oh?" Her eyebrows shot up at this information.

He shrugged, the fingers of one hand smoothing the perfectly fitting black leather glove on his other hand. "You must allow me to be interested in the comings and goings in my own house, my lady."

"I'll allow you to have an interest in anything you please, my lord. I'm merely surprised you should possess an interest in me. And where are you bound today?" she asked with a sinking feeling in the pit of her stomach.

He displayed white, even teeth that enhanced his perfection. "Why I'm bound for Foxrun, of course."

— ♥ —

Gideon knew he shouldn't tease her, but it was simply too difficult to resist.

"Ah," she temporized, quickly masking her dismay. "I wish I'd had a few days to prepare an appropriate welcome," she said, her pale cheeks flushing in a way that was bloody adorable. He knew she'd been married to the last earl for eight years, so she had to be in her mid-twenties, but she looked no older than eighteen to his jaded eyes.

"Oh come now, my lady—surely I don't need to stand on ceremony in my own establishment?"

Her eyes widened slightly and Gideon knew he'd communicated his meaning: that she should never forget just *whose* house it was. It was small and mean-spirited of him, but he didn't care.

"I would have expected business to hold you in London," she said.

Ah, I daresay you wished *it had.*

"Beeky says I'm likely to receive a special writ a few weeks into the session."

She bit her lower lip, as if to stop it from quivering—or perhaps curving. "Beeky?"

"Is that bad of me?" Gideon asked.

This time she didn't try to hide her smile and its effect on her features was breathtaking.

"It is *very* bad of you," she said. "Although I daresay he will bear a pet name if it means improvements to Foxrun, rather than encumbrances."

Was that a slight—very slight—tone of praise in her voice? Gideon refused to be flattered.

Her servant, a crabby looking woman with an alarmingly red nose, came from the direction of the first-class car. "Everything is stowed, my lady."

Lady Taunton nodded before saying to Gideon, "It appears we are about to board so I will take my leave for now."

"Don't be silly, my lady, you must travel with me—in my car." He gestured to the private railcar they were standing beside.

Her expressive gray eyes widened and she stared through the window of the car almost as if expecting to see something scandalous going on inside. He snorted. He supposed his detractors—who were legion—would've wasted no time telling her about his sexual exploits.

"This car belongs to my syndicate," he explained, amused when her pursed lips eased slightly—as if that meant it couldn't possibly be a rolling palace of debauchery.

Good thing she knew nothing about Gideon's associates.

"Please," he said, "I insist you join me. I shall rattle around like a pea in large pod otherwise." That was a blatant lie. He'd actually planned to make thorough use of the railcar's master bedroom, which was equipped with all manner of delightful items—including two "chambermaids" he'd brought along for his amusement.

31

Gideon decided he'd much rather have the delectable countess's company for the journey, although she'd likely—and tiresomely—insist on remaining fully clothed.

He waited for her response.

Lady Taunton nodded slowly, clearly understanding it would be bad form to sneer at a courtesy from the man to whom she stood in such debt.

Gideon should have felt like a heel for exerting such pressure, but he didn't.

Instead he gestured to the Friday-faced maid hovering beside her. "Your woman will, I'm sure be comfortable in her first-class compartment," Gideon said when it looked as if her maid thought to join them. Oh no, that wouldn't do at all.

It took him only moments to detach Lady Taunton from all that was familiar and install her in the luxurious private car. Gideon smiled at the glares he received from Lucy and Susan—his now-disgruntled playmates—as Jackson, his valet, led the two women toward another car.

A trip in first class would not kill the two whores and might actually encourage them to display more gratitude in the future. Besides, they were employed for his pleasure, and they would do well to recall that.

Thinking about women and ingratitude made Gideon's lips tighten as he mounted the steps to the car. Victoria had only been the first of his mistresses that he'd discharged.

He'd found no similar breaches of contract with either of his other, older and wiser, mistresses. What he *had* found, however, was that Lydia had become so reliant on gin these past months that mounting the stairs to their bedroom had left her red-cheeked and winded. While Gideon enjoyed liquor as well as any man or woman, he drew the line at that which was unhealthy.

He'd known—even before arriving at his third mistress's house—that he would discharge Theresa, as well. Not because she'd committed any infraction, but because he was fatigued by the entire process of keeping women for his pleasure.

He'd vowed to never employ another mistress. It was too much bother for too little return. You'd think they'd enjoy a little liberty from him, but instead, they got up to mischief like Victoria had, or merely sat at home drinking their heads off, like Lydia. While it was true that Theresa had neither been fucking other men nor drinking, he'd kept her for almost five years and had been bored with her for at least four and a half of them. And so he'd decided she'd earned her retirement.

He'd not even been bothered to have one last night with her before turning over the appropriate papers to her small but smart townhouse, complete with furnishings and a generous allowance.

Once he'd divested himself of three mistresses and two properties, he decided it was the perfect time to visit his most recent—albeit involuntary—acquisition: Foxrun.

Jackson returned to the railcar as Gideon was pulling off his gloves. "Are the ladies happily settled?" he asked, his gaze on Lady Taunton, who'd taken a seat in one of the plush leather club chairs and was gazing around the luxuriously appointed coach in some wonder.

Jackson took Gideon's gloves and hat and then helped him with his coat.

"They are settled, my lord. But not exactly happily."

Gideon chuckled, amused by the thought of the two girls stewing away in first class when they'd hoped to get up to antics in the private railcar. They'd become spoiled, and it was all his fault. He'd taken both on several trips recently in his private railcar—which was currently in for refurbishing as he'd come to dislike the red and gold interior that he'd allowed Lydia to choose several years ago—and now the two whores had developed *expectations*.

Lady Taunton looked up when he joined her. "This is magnificent, my lord."

Gideon found her obvious admiration more than a little pleasing, and her smile set off a strange thumping in his chest; Lord but she was lovely when she wasn't judgmental and starchy.

He lowered himself into the chair across from her. "You've not been in a private car before?"

"I haven't, but I'd heard about them from my husband. Taunton often travelled with Lord Hastings, who keeps his own car."

"The Marquess of Hastings?" Gideon asked, and then wanted to bite out his own tongue for asking such a gauche question.

33

But she appeared not to notice. "Hastings was Master of the Quorn until a few years ago and Taunton was a Melton man, through and through, so the two often travelled up from London together."

Whatever the hell all that meant.

"Do you hunt, my lord?"

"I do not," he said, unable to keep the irritation from his tone. Fucking fox hunting. Oh, he wasn't against it in principle. No, he hated it because *he'd* never be invited to hunt with the bloody Quorn even now that he was the Earl of Taunton. Not that he was a good enough rider in any case. Riding had been, Gideon had to admit, the least of his priorities once he'd begun to make money. Although that would have to change now that he owned a great country estate. He smiled at the thought of inviting his business associates out for a hunt party. Why not?

"I'd like to give a hunt party." His announcement was as much news to him as it was to the startled woman across from him.

"I see. Er, at the beginning of the Season?" Her amused tone told him that his whim was an odd one. Well, what of it? She'd better become accustomed to his whims or she could find herself some other *free* place to live.

"The people I'll invite don't order their lives by the Season, my lady."

She stiffened at his chastising, superior tone, no trace of her smug little smile remaining on her lips. "We've not done much entertaining in recent years," she said, and then added hesitantly, "I'm afraid there will be nothing with the local pack until the autumn, my lord. But I daresay your friends will discover that the surrounding areas have other pleasures."

Gideon had no idea what to say to that.

"How long were you married, my lady," he asked, although he already knew the answer. He could see by her pinched expression that she found his question excessively forward.

Good.

"A little over eight years."

And no children. Gideon had looked into Taunton before leaving London and learned the man hadn't kept a mistress. He'd asked Smith about him, but Smith didn't even recall fucking the man.

"You're a slattern, you know that?" Gideon had accused him. "It can't be every day you bugger an earl, Smith. I find it difficult to believe you can't recall it?"

"Are you offering to do something to jog my memory, Gideon?" Smith had asked, amused by his insulting words rather than offended.

"Not bloody likely," he'd muttered. "You won't be enjoying a *second* Earl of Taunton."

Gideon had played with Smith a few times in the past, but the older man was too bloody rough and wild, even for his tastes. It irritated Gideon that his business partners were always pointing a finger at *him* when Smith was a far worse whoremonger.

But that was neither here nor there.

Without Smith's help, he'd had to do his own prying into Taunton. The main thing he'd learned about the dead earl was that he'd enjoyed the tables and the ponies.

Gideon let his gaze flicker over the widow's threadbare traveling suit; it was clear that's where all his money had gone.

He looked up and met her chilling stare—so, she'd noticed his inspection? Not that he'd gone to any pains to hide it. Gideon smiled, enjoying her displeasure. That was another thing she'd better become accustomed to—how much he liked to *look*.

"Do you have family near Foxrun, my lady?" Again, he already knew the answer, but he wanted to hear her speak. She had a lovely voice.

"My brother lives outside the village of Hawkesley. He is married and the father of seven children. My parents are both deceased but there is the usual assortment of relatives scattered here and there, nobody I am particularly close to."

Gideon was impressed by her dismissive attitude. He wouldn't have been able to resist puffing off about being a marquess's daughter, having a marquess for a brother and "assorted" relatives that included a duke. Her blood was as blue as it could be, yet she didn't appear to give a toss. Gideon reminded himself that *some* blue blood also flowed through his own veins, but the reminder was less than convincing.

"And what of you, my lord? Do you have family in London?"

Gideon's eyes narrowed at her question, but he could see no spite in her smoky gray eyes.

"I have no immediate family, period. My mother had a younger sister but her marriage took her off to Northern parts and I've not seen her since I was in short pants." He hesitated, and then added. "I only had the one brother, and he died years ago." And what a bloody relief *that* had been, he could have added, but did not. Gideon drummed his fingers on the arm of his chair, oddly uneasy. And why was that? What was it about this female that was making him restless?

Perhaps because this is the first time you've actually spoken to an attractive woman without shoving your cock in her body?

Gideon couldn't help smiling—both at the mental voice, which sounded suspiciously like his judgmental business partner Chatham—and also because the accusation was true.

Naturally now that the subject of fucking had been brought up, he couldn't help visualizing the countess naked, bouncing up and down on his pole.

Her flush, which had just begun to subside, flared with a vengeance at whatever she saw on his face—lust, most likely. For a woman who'd been married eight years she blushed easily. Of course Taunton had likely mounted her under cover of darkness once a month, if not less.

"Perhaps you might share what you find so amusing, my lord?"

Gideon studied her pursed lips and wondered what she'd say if he *did* share his thoughts. In a more playful mood, he might have done exactly that. But the truth was his mood was considerably *less* than cheerful. It embarrassed and surprised him to admit it, but the business with his mistresses had left him feeling less than his chipper, carefree self.

That was the *last* thing he'd ever admit to this superior female.

Instead he raised a matter of business. "I would be indebted to you, my lady, if you could help make an inventory of what the house lacks—linens, furnishings, and the like." He waved his hand to encompass everything. "I was quite serious about wishing to invite my business acquaintances. But I've not got a clue about household matters."

Rather than look annoyed, she smiled. "I would be pleased to assist you. I'm afraid it has been some years—well-before my husband's time—since the house or its contents have received any, er, improving attention."

Gideon could just imagine. "I assumed as much. If you focus your attention first on four guest rooms, the dining room, and a few common rooms, that would be most helpful."

"I'm afraid you might find the kitchen is the room that is most in need of repair, my lord."

"You can leave that to my chef, who'll be down sometime within the next week or so." And who would likely give his notice at whatever gothic monstrosity he found. Gideon cut her a quick look when she didn't respond. "I suppose there is a cook?"

"Yes, my lord."

"I trust the arrival of my chef will not put his or her nose out of joint?" Not that he cared. He was excessively particular about food and the last bloody thing he'd tolerate was a yokel who thought boiled turnips the height of fine dining.

"Well, to be honest, Cook is rather past her time. If you like—" she stopped.

"Yes? If I like?"

"I was going to offer to speak to her, or to any of the servants you might wish to discharge. I'm ashamed to admit that there are several who should have been pensioned off some time ago but were not, er, for lack of money."

He filled in what she left unsaid: Because her spendthrift husband was too busy wasting the ready on horses and at gaming tables to see to his business.

Gideon scowled. He *despised* these effete fools who let fine properties fall to rack and ruin and drove their servants to the bloody poorhouse.

"I didn't mean to offend you, my lord."

Gideon realized she'd misread his sour expression. "You didn't." *It was your idiot of a husband.* "I daresay you're worried I'll give them the sack."

She blinked, her mouth tightening into a pucker.

"Don't worry," Gideon told her with a laugh. "I shan't leave anyone destitute. But it would be far better for you to deal with the servants, if you don't dislike it too much," he added. He studied the nails on his left hand, which Jackson kept in lovely condition. "I have a devil of a time keeping a staff in London," he admitted, and then cut her a quick

37

grin. "Although I couldn't say *why*." Oh yes he could. If there was anything more prudish than a member of the British servant class, he could not think of it. His people were always leaving in a huff over minor matters like encountering Gideon plowing one of his special chambermaids in the foyer, or—on memorable occasion—in a linen closet. Ah well, good riddance.

"I should be pleased to manage the servants," she answered, prudently leaving the second part of his comment unanswered. "Indeed, I will be pleased to offer assistance in any way you need."

Gideon somehow doubted she would be pleased to assist him in the way he was currently needing.

"You are very kind," he told her, and then stood. "I shall have my man bring tea, if that would be acceptable?"

"Oh, yes. Lovely."

Gideon bowed. "If you will excuse me a moment."

He found his silent servant sitting at the back of the carriage reading.

"Bring Lady Taunton tea, Jackson," he instructed. Gideon wished he could read on a train, but it made him ill. Frankly, he wished he could read anywhere, but he was simply too restless.

"In which compartment did you put Lucy and Susan?"

"They are in the third up on the right, my lord. I did as you bade me and purchased all four seats in the compartment."

"Excellent. Tell my lady I shall return in half an hour and not to hold tea for me."

"Very good, my lord."

If his behavior surprised Jackson, the man never showed it by so much as a flicker of an eyelid. He'd been with Gideon for over a decade—the first servant Gideon had engaged when he could finally afford to do so. Although Jackson attended him almost twenty-four hours a day, Gideon knew nothing about him other than he was efficient, obedient, and extremely reserved. He also had no hard and fast lines in the sand about valet duties, which had often proven quite useful—and enjoyable—over time. He was perhaps five or six years older than Gideon, kept remarkably fit, and always did what he was told to do without question. They got on swimmingly.

38

Gideon unlocked the door to the private car and stepped over the gap into the first-class cabin. There were not many passengers at this time of the week so he was surprised the company had put on so many cars—bad management. He'd have to tell his partners to reconsider their unwillingness to invest in trains, he sensed there was money to be made.

Being a nosy bastard, he glanced into each compartment he passed.

He also thought about what he was doing: breaking off a conversation with a woman in whom he'd genuinely been interested— at least as far as she could assist him when it came to his new property—to go cavort with two whores.

Gideon felt a bit sheepish at the admission, but that did nothing to bring down his erection, which even the prissy countess would have soon noticed, given his preference for closely cut trousers. The sad truth was that his brain got muzzy when he needed to ejaculate.

"There's something wrong with you," Edward Fanshawe told him with irritating frequency. The last time his oversized business partner had said that was only a month ago. They'd been returning to London after a business trip in Liverpool. Gideon had just suggested they break their journey to investigate a whorehouse in a town along the way.

Gideon usually ignored his partners' ribbing, but, for some reason, he'd been arrested by Edward's assessment that day.

"Do you really believe something is wrong with me, Edward? Or are you just saying that to be a superior bastard—now that you've got a wife at home who is willing to do things most men wouldn't even dare to suggest to their mistresses?"

Edward had frowned and Gideon had known he was deciding whether he or not he should thrash Gideon for commenting about his wife's sexuality. Considering the man had *invited* Gideon to fuck her, it seemed like a moot point. Still, Edward could be a bit touchy when it came to his wife. Gideon didn't blame him; a woman like Nora Fanshawe might be enough for Gideon to consider marriage. Almost.

"I *do* think you might have a bit of a—" Edward had considered Gideon with a clinical look. "Well, you do seem a bit *obsessed* with sex."

"So what? Aren't you? Don't you think of fucking? Of getting sucked off?"

Edward had sighed. "Of course, I do, but I can restrain myself."

"Why the hell would you do that? We are filthily, revoltingly rich—we no longer have to exercise restraint. We can do whatever we want, whenever we want, to whomever we want."

Edward had chuckled at that. "Oh, Gideon."

"What? Why are you laughing? It's true—I've never met a woman I couldn't have, either with money or promises of heavenly pleasure."

"One day you will—if you are lucky."

And that was all the bastard would say on the subject.

Gideon was so caught up in his thoughts he almost walked right past the girls' compartment.

He opened the door and grinned. "Hello ladies, did you miss me?" Both women studied him through narrowed eyes and he laughed. "Sorry to toss you out of the private car, darlings, but family first, and all that." He pulled the shade down over the window in the door and was going to pull down the one on the other side but decided he might like to watch the scenery while enjoying his pleasure.

He lowered himself onto the seat opposite the women and surveyed them from beneath his lowered lashes. They were pouting, and he could see they'd talked themselves into being genuinely affronted. He'd clearly given his whores too much latitude in their dealings with him. It was probably time to start over with new ones and train them properly this time.

But not just now.

He pulled out his watch, opened the cover, and set it on the armrest before looking up. Whatever they saw on his face made them both sit up straighter.

"I can see you ladies are displeased with the situation."

"Oh, no, my lord, not at all," Susan hastened to assure him.

"We're very comfy here, my lord, quite happy," Lucy said, speaking over the other woman.

His lips pulled into a smile his servants hated to see. "Why, that is *such* a relief, because it occurred to me that *if* you're unhappy I might put you on a train back to London at the next stop. I could pay your wages for the next six months, while you sought new employment."

Gideon knew he should feel like an ogre for the frenzy of apologies his words set off, but he didn't.

Instead, he pointed to the floor between his spread feet, amused by the scuffle that took place as the women fought to occupy it. Good, that was very good. It was time they recalled *why* they were paid more than his bloody butler for a few hours work every week.

Lucy won the battle to kneel and Susan pouted across at him. "What about me, my lord?"

"Lift your skirts and show me what you've been keeping warm for me."

She grinned as she tugged her dress up over her knees. Gideon smiled down at Lucy, who was licking her lips—not an entirely convincing display of desire, but good enough for the moment. "Don't let me stop you, darling."

Her fingers flicked open his trouser buttons and, in mere seconds, he had a hot, skilled mouth sucking the fat bell end of his cock. Gideon grunted with pleasure as she prodded his slit with the pointed tip of her tongue.

Yes, very nice, indeed.

Susan, meanwhile, spread her legs, exposing far prettier scenery than that outside the window.

"That's lovely, darling." Gideon shifted his hips to become more comfortable, weaving his hand into Lucy's thick blond hair and exerting only the slightest pressure. She slid down his shaft until his cock rubbed the back of her throat.

"Mmm, yes," he whispered, pulsing his hips, her signal to do that wonderful thing she did with her throat.

"Touch yourself for me, Susan," he encouraged, his balls clenching when she skimmed a slender finger around and around her rapidly stiffening bud—her swollen sex proof that not *all* their actions were a theatrical performance. "Pretend it's my hands and slip a finger inside. Yes, very good, nice and slow and deep."

Gideon gave a lazy smile of approval and released his hold on Lucy's head. She was too well-trained to move until he finally tapped her jaw, allowing her to swallow and breathe without his erection impaling her—at least for a moment.

"Make it last, darling," he instructed.

Gideon gave himself over to pure pleasure as she began to worship his shaft, sucking him hard enough to hurt, just the way he liked it.

41

She was a lovely girl, her blond locks lightened a bit more than nature intended, but the effect enhancing rather than glaring. Her plump lips and clever tongue were skilled and she worked him with abandon.

He was as thick and hard as a barge pole, but still his juices would not flow.

He clenched his jaws against the howl of frustration that threatened to tear out of him. Just what did he have to do to come? What?

He squeezed his eyes shut, blocking out everything but sensation, as if he could *concentrate* himself into having an orgasm.

Relax, Gideon, relax. Think about how good this feels.

It wasn't difficult to think about his rock-hard erection or the soft, wet mouth moving up and down on it.

Yes.

And then an image started to form.

Gideon held his breath as the gray and white squiggles behind his eyelids formed into something—no, *someone.* Yes—yes—it was . . . the countess. And she was kneeling between his thighs, that lovely mouth of hers stuffed full of *him.*

"Yes," he whispered, his hips beginning to pulse.

His orgasm, which had been as elusive as a moth hovering just outside the light, began to build. Anxious excitement joined weeks of unsatisfied lust and every muscle in his body tensed. "Yes," he encouraged softly, treating his impending climax like an easily startled forest creature that needed to be *lured* closer.

Imagine the countess, not your orgasm. Her, just imagine her.

He painstakingly built her full, pouty lips and charming little nose before moving on to her ripe, shapely body, taking his time over the pleasing swell of her breasts.

He stripped off her hideous black gown and beneath it she was wearing something naughty—stockings held up with pretty suspenders—perhaps even a black corset for mourning. The thought momentarily distracted him; did women wear mourning undergarments?

Gideon shook his head, discarding the foolish question and scrambling to keep hold of his carefully contrived image. Yes, Lady Taunton kneeling before him, encased in a snug corset of black leather.

He grunted as a bolt of pure lust shot from his balls to the head of his cock. Yes, black leather—and she'd be laced tight, cruelly so. Perhaps she'd even wear a collar and he would attach a short lead to it. He'd wrap the leather strap around his fist and keep her head pulled low, her willing lips pleading to service him and—

"Fuck!" he hissed through clenched teeth, throbbing so hard it hurt. He jerked into that stern mouth of hers with sharp thrusts, thrilling at the force building inside his body.

But not yet; he didn't want to come yet. *No, please, no,* he silently begged—or was he praying? Not yet, *please.*

Deft fingers—the countess's fingers, he reminded himself—pulled at the taut skin of his sac as she massaged his aching balls.

He shuddered, fighting to halt the growing tide, and losing. Her hot sucking mouth was too much—*too much*—and he fucked into her with brutal thrusts.

Yes, yes, yes.

As always, his savage jerks alerted her to his impending climax—God, she knew his body so well—and she took him in her throat's embrace and swallowed in a rhythmic massaging motion that tore the orgasm out of his body.

Gideon embedded himself deeply and held her full of his cock, emptying his balls in violent, hot jets down her throat, coming so hard he *hurt.*

God yes!

A sound—barely audible—plucked at him, pulling him from his climax even as his prick continued to spasm. His heavy eyelids fluttered open in time to see a horrified face in the gap of the open door—just before it shut with a sharp *snick.*

He blinked down at the blond head bowed before him, momentarily confused.

Who the hell—?

Oh, that's right: it was Lucy—not Lady Taunton. Gideon swallowed the sharp pang of disappointment and—

Ah!

Lucy gave him a soft, sucking stroke, milking the last of his seed, her clever mouth overpowering his addled brain, making Gideon forget everything, including the mysterious face in the doorway. He shuddered and collapsed back against the seat, pushing Lucy's head off his now painfully sensitive organ.

He closed his eyes and cupped his loose balls with one hand. *Sleep. Just a little sleep.*

But something kept him from sliding into bliss: a face, yes, *that* face. Where had he seen that bloody face before? Where?

Gideon absently tugged at his sac while his befogged brain struggled for a match. An older woman—dressed all in black. It was—Thursday! No, that wasn't right. It was Thursby, or something of that sort. Yes, that's who it was: Lady Taunton's maid.

His lips curved into a lazy post-coital smile and he chuckled weakly. So, just what would Thursby tell her mistress?

Chapter Four

"I've ordered a carriage to meet us," Lord Taunton told Alys as he handed her down from the luxurious railcar.

Alys's hand tingled at his touch—even though there were two layers of leather between them. "That is very kind of you, my lord, but I arranged for a ride from Foxrun." She peered at the waiting vehicles but couldn't see the gig. It looked like Old Thomas was late. Alys supposed the doddering coachman would be one of the first servants his lordship would sack. She shivered.

"Are you chilled, my lady?"

Alys cut him a startled glance; he didn't seem like the type to be solicitous of anyone's needs but his own.

"Would you like my coat over your cloak?" he offered, his hands going to the buttons of his navy cashmere overcoat.

"Oh, no thank you, my lord."

He nodded, one of his odd, teasing smiles twisting his lips. "Don't worry about your gig. Jackson will stay behind to manage that," he assured her with a casual arrogance that left her oddly breathless, as if he never for a moment entertained the thought that he might not get exactly what he wanted.

"My lady?" he said when she hesitated.

"But my maid, Thursby. She'll be expecting—"

"There are two carriages, the second one for the servants and baggage." He sounded impatient and Alys saw he was still extending his arm. She laid her hand on the navy wool and allowed him to lead her away from the train, feeling rather like a leaf carried along on a strong gust of wind as he bore her out of the station and toward a luxurious black coach—no, *two* luxurious black coaches.

Before she knew it, she was installed in the carriage, a rug over her lap, and the carriage rolling smoothly away from the station.

His lordship sat back-facing, his expression distracted in the lamp light, his gloved fingers idly drumming. He appeared to be a restless sort. Indeed, he'd somehow managed to find a way to disappear for half an hour even on a moving train. Well, he was a *business*man, so she supposed he'd likely been doing something, er, business-y.

"This is a lovely carriage," she said, her urge to make idle chatter surprising. In general, she despised chit-chat.

"Hmmm? Oh, yes, this coach." He looked at her as if he'd forgotten she was there. "I ordered them delivered from Bristol but these are job horses. Which brings to mind something else—do you have a stable master who knows the front of the horse from the back?"

"Indeed, Jonathan Silber is highly respected. He is also a younger man— a few years younger than my late husband."

"And how old was that?"

"My husband was three-and-forty when he died."

He nodded, his jaw working back and forth, his eyes flickering to the window. Alys thought he was going to ask her age, but instead he said, "Town seems to have disappeared rather quickly." He leaned closer to peer out the glass.

"Have you spent much time in the country, my lord?"

His head snapped around. "No, why do you ask?"

"No particular reason." My, but he was a sensitive man—and in ways Alys did not quite understand.

He turned back toward the darkened window. "I've spent little time outside cities," he admitted rather grudgingly. "It seems very . . . quiet here. What do you do for entertainment?"

"Nothing of late, as I'm only recently out of mourning."

"Ah. When did the earl die?" Before she could answer he turned to her. "Or shouldn't I ask you that?"

"It's not a secret, my lord. He died a little over thirteen months ago." Sebastian had actually died a lot longer ago for her, but that was hardly something a person mentioned to a far-too-handsome-oddly-seductive-and-awkward stranger.

Alys smiled to herself at the label.

"Why does that make you smile?"

Alys's face heated. "Oh, no, it doesn't—"

He turned away. "Never mind; that was another rude question."

She happened to agree, but now that *he'd* agreed, she felt rather belligerent. "Do you always ask and answer your own questions?"

He gave her one of his disarming smiles. "All right, then. Go on and tell me what you were thinking."

Well done, Alys. What will you say now?

"Er, I was wondering what made you change your mind and decide to visit Foxrun."

His smile turned mocking. "No, you weren't thinking that." Her mouth opened. "But that's all right. I decided to visit Foxrun because I was bored."

She raised her eyebrows.

"What? Don't you ever get bored?"

"Not that I can recall."

A sharp bark of laughter escaped his sensual lips. "Oh, come now—you *never* get bored?"

"I don't know why that's so difficult to believe. My days are full and busy." *My nights, on the other hand . . ..*

"What do you do?"

Alys could see she'd better become accustomed to his direct questions. "I see to household and servant matters, I work in the gardens, I visit the various tenants, I'm active in parish matters."

He merely grunted.

"What do *you* do all day?"

He looked startled, but then a slow, sinful smile curved his lips and her own face heated in response, although she had no idea *why*. "I work with three other men and we purchase businesses that are failing and restructure them. We each have our own specialty. Fanshawe is usually the man who spots the venture. Chatham evaluates the financials. And Mr. Smith—well, Mr. Smith keeps things running."

"And what do you do?"

"I'm an engineer. I'm good with numbers, mathematics, machinery, that sort of—"

The carriage jostled wildly to the side, knocking Alys from her seat. Before her knees could hit the floor, strong hands slid around her torso and pulled her up.

"What the devil was that?" he demanded, staring at her as the carriage jolted to a stop, apparently unaware his hands were still under her arms, his thumbs pressed hard beneath her breasts.

Alys swallowed with some effort. "Er," she glanced down.

"Oh, sorry," he said, not sounding particularly sorry as his hands fell away.

The door opened. "Are you all right, my lady, my lord?"

"What happened?" the Earl asked the groom.

"It was a large limb—it must have only just fallen because it wasn't on the road on the way out."

"Is the coach damaged?"

"Not that I can see, my lord."

He grunted. "Very well, carry on, then."

The door closed and they looked at each other.

"We're almost home, my lord." Alys murmured, wondering how long she would feel his strong warm hands on her body.

—❤—

Gideon's hands felt as though an electric charge had passed through them.

He'd experienced physical attraction for women before. Hell, he experienced it at least five times a day, but nothing to compare to this. He couldn't tell whether she'd felt it, too, or whether she'd just been offended at the way he'd handled her.

He'd not known that hands could have their own memories, but his thumbs fondly remembered the curved underside of her corseted breasts and they kept reminding his brain of the feeling.

Yes, she was certainly shapely.

The carriage moved on to a different substrate—gravel, perhaps— and he saw lights flickering ahead.

"That is the gate house. Mr. Wallace is the keeper. His wife used to live with him but she passed away a few years ago."

The carriage slowed and Gideon let down the window. A bent old man stood beside the open gate, his hat in his gnarled hand.

"Good evening, Mr. Wallace—well met," Gideon called out as they rolled past. The last thing Gideon saw before the carriage rounded a gentle curve was the man's big, toothless smile.

He looked at Lady Taunton—*Alys*—who was watching him with cool speculation. "Mr. Wallace looks as though he is barely up to managing a bowl of porridge. Hardly who I'd want holding the gates between me and the Saxon hordes," he said.

She gave a choked laugh and Gideon felt as though he'd just achieved something—like inventing the combustion engine—by making the haughty woman chuckle.

"Exactly what does a gate keeper do?" he asked.

"Oh, not so much anymore, of course. But he does keep the gate in good repair as well as helping with the grounds." She frowned slightly. "Perhaps you will think the position not worth filling but—"

"Too hasty by far, my lady. If I've got a gatehouse, I'll want to have a gatekeeper."

She smiled. "Oh? So the fact you have a weapon room will mean you engage a master of arms?"

Gideon enjoyed this example of her ready wit. "A weapon room? How intriguing. And is it full of weapons?"

"It's rather sparse these days. There are several sets of armor that are said to be excellent examples of their type, but mostly the room just houses Sebastian's hunting rifles."

Gideon experienced a frisson of something not entirely pleasant at hearing her use her dead husband's Christian name. Sebastian? It was a name that annoyed him—he'd known a Sebastian at the orphanage and the boy had ribbed Gideon endlessly—before he'd finally taken matters into his own hands.

A mammoth black shape loomed up outside the window.

Gideon blinked. "Good God," he muttered. "It's a bloody castle."

There was a moment of silence before she spoke, and Gideon realized she was likely shocked by his language.

"It began as a castle. The original structure dates to 857. Thankfully the family quarters are in a wing that was added at the end of the eighteenth century."

His. All this was his? Well, at least for his lifetime. The bloody thing was entailed, of course. When the carriage rolled to a stop Gideon opened the door without waiting for the footman, flicking down the steps himself and handing out Lady Taunton.

He wanted to touch her hand, even through gloves. Yes, again he felt the odd bolt of electricity.

Her lips curved into a lovely smile, which he at first thought was for him. But then he realized her eyes were on something behind him and turned. A rather straggly line of servants stood waiting for his inspection. Even in this low light he could see the gray and white heads were many.

"Shall I make the introductions?" she asked.

"Please do." Gideon felt oddly nervous—a unique feeling for him. These people were *his* people. There was something about country servants that felt much more *permanent*. He grimaced as he realized he'd have to try and keep his fucking more private or he'd have a rash of heart attacks among this crowd of geriatrics.

"This is Tickle and Mrs. Tickle."

Gideon nodded at a pair of old fossils whose bones creaked as they bowed low. "It's an honor, my lord," Tickle murmured in a dusty voice.

"Thank you for greeting me in full force at such an uncivil hour," Gideon murmured, nodding to Mrs. Tickle.

"This is Poulson, the under butler."

Gideon stopped remembering names after that. For a faltering estate there were upwards of forty servants. He knew from reading the information Beeky gave him that many of them had no place else to go and had not been paid in years. It would cost a fortune in pensions to staff the place properly. Luckily he had several dozen fortunes to spare.

When they reached the end of the line—a boot black no bigger than a minute—Lady Taunton turned to him. "I daresay Mrs. Tickle has readied the master's chambers for you, my lord." She hesitated and flushed. "I hope you do not mind if I continue in the mistress's room until we can make one of the guest rooms ready."

Gideon opened his mouth to tell her she could bloody well stay in the master's chambers if she wanted them. Of course they'd have *him* in them.

Instead he said, "Ah. So they're all in bad shape, are they?"

"I'm afraid so. We've not hosted guests for some years. The only rooms that have been occupied were the master and mistress suites."

"Well, I'm sure with my money and your abilities, we'll have plenty of habitable chambers soon."

She lowered her eyes. "Thank you, my lord."

He'd already been half-erect as he took in the grandeur—albeit faded—of his new possession. But her humble, almost submissive, gesture made his cock as hard as the stone wall of his castle. Luckily the second carriage came rumbling up and nobody noticed his bulging trouser front.

"Would you care for tea, my lord? Or perhaps a cold supper?"

They'd eaten a sumptuous meal in the private car—Jackson's culinary skills were impressive, so Gideon wasn't eager to sample the country cooking. "Tea would be nice. I'd like it if you joined me."

"Oh, of course. The library is quite the nicest room in the house, my lord."

"Tea in the library," he said to the hovering Mrs. Tickle as he stripped off his gloves and one of the ancient footmen helped him off with his coat.

The housekeeper bobbed a stiff curtsey and then scuttled off, leaving Gideon free to stare at the suits of armor, arched ceilings, and stained-glass windows he could see were magnificent even in the dark.

"The library is this way, my lord," Lady Taunton's words called him from his gawking at the cavernous entry hall.

"This must be very old," he said somewhat stupidly as he followed her up the stairs.

"Yes, this section was built when the castle was converted into a dwelling—1147."

The banister was as big around as his waist and intricately carved. Below his feet were stone steps with a depression in the middle, where peoples' feet—his ancestors'—had worn down the flagstone.

His ancestors. Gideon shivered.

"I'm afraid you'll find Foxrun drafty and cool even in the heat of summer. The stones retain the cold. But your chambers are on the south-facing side of the family wing, which are generally sunny and pleasant."

She paused in front of a set of double doors that looked to be at least eleven feet high.

"Good God," he muttered under his breath.

He thought he'd spoken quietly enough, but she turned to him and smiled. "Yes, they are impressive, aren't they? After almost a decade I still marvel at their beauty." She traced a hand over the intricate bronze strapping and wooden carvings. "It's even more beautiful inside," she teased.

Gideon laid his hand on a big bronze handle and pushed.

51

❤

Alys couldn't help liking the arrogant man as he gawked at his new home. Foxrun deserved to be gawked at and admired.

"Bloody hell," he said, standing frozen in the doorway.

Her face heated at his vulgar language, but she certainly couldn't fault his sentiment. The library at Foxrun was the most spectacular private library she'd ever seen. Not that she'd seen many, of course, but it was nicer than her father's and also her grandfather's—the Duke of Lampton—library.

Lord Taunton's lips were parted. "This is—" He shook his head as he turned in a circle, his eyes on the books that went up and up and up. Finally, he threw up his hands, his expression one of awe.

Alys smiled. "It is a one-of-a-kind room." She gestured to the almost gauzy looking staircase that led to the mezzanine level, and then up to another, far smaller platform. "I'm afraid the stairs have not been usable in many years—long before I moved to Foxrun."

His eyebrows descended and his angelic features became those of an avenging angel. Alys decided she would not like to draw this man's anger.

"I shall have to find carpenters who can replicate or repair such woodwork," he said almost to himself. To her he said, "Is it insect damage?"

"Yes, part of it. Some is just fragile old wood—it dates from the 1390s."

"You know a good deal about the house."

"I'm very fond of Foxrun. I daresay you'll think me fanciful, but it has a great deal of character."

One corner of his mouth pulled into a smile that made him look wicked. "I wouldn't have suspected you of whimsy, my lady."

"But then, you don't *know* me, do you, my lord?" she said archly. Before he could answer Alys added, "I beg you will excuse me for a moment. I'm going to check on your chambers but will return shortly."

He nodded, his attention already back on the room.

Alys moved toward the door, realizing she'd be opening it for herself. That was something not even Sebastian—with his selfish, indulgent manners—had ever neglected to do. Still, if it came down to a choice between the new earl's discourtesy and his plump pockets or

52

Sebastian's exquisite manners and debauched habits, she knew which one she'd choose.

She opened the door and almost bumped into two young women.

Alys frowned. "And who might you be?"

Both women gave her smug, dismissive looks. "We're his lordships private maids, my lady."

"Is he in there?" the second one—a woman with unnaturally bright blond hair and lip rouge—asked abruptly.

Alys was shocked into silence, which didn't seem to bother the women.

"That sour bird Thursby said 'e was in the library," the raven-haired woman added, her bold eyes flickering over the double doors. "Crikey, looks like a bloody cathedral."

Alys gasped at her vulgar language and arrogant demeanor, momentarily tongue-tied.

"Go on then, Sooz, I'm that knackered. Let's find himself and see where we'll be kipping."

The brazen brunette smirked and looked over Alys's shoulder into the room before turning to her colleague. "Yep. His lordship is in here."

"If you'll excuse us," the blond muttered, shoving past Alys.

The brunette grinned at Alys. "Sorry about Lucy, ma'am, she gets a bit crabbed when she don't get enough sleep." She winked and followed her friend, disappearing into the room without a backward glance.

Good Lord! What in the world was this?

"My lady!"

Alys gave a small shriek and spun around. "Goodness, Thursby," she said, her hand resting over her pounding heart. "Need you *yell?* You gave me such a scare."

Thursby grabbed her elbow and pulled her down the hall so vigorously that Alys had to run to keep up. "Thursby, what is wrong with you?"

"Did those two—*maids* go into the library, my lady?" she demanded, not slowing her pace.

"Yes, they claim to be his lordship's personal maids."

Thursby gave a choked snort as she yanked open a door, dragged Alys inside, and shut them in utter darkness.

"Thursby, this is a *linen* closet. What is going on?" Alys gave a suspicious sniff. "Have you been drinking?"

"Just a nip, my lady."

Alys frowned and prepared to deliver a scold. "You should—"

But Thursby was having none of it and rolled right over her. "I've got something you should know, my lady—and I need to tell you *right* now."

— ♥ —

"Cor! Take a gander at this desk, Sooz, it looks like it belongs to a king."

Gideon flicked a glance of annoyance at the two noisy whores, who'd not stopped talking since entering the room—a room that felt more like a cathedral than any he'd been in. He stared at the stairs he could not use; they resembled something out of the land of faerie.

A hand slid around his waist and dropped to his crotch.

"Here, then, what's this my lord? The earl's scepter?"

Gideon pushed her hand away. "Not now," he said, his gaze riveted to the colossal rose window overhead. It *was* a bloody cathedral.

Susan came to stand before him, her full lips curved into a wicked grin. "Are you going to fuck us in each room, your lordship?"

Lucy laughed and came out from behind him. "That might take bloody months."

Gideon felt as if he were being buzzed by noisy insects. "What are you doing here?" he demanded.

"We thought you'd like your usual, my lord."

His usual was fucking one woman from behind while she pleasured the other.

Gideon's cock didn't even twinge at her suggestion. "Not tonight." He would have laughed at their expressions if he'd not been so irritable.

Lucy, the smarter of the two, recovered first. "We'll go up and warm your bed for you, then."

Gideon was about to nod when he recalled his room was the master's and in close proximity to the mistress's.

Well, what of it? his baser self—the part usually giving the orders—demanded.

Gideon had fully expected to fuck Lucy and Susan as freely, often, and openly as he had in his London house. But behaving like that in this place? He glanced around at the majestic beauty. Well, it didn't *feel* right. Besides, three-quarters of his staff were as old as parts of the building, he'd be hip deep in bodies if he carried on in his usual way.

"My lord?" Susan had come up before him and was lightly massaging his cock, which was grudgingly responding.

Gideon removed her hand. He could just imagine the screeching that would ensue if the widow Taunton came back with her tea tray just now.

"Go to your rooms. I'll send Jackson to fetch you when I want you." He scowled at Susan when he saw the way her bodice was unbuttoned. "And straighten yourselves up—remember you're supposed to be housemaids, goddammit, not whores."

They both tried to adjust the low-cut bodices of their uniforms— uniforms designed by *Gideon*, as a matter of fact—but didn't look pleased.

Gideon had enough experience with women to know there was a storm brewing. Fine, as long as it wasn't tonight.

"But where do we stay?" Lucy pouted.

Gideon strode to the magnificent brocade pull and gave it a yank. While he waited, he skimmed some of the shelves. It looked as if the collections of each master had been bound differently. How interesting. It was easy to see which were the newest and he took one of the books off the shelf and flicked it open: The Fourth Earl of Taunton. He closed it and examined the red calfskin binding, gold letters and a black spine. Handsome.

"You rang, sir?"

He turned and found Mrs. Tickle swaying in the doorway. Good God, didn't she have somebody *younger* to answer his summons?

"Lucy and Susan are my personal maids—they see to my chambers and such. Will you please show them the servants' quarters?"

Gideon didn't bother turning at the outraged squeaks.

Mrs. Tickle examined the two young women with a suspicious glint in her rheumy eyes. "Of course, my lord. If you'll follow me."

The women went, but not without a half-dozen resentful and imploring looks at Gideon. Well, Lady Taunton said there were no appropriate guest quarters, so they'd just have to make do. Besides, it looked as if the house might actually need a few more maids—at least until he could hire new servants. The women could bloody well earn their keep for a change.

The door swung open and a footman and maid entered with a tea tray. Gideon frowned as the man set down the tray and the woman began to prepare the tea. "You can leave that; Lady Taunton will be returning shortly."

The girl flinched and flushed—she didn't look more than fifteen. "I'm sorry my lord, but my lady said to tell you she'd become involved with a domestic matter of some importance and will not be able to join you." She stood frozen with the teapot in her hand, her eyes anxiously sweeping his face.

Gideon snorted. A domestic matter of some importance? That sounded like an excuse if he'd ever heard one. Well, what did he care? "I like my tea black and strong."

He'd have tea in his new library alone. By himself. And he'd bloody well   enjoy   it.

Chapter Five

A hideous screaming sound yanked Gideon bolt upright.

"What the bleeding fuck was *that*?" he yelled before his eyes were even open. "Oi!" He prodded one of the two lumps in his bed. "Did you hear that?"

Beside him, either Lucy or Susan moaned and shifted.

"There it is again," he said, shoving aside the bedding. He forgot that he needed to use steps and hopped down off the high bed, jamming his spine when he landed too hard.

"Dammit!" He rubbed his lower back, strode to the window, and pulled open the heavy velvet drapes.

"Good God," he muttered, sneezing at all the dust the action generated, staring through a veritable flurry of dust motes into the bright morning light. He glanced at the ugly china clock on the nightstand: eight o'clock. He'd slept in. He scratched his belly idly as he looked out over the scene.

Hmmm, some sort of flower garden with a big fountain. Quite pretty. He yawned and absently stroked his morning erection as he looked past the gardens, the expanse of lawn, and toward a silvery ribbon that must be a stream. There was a wood to the east and the sunlight was streaming through it.

A flicker of movement caught his eye and he glanced down to see Lady Taunton, staring up at him, her jaw hanging open.

Gideon glanced down at himself and confirmed that he was, indeed, naked and hard and then smiled down at her and waved, with his free hand.

She fled.

He chuckled as he turned around, hearing the screeching sound again—a cock's crow, he now realized. He grinned at the memory of her ladyship's horrified face. Well, she'd been married—it wasn't as if Gideon had showed her anything she'd not seen.

He padded back to the bed and considered the two sleeping lumps. He'd sent Jackson for them last night, when he'd been unable to sleep. As was usual these days, he'd fucked them for hours without ejaculation. But he was hard right now—the sight of Lady Taunton's plump-lipped, wide-mouthed stare fresh in his mind.

He gave himself a few experimental pumps—yes, he was dangerously close to spending after no more than a glance at the bloody woman. Christ! What the hell was wrong with him? Why *her?* Gideon scowled down at his erection, but it simply stared dumbly back at him.

Well, so be it.

He'd consider the annoying possibility that he could *only* come when thinking about Lady Taunton *later,* when he was less distracted.

He located the padded steps and crawled up onto his great bloody bed.

Once on top he slipped beneath the blankets and reached out toward one of the lumps. He encountered a fleshy bottom: ah, felt like Lucy.

"On your hands and knees, sweetheart," he murmured.

She groaned sleepily but complied.

Gideon knelt between her thighs, nudging them far apart, and then slid his hands beneath her hips. "Up," he ordered, raising her bottom to the perfect height for his use.

"That's a good girl," he praised, slipping his middle finger into her tight entrance and playing with her until the room was filled with the sound of wet friction. As usual, her responsive body was ready quickly and he could tell by her heavy breathing that she was awake and wanting.

He nudged her shoulders down, until they rested on the bed, and stroked her wet slit with his cock, caressing her clitoris with his other hand.

He closed his eyes. "Yes," he murmured as he positioned himself at her swollen opening and then sheathed himself with a savage thrust.

She wriggled. "Mmm, my lord, that feels so—"

He kept his eyes closed and swatted her arse. "Don't speak," he ordered, the carefully curated image of Lady Taunton flickering dangerously, like a reflection in a pond. He began fucking her with long, lazy strokes while he reassembled Lady Taunton's surprised face in his mind's eye.

She had looked countrified—a big floppy hat to protect her from the sun. He knew that her gown, although he'd not seen it, would be an old one. She held a basket of some sort over her arm and a pair of shears in her gloved hand.

"Yes," he whispered as the vision began to sharpen. He thumbed her slick pearl with more vigor.

Her mouth—open in surprise—quickly shifted into a wicked smile of pleasure as he teased her: *Yes, Gideon, please,* she'd say in her hard as diamonds accent. *Fuck me hard; make me come, my lord.*

"With pleasure," he grunted, driving into her with brutal strokes.

Her passage was slick and hot and tight and she knew just when to clench, working him on the inward stroke, releasing him on the outward, her body like a well-tuned piece of machinery. She shook and contracted with the violence of her pleasure.

His own orgasm took him by surprise, barreling from his balls to the head of his cock before he could stop it.

Too soon, it was too damned soon.

He buried himself deep and pumped her full, shuddering with the force of each jerk and spasm "Take it," he grated through clenched jaws. "Take it all … *Alys,*" he murmured as he collapsed onto the warm supple body beneath him.

He slid into sleep, still hilted inside her.

─ ❤ ─

Alys walked for miles.

Every time she considered turning around, she saw *that* again—*him* again.

He was—he was—*shameless!* Standing in front of the window with his god-like body as naked as the day he was born. Proud and *erect*. And then smiling at her and fondling himself when he *knew* she could see him.

You could have looked away—you'd been watching him from the moment the curtains parted, at least half a minute before he saw you.

"Oh shut up," she muttered, lifting her mud-covered hem as she struggled over a stile.

You became excited. Wet, her mental tormentor accused.

59

She closed her eyes, as if that would stop the sensations, and promptly tripped on a root.

"Oh God." Alys fell to her knees, cradling her head in her hands: she *had* become aroused.

Keeping her eyes closed was worse, because then she saw—in her mind's eye—the scene that Thursby had described in *scandalous* detail.

But instead of disgusting her through and through, it made something—her annoying female parts—pulse and throb. She'd experienced this sensation before, of course, but usually it only came to her in the middle of the night—waking her in the grip of exquisite pleasure. When she tried to go back to sleep to recapture it, it was always lost.

She'd also felt something similar, on occasion, when she'd ridden astride. She'd wonderered if that was why women were made to ride side-saddle? Because men wanted to deny them such pleasure?

Merely looking at Gideon Banks had given her that sensation— seductive, painfully pleasurable, and wanton.

What was she going to do? She couldn't live in a house with him. Did he really believe he could keep two whores and masquerade them as maids?

Of course he believed it! And of course he could do it: he was Lord Taunton and he was ridiculously—*obscenely*—wealthy. He could do anything he wanted and likely would.

Alys stood and started back toward Foxrun. After all, she had nowhere else to go.

That wasn't true; the truth was that she wanted to go back. Why? Because she'd promised his lordship that she'd take an inventory of the house. He'd behaved like it was a favor he was asking, but the truth was that her heart had leapt at the thought of all the things she could do to Foxrun with his money.

Every year the furniture had become more battered and broken, needing care and not receiving it. The roof—a nightmarish expanse of leaks and cracks—would require tens of thousands of pounds alone.

She'd made do with old Jenks the gardener and three boys from town. With only a handful of maids she'd been spread thin even just keeping a few of the common areas clean.

But with Gideon Banks's money?

Alys laughed out loud; she was just as bad as women who bartered themselves for jewels and gowns, except for Alys it was this house, always this house, these lands, and the people who'd made her life bearable for almost a decade. Oh, none of them were her social equal and there was nobody she could confide the truth in—not even the vicar and his wife—but they were the closest thing she'd had to friends—to family.

When she'd first been married there had still been a little money to entertain the local gentry at Foxrun. But that had run out by the second year. Without money, she'd not been able to accept invitations—how could she when she could never reciprocate?

Every year Sebastian gave her less and less money for Foxrun. Every pound and pence he spent on the house—and there were few enough— he spent grudgingly.

After Sebastian died, she pried into his locked desk, where the old steward had kept the books and looked at Foxrun's long-neglected ledgers. She'd almost exploded with fury at the amount he spent on horses, gambling, clothing and other pleasures. All those years he'd taken and taken and taken from Foxrun and had given nothing in return.

At least Gideon Banks, for all that he was a degenerate reprobate, appeared willing to pour his money into both the house and lands.

Alys could tolerate a lot for that—she could tolerate his exhibitionism and cavorting with whores in the next bedchamber if he were going to help bring Foxrun back to her former glory.

She climbed over another stile and stopped at the top to enjoy the view: Foxrun rising up before her like a magical castle. And it *was* magical, but it demanded money like mythical dragons demanded jewels and gold.

Alys knew it was not normal to love a house, but what else did she have to love? As much as Sebastian tried to blame their childless state on Alys she knew it was likely Sebastian who was responsible. After all, she was his second wife and there'd not been a child or even a miscarriage from either marriage.

As she tramped through the dew-dampened vale she considered her only prospect other than living in the Dower House: marriage. She was

61

out of mourning and free to give herself to another man, perhaps one who might give her a child.

She knew the local squire, Sir John, a recent widower perhaps ten years older than Alys, was looking for a wife to help care for his brood of children. Sir John had spoken to her several times in the months after Sebastian's death. Of course they'd done all their talking outside the church, in front of the eyes of the entire congregation, so she couldn't be *sure* of his intentions.

He seemed like a kind man but when she tried to bring up his face, she could only summon the image of a certain naked cit-turned-peer.

Alys growled at her idiocy and yanked a handful of tall grass, and then immediately felt bad for taking out her anger on blameless flora. As she crested the second rise, she stumbled and then gawked at what she saw lining the drive: men with ladders and scaffolding. *Dozens* of them, spreading out around Foxrun like ants surrounding a much larger foe.

She paused to watch the commotion. While the front of the drive was hidden by the house, she could hear and see wagons rolling in; she counted *ten* wagons before she resumed her journey, walking faster now, her heart beating with excitement. How had he managed such a miraculous feat?

Money, that's how.

Alys heard him before she saw him, his flat London accent carrying like the metallic clang of a hammer.

"I'll want you to do section by section," he ordered a stout man who stood beside him, staring up at the new earl with his mouth agape.

So, Alys wasn't the only one he affected that way.

"I know what you lot are like—even a whiff of rain and you're not working. I don't want to find myself bloody roofless all over the damned castle. Do we understand each other Mr. Floyd?"

Mr. Floyd scratched his head. "A'right, my lord."

"Good. Now where is that fellow who's come about the beetles?"

A tall, soberly dressed man stepped forward. "That would be me, my lord. But I'm actually not here about the beetles so much—"

Lord Taunton lifted a staying hand. "I specified in my letter I wanted to make certain the place wasn't being eaten by beetles."

"Well, yes, of course, my lord, but I'm also a—"

Lord Taunton raised the hand higher. "Can you, or can you not, find out if we have *beetles* in this house?"

Alys had to bite her lip to keep from laughing. What the devil had gotten into the man about beetles?

"Yes, my lord."

"Good, do so." He turned on his heel and spotted Alys spying on him.

She recalled the last time she'd seen him, mere hours earlier, and her face scalded.

He grinned and winked, as if she'd said something amusing, and then turned back to his crowd of tradesmen.

"Now, which one of you lads is the glazier?"

⊸ ♥ ⊢

Gideon was studying the layout of Foxrun's farms when a sharp knock made him look up.

It was Lady Taunton, and she was frowning. She was also dressed for the evening in a spectacularly unmodish gown. "Will you be coming to dinner tonight, my lord?"

Gideon squinted at the clock. "At six o'clock?"

"Yes, my lord. Six o'clock."

"Good God. Who dines at six o'clock?"

"That is the dinner time that has always been observed. If you wish to change it, perhaps you might do so *after* tonight, as cook has already prepared the meal."

He frowned at her snappish tone. "Very well, very well—don't fly into a pelter. Have Cook hold it half an hour and I shall rush my toilet, if that is all right with *you?*" He gave her a snappish look to match her tone.

She huffed and spun on her heel.

Jackson was waiting for him when he made his way to what was called the family wing.

"Did you know dinner was at six?" Gideon asked as he pulled off his cravat and shrugged out of his coat.

"Yes, my lord." Jackson had a face that could earn him a decent living at any gaming house in the country. He'd hardly even twitched an eyelash upon learning Gideon was an earl. Indeed, Gideon suspected the man had known of his ascension to the peerage before he had.

Jackson had Gideon shaved, washed, dressed, and down in the dining room—after two wrong turns—a mere thirty-eight minutes later. Hell, it was his damned house; he'd show up at the table whenever he wished.

He arrived in the dining room—a Teutonic cavern that brought to mind boars roasting and pewter tankards of beer along with bearded thanes and lusty wenches—to find Lady Taunton already seated.

"Sorry to keep you waiting, my lady. You may serve," he told Tickle, who was hovering near the door.

A footman pulled out Gideon's chair before taking his position behind it. He looked at Lady Taunton, who was at the foot end of the table. "Do you always dine this way?" he shouted.

"I usually dine alone."

He digested that while his footman filled his glass with something red. Gideon took a sip and almost spewed it all over the table. "Good God! What the hell is this?"

She'd just taken a drink—and apparently *swallowed* it—and frowned at him. "It is from the cellar."

"Yes, but did it come in a bottle? Or was it scraped off the floor?"

Lady Taunton frowned. "I'm sorry it doesn't meet with your standards, but it is what we have."

He *harrumphed* and made a mental note to add wine to his list of items to purchase. Which reminded him. "So, how did the household inventory progress, my lady?"

She brightened at the change of subject. Gideon had noticed she looked happier any time Foxrun was mentioned. It seemed an odd attachment, especially for a woman who would have to leave whenever he decided to get married—not that he saw that ever happening. But what did he know about women like her? Perhaps such an attachment to their husband's houses and lands was a common affliction.

"I've drawn up lists for your inspection. Separate ones for bed linens, draperies, new carpets in—"

Gideon grimaced. "Lord. I don't need to look at them or hear about them. Just order what you want and have the bills sent to me."

Her lips parted and he immediately thought of what he'd like to put between them. He snorted; little chance of *that* ever happening.

"You don't want to look at pattern cards? Samples?"

"I'd rather drive a rusty spike through my forehead."

Her jaw threatened to unhinge.

Gideon sighed and forced himself to speak less carelessly. "I beg your pardon. What I meant to say is that I trust your judgement." He smiled in what he hoped was a conciliating manner. "I daresay it is irreproachable."

Instead of returning his look, she regarded him through a lens of disapprobation and suspicion, even more so than most women did. She clearly sensed something was not right with him—that he was *not* suitable cloth from which to fashion an earl—and she was correct in her assessment.

Gideon doubted she would ever do much more than tolerate him and that for the good of Foxrun.

Well, he would milk that weakness shamelessly.

"You may consider yourself officially in charge of all items and issues that occur beneath the roof and between the walls of Foxrun. So, carpets, furniture, linens, frippery, et cetera, et cetera. Are we agreed?"

She nodded slowly, her expression still one of suspicion.

"I sent a telegram this morning. There will be two master carpenters arriving along with DuValle, my chef. I've also sent one of my associates, Mr. Smith, a request to hire a butler, housekeeper, and four footmen who have been trained to exhibit discretion." He didn't tell her he would station the men around him so that his libertine tendencies wouldn't inadvertently slay the locals with shock.

"Mr. Smith has the best run house I've ever seen, so he's a perfect man to make such important selections. If you can think of any positions that require skills you won't be able to satisfy from the local populace, let me know and I'll send another request."

"Oh, special skills? Perhaps more chambermaids?" she asked, her treacly sweet sarcastic tone one he'd not heard before—and also one he quite liked.

He gave her a lazy smile. "I am always on the lookout for a good chambermaid," he admitted.

She made a strangled, choking sound, her nostrils flaring.

Gideon's cock thumped at the spark of barely restrained anger in her dark eyes. For some reason it aroused him to know that *she* knew what he got up to in the room right next to hers. Yes, it aroused him a great deal. It was likely that Lucy and Susan would get very little sleep tonight.

But that was for later.

Gideon dragged his attention back to business. "I'd like to hire the rest of the servants from the surrounding area," he said, reluctantly leaving the matter of chambermaids behind for the moment. "If you could make it known that I will be interviewing for every position other than housekeeper, cook, and butler I should be much obliged." There, he could see that information made her happy and erased thoughts of chambermaids from her mind. At least for the moment.

"Of course, my lord. I must admit we've been losing a shocking number of our young women and men to jobs in the cities."

"Well, agriculture is dead, and it shall not be coming back soon," he said, picking up his wine, recalling what was in the glass just in time, and setting it back down.

"I thought tariffs were being considered?"

Gideon snorted. "You'll not see such under Gladstone, and it's just as well: agriculture in Britain is on its way to extinction. We are a nation of industry now; it is for others to grow our wheat and corn."

She set down her glass, her forehead furrowing in a fetching fashion "But I thought you meant to make improvements to the tenant farms."

"Oh, I do—make no mistake about it. But Foxrun will never subsist on her rents again, not with the ever-decreasing prices of agricultural goods."

"Then . . . why?"

He smiled. "My dear Lady Taunton," there was her lovely blush again, "Foxrun is *my* country estate and I will operate it as such. That means it must have farms because country estates have farms. That does *not* mean I'm so deluded as to believe it will ever support itself." He shrugged. "That is what my business is for."

The door opened and Tickle entered with another footman and two maids, all bearing platters.

As they set the dishes out on the table, he felt his face shifting into a frown. Everything—every single dish—appeared to be some shade of color between gray and dun. Gideon poked at a nearby item that resembled paper pulp slathered over a block of wood. He looked up to find Lady Taunton regarding him with a questioning expression.

He laid down his fork, his eyes flickering over the horrifying number of brown dishes. He'd always been a fussy eater—even when being fussy had meant going without—and his stomach roiled as he looked around at the food on this table.

"I cannot eat this."

All eyes focused on him, yet nobody spoke. Gideon wondered if this was what it felt like to be king—commanding such utter attention? The thought cheered him.

"I'd like bread, cheese, and perhaps some fruit." He directed the words at Tickle and enunciated them clearly.

The old man's jaw dropped—not nearly so handsome an expression on an ancient man as it was on Lady Taunton—and he hesitated, his eyes flickered from Gideon to the food to the countess to Gideon. It seemed like the old gaffer might run the circuit all night long but, fortunately, Lady Taunton stopped him.

"I believe his lordship prefers a light dinner, Tickle. Please inform cook to add some of our excellent ham and a flagon of cider along with the rest."

The old man nodded shakily and left the room, his expression lost and shaken.

Gideon felt a bit like a pillock for sending him hoofing. "Couldn't somebody else—perhaps somebody *more youthful*—do the fetching and carrying around here?" he asked.

"That's an excellent idea, my lord. Perhaps we might discuss that," she said, giving the two remaining servants a significant look.

Gideon frowned. "Discuss what?" he asked rudely

"That item on your list you asked me to address?" she prodded. "Along with the inventory?"

Oh, the pensioner matter.

"Ah, yes, that," Gideon said, feeling rather thick. "Leave us," he told the footmen. "Go bring up whatever Tickle finds—don't let him carry anything heavy," he added.

Lady Taunton waited until the door closed before speaking.

"Now, you were saying?" he asked.

"First, I apologize for the food. I'm afraid I hadn't noticed quite how much Cook had slipped." She caught her plump lower lip with even white teeth and shook her head.

Gideon's gaze riveted to that pillowy lip.

She released it and her spell along with it. "Er, what?" he said.

"I said I hadn't noticed the quality of Cook's meals."

"You eat this every night and yet you didn't notice?"

"Oh, no. I usually eat some gruel, toast, and tea in my room."

Gideon shivered. "Good Lord! That's dreadful," he said, aghast.

"I don't think everyone places as much importance on food as you might, my lord. Most people around here are largely concerned with getting enough of it."

Amazingly, Gideon felt his face heating. "Yes, Lady Taunton, I'm aware of what *most people* think about food—I spent the better part of my formative years in an orphanage." It was gratifying to see *her* face darken. "But I'm now a revoltingly wealthy man and one of the things I like to spend my money on is food that will not cause me to become ill. DuValle will arrive shortly, but until then, I'd rather go without food than face this," he gestured to the rapidly cooling and congealing dishes.

"You won't have to go without, my lord. I shall pass the word along to cook."

"While you're at it, you might as well tell her she's about to be pensioned off."

She hesitated and then asked. "Might I tell her the, er, details of such a pension?"

Gideon shrugged irritably. "Do whatever is usual."

"And what would that be?"

"How the devil should I know?" he demanded, vaguely aware he was behaving like an irascible arse. "Surely your husband allowed *some* servants to retire? Or did they all just die with a platter or dust mop in their hands?"

Her lips parted in shock and it reminded his cock of this morning. Heat and tingly pleasure gathered in his groin as he stared at her mouth.

"That was *horrid*, my lord."

"What?" he asked.

"What you just said about the servants—it was horrid."

"I beg your pardon," he said, not really meaning it. After all, he suspected he'd be using the memory of the way her face looked right now as a masturbatory aid later on in the evening.

Just what the devil *was* it about this woman? Whatever it was, he found it excessively irksome that thoughts of her seemed to be the key to his orgasms at present. *He* was the only person who should be in charge of his orgasms.

Yes, *bloody* irritating.

"That was most callous," she said, stabbing at something on her plate with a fork and probably wishing it were his head.

Gideon frowned—what the devil *had* he said? Ah, yes, now he remembered. "I already begged your pardon. Here, I'll do it again: I beg your pardon—and that of the servants I wronged with my callousness. Am I forgiven now?"

Luckily the door opened and Tickle entered with the two footmen, both bearing trays loaded with fruit, bread, and, yes, some slabs of ham. Well, that looked rather good. His stomach growled.

Gideon rubbed his hands together. "Thank you, Tickle, this is perfect." He looked up and raised a brow at Lady Taunton, who was watching him with her judgy, frowny look. Gideon wondered what she'd say if he told her exactly how he planned to employ the memory of *that* expression when he was alone.

Instead he turned to the butler, "Oh, Tickle," he said as the old man shuffled toward the door. "In the future please set Lady Taunton's cover beside mine. I'm liable to become hoarse shouting down the table."

"Very good, my lord." The door *snicked* shut behind him.

Gideon sawed off a chunk of ham and popped it into his mouth, groaning with pleasure as he chewed. The barbaric response drew both a blush and, surprisingly, a smile.

"It is cider-glazed ham. A specialty here. As is the apple cider."

Gideon washed his food down with a mouthful of said cider. "Ah, that's right—famous Taunton cider." Gideon noticed her eyes flickering over his sumptuous repast and stood, quickly reorganizing a platter until it held samples of everything, and then strode toward her, pleased by the way her eyes widened. Oh, she was a lovely woman, condescending looks, or not.

"Here, I've plenty to share." He plunked the tray down beside her, enjoying the weight of her eyes as they flickered over his person. Gideon knew the cutaway tailcoat flattered his broad-shouldered,

69

narrow-hipped build more than any other style, and his black, slim-fit trousers did nothing to hide his tumescence.

Her throat tightened convulsively as her eyes moved up his body. "Thank you," she said, her voice somewhat ragged as their eyes locked.

Gideon forced himself to give her a cool smile and limp back to his chair.

Chapter Six

It was Jackson who told Gideon about the peep hole.

It was his third night at Foxrun. He'd been out inspecting the tenant cottages and had not finished until after dark. He'd sent word to the house that Lady Taunton should dine without him and had, instead, taken his meal at a pub called The Jolly Taxpayer.

He'd made his rounds today with a local builder named Mr. Pendleton, a man who'd grown up in the area and was familiar with the cottages and most of their inhabitants. It had been Pendleton who'd suggested the pub.

"They've got a cider that can't be beat and the innkeeper, Mr. Thomas, makes his own cheddar."

Gideon had felt every eye on him when they walked into the taproom, which had hushed with comical celerity.

A chap in a crisp apron—who'd turned out to be none other than Mr. Thomas—rushed out from behind the bar to greet him.

"What an honor, my lord," he said after Pendleton introduced them, bowing low.

Gideon had received the same marked deference all day from his cottagers but didn't believe he'd ever become accustomed to it—not that he didn't enjoy it. No, he enjoyed it immensely, but it still left him feeling oddly uncomfortable.

He and Pendleton had taken what must have been the table of honor—near the cavernous hearth. Over the next hour the villagers—many his tenants—had come to pay their respects.

Gideon had instructed Mr. Thompson to put all the drinks for the evening on his bill and had left to loud and happy cheers.

He'd returned to find Foxrun shut down for the evening. He'd not wanted to miss dinner with Lady Taunton, but it was probably for the best as he seemed destined to misbehave around her. He'd been unable to resist going to the same window—again in his birthday suit—the second morning. He'd been disappointed to find himself without an audience.

But then tonight Jackson informed him of the peep hole.

He was undressing Gideon when he told him the news, his lips barely moving, his words almost inaudible. Gideon had stiffened and only *just* kept himself from stalking from the dressingroom to stare at the peep.

"Over the bed, you say?"

"Actually, it is tucked into the scrollwork in the headboard."

Gideon shook his head as he dropped into the dressing room chair and Jackson removed his boots. He'd worn breeches and riding boots today but had—fortunately—not needed to display his horrid equestrian skills as Mr. Pendleton had arrived with a gig—yet another countrified mode of transport Gideon would need to master.

"Good God, Jackson. How did you discover this?" Gideon asked.

"I was coming back up with your lordship's laundry earlier in the evening when I saw one of the panels in the hallway move. Rather than enter your chambers I entered the room across the hall—an unused suite of rooms—and waited." Jackson's lips curved ever so slightly—perhaps the first time Gideon had seen the man get even close to a smile in over a decade. "I waited for a quarter of an hour before the panel slowly opened."

"And," Gideon prodded, annoyed by his valet's sudden lapse into theatricality.

"Lady Taunton glanced up and down the hallway before stepping out and hastily closing the door. She then went to her chambers. It took me three or four moments to find the catch." Gideon heard the smugness in his voice. "The corridor passes behind both your and her ladyship's chambers. A small stool stood in one area, which is how I discovered the peep. There is another one down the hall a—peep, not stool. I looked through it and saw it was indeed in roughly the same position in her ladyship's bedchamber."

Gideon shook his head and stood, his hands going to the placket of his leather breeches and then stopped. He turned to Jackson, his mouth curving into a smile. "Did you . . .?"

Jackson nodded solemnly, an uncharacteristic twinkle in his eyes. "I placed a piece of string at the bottom of the panel." He paused for effect. "It had been moved when I went to fetch your can of hot water."

Gideon grinned. "Ah, so I have an audience."

"So it would seem, my lord."

Gideon was so bloody hard he ached. What he wanted to do was go out into his bedchamber and fist himself for her viewing pleasure. But really, after all the effort she was going to she deserved more of a show. "Go fetch Lucy and Susan."

"Very good, my lord."

"And tell them to dress for an evening of exertion." The women would know exactly what he meant.

—❤—

Alys was the lowest form of life: a spy. A sneaking, peeping, spy.

Well, what of it? She got little enough pleasure in life. Besides, the way his lordship displayed his naked, hard, muscular body at his window in the mornings—yes, she'd seen him again, thanks to some careful planning, although he'd not seen *her*—told her that he *wanted* her eyes on his body. Or anyone's eyes, likely.

She'd resisted the urge the last two nights, but she could resist it no longer. So, she'd sent Thursby off to bed early with her sniffling cold and lingered and loitered around his lordship's rooms like some sort of lurking pervert. She'd known he'd not be home for dinner—indeed, she'd been pleasantly surprised by his courteous message to that effect—so she'd not expected him until late, although not as late as this. She'd flapped back and forth not once, but twice. This second time she *knew* he was in there because she heard him arrive when Mr. Pendleton's gig clattered into the courtyard. She'd had to hurry to get into the passageway before he entered his room.

It occurred to her, as she stood on the stool, her eye plastered against the hole, that she would burn in hell for such behavior, but that wasn't enough to peel her away. She pulled an apple out of her dressing gown pocket and nibbled as she waited, her heart pounding in expectation.

The moment he strode into the room Alys lowered the apple and stared. He was dressed for riding and his clothing had been cut as closely as every other garment she'd seen on him. His riding breeches were black leather rather than buckskin and something about that seemed wicked and erotic. Her sex, already sensitive with anticipation, began to thump and she instinctively clenched her muscles, which just made the throbbing worse—or better, depending on how one looked at it.

His blond hair was overlong and brushed the collar of his black riding coat. His profile was toward her and she had to admit it was as exquisite as every other part of him. High chiseled cheekbones, an aquiline nose, and a firm chin gave him his "angelic" aspect, his full lips providing the "fallen" part.

Alys was surprised—but pleased—that he sported no facial hair, and guessed he was perfectly aware of his fine features and took pains to display them, rather than shroud them in moustaches and muttonchops.

He shrugged his muscular shoulders and his valet removed his coat, leaving him standing in his shirtsleeves and waistcoat.

His breeches fit lovingly over his narrow hips, the black leather stretching taut across his bottom which—she had to admit with a painful gulp—was quite shapely. Had she ever noticed a man's bottom? Sebastian had been a sporting man so he'd been fit and muscular, but he'd been stout by nature and his bottom had been squarish and broad, his shoulders rather narrow—nothing to compare with the classical physique of the man she was currently ogling.

Lord Taunton—*Gideon, go ahead and call him by his Christian name as you're about to watch him take his clothing off and*—

Alys squeezed her eyes shut and shook her head, as if that might shake away what she was doing and what she *hoped* to see: this *cripplingly* sensual man cavorting with his two prostitutes.

She swallowed loudly and opened her eyes just in time to see his lordship striding into his dressing room, his valet behind him.

"Well, drat," she whispered. The peep was over the bed, which made it perfect for viewing what transpired in the bed and that area right in front of it—the fireplace and settee and two chairs around it—but the rest of the suite was beyond her view.

She resumed eating her apple, pausing again when Jackson—Gideon's rather sinister-looking valet—stepped out of the dressing room and left his master's chambers.

Alys squinted and leaned closer, as if that would somehow allow her to see through the wall into the dressing room. But then he stepped out into the bedchamber. The apple slid from her fingers and hit the floor with a dull thud.

"Oh Lord."

He wore only his breeches—and he'd unfastened the catches, which allowed them to slide further down his narrow hips, exposing a remarkably tantalizing V of muscles. He extended his arms above his head and stretched in a way that sent every muscle in his body rippling—and also caused his breeches to drop even lower, until they exposed just a glimpse of dark blond curls.

Alys felt as if her eyes were fogging up. He lowered a hand and lazily stroked the muscular ridges of his belly, his fingers slipping beneath his placket and—

Oh. Lord.

He shifted his obviously erect member and heaved a sigh, his body flexing with pleasure. And then he turned his back on her and sauntered toward the small sitting area.

"Oh, please, God, don't let him sit in that chair . . . no, no, no," she whispered as he began to lower his bottom into the chair whose back faced her.

But then, quite suddenly, he seemed to change his mind, heading instead toward the fire. He leaned his forearm on the mantle and took up the poker, the fascinating musculature of his back rippling as he stirred the glowing embers.

Alys realized her entire body was clenched into a knot and forced herself to relax, swallowing repeatedly and taking deep breaths. She would have some kind of seizure if she didn't breathe and calm herself.

He replaced the poker and was leaning his head against his forearm, the position inadvertently displaying his body—his narrow, corded waist and the flaring muscles of his back and shoulders—to perfection.

Never in her life had she felt so alive—especially parts of herself she generally ignored, the muscles in her own belly tightening, her sex swelling and becoming noticeably hot.

The door to the bedchamber opened and Jackson ushered in not *one* but *both* women.

Alys gaped. What could one man possibly do with *two* women?

And then she noticed what they were wearing—how dare they traipse through the hallways wearing their only dressing gowns!

Jackson disappeared into the dressing room again and Gideon turned from the fireplace toward the two women. He must have said something funny—sound did not travel through the glass-filled peephole very well—because they chuckled as they walked toward him, their hips swaying in a way no chambermaid would employ, their bodies clothed in dressing gowns no chambermaid could afford.

He stopped them with a casual flick of his hand, their backs facing Alys and, inconveniently, blocking all but Gideon's head and shoulders from her view.

Again, he spoke and both women must have tugged at the sashes on their robes because the silk garments loosened and they shrugged them off with identical motions.

A gasp slipped out of her as the garments fluttered to the floor. Both women were identically attired—if that was the proper word for it—in only black corsets.

Gideon's sinful lips curved with approval and he twirled a finger around in the air.

They turned for him in slow circles, which is when she noticed the corsets were of a special design that lifted and exposed their astonishingly large bosoms.

She swallowed hard, her throat hurting as she stared at their perfect figures. The sour stew in her stomach was largely composed of jealousy—or envy—or perhaps both. But it did nothing to dampen her arousal. Quite the reverse. Instead of seeing them, she imagined herself dressed like that. What would she look like?

Her hand unconsciously went to her own waist, tracing a path up to her loose breasts, which were nowhere as large as Susan or Lucy's.

She'd had Thursby undress her before sending her away. She wore a heavy flannel nightgown—the nights were always chilly at Foxrun—and an older brocade robe. Neither garment, she knew, would elicit the smug smile of approval from the man currently studying the two women with all the cool expertise her dead husband had used to appraise his cattle. Was this how Sebastian had looked at his mistresses, too? Had her husband used *two* women at once, as well?

Gideon gestured to one of the women—Susan—and all thoughts of Sebastian fled as the woman went to the settee—which sat at an angle that, thankfully, allowed Alys to see.

Rather than sit, she knelt on it, her back to Gideon, and placed her hands on the high back, and then, very deliberately, spread her knees and canted her bottom up toward him, exposing a part of her body Alys had never seen—not even on her own person.

"Oh my goodness." Alys's heart pounded so hard she felt it at pulse points she hadn't known she possessed.

Just then Jackson emerged from the dressing room, bearing something in both hands.

The brunette went to take whatever it was and when she turned Alys saw they were straps of some sort—like the leads of a bridle, long strips of leather.

Still facing away, Gideon took one strap and bent to slip it around the kneeling woman's ankle. Alys watched in open-mouthed shock as he tugged on the leather strip, spreading her wider, and then secured the other end with a quick slip knot to the wooden settee leg.

He did the same with her other ankle, pausing to tilt her bottom toward him in a way that left Alys in no doubt of what he would soon be doing.

He quickly bound her wrists, moving around to the other side of settee to tie them to the other legs, bending her over the wooden sofa back to secure her. When he stood, she gasped: the shiny crown of his penis extended above the low-slung breeches and pressed against his hard belly, which glistened with wetness.

She watched in a trancelike state as he tied Susan's second wrist and then stood, coming around the settee until his back was once again facing Alys. He slid a hand between the bound woman's thighs and her own sex tightened and sent her hurtling toward the exquisite sensation she'd been experiencing in her bed the last two nights, but only after a good deal of rubbing. She squeezed her eyes shut as her body shuddered with pleasure, wave after wave washing over her.

Still trembling with tiny aftershocks of pleasure, she forced her eyes open, afraid to miss—

"Ah, God—" she whispered, horrified by her blaspheming.

He'd turned in profile to face the brunette, who came toward him and sank to her knees gracefully. She leaned toward his placket, until her mouth was hovering just above his exposed crown, and then she stuck out a tongue and *licked* his organ.

Alys gripped her sex with one hand, as if that might stop what had already started to build again.

Gideon shuddered at the woman's gesture and he said something as he gazed down at her, one hand slipping into her hair while his other still moved between Susan's spread thighs.

Alys watch enrapt as the woman unbuttoned his placket and his breeches slid to the floor allowing his erect breeding organ to spring free. Without hesitation the woman lowered her mouth over the swollen head, taking only that part of him into her mouth, her cheeks hollowing with the force of her suction.

Alys's mind responded with revulsion: how *could* she do such a thing?

But her body felt otherwise, and she shook with the force of what she was failing to suppress, the clenching and swelling almost primitive in its forcefulness, even as her brain rebelled at the low animal behavior she was witnessing.

She'd found that book in the library—the one with all the drawings—so she had some inkling that things of this nature went on. But Sebastian had always behaved like a gentleman with her. He'd bred her regularly when he was at Foxrun, but he'd behaved like a civilized Christian, coming to her in darkness, entering her only long enough to spend his seed inside her, and then bidding her good night.

This? She shook her head, unable to look away. This was . . . well . . . she had to force herself to blink, her eyes dry and scratchy from staring.

Gideon's mouth moved and his hips began to pulse. The woman opened her jaws wider and her head lowered and lowered and lowered—good God! How could she breathe?

Alys could hardly breathe just watching.

Lucy sank as far as she could go, not stopping until her lips rested against the curly hairs at his base. And then they froze in that tableau. Gideon's tight abdomen was flexing with his rapid breaths. And then, impossibly, he spread his feet wider and bent his knees, his spine curving into a C shape as he flexed his muscular bottom, took the woman's head with both hands, and flexed his hips in sharp thrusts—just as if he were *breeding* her mouth.

Lucy's body was pliant, her slightly bowed posture submissive as her big breasts jiggled with the force of his thrusts—*how* could she get any air in her lungs with *that* in her throat?

He held her that way as he pulsed, gazing down on her body as if he were feeding on watching her as much as violating her.

And then ever so painfully slowly, he began to pull out of her, stopping only when her lips tightened around the end. Still with his body curved and knees slightly bent he tilted her chin up so that he might watch as he slid in and out, his muscular bottom and thighs flexing.

He plunged deeper and harder, his forearms tightening as his hips began to jerk with increasingly uncontrolled thrusts. Alys recognized the action—although far, far less savage—from her times with Sebastian and knew his climax must be impending. She waited in horrified fascination to see if he would spend in her mouth. Surely not? Surely even such a beast as this man would not—

He froze, holding her still for a long moment and then slowly straightened, pulling himself out of her entirely this time.

A strand of spittle linked the woman's open mouth and his impossibly long and thick organ. He laughed down at her and used the slick, ruddy rod like a whip, slapping her cheek several times—hard—before pulling away.

He was just *vile*.

And Alys was even viler for wanting to be in there with *him*. Her mouth watered to taste him—to see how much she could fit inside her throat.

She was a disgusting, immoral, repulsive, wanton *pig*.

But oh, he looked so . . . virile, masculine, savage.

His breeding organ was the only real one she'd ever seen. Sebastian had always worn his nightshirt and come to her in darkness, but she swore it had not felt as huge as what she saw before her now. Not only had she never seen her husband's erect organ, she'd certainly never touched it, and she didn't even know whether he'd possessed the slight sprinkling of hair that glistened on Gideon's broad chest.

He patted the kneeling woman's cheek with a gesture of dismissive affection and spoke a few words. She immediately rose and went in the direction of the dressing room.

He stood, as if in thought, absently stroking himself with one hand, while feeling his testicles with the other. For some reason this casual but erotic action seemed even more decadent than what he'd just been engaged in: he was so *at home* in his body, handling himself in ways she'd never dreamed of touching herself.

Until these past few days, she'd only ever felt the itching between her thighs either in her sleep or those few times she'd looked at *The Book*. She shuddered at the mere thought of *The Book* and how she'd embarrassed herself with it. How Sebastian had treated her the night she'd told him about it. What a terrible night.

Ever since that horrible, mortifying evening she'd simply tried to ignore her body. She did a fairly good job of it, unless the sensations came to her when she couldn't help it. Those were the nights she woke in shame to find her fingers wet.

Watching him stroke himself with such confident arrogance also made her realize—quite pointedly—that she was watching another human in their most private environment without their knowledge or permission. Alys squeezed her eyes shut.

She was worse than this man and his horrid, vulgar debasement of those women. She should go back to her room this instant—while the occupants were too busy with their depraved behavior to notice. She opened her eyes and lifted the skirts of her nightgown and dressing gown, preparing to step down. Her eyes drifted over the peephole without her brain's permission and she gasped, leaning closer before she even knew what she was doing.

He held a whip in his hand—a whip of a sort she'd never seen, with many strips of leather, like something she'd once read about, a cat-o-nines she believed it was called.

Alys gave a loud squeak and quickly bit her tongue. In his bedchamber, Gideon cocked his head, as if he might have heard something. Alys cursed her stupidity—quietly—holding her breath. Oh please, Lord, don't let him find me here.

Her own prayer shocked her. Why would God condone such activity, not to mention protect her? He was far more likely to strike her down with a bolt of lightning.

Run now! Run!

But she couldn't, her feet refused to move.

He held still for a long moment, but then gave a slight shrug, and turned back to the bound woman.

Alys watched in stupefaction as he commenced to whip her. The blows looked light enough, but he delivered them without ceasing, his muscular arm falling into a rhythm that was mesmerizing; a rhythm that seemed to pulse through her own body, once again concentrating in her sex.

She had no idea how long he worked, only that his body had become slick from his exertions and the woman he was whipping began to shudder, her back a flaming red, but with no sign of broken skin or even welts.

His blows became harder as her shaking intensified and Alys saw, with a bolt of shock, that she was leaking between her spread thighs, almost as if she—

Just then the woman threw back her head—barely able to move given the nature of her bondage—and Alys heard her hoarse cry even through the thick walls.

Gideon tossed aside his whip and mounted her as quickly and violently as Alys had once seen her father's breeding stallion mount a mare.

He'd bound her low, so he had to spread his feet wide, bending forward and resting one hand on the settee back to support his weight while he thrust savagely into her.

Alys's eyes were drawn to the place between his legs, to where his testicles, no longer pendulous, had drawn up snug to his body as he pounded into the woman's immobilized form without mercy.

Suddenly, every sinew and muscle in his body hardened and he rammed into her with a particularly brutal thrust and then held her as his body spasmed, his hips jerking as he filled her with his seed.

Alys closed her eyes and collapsed against the cold stone wall, her face hot with shame as her body gave up the struggle and shook with the force of her climax.

Chapter Seven

Gideon was up before the cock's crow the following morning, feeling more himself than he'd done in *months,* perhaps even years.

He'd sent the girls packing once Jackson had given him the sign that Lady Taunton was safely back in her room. He'd then fallen asleep grinning and—thankfully—spent and flaccid.

He'd woken up bright-eyed after a night completely free of tossing and turning. And all because of nosey Lady Taunton.

He dressed in his riding kit and headed down to the breakfast room, which he'd seen but never eaten in yet. He arrived to find the room dark and cold. Tickle—somehow attuned to his movements in this vast, rambling house—popped up behind him. Although *popped* wasn't probably the correct verb.

"Ah, good morning your lordship. Er, were you looking for breakfast?"

Gideon thought about saying he'd been looking for the stables, but decided the old man was only trying to be helpful. Besides, after the explosive orgasm he'd experienced last night he felt benevolent toward all of mankind.

"I'm feeling peckish," he admitted.

"Ah."

Gideon waited, but there seemed to be nothing forthcoming. "Perhaps you might send some toast, two eggs, and a pot of *extremely* hot coffee to the library."

"Ah." The old man nodded, as if only now hearing the order. "Very good, sir."

Gideon frowned as he watched the old gimmer shuffle away. Well, the new servants from London would arrive soon and today was the day he'd picked to interview for most of the lesser positions. He turned on his heel and strode toward the library, his thoughts on the servant situation.

Mr. Smith had responded quickly to his telegram, with the good news that his steward was already at work engaging several tight-lipped servants for Gideon. Smith was a sod and managed to have his lovers living right in his house without facing prosecution. If Smith could do it, certainly Gideon could employ some servants of his own to set the tone? He probably should have consulted the man far sooner and would have spared himself a lot of aggravation in London. But better late than never.

He jogged up a flight of stairs, his mind returning to last night's entertainment. His need for decorum had dramatically reduced with the knowledge that her ladyship, whom he'd been foolishly, not to mention uncharacteristically, concerned to protect from his debauchery not only *knew* of his antics but actively sought them out.

Gideon began to stiffen at the memory of last night, already anticipating tonight. He grinned. He was particularly looking forward to staring her in the eye over the dinner table, if not sooner.

He'd been bloody tempted to slip into that corridor and avail himself of the countess's peep after Jackson reported she'd returned to her room. But he simply couldn't bring himself to spy on her. For all that she was getting a free show, he suspected she was the closest thing to a virgin. According to Pendleton, whose lips had moved constantly, the last earl had barely come home four times a year, a fact that had reduced him in the eyes of his tenantry and the local townsfolk as her ladyship was much beloved.

Gideon had shamelessly tweezed gossip from the man, learning, among other things, that this marriage had been the earl's second. His first had lasted for twelve years and ended childless. His lordship had married the current countess when she'd not yet turned seventeen and there had been much speculation in the neighborhood when she, too, failed to produce an heir or even fall pregnant.

Gideon entered the library, pausing as he always did to admire the magnificence of the room. He'd sent a message to London, describing the woodwork to Edward Fanshawe, who'd started out life as a carpenter.

He doubted he'd done justice to describing the artistry of the work, but Fanshawe could see for himself since he'd accepted Gideon's invitation to visit.

He knew he should probably send them a message to push the visit off for a while—a long while, likely—but he'd decided to stick with the plan. Besides, none of them were strangers to a bit of rough living. And he also suspected Lady Taunton would bring the place up to snuff quickly enough—at least three guest rooms and a few common rooms—knowing there would soon be visitors.

He grinned to himself as he dropped into the old leather chair behind his desk and began perusing his day's long list of tasks.

— ♥ —

"Goodness, my lady, you're in a fidget this morning," Thursby observed in a grumpy tone as she finished braiding Alys's hair—badly—and fastened it into the simple coronet Alys favored.

She was glad Thursby didn't usually wake and wander into her rooms until nine at the earliest. Alys had woken at dawn and gone for a mad ride on her mare, Nike. The poor girl hadn't been ridden so hard in years and Alys felt like a brute when she brought her back to the stables, lathered.

"Ah, my lady, took the old gal out for a jaunt," Silber said as he waved away one of the stable lads and came to help her dismount.

He lifted her to the ground easily, his strong hands on her waist never failing to send what she now understood were spirals of sexual stimulation through her body. It was lucky for her that her face was already hot from riding when she looked the long way up to meet his eyes.

Silber was a few years younger than Sebastian but Alys had always found the gentle, humorous man far more responsible and mature. She wished she didn't also find his matter-of-fact touches and powerful body so . . . distracting. No doubt he would be horrified if he knew what feelings she'd entertained toward him over the years.

She gave him an awkward smile. "I shouldn't have been so hard on her," she confessed.

He smiled as he stroked Nike's neck with his massive but gentle hands. "It's my opinion a good hard ride was exactly what she needed."

He looked down at her with the same respectful smile but . . . was that a glint of something in his eyes? Amusement?

Good God! What was wrong with her? Just because *she* was a wanton didn't mean every man she saw was thinking about the things that Gideon Banks was doing.

Silber cocked his head, a crease of concern between his brown eyes. "Is aught amiss, my lady?"

"No, of course not. Give her a double helping of grain," she said as she turned and strode back toward the house, her legs like rubber beneath her heavy habit.

She'd come up to her room to find Thursby waiting. "And where have you been?" she demanded, as if she were the mistress and not the servant.

"Out for a ride."

"Hmmph."

Alys would have liked to fire Thursby, but she'd been forced on Alys by Sebastian because Thursby had once been maid to Sebastian's mother. And now that she *could* dismiss the woman—who was a dreadful maid and an unhappy drunk—she decided it was pointless. After all, she'd tolerated her for years, and where else would the woman go?

"I'll have a bath, Thursby."

After grunting again, the old woman went to order the water and then left Alys to herself.

So, she'd lingered over her bath and then lingered over her usual breakfast, trying to linger even more until she'd recaptured some of her calm and reserve. But now it was past eleven and she could linger no longer, so she rang for Thursby.

"You look tired," the old woman said.

Alys met her maid's red-rimmed but curious eyes in the mirror and was impressed that she'd been able to muster such a bland smile.

"I had a poor night's sleep," she said, no less than the truth.

Thursby's hands froze and an expression of avidity spread across her face. "Was it because—"

"No!" They both startled at her sharp voice. "I heard nothing." That was true, although she'd *seen* plenty.

85

Thursby's jaw worked from side to side and Alys knew what she'd say before she said it.

"It's sinful you being here. You should be in the Dower House like a respectable woman."

Alys had to bite her tongue. Instead she said, "I'm biding my time, Thursby. But I can hardly ask him while he's so obsessed with Foxrun ant the tenant structures."

Thursby grunted and fastened Alys's plain gold cross around her neck.

Alys was surprised she didn't burst into flame at its touch. She was a filthy, wanton sinner. Not only for what she'd watched and reveled in, but for her disgusting thoughts about Silber and her burning impatience for tonight.

"My lady?"

She glanced up to find Thursby frowning. "You don't look well."

"I'm fine," she lied, standing. "Now," she said briskly, "I want to go into Taunton today. I had planned for a shopping expedition to Bath after his lordship picked out the patterns he wanted, but he's indicated he does not care. Therefore, I will buy everything in Taunton."

Thursby sucked in a shocked breath, "That will be—"

"Dear," Alys finished with a grim smile. "Yes, it will be extremely dear, and doubly so when I tell them how fast we want it. But that is what his lordship wants, so that is what he will get." She turned away from her black clad reflection, another black piece of clothing flitting through her head, causing an uncomfortable throb beneath her heavy skirts before she forcibly shoved the image of last night's corsets from her mind.

She'd just laid her shawl on her shoulders when a light knock at the door made her turn.

"Enter," she called out.

The door opened on Susan. The slattern was wearing a whore's idea of a maid uniform and her slouchy posture was insolent, which matched her amused expression perfectly. "His lordship wants to see you in the library."

Thursby gasped behind her and Alys inhaled—and then just kept on inhaling, until she thought she might explode.

Thursby bristled and stepped around her. "How dare he summon her ladyship like a servant! You will address—"

Alys lifted a hand and Thursby stopped immediately. "What is your name?" she asked, even though she'd made it her business to know it. Whatever Susan saw in Alys's eyes made her straighten slightly.

"Susan, er, my lady." She dropped a hasty, clumsy curtsy.

"Thank you, Susan. You may go."

Susan shut the door so quickly she almost snapped her nose off.

"That *slut!*"

"Thursby!" Alys snapped. "I will not tolerate such language."

"How can—"

"I don't wish to speak of it."

"But surely you'll—"

Alys frowned and her maid sighed and stomped away.

Alys's legs wobbled as she made her way toward the library. Would she even be able to look him in the eyes after what she'd seen last night? Oh God, just thinking about his body and the things he'd done with it left her positively weak.

You want him to do those things with you.

"No!" she blurted, startling herself.

Oh yes.

All right, so it was true. She'd tossed and turned all night imagining herself with him—doing those *things*.

You need to go see the vicar.

Alys grimaced at the thought, realized she'd passed the library, and turned around.

Just go in there, she told herself.

Just—

The door swung inward, revealing the object of her ruminations. He gave a start when he saw her, his gorgeous face wearing a look of pleased surprise—but all she could see was his feral grin of pleasure from last night.

"Er."

"Ah, my lady. I was just about to head to the weapon's room."

Her eyebrows shot up. "You were?"

"Yes, today is the day I'm interviewing for the servant positions— remember? Tickle said the armory would be the best room to speak to people, being that it's large and on the ground floor." His smile turned to that grin he'd sported last night—when he'd sported nothing *but* a smile. "He also mumbled something about Mrs. Tickle, dirty boots, and carpets."

Alys tried to think of something, anything, to say, but could only nod.

His brow furrowed. "I say, I hope I haven't over-stepped? I asked you to join me with the interviews because you're so knowledgeable both about the house and our servant needs, but if you're not feeling quite the thing—"

"No, of course I'd be glad to help. I'm sorry, I'd forgotten it was today."

"Well, don't worry about it if you've made plans."

"Oh, I was just going to visit the draper in Taunton and choose some fabrics."

He frowned, this time not with concern, but irritation. "I'll send somebody for them—they can come out with their," he churned his hand in the air, "Well, whatever." He seemed to realize they were still standing on the threshold to the library and pushed the door open and called out after his shoulder, "Lucy, go down to the kitchen and have somebody trot off to Taunton. Tell them not to return without the draper and his entire bag of tricks."

There was an exceedingly long pause, during which time his lordship's expression turned thunderous. He'd just opened his mouth to say something when an exaggerated sigh stopped him.

"Yes, *my lord*."

The silence that followed this shirty response was deafening.

His lordship's jaw worked back and forth and Alys though he might explode. But he seemed to recall her presence just in time and whipped around, catching her gawking. He gave her a smile, forced this time, and shut the door with a sharp click.

"Well," he said, gesturing toward the stairs, "Shall we?"

❤

It looked like the entire town had turned out. While it was true there were many seeking work in the village, it also seemed like every person who needed a job had brought a small audience with them. Everyone wanted to see the new earl, one of the wealthiest men in Britain. And the new Earl of Taunton did not fail to put on a show.

The first thing he did was order the kitchen to provide tea and biscuits. For everyone.

Upon hearing his bellowed order, Alys excused herself and made her way through the growing crowd until she saw just who she'd been hoping to find, Jerry Harlow, the baker's seventeen-year-old son, who was desperate for a position in his lordship's stables.

"Hello, Jerry."

"My lady." He dropped an awkward bow, his eyes jumping around to take in the luxury of the ancient corridor he was waiting in.

"Will you do me a great favor?"

"Yes, 'course, my lady."

"I need you to get Silber to hitch up the gig and run you into town. Take everything at your parents' bakery and tell them to send a bill to his lordship. Stop at The Jolly Taxpayer and fetch a keg of cider and another of ale."

Jerry's eyes slid nervously toward the line ahead of him.

She smiled. "Don't you worry, when you get back, I'll introduce you to the earl before you'd ever reach the front of the line."

He grinned and nodded, his thick brown hair flopping. "Aye, my lady."

"Good, now hurry!"

She next went toward the kitchen, encountering a stricken looking Mrs. Tickle halfway there. "Oh, my *lady*! Tickle tells me his lordship—"

Alys laid a hand on her arm. "Don't worry, I've just sent Jerry Harlow into town to his father's bakery."

Poor Mrs. Tickle sagged so quickly Alys feared she would collapse. "But his lordship will expect—"

"I'll deal with his lordship."

When Alys arrived up at the table the earl was chatting with Nelly Benson's twin daughters. Alys stared hard enough at his lordship to burn holes through him. But—amazingly— he appeared not to have noticed they were nubile fifteen-year-olds. At least his lascivious leer was nowhere in sight. Indeed, he was behaving positively avuncularly.

"Hello girls," Alys said as she settled into the chair beside him.

The girls dropped identical curtseys, "Hello my lady."

Somebody, likely the footmen at Mrs. Tickle's direction, had brought in a heavy trestle table and two thronelike chairs. She felt like a fifteenth century liege lord taking tithes from her vassals.

Gideon turned to her. "These young ladies say they are interested in chambermaid positions," the corner of his mouth pulled up and her face heated at what she saw in his eyes.

Her mouth tightened, both at his wicked look and her own body's reaction. "We do need chambermaids. But these are not your type, my lord."

All the humor drained from his face and his pupils shrank to pinheads, his lips suddenly thinning. "I'm going to pretend you did not just say that to me," he said, his soft voice sharper than the lash he'd wielded last night.

Alys felt a rush of shame at his words.

He was correct to be angry: he might be engaging in deviant sexual antics, but he was not doing so with young girls. The women he'd brought with him were well above twenty and clearly skilled in their business.

"You're correct, my lord. I apologize. That was unworthy."

He nodded and turned back to the girls. "Go see Mrs. Tickle—the footman at the door will show you the way. If she wants you, she'll tell you when and what to do." He turned to Alys with a questioning look. "Any idea what wage a chamber or parlor maid makes?" he asked under his breath.

Alys smiled at the girls. "I daresay Mrs. Tickle will want you to start out in the kitchen and work your way up."

"Yes, my lady," the girls said, unsurprised at her words.

"A tweeny position is £10 per annum."

The girls grinned and dropped another curtsey. "Thank you, my lady, my lord."

The earl turned to her as the girls scuttled off. "Good God! £10?"

"That is a generous wage, my lord—exceptionally so."

His lordship shook his head in disgust and then called out, "Next."

Chapter Eight

For the first time in longer than he could remember, Gideon went directly up to bed after dinner, undressed, dropped face-first into bed, and fell into a deep, dreamless sleep.

He woke alone, just before first light, the bedding hardly disturbed. The experience was . . . singular.

Then he recalled his plans for the last evening—putting on another show for Lady Taunton—and groaned. "Damn and blast!" And he'd had something rather delicious planned for her, too.

Gideon didn't know *why* yesterday had been so exhausting. He'd done nothing physical, just sat and talked to strangers. All. Day. Long.

Lady Taunton had sat beside him for most of the day, only disappearing briefly a few times, which usually preceded the arrival of food and beverage. Really, the woman was a bloody marvel. Gideon had realized immediately after he'd ordered food and drink for a hundred people that perhaps he might have misspoken, especially given what his cook had shown him the one time she'd prepared a meal. But, again, it had been Lady Taunton who'd saved the morning, somehow managing to magically create the most delicious baked goods.

Again, at luncheon, there'd been hearty sandwiches of marvelous Taunton cheddar and cider-glazed ham.

By the time they'd seen the very last petitioner—yes, they spoke to *everyone*—it had been past dark.

Once again, the countess had seen to his gastronomical needs and a meal arrived, unsolicited by him, in the library, where they'd gone to compare their notes from the day.

They'd eaten a hearty stew with fresh bread while looking through their lists.

"I count thirty-seven new employees," Lady Taunton said after taking a genteel sip of cider. "And you, my lord?" she urged when Gideon simply stared.

"Oh, er, yes." He squinted at the sheet. "Are you including that last lad—Joe Jensen, I believe his name was?"

She frowned down at her page. "No, I missed him." She made the *tsking* sound he found adorable.

She looked up at him and smiled. "You are asleep at your desk, my lord."

He blinked. "I most certainly am *not.*"

She laughed and the sound swirled in his belly. Gideon frowned; he was an idiot—it was likely *cider* he felt swirling.

She stood. "I never expected engaging employees would be so exhausting. I suppose that is why many people employ both house and land stewards.

Gideon groaned. "Good God! Two more positions?"

Again she laughed, this time the swirly feeling dropping down lower, in the neighborhood of his cock—one of Gideon's favorite neighborhoods.

"You might want to give more thought to such positions. Aren't your new butler, housekeeper, and footman—"

"Four," Gideon said.

"*Four* footmen arriving shortly?"

"Mmm-hmm." A huge yawn distorted his face. "I *do* beg your pardon," he said, and then realized she, too, was yawning. "Off to bed, Lady Taunton, we can finish this discussion on the morrow."

And then he'd gone up to his room, Jackson had peeled him out of his clothing, and he'd climbed the ladder to his bed and collapsed into it, sleeping without waking even once.

Gideon shook his head. Such wholesome, healthy behavior was not normal and likely wasn't good for him, either. He turned to look at the clock—it was barely past five o'clock. The charwoman would be moving about, so he could hardly summon Lucy and Susan.

Thinking their names reminded him of Susan's behavior yesterday and he frowned. The whores were becoming unmanageable. He had half a mind to send them back to London. But then of course he'd need to have two more brought down. Gideon always employed two because he tended to wear them out.

Not last night, the snide little voice mocked.

He bristled at that. *It was just one bloody night. I'll be back in the saddle again this evening—you'll see.* And then he felt like an idiot for arguing with himself.

The word *saddle* made him think: why not go for a ride as he was up so early? He'd had two riding hacks sent over from Taunton but hadn't tried either of them. A ride early in the morning—without anyone watching his clumsy horsemanship—might be just the thing for him.

He pushed back the bedding and hopped out of bed. Yes, a brisk early morning ride would be just the thing to begin the day.

→ ♥ ←

"The second early morning this week, my lady. Nike will be pleased to see you." Silber smiled down at her, his grin remarkably fresh for so early in the day.

Alys returned his smile and flicked her whip, tapping her worn leather riding boot. "Keeping you hopping, am I, Mr. Silber?"

He chuckled. "I'm pleased to be able to earn my crust. I'll be back in half-a-blink, my lady."

Alys watched him turn and walk toward the stalls, appreciating the broad expanse of his shoulders. He was a *gigantic* man, far bigger than Lord Taunton's lithe, muscular person. Alys wondered what he looked like without any clothing—

A wave of shame hit her. "What *are* you doing?" she hissed at herself.

"Yes, what *are* you doing?"

She yelped and spun. "You!"

Gideon grinned and held up his hands. "Me."

"What are *you* doing up so early? I thought you usually weren't up and about until noon?"

"*Tsk, tsk, tsk,* my lady." A truly wicked grin spread across his face. "I think you know I'm *up* and about far earlier than that."

Alys gasped.

"Ah, your lordship, what a pleasure to see you this fine morning."

They both turned to find Silber smiling down at them, amusement glinting in his eyes. Had he *heard* what his debauched employer said?

"Good morning Mr. er—"

"Silber, my lord." Silber dropped a remarkably graceful bow for a man his size.

"Ah, yes, Silber. Her ladyship says you know your way around cattle."

"I like to think so." The big man patted Nike's neck, his hands deftly slipping a bridle over her bowed head. Horses, Alys knew, loved the man.

"Is there anything decent to be bought around Taunton?" Gideon asked.

Silber cut him a quick glance, his hands moving all the while, efficient, gentle, and deft. "What might you be looking for?"

Gideon smoothed the already smooth leather of his gloves, stroking every finger. It was a nervous motion Alys had seen before. Did Mr. Silber make him nervous?

"I need carriage horses and some decent riding stock—enough variety to please and accommodate any guests I may invite. Something for me, as well." He paused and gave the other man a self-mocking smile. "I won't lie to you, Mr. Silber, I'm a poor equestrian at best."

Silber gave a low, easy chuckle as he lifted Alys's saddle blanket onto Nike. "I doubt you have much need to ride in London."

"Yes, you are correct. I have not done much riding." Gideon flushed with either relief, or pleasure, or both and Alys realized what a truly kind and gentle giant Silber was to set the earl—a generally arrogant obnoxious man—at ease.

"It happens that I do know of some excellent stock around these parts, my lord, we've got some fine breeders. It would be my pleasure to bring a selection of mounts here for you to try before you make any decision."

A sleepy stable lad came wandering around the corner, rubbing his eyes with his fist.

"Ah, look who's decided to join us," Silber teased, smiling down at the small boy. "Go fetch master's horse, Jimmy—the bay in the last stall but one."

The boy's eyes and mouth formed stunned circles when he noticed Lord Taunton and he went sprinting off.

As Silber tightened the girth Lord Taunton said, "You seem an easy man to work for, Mr. Silber."

"Aye, my lord. Can't see any use to make those below me suffer— not when I love my job as much as I do."

Lord Taunton's eyebrows arched and for a moment Alys feared he'd say something cutting, but instead, he said, "An excellent motto to live by." He turned to Alys. "Do you mind if I join you this morning?" he asked.

"Of course not." Did she sound breathy?

"Here you are, my lady." Silber walked toward Alys, Nike following him like a faithful hound.

Alys slung her train over her arm.

"Are you ready, my lady?" he asked and Alys nodded, ashamed at how much she always enjoyed this part of her ride.

Silber's gargantuan hands circled her waist and he lifted her like a feather and set her on her saddle, his hands disappearing from her body all too quickly.

Alys knew her face was flushed and she felt Gideon's eyes upon her as Silber checked her stirrups, his hands hard and warm through the leather of her riding boot as he shifted her ankle and tightened a strap.

Alys was torn between her beloved ritual of watching Silber's battered, capable hands—he was so close she could smell the sweat, leather, and horse on him—and looking up at the man she knew was watching her.

Lord Taunton won and she looked up.

Gideon Banks was staring at her with pupils so huge his eyes were black. His nostrils were flared and his jaw was flexing. As if pulled by heavy weights, her eyes dropped to his hips; the long, hard ridge of his erection was pressed against his snug leather breeches.

━ ♥ ━

Fuck!

Gideon's erection was like iron, and the cause of it was crystal clear: Lady Taunton was in a state of high rut for his immense stable master. Part of him wondered if they'd consummated her desire, but he somehow didn't think so.

The man looked far too comfortable and easy to be harboring either unrequited *or* requited lust for the mistress of the house.

Jonathan Silber—Gideon knew his name, of course—he knew the names of every person who worked for him, even the new ones—was one of the most likeable men he'd met in recent memory. Comfortable in his own skin to a degree one rarely encountered, he seemed contented to use his skills without making a spectacle about them.

Gideon had to admit that *wasn't* something he'd learned yet—*not* boasting—and might never master.

Not only was Silber pleasant and gentle, but the man was a bloody ox, his body even bigger than Gideon's partner's—Edward Fanshawe.

Gideon had given a great deal of thought to his feelings about other men, especially when it came to his body's reaction to seeing them naked or watching them fucking. He didn't *believe* he was a sod—because he certainly enjoyed women—but he'd both taken pleasure from, and given it to, other men.

So, perhaps that *did* make him a sod?

He mentally shrugged. He'd long ago decided he would never feel guilt for his sexual appetites. The truth was he enjoyed fucking fine human animals, no matter the gender, and he imagined Silber would strip to considerable advantage.

His deviant brain already had the gargantuan man mounting Lady Taunton from behind, just like a stallion, his massive thighs and arse flexing and pumping. Doubtless he'd have an enormous cock—horse-like, of course—and he'd employ it with the same competence he appeared to do everything physical.

Gideon was also part of this fantasy—that went without saying—but he couldn't help appreciating the image of the stable master's powerful body covering the woman across from him and plunging into her.

As Gideon took in her quickened breathing and flushed face he *knew* she was envisioning something similar, if not nearly so graphic. Yes, if there was one human emotion he recognized above all others, it was lust, and Lady Taunton had it in spades for her big servant.

The woman in question tore her eyes away from Gideon's ridged placket with visible effort.

"I shall meet you on the drive," she said without looking at his face, urging her horse on in that effortless way that people like *her* seemed to possess in the saddle.

Gideon watched her go, appreciation vying with envy as he shifted his cock.

"Her ladyship is a prime horsewoman," Silber commented mildly as he took the saddle the boy brought to him and lifted it up onto the placid-looking bay.

"Born in the saddle, I'm sure."

Silber laughed. "Near enough."

Gideon grunted.

"She used to hunt with the Taunton pack, her first few years here."

"Oh? But no longer?"

"No longer," he agreed.

"His lordship still hunted, I gather."

For the first time the man's expression was something other than pleasant. "Oh, aye, his lordship hunted."

So, Silber hadn't liked the last earl much. Interesting.

"All right then, my lord," Silber said, "Need assistance to mount?"

Gideon grinned. "Only if you'll lift me up like you did Lady Taunton?"

Silber gave a great bellow of laughter. "Aye, my lord, you're the master."

"I shall attempt it on my own, first." Gideon said with a smirk. "But don't go away just yet."

He mounted without any fuss, he wasn't *that* poor a rider, and then turned his horse toward the courtyard.

"What's this beast's name?" he called back over his shoulder.

"That's Lightning, my lord."

Gideon laughed as he guided the palpably sluggish *Lightning* toward the drive. Lady Taunton had ridden to the end and was on her way back toward him. Gideon felt like a bundle of cloth tied to the saddle compared to her. He didn't like not doing things well, but he supposed he'd best get used to it when it came to riding.

"Thank you for waiting," he said.

"Of course." She looked straight ahead, her profile regal under her plain, masculine top hat.

"Silber says you used to hunt," he said when it seemed she was contented to ride in silence.

"I did."

"Why did you stop?"

She turned slowly toward him. "Are we having a conversation about something other than house or land business, my lord?"

He blinked at her arch tone. "Why? Would that be unusual?"

"Most."

Gideon laughed at her saucy look and brief answer. "Well, if we don't talk about anything other than *business* it's not for a lack of trying on my part."

She snorted softly at that.

"What? It's true. The few times I've asked you about yourself or your past you've looked daggers at me."

"Tell me, my lord, just how does one *look* daggers?"

"You're doing an excellent job of it right now."

To his surprise, she laughed.

"That's better. Now, why did you stop hunting?"

She turned back to the road. "It was an issue of expense; a good string of hunters is expensive."

"Yet the earl continued to hunt?"

Her lips twisted into a mocking smile. "Yes, he did." She turned to him. "He also gambled and bet on races and, I suspect, kept a mistress."

Gideon's lips parted to tell her that was the one thing her dead husband hadn't been guilty of, but he didn't—it wasn't any of his concern.

She gave him an amused look. "You appear surprised that I would say such a thing?"

"That's because I am," he admitted.

"You're surprised to hear Taunton was keeping a woman?"

"I know nothing about that, but I'm exceedingly surprised you would mention it to me—a relative stranger."

She gave a low chuckle that curled around his body and settled in his balls. He shifted in his saddle, reminded of why he didn't enjoy riding as much as he always thought he would.

"Why did you laugh?" he asked when it appeared she wouldn't elaborate.

"No reason."

What a little liar she was! Gideon knew why she told him and suspected she did, too. It was a version of pillow talk, even though they'd never actually shared the same pillow. Still, watching him a few nights ago must have lowered her defenses. He cursed himself for falling asleep last night and cheating them both out of a second show. Well, there was tonight and every night after.

"Will you tell me a little about the guests who are coming to stay at Foxrun?"

Ahh, so she'd run shy of the dangerous subject.

"My three partners and Mr. Fanshawe's wife."

"She is the painter—Natalie Hartwicke."

"She is, although she goes by Nora Fanshawe in all other aspects of her life." Thinking about Nora as always made him recall that night at the Birch Palace. Which led to uncomfortable physical reactions, so he thrust it aside—with reluctance. "She is a very . . . unusual woman."

"In what way, my lord?"

"Well, there's the fact she is a painter of some eminence—a woman succeeding in a male dominated sphere. But there's more than that. Nora is—" how did one describe such a woman without getting one's face slapped in the process? "Well, she is unique. There is, I'm sure, nobody else like Nora Fanshawe." If there was such a woman, Gideon bloody well wanted to meet her.

"You sound quite enamored."

Gideon looked up at that. Lady Taunton's mouth was curved in a rather hard smile, almost as if she were . . . jealous? No, surely not. Likely that was judgement he saw in her eyes.

"I've heard the rumors swirling about her," she said when he didn't respond.

"Ahh. Rumors. You didn't strike me as the rumor-mongering type."

It was amazing how fast her cheeks turned fiery. "I didn't need to go searching for them, my lord. After all, her name was bandied about along with Mr. Fanshawe's and Lady Catherine's for months."

"That's true," he agreed in a tone that said he would not contribute to such gossip.

"Tell me about the other guests."

"Mr. Smith will be coming by himself. By the by," he said. "Mr. Smith just goes by that: Mr. Smith. Even the rest of us don't know his Christian name."

"Surely you're joking?"

"No. That's all he'll give us. Of course we like to amuse ourselves imagining names for him." Gideon snickered as he recalled some of his last guessed names. He always chose the most outlandish names, enjoying the usually unreadable man's irritation. They went through the alphabet, each taking a turn. His had been A and he'd come up with the name Algernon, which had set even Edward Fanshawe rolling with laughter.

"Stephen Chatham is the last, but not least, of our number." He hesitated, trying to think of a way to describe the brilliant but almost pathologically reserved man. "He is no doubt the smartest of the four of us. It is difficult to say what his motivation for making money is. He appears to live fairly humbly." Gideon shrugged. Stephen was no less a mystery than Smith.

"And will he be bringing a guest?"

"I doubt it, but it would be best to have a room ready just in case— preferably one adjacent to his. I suppose the same goes for Smith." When she made no sound he turned to her, beyond amused by the stiff expression on her face.

"I know my friends are not what you are accustomed to."

She snorted.

"Very well, it's likely they're not what *most* people are accustomed to, but I didn't work as hard as I have to pretend I'm somebody else. While my guests may be on the, er, *bohemian* end of the spectrum, they are not animals and comport themselves decently in front of staff and our neighbors." He paused for effect. "What they do behind closed doors is their own affair."

Gideon let her stew on that, wondering if there were little peep holes in every room in the house. If so, that could be quite entertaining. He wouldn't have any compunction about spying on his partners and their lovers the way he did about Lady Taunton.

Yes, he needed to discover all the little hidey-holes. He'd been terribly remiss exploring his house, too busy pouring coin into it.

"Will the guest chambers be ready by the time they arrive?"

"I believe so. The draper from Taunton's is most . . . inspired."

Gideon snorted. "He should be for the money I'm offering."

"That was clever of you to set him and his seamstresses up in the rooms," she said.

Gideon laid a hand over his heart. "Praise from *you*, my lady?"

"On another matter, will you speak to those servants I've told about their pensions? I daresay you'll want them around for a few days to help the new servants who arrive from London. They were all, without exception, *very* grateful for your generosity and—"

"Good God. Do you mean I have to let them all *thank* me?"

"Well, that would be the right thing to do."

"Ha! I expect you mean that would be the *lordly* thing to do."

"Yes, that too." Her lips twitched slightly. "We shall take this path up ahead. It leads into the vale." Her eyes flickered over him, assessing. "You have a better seat than you indicated."

He was annoyed by the pleasure he felt at her words. "I'm adequate to ambling along, but anything over this speed will give you much amusement."

She opened her mouth, and then closed it, pursing her lips.

"What? Go on and say it. Please don't feel that you need to check yourself in my presence."

"I was just going to say that if you like, I could offer you a few words of advice on your position."

"I would love anything you could offer on the subject of positions."

She frowned and Gideon could almost hear the gears grinding away as she tried to figure out whether he'd said something shocking. She appeared to dismiss it. "Let's see you trot."

Gideon nudged the horse's flanks.

"Where is your whip?"

"Er."

"Always have your whip."

"I don't particularly like the thought of using a whip on a dumb animal." *But I'd very much enjoy using it on* you, *my dear.*

She looked at him as though he were an idiot. "You do *not* beat a horse with your whip, my lord. You use it for direction. That is what they've been trained with—using your heels or knees as a *prod* is merely confusing to them." She pursed her lips and then sighed. "Pull up and observe."

Gideon stopped his horse and Lady Taunton flicked her crop—a very unusual variety he'd not seen before—a type of horn or antler on one end with a long lash. The end tapped her horse's arse, sending the beast smoothly into a trot, her own posture flowing—almost *rolling* along with the beast.

She rode in a tight circle around him, keeping her mount at a trot. "You'll notice my posting is different from what you do—that is a matter of saddles. But the action is the same in theory. You are not working against the horse but using the momentum. The upward portion of the post relies on the horse's motion. You control the downward, using the muscles in the fronts of your thighs, rather than the rear." She pulled up beside him. "I could show you better if I were riding astride."

"Why don't you?"

"Ride astride? Because it is—well, it is unseemly."

"Ah. Well, I must say I think riding side saddle looks bloody awkward, begging your pardon."

"Riding astride is easier."

"You sound as though you speak from experience?"

She pursed her lips and her mouth pulled up on one side. "Yes, on occasion."

"I see. And it would be easier to teach me if you were astride?"

"Well, yes, but Silber could instruct you better. He is the best rider I know."

Ah, Silber again. Gideon smiled. "Perhaps you both might instruct me—I daresay I could use all the assistance I could get. Unless you are unwilling to be *unseemly*."

She hesitated. "I don't mind riding astride if there are no others around."

Gideon could tell by the sudden stiffening of her shoulders that the thought of being seen in breeches titillated her. He wondered if it was the thought of *him* seeing her, or her strapping servant, that was pleasing her most.

Well, he'd have a very enjoyable time figuring that out.

Chapter Nine

Alys was directing the servants with the rearrangement of one of the guestrooms when Lord Taunton strolled into the room.

"Here you are," he said.

"You needed something?"

He gave one of his sly smiles—the type that always made her feel as if she should slap his face.

Liar, you want to do something else to get that look off his face.

"I wondered why you were not at dinner."

She frowned. "I told Thursby to send down a message."

"Oh, she did, but all she said was you were detained." He glanced around at the large study with obvious interest. "This is looking very nice. That carpet will look well with those green drapes. The room seems . . . bigger than I recall."

"That is the result of a thorough cleaning. I don't know why it is, but removing dust always makes a room look larger."

"The floors and furniture are positively glowing."

"Perhaps you'd like me to send the maids into your chambers?" She gave him an exaggerated look of mock comprehension. "Oh, wait—you have your own chambermaids. You don't need any assistance."

He cocked his head, his slow smile spreading over his face. "I think my room could use a thorough cleaning—you're correct. Have them do it tonight." He grinned. "Perhaps you might supervise?"

She snorted.

"Do you plan to be at this all night?" he asked, gesturing to the general area around them.

"No, I shall dismiss everyone after this room is done. That will leave only two for tomorrow." *And it shall leave me time to go see what you get up to tonight, my deviant lord.* Her face heated at the mere thought, but she couldn't find it in herself to deny it: she would be glued to that peep hole tonight, there was no point in lying.

Gideon wore a concerned frown. "Will we be ready for my friends two days hence? Or should we hire some day workers?"

"No, we'll be ready."

"Excellent. Thank you so much for your efforts." He hesitated and then said, "I did send Mr. Floyd over to the Dower House and it is next on his list. I've told him to bring in more workers and he's grudgingly agreed to work with two additional roofing companies from Bristol. You might want to take a look at the furnishings and place orders for anything you need while you're doing so for Foxrun."

Alys realized she was gaping. "Why, th-thank you, my lord. That's very generous—and rather more timely than I'd hoped for."

"Yes, well, they're working far quicker than I'd anticipated." He stifled a yawn. "I do beg your pardon. But it's off to bed for me, I'm afraid."

Liar.

"Good night, my lord." Once he'd gone, she turned to the servants who were positioning the big rug. "Once we finish with this, we can stop for this evening," she said, fervently hoping to motivate them with that information.

┥ ♥ ┝

Alys was frantic by the time she finally managed to shove Thursby out the door.

"Somebody," the old lady said—and Alys knew who *that* meant—"should speak to him, my lady. These—these *women* are just—"

"Thursby," she said sharply, cutting off the woman's slurred, wild-eyed speech. "It is *his* house. You must take hold of yourself and stop your complaining." Alys yawned. "Now, I've had a full day."

The old woman's face twisted. "Oh, aye! I can see what you're about. No better than you should—"

"Out." Alys had to bite down on her lip to keep the flow of anger inside. She'd dealt with the old woman's vitriol for almost a decade. She could deal with it again tonight. Besides, it wasn't as if she could afford to pension her off—even if she could, where would she go? Thursby had grown up on the grounds of Foxrun, the daughter of a butler of yore. How could Alys ask for a cottage for the bitter old drunk when so many others, who were more deserving, were living in squalor? No,

104

they were stuck with each other and would likely live out their days together as querulous old crones in the Dower House.

Thursby tottered around her room fussing and puttering about until Alys wanted to scream, before finally shuffling off and leaving her alone.

The second the door closed behind her Alys sprang from beneath the covers and shrugged into her heavy, quilted dressing gown. She'd brought two apples tonight and wore her heaviest nightdress—it was cold in the narrow corridor—as well as the ugly but warm slippers her sister-in-law had sent her last Christmas.

Alys peered out the door, careful to look both ways and listen, feeling like the spy she was. When she was sure it was clear she ran with undignified haste to the panel and felt for the catch, which for a moment she couldn't feel. Was this the wrong panel? Was it—voices came from the direction of the servant's staircase and her fingers were frantic.

She located the catch just as the voices approached the top of the stairwell. She shut the door almost all the way before pulling it closed with painful slowness and scampering down the corridor toward the stool.

Her heart was pounding so loud she swore she could hear it echoing in the hallway. She climbed up on the stool.

"Oh my," she whispered. A huge copper bathing tub had been set in front of his lordship's fire. And his lordship was in it.

She swallowed. He was reclining against the sloped back, his eyes closed, while the two women bathed him, like some sort of barbarian emperor.

All three of them were naked, at least mostly.

The tub was at such an angle that she could see his face and chest. One woman faced her direction—Lucy—while the other—Susan—knelt with her back facing the peephole. Alys pressed her eye hard against the glass. Susan was wearing some sort of . . . well, she didn't know what it would be called. A wide black strap ran between her thighs and was pulled tight enough to spread her buttocks. It was fastened to a black belt that as cinched just as tightly around her tiny waist. It looked uncomfortable but . . . unspeakably erotic and Alys swore she could feel the snug straps against her own swollen lips.

Alys had given up mentally flagellating herself for her body's reaction. She was here, she knew *why* she was here—to be titillated—and there was no point in denying it. As to *why* she found such depraved sights arousing? Well, that was something she could think about later. Likely while praying in church this coming Sunday.

Not if you turn into a flaming cinder on the front steps.

She snorted at the dry voice.

The women soaped and scrubbed his entire body, paying particular attention—it appeared to Alys—to his midsection, which was unfortunately hidden by the side of the tub.

Jackson came out of the dressing room and went to the door. When he returned, he held two cans of water. Lord Taunton pushed himself up from the tub, like some sort of god rising from the ocean. Alys had to swallow several times—something she felt like she was continually doing to keep from drooling—when she saw his member. Yes, it was as thick, ruddy, and long as she remembered.

Jackson lifted a can and poured it over his master's back and shoulders while the women slicked the water over his skin, Susan's hands brushing against his erection in the process.

For the first time Alys really looked at the valet. He had a very featureless face, his salt and pepper hair exceedingly close cropped, his black suit as closely fitted to his powerful body as his master's was. She'd not noticed before, but he was half a head taller than Gideon, with shoulders like an ox. He was, she had to admit, as appealing as his master in his own way: brawny but silent and menacing. And completely expressionless in the midst of the most sensual tableau Alys could imagine.

What *was* he thinking of this man he served? Was he aroused, as well? Alys could not see his hips from her vantage point, but how could he not be?

The women rose and took two bath sheets from a stack by the fire while Jackson poured the second can over Lord Taunton's hair, washing away the soap. The water ran down his body, sliding over the hard muscles of his chest and abdomen in a way that made her salivate to *lick* those taut, defined ridges.

Oh yes, she was entirely lost.

Once Jackson finished, he picked up the cans and disappeared in the direction of the dressing room. What did he make of Lord Taunton's activities? Was this type of thing normal? Is this what Sebastian had done in London? Did he employ women to wait upon him like the body slaves of old?

And why was the thought of Sebastian behaving this way enough to cool her ardor?

Gideon stepped from the tub and stood with his hands on his hips as the women dried him. Lucy, she saw now, was without clothing. Alys squinted. It looked as if she had less pubic hair than was normal—or certainly less than Alys had. Surely the woman did not *groom* herself down there?

Gideon said something to Lucy and the woman turned and bent over, her feet spread wide.

Jackson reentered the room and handed what looked to be a small bottle to Gideon. He pulled off the top and Lucy reached back and took one buttock in each hand, spreading them.

Alys had to breathe through her mouth to get enough air and her eye fogged up the peephole and she had to rub it with her finger.

Gideon dropped into a crouch, his erect organ jutting out in front of him, and he poured a long stream of oil at the top of her crevice and then handed the bottle to Susan, who stood across from him, wearing only the odd strap of a garment, still and servile.

Gideon slid his fingers between her lips.

Alys's body clenched in sympathy—in yearning. Although she couldn't see his fingers, she could see the corded, powerful muscles of his forearm flexing. And then his arm began to move back and forth, working her with rhythmic thrusts, his body clenching as he pumped her harder and harder. Still she remained in her position, her hands jerking on her spread cheeks and pulling them wider.

Gideon stopped when she visibly shuddered, her climax apparently strong. He moved his hand to—good *God*—was he—

Yes, even from a distance Alys could see what he was doing, his finger massaging her back puckered hole. Yet another part of the human body Alys hadn't even *seen* before.

Nothing in the book she'd found that summer talked about any of this and Alys realized she was pressing her face so hard against the wall that the brick had scored a mark on her forehead.

She didn't care.

He must have spoken to Susan because she poured more oil over the other woman, Gideon's fingers massaging, lightly probing, their motions mesmerizing.

And then he paused and she realized what he was about to do: he was going to breach her.

He used the smallest of his fingers and she could tell by Lucy's reaction when it entered her body because she tensed. He stroked her thigh in soothing motions with his other hand, but his finger stayed in place. More oil and more probing, he twisted his finger, easing it in joint by joint.

Warmth slid down Alys's thigh and she bit her lower lip so hard she could taste blood. Susan poured more oil and he kept gently thrusting. Alys shuddered when she saw him pause and gently insinuate another finger.

And then he stood, leaning over her, his free hand beneath her body—Alys knew *where* that second hand was touching her—while he slowly invaded her. Lucy shuddered and stiffened, her pale skin a splotchy red by the time he'd added a third finger.

He stopped and spoke to Susan, who came to him with a—Alys squinted at whatever it was Susan handed Gideon. It looked like a—well, she didn't know what to call it. A cork or plug of some kind, with a flanged end.

Susan poured oil over the plug and then he took it and placed it against Lucy's back hole.

Alys squeezed her eyes shut. "Oh my goodness," she whispered, her own hole clenching.

You're missing it, Alys!

Her eyelids rolled up like shades, just in time to see him push the plug all the way in. The flange, she realized, was to stop it.

Who would have ever *thought* of such a thing? And *why?*

Gideon gave her a hard slap on the bottom and Lucy stood, shifting her hips in a fetching way, as if adjusting the plug inside her.

She was, Alys saw, smiling.

Could such a thing *feel* good?

Gideon went to sit on the big chair that faced the peep hole so perfectly it might have been placed there.

But, no. That was her imagination.

He sat in the chair, thighs wide spread, and his hand on his shaft as a thin strand of liquid leaked from the smooth, bulbous head. He made a beckoning motion and Lucy went to him, and then turned when she stood between his thighs.

She began to squat and Alys felt like her eyes might roll out of her head.

Lucy's surprisingly muscular thighs flexed as she lowered herself over Gideon, who held his member in one hand. She squatted lower, until his penis touched the spread flesh of her sex. Lucy used one hand to guide him to her entrance and then took the thick shaft inside herself.

It was—well, it was a revelation. So that is what it looked like? No wonder it had hurt so much when Sebastian first came to her. Had he been as large as Gideon? Because Gideon looked obscene, and Lucy appeared far too small to take him.

Lucy had her lower lip between her teeth and threw back her head as she accepted him deeper, until she was resting her bottom on his pelvis.

He leaned forward and kissed the side of her face, his arms sliding around her body and taking a breast in each hand. Alys shivered, her nipples tight and hurting as they chaffed against her heavy flannel nightgown.

He pulled Lucy back against his body and then pushed his knees between hers, using them to spread her wider and wider and wider, until Alys had a perfect view of his organ impaling the other woman.

He ran a hand from her breast down her belly, his fingers stroking her entrance, which was stretched tightly around his shaft. He pulsed his hips, sliding in and out of her body as Lucy squirmed in his arms. He stroked her from breasts to hips, pulling cruelly on her nipples, his legs spreading her thighs ever wider, until it seemed she would split in half. All the while he pumped, his thrusts growing sharper, deeper.

And then again, he stopped abruptly, visibly panting as he said something to Susan who'd been standing behind him, rubbing his shoulders and chest. She came around the couch and knelt between their twined thighs and bent low. Alys could only see the back of her head, but she knew what the woman was doing: she was using her mouth on their joined organs.

It was the most filthily erotic sight she'd ever seen and by God she wished she were closer.

Gideon resumed his thrusting, his motions so jerky she knew he must be close to his crisis. He gave only a few more violent thrusts and then he threw back his head, his hips lifting both their bodies off the chair as he shuddered and spasmed.

Alys closed her eyes, her own fingers drenched between her shivering thighs. She lost count of how many times she'd reached that precipice and gone over.

It was hard to open her heavy lids, but she managed just in time to see Gideon take his organ out of the other woman, it was not as hard, but still ruddy and very slick. Susan leaned forward and took him into her mouth.

Alys jaw dropped as the blond woman lapped at him like a cat, cleaning him. Cleaning the other woman's juices from him. Her body shook her so hard she stumbled off the stool, barely catching herself to avoid turning her ankle.

All those climaxes sucked away her energy and left exhaustion and a bone deep disgust in its place. Some of the disgust was for the depraved man in that room, but more was for herself. A woman depraved enough not just to watch, but to want all of that for herself.

Chapter Ten

The shrieking began in the middle of dinner, just before the sound of glass shattering.

Alys and Lord Taunton were discussing when they might be able to put tenant families in the four cottages that would be the first to get new roofs when the blood-curdling scream caused Alys to set her wineglass down on the edge of her plate and send ruby liquid spilling across the brand new table linen.

"Oh, goodness," she murmured. One of the footmen lunged forward and picked up her glass and mopped up the spill.

Gideon was already half-way to the door when it flew open. Mrs. Tickle stood in the doorway and Alys would have sworn her gray hair was standing on end.

"What is it?" Gideon demanded.

"Bats, my lord. Hundreds—no, *thousands* of them." And then she fainted dead away.

Gideon was the one who caught her, even though one of the footmen was closer and Tickle was right behind her.

He scooped her up just like a child, cradling her in his arms. He looked . . . well, he looked like a fairytale prince. Or at least what Alys had always imagined a fairytale prince to look like: blond, tall, muscular, beautifully handsome—and so heroic.

A slight dusting of scarlet made his sharp cheekbones appear even more sculpted. "Er." His face creased with mortification and his obvious discomfort was beyond charming.

Alys decided to have mercy on him. "Come with me, my lord. You can lay her down in the Rose Salon."

Her order seemed to wake up the other men. John, the younger of the two footmen, sprinted down the corridor to open the door to the Rose Salon where his lordship gently laid Mrs. Tickle on a settee covered in rose silk that had seen better days.

Gideon looked at Alys, hesitated, opened his mouth, and closed it again.

"You go see to the bat situation, my lord. I'll see to Mrs. Tickle."

He was out of the room as if he'd been shot from a cannon, the other men not far behind him.

So, his arrogant lordship became nervous around fainting women. No doubt he reacted similarly around crying women. Alys filed that helpful information away and took Mrs. Tickle's hand, which was as fragile and delicate as a bird's wing.

A maid came running into the room—one of the new tweeny twins. "His lordship sent me to help, my lady."

"Please fetch Thursby and tell her to bring along her smelling salts." Alys could only hope her maid was not in need of smelling salts herself, and already insensible or unconscious from gin.

"Yes, my lady."

"Arggh." Mrs. Tickle shifted. "Wha—what happened?"

Alys patted her hand. "I'm afraid you fainted—after saying something about bats."

The woman blanched and Alys feared she might pass out again, but she rallied. "There must have been a nest of them in the south wing—just above the chapel."

"Where they were stripping off the lead roofing tiles today?"

Mrs. Tickle nodded, shivering. "I was in there securing the windows—those workers are so careless—when they came pouring out of that hole in the ceiling—the one Mr. Floyd made to check for rot. Thousands of them." She whimpered.

"There, there, Mrs. Tickle."

"You need me, my lady?" Thursby's cheeks wore bright red circles that proclaimed she must have run the entire distance from Alys's chamber. She carried a small satchel. "What happened? I heard screaming—"

"Mrs. Tickle needs you, Thursby. She fainted, perhaps you might sit with her." Alys released Mrs. Tickle's hand and stood. "Thursby will take care of you," she said to the older woman, who looked justifiably skeptical about being left in the hands of a well-known dipsomaniac. "I'm going to check on the bat situation."

Thursby sank down on the settee and cut Alys a horrified look. "Bats."

Both women shrieked as Alys headed for the door. "No, they're vermin—rats with wings!" Thursby yelled.

"I thought those were pigeons," Alys said with a smile, not slowing her pace.

"My lady!"

She ignored the women's wailing and followed the sounds of the screams and commotion and excitement.

—❤—

Gideon knew there would be no sleeping at Foxrun until every last bat had been tracked down and ejected. At least that was the message that Alys—because, really, what was the point of standing on ceremony, at least in his head, when the woman had seen him naked and in action—had passed along to him.

"Why aren't *you* scared?" he'd asked, his eyes following the remarkably speedy progress of his rather stout laundry woman as she ran screaming from the servant quarters.

"I'm made of sterner stuff, my lord. Besides, they're just bats."

"Just. Bats." Gideon shook his head. "I wish all the other women felt that way."

She aimed a significant look at Cedric, one of the new footman, who was lurking behind a door clutching a poker. "Women *and* men," she corrected, looking happy, as if this were a half-day holiday rather than a verminous infestation.

Gideon gawked at her as if somebody had climbed onto his chest and was jumping up and down. *Good God!* She was bloody lovely when she smiled.

This was not good. Not good *at* all.

She chuckled at whatever she saw on his face and turned away.

"Where are you going?" Gideon's face heated at the slightly hysterical note in his voice.

"To bed. I'm going to get an early night. I have to go into Taunton in the morning," she reminded him.

He sputtered. "But it's not even eight o'clock."

"I've had a long day. I daresay I'll sleep like the dead tonight."

Gideon knew *that* for a lie. The little spy had been at the peephole all the way until the end last night—so Jackson had said. Quite an education she'd received. It had taken her until after five today before she'd looked him in the eyes.

"You'll be able to sleep through this racket?" he demanded.

"Like a babe."

Gideon watched her walk away, wishing—not for the first time—that he didn't live in an age where women wore bloody bustles and cages and fifty pounds of fabric.

An ear-piercing shriek drew his eyes to the servant stairs.

Lucy, with Susan almost on top of her, were thundering down the stairs with mouths wide open and eyes squeezed shut. They were lucky to collide with Randolph, the other young footman he'd just hired, a giant man who absorbed the impact as if they were flies rather than full-grown women.

"Here, here, then," Gideon said, helping the boy set the women on their feet.

"I am *not* sleeping in this house," Lucy snapped, glaring at Gideon as if *he* were a bat.

"Me either," Susan added, her eyes glittering with hostility. "First plaster falling off the ceiling onto my 'ed all night, freezing cold water to wash in—"

"A rickety bed with a mattress made of nettles," Lucy cut in.

"And then a—"

Gideon held up his hand, the imperious gesture working well even in such conditions. "I've heard all this before," he reminded them.

Susan stomped her foot. "I can't live 'ere any longer, my lord. It's—it's *savage*."

Gideon stared at her until she dropped her gaze. He tried to decipher the emotions he felt at that moment and decided that irritation outweighed everything else combined—closely followed by relief. The whores hadn't stopped complaining since the day they arrived at Foxrun. And the other servants despised them for their airs and obnoxious behavior.

Most importantly, however, was the fact neither of them was capable of bringing him sexual satisfaction. Oh, he was having one hell of a time using them in his shows for Lady Taunton. But without her

114

ladyship's presence on the other side of that peephole Gideon would still be fucking all three of them raw every night, to no avail.

As it was, he could toss one off on his own without hardly any effort—he knew that because he'd done it a good half-dozen times already—just *thinking* about Alys right next door to him.

And his hand, he suddenly decided, was a hell of a lot less bother than two whiney whores.

After these two were gone, he could sent word to his secretary, a beaten-down and harried looking man by the name of Watkins. Watkins could go to the Birch Palace or Toscas and hire two more *chambermaids* for him. This time he'd begin their training on the right foot: *no complaining* about his house and the understanding that they actually had to tidy up his bloody rooms every once in a while.

Yes, two new whores were exactly what he needed.

"Randolph, I want you to take these ladies to the The Jolly Taxpayer for the night and book them on the first train to London in the morning."

"Now?" Lucy shrieked.

Gideon turned on his heel.

"Oh, my lord, please," Susan begged. "Lucy didn't—"

Gideon just strode into the heart of the bat storm, where he knew he would be utterly safe. At least from *these* particular women.

❤

Alys was running late. She'd hoped to get into Taunton to purchase a few last-minute items at the emporium before this evening.

"We will be *late*, my lady," Thursby nagged as they hurried down the main staircase.

"It will be fine, Thursby, I've—"

"Good morning, ladies."

Alys stopped, Thursby beside her, both of them staring down at Gideon, who stood in the middle of the enormous entry hall, dressed in his town clothing.

"My lord," Alys said after catching her breath at the magnificent sight, resuming her journey at a more moderate pace. "Are you going somewhere?"

"I decided to accompany you into Bristol."

Thursby squeaked.

115

Alys ignored her. "But I hadn't planned to go into Bristol—just Taunton," she said as she pulled on her best gloves, lavender kid that she'd purchased for mourning.

"Oh come, it will be a little jaunt to break up the monotony."

Alys laughed. "You found last night monotonous, did you?"

"It's less than two hours away and there are far more shops to choose from. Besides, didn't we need to order more silver from somewhere?"

"Well, yes, but—"

"Perfect. We'll be back well before dinner and their train isn't expected until after eight."

"My lady," Thursby began.

"Come, I insist. I've taken the liberty of having the carriage brought around." Gideon gestured for Alys to precede him. "Take Mrs. Thursby's bag, Jackson."

Somehow Alys hadn't noticed the tall, powerfully built valet standing in the shadows. After these last few nights, she looked at him in an entirely different light. Of course she seemed to be looking at *every* man in an entirely different light. She'd even eyed Cedric—the young footman—this morning when he'd brought her the morning post; he was a fine looking young man.

Thursby bristled. "I don't need any help, my lord."

"Of course you do." Lord Taunton raised his eyebrows. "Jackson."

Alys could feel Thursby boiling as she trotted behind her. The carriage was ready and waiting, the steps down and door open. Lord Taunton handed Alys, and then Thursby, inside before entering. "You sit with her ladyship," he ordered Thursby, taking the less desirable seat himself while his valet climbed up on the box with the coachman. Lord Taunton rapped on the roof once he'd settled.

"How late were you awake?" Alys asked, knowing *exactly* when he'd gone to bed—two thirty—because she'd stayed awake listening for him. Once the door to his room had closed, she'd scurried like the rat she was to the secret hallway.

"A little past two."

"You must be exhausted."

"My energy is boundless." He grinned.

116

She knew *that* was a lie because she'd watched through the peephole as he pulled off his clothing without the help of Jackson, whom she supposed was still assisting with the bat situation. Alys had barely caught a glimpse of his naked, muscular body before he'd crawled into bed and snuffed out his candle. To say she'd been disappointed that she was not to get her nightly performance was an understatement.

And then this morning, Thursby had actually arrived before eight and told her the shocking news.

"His lordship sent those two *maids* of his back to London."

"He discharged them?" Alys demanded, shock and disappointment stabbing her in almost equal measures.

"I don't know if he discharged them, but he certain sent them away. No doubt his London house is crawling with such females."

Alys wasn't sure what to think about the departure of the two women. Wouldn't a decent, virtuous woman be pleased that he'd dismissed his whores? So why did she feel such a sense of . . . *something?* Something that was not relief or satisfaction, but—

"And you, my lady? Did you have a good night's sleep?" he asked.

"I slept like an infant. I understand you were able to get the bat cavern closed up last night."

He grimaced. "Yes. And a more disgusting activity I hope never to encounter." He shivered. "Jackson says we shall have to burn our clothing. He even suggested burning our hair."

Alys laughed.

"I'm pleased to amuse you."

"Had they been up there long, then?"

"Years—centuries. Eons."

Alys laughed again.

Thursby cleared her throat, and Alys wrenched her gaze away from him and looked out the window.

Why was he coming with her? Why had he sent his women away? Would he be employing new females? Beside her, Thursby sneezed.

"Are you not feeling quite the thing, Miss Thursby?" the earl enquired, his mien one of concern, but Alys suspected he understood the true reason behind her maid's 'illness.' "Are you sure you wouldn't rather go back to Foxrun than drag yourself all the way to Bristol?"

Thursby looked like she wanted to wave a cross in his direction. "It's nothing that will take me away from my duties, my lord," she declared virtuously. The message was clear: watching Gideon Banks was her duty.

The man in question looked pleased by the prospect rather than daunted.

"It's fortunate that my private car was delivered to Taunton just yesterday," he said, his attention moving back to Alys. "We shall be able to travel to Bristol in comfort, my lady."

Alys knew Thursby would be thinking about the last train trip with this man, and how his lordship had deftly separated them *that* time, and what he'd done during the journey. Thursby would know he had no women to service his needs this time and would be thinking of what he might do to amend that lack. No doubt her addled brain was spinning trying to find ways to thwart him.

Alys, wanton that she was, was thinking of ways to aid him. Yes, there was no denying it. Something had happened to her after that first night she'd watched him and the second night had just made it worse—had made her body's demands worse. It was as if a process had been set into motion—one that could not be halted until its completion. But what *was* the completion?

As if you didn't know.

She grimaced at the wry voice and studied Gideon from beneath the protection of her lashes, an activity she'd only ever read about in books and never dreamed she would one day employ. Her life had become so . . . invigorating.

Did he sense that change in her? How could he? He didn't know she'd spied on him. To Lord Taunton she was the same black-clad proper widow she'd always been.

Thursby swore he'd not seen her peek into his compartment that day—that he'd been too *consumed* by his activities.

No, Gideon knew nothing about her or what was taking place in her mind and, more disturbingly, her body.

Alys had to dig deeply to mine the courage to lift her gaze.

Lord Taunton was staring at her, and he was no longer smiling. His face was hard and stern, his jaw taut, his eyes the darkest of blues.

Alys swallowed and it came out a gulp. He looked implacable, like a man who always got what he wanted.

The question was, what did he want?

─ ♥ ─

Gideon knew it was petty of him, but he couldn't help taking pleasure from sending Alys's sour maid off to the first class car with Jackson as her escort. The journey to Bristol was slightly under two hours so Gideon would manage without him.

He handed Alys into the car himself and gave the stationmaster—who'd come to see him personally—a nod along with a fat gratuity. "Thank you for your haste Mr. Snively."

The stationmaster smiled and bowed. "Anytime, my lord. *Any* time."

Alys was staring around at the car, her expression one of surprised wonder.

"You like it?" he asked.

"It's very elegant."

"You sound so surprised," he said mockingly. But he was surprised, himself. He'd asked Nora Fanshawe to give the orders for the car's interior and the result was—well, he supposed artistic was as good a word as any.

It was a masculine color palate, all rich browns with touches of black and dull gold. It amused him to see she'd included heavy metal rings in convenient, but discrete, locations. Gideon thought about the very private bedroom at the back of the car; Nora would have made sure that was equipped for his particular tastes, as well.

His prick had begun to swell, even though he knew good and well he would have no way to relieves his suffering on the brief journey.

"Would you care for tea, my lady?" he asked.

She'd chosen to sit on the small brown leather tufted settee that faced forward. "And will you make it, my lord?"

He smiled. "I can do that much—do you doubt me?"

"No, you strike me as a most self-sufficient type. But I don't need any tea, I just had breakfast."

That was just as well. Gideon could make tea, but it had been a long, long time.

He took the black leather armchair across from her. "Have you spent much time in Bristol?"

"Not very much. I generally go to Bath if I'm going for a few nights, but I'm sure Bristol's warehouses are far more likely to have what I want on such short notice than anything I could find in Taunton." She frowned. "You never said what business you have in Bristol, my lord?"

"No." He smiled. "I didn't." She sighed and Gideon relented. "I have a few errands. One is to visit a woodworker my business associate, Fanshawe recommended. He says the old man—although curmudgeonly—would be whom he would choose to restore woodwork. I shall take a look at his work and arrange to have him out to Foxrun if he suits. By the by," he said, "did I ask you about the silver?"

"Not to worry, I've been carrying a spoon in my reticule for days. I'm hopeful they will be able to make something close enough to match it. The set is very old and I wonder if such craftsmanship still exists." She cut a glance out the window, her hands tightening on her small bag.

Gideon didn't want to ask, but he had to. "Why don't you tell me what happened?"

Her eyes widened. "I'm sorry?"

"About the silverware. Every time you speak of it, you get a . . . *haunted* look."

She seemed to deflate before his eyes. "I'm sorry, my lord. I should have told you before—that silver belonged to the estate—it should be yours—"

"Don't worry about that. What happened?

Alys swallowed audibly but couldn't seem to speak.

He leaned toward her. "You don't need to tell me anything you don't want to. I don't hold you responsible for the condition at Foxrun." He snorted. "Well, except I give you credit for holding it together."

Her smile was slow to come, and it was more of an expression of relief than happiness. "I was at Foxrun by myself when it happened and Sebastian hadn't been home for months, much longer than he'd ever stayed away before. I was out riding early in the morning," she shuddered her breathing speeding up.

120

"Easy," he soothed, wishing he had the nerve to touch her hand, or somehow comfort her.

She swallowed and her jaw shifted from side to side. "I used to ride every morning, until—Well, there were two men waiting for me in the woods—"

Gideon's hands fisted. "Did they—"

"No, no—it wasn't like that, although—" she shook her head, as if to shake something unpleasant away. "They wanted money. They said Sebastian borrowed from them at Newmarket and that he'd lost everything." She chewed her lip, her eyes on her hands. "They said they couldn't find him, so they were giving me the message. The amount of money they spoke of was—well, it seemed astronomical to me." Her eyes looked haunted. "Three thousand pounds. Three *thousand* pounds—on horses!".

Gideon didn't know if he wanted to laugh or cry at her reaction. To him three thousand pounds was . . . well, it wasn't nothing, but it certainly wasn't much. He couldn't stand it any longer, he took her hand before he knew what he was doing. He expected her to jerk away, but instead, she squeezed his fingers hard enough to hurt.

"I *had* to let them into Foxrun—at night. I gave them the few jewels I had, but I had nothing approaching that amount. I offered them my wedding ring—a family heirloom, and they laughed. They said it was glass, along with everything else in the family vault. So they took most of the silver along with the carpets in several of the rooms that were worth a great deal, and even a few paintings. They said that was only a fraction of what they were owed and they would be back for more if Sebastian didn't go to them." She came out her trance, noticed she was holding his hand, and released him. "I'm sorry," she said, "I don't know why it upsets me so even now."

"Of course it upsets you," Gideon said, "You did the right thing giving them what they wanted. They were thugs and they were in your house—it was wise to get rid of them quickly. What did Lord Taunton say about it?"

"I sent a telegram to London but never heard back from him. And then he died less than three weeks later."

"Good God, Alys—"

She startled.

121

Gideon grimaced. "I'm sorry, I shouldn't have—"

Twin spots of color darkened her cheeks and her eyes were dewy with unshed tears. "Please, it's foolish to stand on ceremony when I'm willing to share such mortifying details of my life. Please, call me Alys."

"Gideon," he said distractedly, his thoughts stuck on what she'd said. "I hate to mention this, but—"

"You're wondering if they ever got paid?" she asked.

He nodded.

"I don't know." She sat back in her chair. "They never came back and it's been over a year since his death. I suppose he must have paid them."

"The earl died while hunting?"

"Yes, why?"

Gideon didn't want to have to say the words, but she took his meaning anyway.

"No—that's not possible." She shook her head vigorously. "He was riding with the Quorn—there were dozens of others about. Besides, Sebastian took a fall. How could somebody arrange that?"

Gideon kept any ideas he had about that to himself, deciding to let the matter rest. But he would ask Smith about it when he came to Foxrun. If Smith didn't know about it already, he'd be able to find out: the man knew everything.

They rode for a while in silence, each busy with their own thoughts.

"What was the second thing?" Alys asked.

"Hmm? I beg your pardon?"

"The second thing in Bristol you were going to see about? You said the first was the woodworker."

"Ah, that." He grinned. "Well, that's a private matter."

She stared, her jaw moving slightly, as if she were engaging in an argument with herself.

Gideon could *smell* her burning curiosity. He certainly was not going to assuage it without getting anything in return.

So he smiled, relaxed against the plush brown leather, and watched the   passing   scenery.

Chapter Eleven

Alys had never shopped with a man before. She'd not done very much shopping, at all—at least not for some years.

She didn't know if all men shopped like Gideon—with the enthusiasm of a child—but she *did* know not all men spent as much money as he did.

"Is he mad?" Thursby whispered in Alys's ear as his lordship marched through the large furniture shop pointing at items, with the harried—but delighted—manager of the store sprinting behind him.

Thursby sneezed into the handkerchief she was holding against her mouth.

"Thursby you should have stayed at home. Or at least rested in the railcar," Alys chided as she took in the other woman's watery and red-rimmed eyes. She felt dreadfully guilty—the poor woman really *was* ill, not just jug bitten.

"And leave you here with *him*?"

"Shh! What do you think he will do in the middle of the Bristol shopping district?"

"I don't know, my lady." She sniffed loudly and sneezed. "But it took less than two hours in a train car with him for you to begin calling him *Gideon*."

Alys's face got hot. "Oh, hush."

"What do you think his lordship would have thought about this?" Thursby hissed, causing all the sympathy Alys had been feeling toward her to dissipate in an instant.

"My husband is dead, Thursby. And what he might have thought is certainly none of your concern."

"His lordship entrusted me to—"

"To *spy* on me," Alys finished.

Thursby gasped, her eyes wide and offended.

"Do you think I'm really so stupid as to not have known that all along? No, don't answer that. Just hush."

Thursby gave an indignant squeak.

"What do you think of this?" Gideon called from half-way across the large room.

"Barbarian," Thursby muttered as she followed Alys to see what he'd found now.

"Isn't this interesting?" he asked, pointing at a painted oak cabinet.

Alys leaned closer to see what the scene was. "Is that St. George?"

"Yes, my lady—you've got an excellent eye," the clerk added unctuously. "It is an exceptionally fine piece. A furniture maker named William Morris."

Gideon ignored the clerk. "How did you know it was St. George?"

"The dragon was my first hint," she said drily.

He narrowed his eyes at her but said to the clerk, "We'll take it. Do you have any other furniture with dragons?" His lips twitched.

Alys laughed before she could stop it.

"Saints preserve us," Thursby prayed beneath her handkerchief.

Alys ignored her. "Where will you put it?" she asked as she accompanied him down another aisle.

He leaned low and whispered. "I haven't a clue. What the devil is it for?"

"You *bought* something and you have no use for it?"

"Exactly. Don't you ever do that?"

"No. No, I don't."

He cut her a sharp look but said nothing.

It took another three-quarters of an hour before Gideon was done decimating the shop and took out his pocket watch. "I'm parched. What about you?"

"I could use a little refreshment," Alys agreed.

"The Royal does a lovely early tea, my lord," the clerk volunteered.

"Excellent, that's just across the street."

Alys took his arm while Thursby, who seemed to become worse—in more ways than one—by the minute, trundled behind them coughing and sniffing and sneezing.

"That was all the rugs, wasn't it?" Gideon asked.

"Yes, and more besides. Where in heaven's name will you put that remarkably long runner?"

He shrugged. "We can always cut it into pieces and put it several places." Alys gasped and he grinned down at her. "You're so gullible. I actually thought it would look nice in the gallery."

Alys considered that. "It might," she conceded.

"High praise, indeed. What remains on your list? The silver?" he asked.

"Yes, silver and there is also a draper who might have a fabric to match that of the library curtains, but I don't think we shall have time."

"We are not getting new curtains?"

"Only six are sun-damaged enough to need replacing, the others are—"

He waved a hand—a monarchic gesture she'd noticed he employed frequently. "Replace them all, I don't care for the color."

A watery snort came from behind them.

Gideon leaned close to Alys and whispered. "I fear Mrs. Thursby will go to her death protecting your honor. You will have to exert some force to get her to go back to the railcar. She can rest in the comfortable bedroom."

Alys's face heated at the word *bedroom.* "I shall speak to her once we reach the hotel."

"That would be . . . delightful. I will secure one of the hotel's private dining rooms for our pleasure."

"Oh, you needn't—"

"Oh, but I *need.*"

Alys stumbled slightly over a cobble and his hand, strong and warm hand, took her elbow.

"Steady on, *Alys.*"

━ ♥ ┝

Gideon spoke to the concierge about a private dining space while Alys argued with her maid.

He'd foolishly thought there would be more time and had anticipated visiting the specialty brothel that Smith had suggested, just to have a look around. He wouldn't engage replacements for Lucy and Susan without trying their services, first, but it would be good to inspect the premises, even though it had come highly recommended by Smith when he'd learned how near Foxrun was to Bristol.

"Given your eclectic tastes I think you will find it very . . . enjoyable," Smith had informed him, wearing his signature smirk and smoking one of the detestable cigars that he favored.

"What do you mean by *eclectic*?" Gideon had asked suspiciously.

"Dear Gideon, please remember to whom you are speaking."

Well, that had been fair enough. Gideon and Smith had done quite a bit of playing together during their early years—and especially once they'd made enough money to allow their desires free reign. Indeed, Gideon had been rather disappointed when Smith began to slow down—which happened around the time he met Nora's good friend, Charles Smith. Gideon knew Charles had once been a whore at the same brothel as Nora. He'd long known that Smith liked men and women as the two of them had often shared whores of both genders over the years.

Gideon's lips twitched at some of those memories; the man knew how to fuck and had taught Gideon more than a few things along the way. He liked Smith a great deal, for all that he was such a mysterious, secretive bastard.

"I apologize for keeping you waiting, my lord."

Gideon looked up at the sound of her voice; Alys was looking a bit harried.

"Gave you a difficult time, did she?" Gideon offered his arm and she laid a dainty, leather-sheathed hand on his sleeve. Gideon wondered how that small—but very feminine—gesture could possibly be more erotic than Susan sucking his cock, but it was.

"She did give me a difficult time," Alys chewed her lip. "You say Jackson will be there to admit her?"

"Yes, he seemed concerned there was a problem with the new ice box and has probably dismantled half the train by now. Don't worry, she'll be safe with Jackson." He had no idea what type of woman his valet liked—or even if he liked women at all—but he suspected elderly gin drinkers were not in the running.

"I don't know why she had to be so argumentative, she quite wore me out," Alys muttered.

Gideon's imp of the perverse, never far from his shoulder, prodded him viciously. He leaned down and whispered. "I daresay she can't forget what she saw when she peeped into Lucy and Susan's carriage that time."

Her entire body stiffened, answering his question as to whether Thursby had shared such shocking information with her young mistress.

"Alys?" he asked gently when she'd stopped walking.

The word seemed to release her from her stunned stupor and she accompanied him into the private dining parlor, dropping her hand the instant the door closed behind them.

Gideon seated her in silence before taking his own seat.

Her face was the color of a beet and she was breathing hard.

"I'm sorry," Gideon said, reaching for her hand without thinking.

She snatched it away and then hid both under the table. "How long have you known?"

Gideon shrugged. "I saw her face in the open door."

"Why didn't you *say* something?"

He laughed. "To *whom*? Besides, what should I have said?" Gideon asked. "Why didn't *you* say something? That seems precisely like the sort of thing you'd scold me for."

"I *do not* scold you."

He smiled.

She flushed even darker, inhaled deeply, opened her mouth, and then shook her head and exhaled.

Gideon chuckled. Just then the door opened and servants entered bearing tea and several plates of sandwiches and biscuits.

Neither of them said anything as the food was laid out.

"Will there be anything else, my lord?" the head waiter asked.

"My lady?" Gideon asked Alys.

"No thank you, this looks lovely."

The silence was deafening after the door closed. Gideon could not tell from her expression whether she was horrified, angry, terrified, disgusted, or all four. The ground felt far too shaky to walk on, so he merely watched as she performed that feminine ritual that was tea preparation.

"Can I make you a plate?" he offered.

"Yes, thank you," she said woodenly.

He piled two plates with cakes, biscuits, and dainty sandwiches.

127

He'd ordered a special menu they offered called a petit fete champetre. Even Gideon, with his pitiful schoolboy French, knew that meant it was a picnic-style tea.

"I want to know the second thing."

He looked up from the excellent thin-sliced ham, fully aware of what she meant. But did *she* know what she meant? And more important, just how far should he go with this woman?

His conscience, which he'd not heard from in decades, popped up out of nowhere. He'd already contributed to her debauching by doing things for her viewing that even some whores hadn't seen.

Gideon sighed. "I shouldn't have teased you about what happened on the train. I know my habits and proclivities must be horrifically shocking to you and—"

"I'm a woman grown and was married almost a decade," she reminded him, her expression that of a mountaineer setting out on the most challenging climb of her life. "I hardly need your protection when it comes to such matters. Nor is it your concern."

Gideon didn't laugh. Instead, he took the cup of tea she offered and wondered just how many other peepholes there were inside that house. He could hardly forbid her from using them. But what would happen if Smith ended up bringing Charles with him? Or if she saw Fanshawe and Nora? Or, even worse, Gideon joining one of those two couples— something that had happened on more than one occasion in the past?

Besides, wasn't she correct? It wasn't his responsibility to protect her. And if she watched, didn't that mean she was interested? She *was* a grown woman, not a schoolgirl—no matter how much she might look like one.

But she wasn't looking like a schoolgirl right now. Right now she was every inch a woman and she was glaring at him.

He shrugged. "Very well, I take it you want the words with the bark still on them?"

She nodded.

"I discharged Lucy and Susan so I *was* going to a local establishment to, er, well look about."

She made an odd gurgling sound, her face so red he worried she would lose consciousness.

"Perhaps you should breathe," he suggested nervously.

128

"I'm fine!" she snapped. "You needn't worry you'll have another unconscious woman on your hands, my lord."

He flinched at both her tone and at the title. Were they back to that?

"Have you been to Bristol before?" she suddenly demanded.

"No."

She shook her head. "How does a person even know of such places?"

It was not the question he was expecting; it was a *far* better and easier question than what he'd been expecting.

He shrugged. "Men talk."

Her lips were tightly pursed and she turned her cup round and round.

Gideon hesitated a moment, and then decided he'd better tell her the truth sooner rather than later.

"I owe you the truth because you will be living in the same house with me—at least until such time as the Dower House is ready for your occupation. I'm sorry I've been released into your world, Alys. I'm a bit shocking in my behavior even for men who are . . . well, more like me than others and—Bollocks," he muttered. "I'm sorry," he said when she recoiled at the vulgar word. "I'm making a hash out of this because there simply isn't a way to pretty it up. I'm the sort of man who enjoys a certain kind of woman. Often." He shrugged. "Likely I enjoy such activities to an unhealthy degree, but that has been the case since I was a lad. I'd like to tell you I'll lose all interest in women like Lucy and Susan and become fascinated with beehives and sewer drains now that I possess a country estate, but that would be a lie. I am who I am."

Once again she surprised him.

"Thank you."

He blinked. "I beg your pardon?"

"Thank you for speaking honestly to me."

Oh darling, I haven't even skimmed the tip of the iceberg when it comes what I want to say to you.

Instead of saying that, however, he chewed the inside of his mouth and decided now was as good a time as ever to ask something he'd been pondering. "Do you have any plans for your future? Are you just content to live a quiet life in the Dower House?" He paused and then decided to plunge on. "I'll be fixing the London house and you're more than welcome to visit as often as you want, or even live there if you should decide you wish to move in society. I own another house—three, in point of fact—so that one can be yours, alone. You're still a young and *very* comely woman, surely you don't wish to molder away out in the country?"

Her pale cheeks darkened at his compliment, but she seemed determined to ignore it.

"Living in the country—a quiet life—is all I've ever known. Before I married and moved to Foxrun—just before I turned seventeen—I lived at my father's country house." Gideon could see she was struggling with what she was saying and he didn't ask the questions he wanted to ask: like what the hell she'd thought marrying a man almost twice her age when she'd been so young.

"My father was a deeply religious man. He was the younger son and was in seminary when his elder brother, the marquess, died suddenly. I don't think my father ever got over that. He married my mother shortly after leaving the seminary—because it was what he was supposed to do—and set about being a marquess and landlord and father rather than a clergyman, as he'd always wanted.

"But he never really left that part of his life behind him. Indeed, he ran our household like a religious order, one where abnegation and humility—especially in his wife and children—were required. He'd known Sebastian's uncle in seminary and that is how he came to know Sebastian." She shook her head. "I don't know why I'm telling you this, I—"

"Because I asked about you. Surely there can be nothing wrong in two cousins sharing their stories."

She snorted. "You know we have no blood between us."

"Yes, but we have both been thrown into a position that makes us fast family."

She held his eyes for a long moment. "What does any of it matter?"

"It matters to me. I should like to know," he said, discovering that was very true after he'd said it.

"Very well." She sighed. "My family suffered with the times as much as any other landed family, but my father and his father before him were prudent and I had an exceptional dowry for a woman of my status—although nothing to what so many American girls have brought to England."

"Sebastian, I learned after we were married, was a dreadful snob about such things. He viewed marrying an American heiress on the same level as marrying one of his horses—worse, actually, as he at least knew the bloodlines of his cattle. So, I was perfect for what he needed: young, ignorant, biddable, of good blood, and comparatively well-dowered."

She grimaced. "It shames me to admit it now, but Sebastian was handsome, charming, and I flung myself into love." She gave a mirthless laugh. "I can claim it was my sheltered upbringing—he was the first man I'd seen aside from older friends of my father's. I was kept at home—schooled by our family chaplain."

"Good Lord!" Gideon blurted, horrified by the notion of having his own personal clergyman.

She chuckled. "Yes, we had our very own church—built hundreds of years ago—so we didn't even need to associate with our inferiors when we worshipped. All this is to say that I was exceedingly innocent and naïve. Sebastian was seventeen years older than me—more than twice my age—and my father was very pleased when he showed an interest in me."

Gideon would wager Taunton had been pretty damned pleased with the notion of an obedient, nubile young bride, as well. Lord! Sixteen? And people accused *him* of being a pervert; at least he stuck to women rather than adolescents.

"I had some qualms," she said musingly. "I worried about how little I really knew him—but I'd been raised to do my father's bidding and he wanted this marriage for me. Besides, marrying Sebastian seemed like a way to get out of the suffocating atmosphere of my home. He appeared strong, gallant, and worldly, the type of man who would protect me as my father had always done with my mother. But he also enjoyed society and town living, so he wasn't as strict and religious as my father."

No, the activity Gideon had seen the earl getting up to with Smith that time wasn't that of an overly religious man.

Alys gave a bitter laugh. "It turned out that Sebastian was profligate in every way and horribly in debt. The money I brought to our marriage allowed him to continue his lifestyle for a few more years, but it was

131

not enough. And he'd never had any intention of bringing his child bride with him to London." She looked at Gideon. "He'd been married once before, you know?"

"Yes, I'd heard that."

"His first wife brought an exceptional amount of money to the union. She was seven years older than him, and although they were married for over a decade, she never became pregnant. I'm sure Sebastian believed he would avoid that mistake by taking a young bride," she stopped and chewed her lower lip, realizing she'd somehow strayed into dangerous waters. She shrugged. "After a few years he accepted there would be no child. It was also rather obvious whose fault it was. He was furious. And, well—"

"Was he cruel—violent—to you?" His anger at the thought surprised him.

"No, but after he gave up hope the allowance he left for me was, well—you've seen Foxrun and the state of it. It was all I could do to keep us in food with a roof over our heads."

She glanced down at the piece of shortbread she'd crumbled on her plate. "I saw him less and less. I didn't miss *him*, but I dearly wanted a child—a proper family. And without him, there would be no children."

Gideon almost smiled at her naivety. Had it never occurred to her she might get pregnant some other way? It appeared not. What must it be like to be so pure in thought?

"Shortly before my father died, he came to Foxrun. Somebody must have told him about Sebastian—about the carousing, the gambling. So, he came to speak to *me* about my husband's behavior. He was livid that I was bringing shame onto our family by—"

Gideon held up a hand. "Wait a moment—he was angry with *you?*"

"He told me a man straying was the fault of his wife and that I was failing in my wifely duty."

"That's bloody bollocks!"

She gave him a weary smile, clearly too distracted to be shocked by his language. "You had to know my father. He was . . . well, he was fond of the Old Testament. He told me I needed to exert myself, to be the kind of woman a man would stay at Foxrun for." She glanced down at the table. "I was not yet twenty—and so isolated. Without money I could not entertain—or accept invitations I could never return. I had *no one* to ask about this most mortifying subject. *No one.* But one day I was searching through the library for something to read—there are lots of books, but so few novels—when I came upon a book that was hidden behind several others. It was—"

"Sensual in nature?" Gideon guessed.

She nodded, her expression one of embarrassed misery.

"The next time Sebastian came to Foxrun, I didn't wait for him to come to me: I went to him." Her voice was a ragged whisper. "It was the only time he ever laid hand on me—he struck me across the face and called me a wh-whore."

Gideon had to grit his teeth not to let out a string of curses; what a bloody hypocrite!

"He accused me of being unfaithful—he said I could only have learned such wanton behavior from some other man. He was enraged—violent—positive I had a lover. He threatened me with horrid things if I were suddenly to prove pregnant when he'd not been home in months. Even after I showed him the book, he didn't believe me. Sebastian told me he'd had enough of my *gallivanting* and sold all but one of my horses as well as my hunters. He was sure that was where I'd found a lover—when I'd ridden with the Taunton pack."

Her voice was thick with regret; Taunton really had been an exceptional ass.

Like anyone else we know?

Gideon grimaced at the accusation; he might be an ass, but he wasn't a hypocrite.

"It was a stupid accusation as he'd been *with* me during the few hunts, but he didn't care. He was so angry that he didn't return for half a year—not even for Christmas." She lifted her cup to her lips with shaky hands. "It was the most dreadful time of my life. My Father fell ill and died and my mother not long after. And then I was alone. My brother's wife had never liked me, nor I her. I f-felt like an orphan."

Gideon made a noncommittal noise of sympathy, aching for her—understanding her feelings of abandonment and loneliness—but tongue-tied.

"I'm not telling you this so you will feel pity for me, I just—well, I just want you to know because—" She gritted her teeth and shook her head, her expression so naïve, young, and confused it made his chest

133

tighten. Gideon guessed that she was probably only talking to him about such a subject because she *had* nobody else to talk to: no friends, family, and her maid was a sot. She was, he realized, one of the loneliest people he'd met.

"Yes?" he prodded. "Tell me why you're sharing this, Alys?"

Her lips parted and Gideon felt himself teetering on the edge of his seat. He saw the moment she changed her mind about whatever she was about to say.

"Nothing," she said, her eyes shuttering. "I just wanted you to know why Foxrun is in such appalling shape."

He remained silent until she was forced to look up. The both knew that was not what she'd wanted to say. But it was not his place to force confidences. This was already more conversation than he'd ever had with a woman in his entire life. He felt . . . raw, just watching her re-live such an ordeal. And, yes, he was a bloody coward so he didn't press her for her real answer.

"Thank you for telling me," he said.

She poured them both more tea and then gave him the fixed, unhappy smile she must have shown her husband for eight years. "Do you think we shall be able to see the silversmith *and* the drapers?"

Chapter Twelve

Alys felt as if she were a toddler at a *ton* party.

Gideon's friends were the most sophisticated, worldly people she'd ever met—not that she'd met a great many people in her life, of course.

Their train had been almost three-quarters of an hour late and Alys had become increasingly anxious as she'd waited for Gideon to return from the station. He'd taken both coaches, of course, and had hired another two from town for servants and luggage.

"Are you sure you don't want to come?" he'd asked Alys more than once.

She *had* wanted to go, but it didn't seem right to force her way in to such a happy reunion of friends.

"I'll stay here, there are a few last-minute things I need to see to."

So she'd stayed. It had probably been just as well as there were the new servants who'd arrived on the same train as Gideon's friends. Alys had thought his cook was coming sooner, but it appeared the high-strung man moved at his own speed. That meant the main hall had been chaos when everyone arrived.

But Gideon had immediately brought her forward—as if she were of paramount importance. "Lady Taunton, let me introduce Mr. and Mrs. Edward Fanshawe."

Alys had been stunned by the rather ordinary-looking couple after all the gossip they'd supplied for the nation's scandal sheets. Mrs. Fanshawe was attractive enough, but not the siren she'd been depicted as in the papers. She did have beautiful blond hair and exceptionally pale eyes. Indeed, if Alys had seen her in public she might have thought the woman was blind.

Edward Fanshawe was almost as big as Silber. But, unlike their stable master, he had harsh, cold features. He was not handsome, but there was something in his dark eyes that was very compelling.

"Thank you so much for having us in your home on such short notice," Nora Fanshawe said, her accent somewhere between Alys's and Gideon's.

Alys thought about pointing out it was Gideon's house, but knew that was foolish: everyone already knew that.

"Yes, thank you," Edward Fanshawe added. "I'm sure Gideon gave you little choice."

"Very droll, Edward," Gideon said. "And this is Mr. Stephen Chatham."

Stephen Chatham was so tall that a person would get a crick in their neck looking up at him. Other than his height, his appearance was average: medium brown hair, cut short and brushed back, clean-shaven like his associates. His eyes were perhaps his only interesting feature, not so much in color as in shape—they were over-large, protuberant, and heavily lidded—almost sleepy looking.

He took her hand in his huge paw and bowed over it. When she looked into his eyes, she swore she felt a cold breeze, as if he were looking down at her from a tall wall of ice. Alys shook herself at the odd fancy.

"Welcome, Mr. Chatham."

"Thank you for your hospitality." The words were pleasant enough, but his reserve was so strong it was almost chilling.

"Stephen did not bring a guest," Gideon said, giving her a quick smile, apparently accustomed to his associate's quelling effect on others.

"Last, but certainly not least, is Mr. Smith."

Alys hadn't even seen the fourth man, who'd been concealed by his taller and broader friends.

"Lady Taunton, it's a pleasure." His teeth were white in his handsome olive face and his dark eyes crinkled at the corners. He was of middling height and his tailoring was exquisite and flattered his slim, athletic physique. "Gideon tells me you were expecting me to bring a guest. I'm sorry, but it is just me. I apologize for putting you to the extra effort."

He was well-spoken and pleasant, but Alys sensed some darker presence behind his attractive exterior. For reasons she did not understand, she sensed Mr. Smith was an extremely dangerous man.

She smiled, even though the hairs on her neck were standing up. "No need to apologize. I do hope your friend is all right."

Smith's expression didn't change, but Alys swore she heard a door slamming shut. "He was called away on business he couldn't ignore."

Gideon stepped into the sudden silence. "I thought you might show our guests to their rooms so they could freshen up—and then maybe tea in the library?"

"A real library, Gideon?" Smith teased. "With books, too?"

Gideon smiled at his friends. "I know it's odd for a man who doesn't read, but it's a comfortable room. Now, I should go and make sure Tickle and Mrs. Tickle meet Bains and Mrs. Harwell and DuValle and everyone else."

Alys was relieved that Gideon had decided to take a hand in what would surely be an awkward situation. The Tickles were ready to step down, but there was still the fact they'd been in service here for fifty years.

"Shall we meet in a half hour?" he asked his friends, who nodded their agreement. "Lady Taunton will show you to your rooms. If you'll excuse me."

"If you'll follow me," Alys said, leading them toward the guest quarters, which were the floor below hers and Gideon's suites.

Nora Fanshawe walked beside her. "What a fascinating house. I'm very eager to see it in the daylight."

"It is certainly unique," Alys smiled down at her, not realizing until she was right beside her just how small she was. At five foot six Alys was a bit taller than average, but the other woman was a good three inches shorter. "I've heard you are a brilliant painter. Do you paint people exclusively? Or landscapes?"

"Brilliant may be a bit strong, but I appreciate the compliment. As for what I paint? Well, I paint whatever catches my interest."

"Did you bring your supplies with you?"

Nora Fanshawe gave her a charming smile that made her rather colorless face seem warm and inviting. "I'm embarrassed to admit I never even leave the house without at least one sketchbook. For this visit I brought my full traveling kit with me."

"Do you allow others to watch you paint? Or is it a private affair?"

Mrs. Fanshawe laughed, the sound low and gravelly for such a petite woman. "I can paint in the middle of a raging thunderstorm, and I would love your company."

It was such an unexpected—and open—gesture of friendship that Alys was touched.

"I shall be able to show you some beautiful places." She stopped outside a set of double doors. "Here we are at your room, Mrs. Fanshawe. Your husband has the adjoining room." She opened the door to her favorite guest suite. She'd had the drapes and hangings done in several shades of blue.

"How beautiful—blue is my favorite color," Mrs. Fanshawe said.

"I thought artists weren't allowed to have favorite colors, Nora—isn't that like having a favorite child?" Mr. Smith teased.

"Nonsense—of course we have favorites," Mrs. Fanshawe said. "We just need to make sure none of the other colors find out and get their feelings hurt."

Alys and Smith laughed at her whimsical answer.

"Your room is through here, Mr. Fanshawe," Alys gestured to the connecting door.

"How old is this part of the house?" Mr. Smith asked.

"This is one of the newer sections and was built in the 1740s."

He stroked the intricate dental molding around the door frame, his fingers as slender and elegant as his person. "Has each Earl of Taunton added a new addition?"

"Thankfully, no. The last part to be changed or remodeled was during the current earl's grandfather's time. By all accounts he was a practical man and focused his energy on bringing the kitchen, laundry and dairy into this century."

"I daresay Gideon will leave his mark," Mr. Fanshawe commented drily.

"Actually, he's already done so with the tenant farms, many of which have not been modernized or improved for well over a century."

"Ah-ha," Smith said, "Our Gideon, a gentleman farmer."

Mr. Chatham and Mr. Fanshawe smirked, as if at some private jest.

"Let's not keep our hostess standing about, gentlemen," Mrs. Fanshawe said. "You'll have to drive them along like cattle, my lady." Mrs. Fanshawe made shooing motions toward the men.

"We're holding matters up, Chatham, onward," Mr. Smith said. "See you two downstairs in half a tick," he said to the Fanshawes.

"You are directly across the hall, Mr. Smith," Alys said, opening the door in question. "Your room is almost a mirror image of the suite we just left."

"It's lovely," he said, looking around at the cool greens and touch of brown. "A bit like a forest. Thank you."

Alys turned to the last guest, whose towering size and silence made her a bit nervous.

His large eyes glinted beneath their heavy lids. "You saved the best for last."

Alys smiled at this unexpected display of humor. "How did you guess? You are along this corridor. I put you all the way at the end as the view over the deer park is magnificent."

He opened the door for her and followed her in, his impassive face giving no sign of what was in his mind as he looked around. They both turned at the sound of activity out in the hall.

"Ah, here comes your luggage and this must be your man."

A tall, slender man dressed in a black suit and wearing the thickest spectacles Alys had ever seen entered the room and bowed to Alys.

"This is Leather," Mr. Chatham said.

Alys had never been introduced to a valet before, but she nodded. "Welcome to Foxrun."

"I'm honored, my lady." The man's lips flexed slightly, candlelight glinting off his spectacles and obscuring his eyes. His face was even more featureless than his master's.

The valet headed toward the dressing room and Mr. Chatham's eyes followed his servant's progress until he disappeared into the other room and then he turned back to Alys. For the first time she saw a glimpse of something behind those hooded eyes, as if speaking to others was not only exhausting, but difficult. "Thank you, the room is perfect."

"You're most welcome."

Alys couldn't help feeling a pang of pity for the other man. No matter how wealthy and powerful he was, it must still be strange not to even be able to speak a polite platitude without a struggle.

Everyone, she realized quite suddenly, was a prisoner of something—or someone.

Alys had first been her father's prisoner and then her husband's.

What a disaster her marriage to Sebastian had been. Telling her pitiful tale to Gideon had made her realize just how grim her life had been all these years.

Alys had considered his question several times today: was she content to live out her life in the Dower House? Was that all she wanted?

Or had Gideon's arrival in her life opened up vistas she never would have dreamed of?

Vistas that decent women—women like the daughter her father and mother had raised—would turn away from.

❤

"All right—let's have it. What happened, Smith?" Gideon followed Smith up to his room for a nightcap after they'd all had tea in the library.

"What do you mean?" Smith asked in his maddening way.

"Why are you here alone?"

"Do you think Lady Taunton would object if I smoked? I'd open the windows."

"She wouldn't, but I would. It's my bloody house, remember?" He snorted at Smith's dismissive expression. "Fine. Go ahead, light one of those foul-smelling sticks. And then tell me what happened." Gideon poured them both glasses from the decanter of fine brandy he'd made sure were in every room.

He took the glasses to Smith, who'd opened the window and was leaning against the frame.

"Thank you, my lord," Smith said, and then gave one of his rare grins. "Tired of hearing that yet?"

Gideon laughed. "Never." They clinked glasses. "Can you bloody believe it?" he demanded after taking a deep drink. "Me—an earl?"

"We always said aristocrats were dissolute bastards; you can probably teach them a thing or two, Gideon."

"I'll take that as a compliment."

"Tell me about the widow."

"Ha! I asked first," Gideon said.

140

"Yes," Smith said gently. "But we both know I'm not going to answer you."

"You're such a bastard, Smith—you know that?"

"Yes."

Gideon snorted. "I don't know why you can poke your not insignificant nose into everyone else's business yet don't deserve the same treatment."

Smith smiled.

Gideon threw up his hands. "Oh, fine. Never mind. But since I missed our last meeting I'm going to go with Barnabus." He enjoyed this game of guessing Smith's first name—although he suspected the man wouldn't confirm a correct guess even if one of them stumbled on it.

"I believe you guessed that one before. Now, the widow."

Gideon sighed. "What about her?"

"The two of you appear almost . . . domestic."

"She's been extremely helpful," he said, realizing his tone sounded defensive. "And she has nowhere else to go until her little cottage is livable." He shrugged. "Surprisingly, we get on."

"Hmm."

"What, Smith. Just bloody say it."

"Have you considered marrying her?"

Of all the things he'd expected, that was surely at the very end of the list. "*What*? Are you mad?"

"No, I'm not. And I can tell by the lack of conviction in your tone that you *have* considered it. Tell me honestly that you haven't?"

Gideon blinked rapidly, as if to clear something annoying from his eyes. He hadn't thought such a thing!

Had he?

"Christ!" he said when he saw the other man was smirking. "Of course I haven't thought such a thing. Even if I had, she's the daughter of a bloody marquess."

Smith clucked his tongue. "And you are one of the wealthiest men in the nation and now a peer."

"I'm also one of the most deviant men in the country."

"I can't argue with that."

"You *are* a bastard." Gideon took another drink. All three of Gideon's partners could read him like an annual profit report. Unlike them, Gideon had never been reticent about talking about himself, his life, his purchases, his . . . well, his whatever. But—oddly—he didn't feel so forthcoming right now.

"I can see she loves Foxrun," Smith said.

"Yes, she does. More than Taunton ever did. Oh, by the way, speaking of wagering. Can you find out for me who Taunton owed money to?"

Smith's left eyebrow crept up. Gideon hated how the man was able to do that. His eyebrows only worked in tandem.

"What happened?"

"Some rough sorts came up here—scared Lady Taunton and demanded payment for Taunton's unpaid racing debts. He ended up dead less than a month later."

"I read he died in a hunting accident."

"He did, but we know how accidents aren't often accidents."

Smith turned to stare out into the darkness. "That's true. I'll nose about when I get back to town."

"Is it my imagination or does Chatham seem happier than usual?" Gideon was not jesting. There was a gleam in the tall man's eyes he'd not seen before, not that his actual behavior was any different.

"I think that must be your imagination, Gideon." Smith took a sip and smiled at him, but Gideon discerned a subtle tightening around his eyes.

Well, well, well! This was interesting—Smith and Chatham having a disagreement over something? Or someone?

Gideon knew Smith would tell him nothing—nor would Chatham. He'd have to see what Edward knew about this.

"I read about your newest acquisition in the paper—that you and Chatham are now the proud owners of some duke's castle? Did you have anything to do with the man dying on a yacht?"

"I'm merely an investor—Chatham is the new owner. As to what happened to the last duke?" Smith shrugged. "I have no clue. You'd have to ask Stephen."

"Yes, but then I'd have to listen to him drone on about it."

They both laughed. Stephen Chatham was a man who rarely said more than ten words a month.

Gideon lifted his empty glass. "One more?"

Smith nodded.

When he returned with their refreshed glasses he said, "She's already had one selfish arsehole in her life, do you think she really deserves another?" He didn't have to tell Smith who he meant.

"That's her choice, isn't it? Besides, what do *you* deserve, Gideon?"

"I think we both know the answer to that," Gideon said, laughing. But Smith did not laugh with him. Instead he stared, smoked and waited.

"Christ!" Gideon shoved a hand through his hair and groaned, letting his head *thunk* against the window frame opposite Smith. "You know me, Smith. I'm not a one-woman man. Hell, I'm not even a five-woman man."

"And how is that working for you?"

Gideon opened his mouth to tell him to go sod himself but Smith was not finished yet.

"Is that what she wants, Gideon? A one-woman man?"

Gideon looked at him, arrested by the question. But then he shook his head. "Of course it is—that's what all women want."

Smith chuckled. "You don't know *what* she wants, do you, Gideon?"

He tried not to bristle at the smug amusement in the other man's voice. "She wants children, a luxurious home, expensive frocks—just what they all want."

"That's not what Nora wants."

That stopped him.

"No," Gideon admitted. "You're right; that's not what Nora wants." Gideon remembered well and good at least one thing Nora wanted— his cock in her body. "Unfortunately, there aren't many Nora's about, are there?"

Smith ignored his question. "Tell me something. Did you discharge your mistresses and leave London in a huff because you were satisfied with your life, Gideon?"

Again, he wanted to tell Smith to sod himself, but then he remembered London—the days and weeks, hell, *months*, and all the fucking he'd done, and just how little he'd liked any of it.

Smith blew out a narrow jet of blue-black smoke and turned his uncomfortable gaze on Gideon. "Any man who fucks as many different women as you do is looking for something Gideon. I applaud that you keep looking, keep searching. But I'm disappointed you keep looking in the same places. Maybe it's time to start looking someplace else."

—◄ ♥ ►—

Alys didn't know why she wanted to go to the peephole tonight. He'd sent his mistresses away. He'd be alone. And after their long day he was likely already in bed, sleeping.

Well, then she could see him sleeping. She was pitiful; she just wanted to *see* him—clothed or unclothed.

She groaned and shoved back the blankets. After enjoying the company of his friends for an hour she vowed she'd not spy on him again. Watching Nora and Edward Fanshawe had been enlightening. Here were two people who'd gone through public trial and came out of it loving each other. *That* was what a marriage should be like.

Yet here she was, slipping her feet into her woolen slippers and heading out to engage in more depravity.

She looked both ways before picking up her skirts and trotting toward the panel. She was glad the guests were on the floor below them. And now that the two women had gone back to London, she only had Gideon and his valet to worry about.

Heartened by that fact, her fingers found the catch on the first try.

She made her way to the peep, feeling like a rat just as she always did. Still the arousal in her body was irresistible.

She stepped into the corridor, closed the door, turned, and then froze. There was a candle flickering in the wall sconce. She clenched her jaws. Had she left a candle burning the last time?

"Good God!" she whispered as she all but ran toward it. She could have burned the house down.

She slid to a stop before turning the corner, her hand going to the sconce

This candle looks almost brand new. The thought occurred to her just before she blew out the flame.

"If you do that, we'll be in the dark."

—◄ ♥ ►—

Gideon got what he deserved for scaring her.

Who would have thought such a small woman could scream so loud? And then her hands flew up and the candle went sailing through the air, hitting the stone wall and plunging the corridor into profound darkness.

The panel door opened and Jackson stood in the opening, backlit, his face in darkness.

"Is everything all right, my lord?"

"Does *everyone* know about this peep?" Alys squeaked.

With the light from the hallway Gideon could see her clearly enough to take her elbow. "Come with me."

"I heard voices on the stairs, my lord," his valet said.

"Go deal with it, Jackson—before they make it up here." He pulled Alys along with him. She wasn't resisting, but she wasn't helping either. "Do you *want* to be caught, Alys? Come along." That spurred her on.

Gideon shut the panel door behind them, hurried her down the hall a few steps, and then opened the door to his room and pulled her inside.

"What are you—"

"Shhh," he whispered, laying his ear against the door. "They're out there."

Her mouth shut with a snap and she put her head against the wood, so their faces were only a few inches apart.

"Can you tell who it is?" she whispered.

He shook his head. "Mr. Tickle for certain. And perhaps Fanshawe."

She squeezed her eyes shut. "Oh no, I'm so sorry, Gideon—I didn't mean for something like this to happen in front of your friends. I'm sure poor Mrs. Fanshawe is shocked and frightened.

Gideon said a silent prayer for his blackened soul and said, "Yes, they're probably both deeply shocked. Especially Nora. You'd better stay put—and quiet."

"I'm so sorry for screaming," she whispered.

Gideon took her hand. "Come away from the door." This time she followed him without a struggle and he led her into the bedchamber before she realized what was happening.

"What are—"

"Shhh."

145

She narrowed her eyes at him. "They can't hear me all the way in here."

A loud knocking on the door made them both jump and Alys made that adorable squeaking sound again.

"My lord?" It was Jackson. "Is everything all right, my lord?"

"What the devil is it, Jackson? I was asleep." Gideon winked at Alys and she scowled.

"It is nothing, my lord. I'm sorry to wake you."

They remained planted to the floor as the voices moved away.

And then she whirled on him. "What were you doing in there?"

"What were *you* doing?"

"I—" She frowned and her jaw snapped shut.

"You were spying."

"No. I was—"

"Yes?" Gideon took a step toward her. When she tried to step back, she bumped into one of the posts on his bed.

He knew that what he was doing was wrong—she was the next thing to an innocent—and a better man would step away.

Instead, Gideon came closer, until he could feel the heat of her body and smell the hint of lavender and faint scent of female sweat. It was intoxicating.

He lowered his mouth until his lips brushed her ear. "Tell me, Alys, did you *like* what you saw me doing?"

Her breathing was rapid, breathy, and so raspy he barely heard her answer.

"*Yes.*"

His eyelids fluttered shut and he sighed—torn between relief and despair. "Oh Alys, do you know what you've done?"

Chapter Thirteen

Gideon was so close that Alys felt the vibration of his deep voice before she heard the words.

His hands slid with exquisite firmness around her waist, just the way Silber's did when he lifted her into the saddle.

Well, perhaps not *just* like that.

"I've wanted to touch you since the first time I saw you," he whispered, his breath hot on the top of her head. "I want you, Alys. I want you so badly it hurts."

His words detonated something inside her and her arms went around his torso before she knew it, squeezing him until he grunted.

"Easy, little one," he whispered, the unexpectedly sweet endearment bringing tears to her eyes.

Alys sighed, melting against him. He felt so very, very, very, very, very good. When had she last held another person like this? When had she *ever* held anyone—ever? Or been held?

"Shhh, sweetheart. It's all right," he soothed, which is when she realized she was shaking *and* crying.

Oh God. How utterly mortifying.

His arm was still around her but he now patted her shoulder with a tentativeness that told her he'd gone from aroused to terrified in mere seconds. She was a crying female, one of his nightmares.

Alys actually *felt* him changing against her belly, the hard ridge softening.

Her father had been right all along: Alys *did* drive men away.

She squirmed in his arms; she never should have come here.

"Alys," he held her lightly, but his embrace was as unbreakable as an iron shackle. "Please," he said, "Don't cry—I promise I won't touch you. I'll—"

"I *want you to touch me, you idiot*," she snuffled into his fine cotton shirt, which she was wetting and likely ruining.

He stood rigidly for a second and then started shaking silently.

"Are you *laughing* at me?"

He made a strangled choking sound. "No, sweetheart, that's the last thing I'm doing.

— ❤ —

Then what the hell are you doing, Gideon?

Gideon startled at the voice—which wasn't one he recalled hearing inside his head ever before. This voice was hectoring, bossy, and sounded nothing at all like any of his normal, fun-loving mental companions.

Er, nothing, he said carefully—thank God only inside his mind.

Take your hands off her and escort her out of your room. Immediately.

But his hands were already sliding around her body before the voice had finished.

Good God! She felt delicious. She wasn't wearing a corset and her breasts were pressing against him in all their glory.

"Gideon?"

He ignored the nagging voice, allowing his fingers to slide down her narrow waist to wide, flaring—

"*Gideon?*"

He blinked. Oh, that wasn't the voice in his head. He shook himself. "I'm sorry, darling what was that?"

"I shouldn't have said that."

"Hmmm?" His fingers resumed their stroking. "Said what?"

"Well, when I said *yes* to your question—meaning I wanted you to—well, *you* know."

Those words made their way through the mental fog and he grinned before tilting her face to his and lowering his mouth over hers, thrusting his tongue between her parted lips. Oh God. She tasted as good as she looked and smelled.

He angled his head, wanting to take her deeper, to explore every—

She doesn't know how to kiss, you oaf.

Gideon squeezed his eyes shut, as if he could block out his own mind.

The voice was gone, but he couldn't avoid the truth: she was such a bloody innocent she didn't even know how to kiss!

He inhaled deeply, gathering every bit of strength he could find, and then carefully put her at arm's length. Her sweet, soft lips clung to him and her body followed his as he pulled away.

"Alys? Alys, sweetheart?" He held her shoulders lightly but firmly.

She blinked drowsily. "Yes?"

"I think this is—ah—I think it's—"

Go on you coward, do the decent thing.

He gritted his teeth at the infuriating voice. "Alys, I'm not a good man—you know that, don't you?" That last part came out a bit whiney and plaintive.

"Wha-what do you mean?" she asked.

Gideon groaned, his cock making it difficult to think or speak. He just wanted to throw her onto his bed and fuck her into next week.

And that's the last thing she needs from somebody like you.

Gideon didn't bother arguing, he just didn't have it in him—especially when he knew the voice—his long-lost conscience?—was telling the truth.

"Listen, Alys. I'm not a knight in shining armor. I will not lift you onto my white charger and spirit you away to a happily ever after. I'm a *terrible* man—a man who could *never* be faithful. I don't *want* to be faithful and doubt I could even if tried." He shook his head, as if she'd tried to argue with him, when all she was doing was looking up at him with those huge trusting eyes.

"Christ!" He stepped back. Maybe if he wasn't actually *touching* any part of her he could talk—or at least think. "Listen to me carefully." He waited until she nodded. "If you come into my bed it means nothing more than what it is: the two of us fucking."

She flinched.

Good. She needed to know what he was—a vulgar, selfish, depraved cit with the morals of a filthy street cur.

"It doesn't mean love and it doesn't mean marriage and it doesn't mean anything beyond the moment."

She cocked her head, as if listening to something Gideon couldn't hear. And then she nodded and said, "All right, Gideon."

"*What?*"

They both startled at his squawk.

149

"Are you bloody mad?" he demanded. "Weren't you listening to a word I said?"

She laid a hand on his forearm and he startled. "I understand. I said that is all right. I don't wish to be married; I just want—" she churned her hand in the air.

"To fuck? You just want to fuck?"

Her soft, creamy cheeks streaked with red.

"Does the way I talk bother you? Because that is what I am, Alys—crude, crass, promiscuous, libidinous, deviant—and other things beside. I like to find the filthiest words in the English language—fuck, cunt, cock, cunny, arse, prick, balls, *come*—and use them with abandon. I like to *do* the filthiest things the human body is capable of doing and the most depraved things the human mind can conceive of. I am *not* a tender lover who will whisper poetry to you. I won't fall in love with you—*ever*," he hissed the word and she flinched, as if he'd thrown stones at her—which is exactly what he was doing. "I *like* fucking and I *like* variety and I *like* discovering new debaucheries—there are very few lines I will not cross, Alys. I will never tie myself to one woman. I am not a one-woman man and I never will be. The only thing I want from you is your mouth, your cunt, and your arse. The only thing you will *ever* get from me is my body and my enthusiasm using it. Do you understand?" His chest was heaving and his voice was breathless by the time he said the last word.

Alys stared up at him with eyes as round as marbles.

There! *Finally* he'd gotten through to her and—

"That's what I want—something physical, animal, those things you were doing to L-Lucy and Susan." She swallowed. "I imagined you doing them to me."

Her words set off a commotion in his head—not to mention in his cock—that was too powerful to ignore. Gideon grabbed her arm and yanked her close, holding her clamped against him from hips to shoulders.

"You are rapidly approaching a place where I will not turn back," he snarled into her ear. "Do you understand?"

"Yes . . . please."

He groaned and ground his erection into her soft midriff. "Do you feel that? It's for you, Alys, only for you—and it's *all* I'll ever have for you."

"Please, Gideon."

He groaned. "All right—you think you know what you want and what I have to offer. Let's hear you say it. I want *you* to tell me—in detail—which of the things you'd like me to do first?"

Her body was so rigid and still that Gideon thought he might have frightened some sense into her.

But then she whispered against his shoulder. "Don't make me say those things, Gideon. Please, just . . . can't you just make me feel like that? *Please.*"

Alys was mortified by her begging, but her body's demands were stronger than her pride.

Gideon's arm relaxed and she thought he was leaving. Instead, he stepped back, his hands at his shirt cuffs, deftly removing the links. His high cheekbones were hard and sharp in the candlelight, his full lips much thinner as he examined her coolly, dispassionately.

"Am I the first man you've seen naked? My cock the first one you've seen hard?" he asked in a tone that was conversational—which was somehow worse than his harsh voice of only moments earlier.

She swallowed and nodded.

"I want you to tell me how your husband took you," he said, his hands going to his waistcoat buttons.

Alys's eyes widened. "Why? Why would you want to hear about that?"

He shrugged. "I just do."

"But—"

His waistcoat was unbuttoned but he made no move to remove it. His eyes glittered and his expression became cruel. "You're the one who told me you were a grown woman, Alys, and if you can't talk to me *like* a grown woman then perhaps this is not a good idea. The last thing I want is to end up with a weeping schoolgirl on my hands and—"

Alys shoved him in the chest so hard he staggered back.

He glared at her. "What the—"

151

"You want me to prove to you that I'm woman enough to be with you—and not a *schoolgirl*? You want to hear the pathetic extent of my *womanhood*?"

Something in his eyes flickered and he opened his mouth.

"Shut up. I'm going to tell you now—everything. Don't worry, it won't take long," she sneered. "My husband came to me in the dark, never more than twice a week—on those rare occasions when he was actually *here*. He lifted my nightgown, spread my legs, and shoved into me. It *always* hurt and sometimes I bled. He would thrust and thrust and it felt like he'd put splintered wood inside me."

Gideon's eyes had narrowed to pinpricks, his jaw flexing.

"But at least it never lasted long—just a few thrusts and he would spend. And then he would take himself from my body, pull down my nightdress, thank me, and leave."

She shoved him again, but this time he was ready for it and stood firm.

"Was that what you wanted to hear? You wanted to embarrass me?" She went to shove him again but he caught her wrists.

"I didn't want to shame you, Alys. But I *do* want to know what I'm dealing with. And if you thought that question was insensitive, you'd bloody well better reconsider having anything to do with me, because that is how I am: heartless, selfish, and cruel. If you leave now, we can pretend like nothing happened and go on with our comfortable existence. If you go, I will never bother you or remind you of this night. You may live here unmolested for the rest of your life if you choose. I will settle a living allowance on you—a decent amount that will allow you to live in a manner you deserve, and as you choose—and you never have to see me again, if you don't want to. Or you can stay... and suffer the consequences. The decision is yours."

Her jaw worked from side to side and she her eyes prickled in a way that heralded tears. She swallowed, refusing to cry in front of him again.

"Do you want to stay, or do you want to go?" he repeated coolly.

She gulped again, breathing hard. "Stay," she said, her face burning and her voice barely a whisper.

His cold expression didn't even flicker. "Then take off your dressing gown."

Alys gaped.

"I *said:* Take. It. Off."

Her hand trembled as she reached for the sash and gave it a shaky tug.

His eyelids lowered and his hands slid beneath the stiff material and he pushed it off her shoulders. When she would have bent to pick it up, he put a finger beneath her chin, holding her in place. His celestial blue eyes had once again gone dark. "Leave it. Turn around."

Alys turned on trembling legs, her heart pounding in her ears. She felt the heat of him behind her, but he didn't touch her.

"Here are my rules, so listen carefully. I'm the one in control—at all times. You'll do what I say, how I say, and you'll do it quickly. Do you understand?"

His menacing tone and arrogant words had an immediate and powerful effect on her body—and not one that she would've expected. Instead of wanting to slap his face, that place between her thighs—the place she had to tease forever to get any pleasure—tightened so exquisitely Alys could barely nod her head.

"Never nod your head. Always answer me—unless your mouth is otherwise occupied—and use my name. Do you understand?"

"Yes, Gideon." Her voice was the husk of a whisper.

"Mmm, yes." His arms slid around her and he pulled her against his hard, muscular body. "I like hearing you say my name. And I especially like instant and eager obedience from my lovers." His breath was hot on her ear and he nipped her lobe—*hard*. Alys startled and he chuckled. "Shhh, little one. I'll never do anything to hurt you. Unless you want me to," he added, his voice pulsing with lust and amusement. "I'm going to take off your nightdress, but *only* if you want me to take it off after everything I've just told you. And *only* if you understand what I want from you and are prepared to obey me, at all times. Otherwise, I'll escort you out and we shall go on as before—as friendly cousins. So, one last time: stay or go?"

She began to nod and caught herself. "I want to stay, Gideon."

"Mmmm." The sound was like the purr of a big cat and he released her, his warm hardness disappearing and leaving her cold. "Stand up straight," he ordered when her body wanted to follow his.

She jerked upright and his fingers worked quickly on the ten buttons that ran down her neck and shoulder. "Lift your arms."

153

She closed her eyes, inhaled deeply, and complied.

He lifted the gown and then all she felt was air around her naked body

"Oh, Alys." Gone was arrogant mastery and in its place was . . . reverence? "Turn around," he said huskily.

Alys's feet were so very heavy. If she turned, he would see her—he would—

"Alys."

Her body shook at his quiet command and she turned.

The room was utterly silent for what felt like years.

"Look at me."

Her head jerked up and her heart did that odd stuttering stagger at the raw desire she saw on his face.

"You are very beautiful. Indeed, you are perfect. The next time you come to me I want you naked under your dressing gown. Understand? I want to tug on that sash and have your body immediately available to me."

Her face could not possibly become any hotter.

He stepped toward her, his hand going to her sex, cupping her. She shuddered but didn't step away. "Good girl," he murmured, one of his fingers probing her lips and finding that sensitive part of her without even looking and giving it a careless flick.

She moaned and then bit her lip.

"Do you understand?"

"Hmmm?"

"Alys, you need to answer me, or there will be no more of *this*." *This* was another flick.

"Yes, Gideon, I understand."

Flick.

"What do you understand?"

She struggled to recall the question, momentarily terrified she'd forgotten it.

"The dressing gown," he reminded her.

"Oh, yes, I am to come to you only in a dressing gown."

"Good," he whispered in her ear, his finger moving faster, sliding over her easily thanks to all the mortifying moisture her body had produced. "You're so wet and swollen and needy," he continued in the same soft voice. "I'm going to keep you in a heightened state of arousal at all times. Whenever you look at my hands—no matter where we are—I want you to think of *this*. I want you to remember how easily and quickly I can give you pleasure." He dropped his voice and his finger moved to the base of her pearl and massaged. Her body became boneless. "Does this feel good, Alys?"

"Yes, Gideon," she said in between shaky breaths.

He chuckled wickedly, his warm, hard body vibrating with laughter as his finger stroked. "This is your clitoris—the source of all female pleasure. I've spent a great deal of time learning about this wonderful little bit of flesh, Alys, and you will be the beneficiary of all my studies."

Alys made that embarrassing sound again and clamped her jaws shut. But her body's trembling was beyond her control.

"Never hold back from me, Alys. I want to hear every whimper, yell, groan, grunt, and gasp." His finger elicited several of those examples immediately, whatever he was doing making her dizzy and weak. "Come for me, little one," he urged. "That's right," he praised as her hips jerked. "Let go and soak my hand."

Her body responded to his crass order almost as much as his skilled touch and explosive, exquisite pleasure spread from that one little spot to every part of her. Even when his finger stopped the waves still came, the bliss a warm embrace.

Alys didn't realize she was falling until his arm slid around her and he lifted her and then laid her on the bed.

He chuckled. "I think you were going to sleep on me, Alys. And we're only just getting started. Now, scoot back, darling," he said, his eyes glinting with amusement as they rested on her thighs, which were clamped tightly together.

Alys backed up before he had to tell her twice. She would have kept right on backing, but he caught her ankles.

"That's far enough." He slid a hand up her legs to her thighs and tried to separate them, but they just pressed tighter together. His eyes met hers and he cocked his head.

She gulped and began to open them.

His hands moved to his bulging trouser front. "Keep spreading until I tell you to stop or until you can't open any further."

He pushed down his trousers and drawers and kicked them aside. His organ was even more impressive close up: long, hard, and arched gracefully against the taut ridges of his belly.

Alys's hips trembled and she could spread them no further.

He took his shaft in his hand and stroked, his eyes on the juncture of her thighs. "Use your hands to part your lower lips for me."

Alys's head buzzed. "I-I beg your p-pardon?"

His hand stopped its stroking and he frowned down at her, looking every inch the avenging angel. "Did my words confuse you?"

She swallowed. "No, Gideon."

"I did not speak in jest when I said I expected instant obedience from you. This is the last time I'll ask you to do something twice, Alys. The next time you can put on your nightgown and robe and go back to your room. And never come back."

His eyes were pitiless, his jaw hard: it would all be the way he wanted, or it would not be, at all. He really would send her away—just as he'd done to those other two women. And then he would replace her with someone else and she would lie awake in the room next door while he did all those wonderful things to some other woman.

Alys inhaled deeply and reached down with shaking hands, her face so hot she thought she might simply faint before she could complete the mortifying instruction. But of course she didn't.

"Mmm." He resumed his stroking, the bead of moisture that formed at the tip slowly sliding down the ruddy, bell-shaped head. He smiled at her. "Do you like watching me touch myself?"

She gulped. "Yes, Gideon."

"Why, thank you, Alys." He grinned, released himself, and climbed up on the bed, using his knees to push her thighs painfully wide and keep her open. "I'm going to give you an orgasm with my mouth and then I'm going to fuck you with my cock. Do you want that, Alys?"

Alys gaped

His eyebrows began to lower.

"Yes, Gideon," she blurted.

He dropped his head, sucked her into his mouth, and all her thoughts fled more quickly than the flash of sunlight on water.

→ ♥ ⊱

Gideon didn't think he'd ever be able to leave her cunt alone.

She was delicious and responsive, coming only moments after he'd put his mouth on her. So, he'd busied himself elsewhere until touching her sensitive bud didn't make her scream.

He explored her entrance, licking and kissing and sucking her until she was shivering, and then probing her with his tongue, using a suggestive thrusting rhythm to let her know what she would soon be getting. And getting.

Once she'd stopped shaking, he rose up on his knees, drinking in her flushed body.

"Slide your hands behind your knees and lift them to your chest—good, now open for me. Oh, yes," he praised, "spread nice and wide—hold them." He wished he had another set of eyes to look at her.

"This is such a wonderful position," he murmured, one hand sliding over her thighs while the other skimmed between her cheeks. He spread her lips with one hand and dropped to his elbows and sucked her into his mouth.

She groaned and shuddered. And, he saw with a grin pulled her thighs even wider. His little sensualist in the making.

Gideon worked her little jewel with tightly pursed lips while he lightly thumbed her back hole with his other hand. Her eyes flew open and her hips thrust up, as if to get away.

He released her swollen clitoris and held her eyes while he thumbed her tight pucker. "Did you enjoy watching me fuck Lucy and Susan back here?" Actually, he couldn't recall which of them he'd had annually.

Judging by her stunned expression, she probably didn't remember, either. She nodded, as if in a trance. "Yes, Gideon."

"Do you want it?" he asked, his thumb pressing harder, but not enough to breech her.

She gulped loudly and said, "Yes, Gideon."

He grinned. "That's the correct answer, darling. But not tonight."

He covered her with his mouth and worked her to orgasm. While she shuddered and whimpered, he used both hands to expose her tight little arsehole to his view. He licked her, breaching the tight ring of muscle with the tip of his tongue. She began to writhe and moan when he pushed inside her, holding her immobile while he fucked her with his tongue.

157

When he could bear his aching balls no longer, he raised onto his knees. She was breathing heavily, but her eyes were open, and they were locked with his.

"Did you like that? Did it make you feel filthy—wanton?"

"Yes, Gideon."

"It pleases me to lick and taste every part of you, Alys." He throbbed at the embarrassment and lust he saw mingled on her face. "But I can't hold back much longer. You can release your thighs—take me in your hand and guide me to your entrance."

Her hand didn't hesitate to do his bidding and something about her wordless obedience gave him a pang of shame. He knew he was behaving like a pig, but it was far better for her to see him at his most obnoxious, depraved, and dictatorial because that was who he was, and all he could ever be to her.

Her hands shook as she placed him against her slick heat. He hissed in a breath and pushed only his crown into her.

"Fuck!" he shouted as she clenched around him. "You're so wonderfully tight," he added on a gasp, pulsing his hips so that he breached only her entrance over and over with his fat, sensitive head.

She stared up at him, wide eyed, her mouth a shocked O at his yelling, which he knew had been loud enough to wake the house.

Gideon smiled and then slid into her slick passage with one long, smooth thrust, giving her something other than the noise level to worry about,

It was her turn to cry out and her back arched as if an electric charge had gone through her, her sheath gripping him so tightly it made him see stars. Or maybe that was because he'd stopped breathing.

"Does it hurt?" he asked when he could catch his breath; he wanted to shock her, but he never wanted to cause her physical pain. Well, not unless she asked for it.

She shook her head, breathing raggedly through her mouth and Gideon gave her a pass on not answering him correctly.

"I wish you could see how beautiful you look wrapped around me," he said, his eyes dropping to where his shaft impaled her. "The next time I'm going to fuck you in front of a mirror so you can watch me sliding in," he pushed, "And then out." He pulled out and her cunt contracted, as if to keep him inside.

158

Gideon grunted. "I love that, little one, your tight sheath squeezing and milking me," he said in a strained voice because he *was* strained, barely able to stop himself from savaging her.

Rather than stroke back into her, he kept himself poised at her entrance, studying her face for signs of distress. He doubted he was hurting her physically, suspecting his vulgar words and behavior were likely more shocking than his prick. Although it *was* an impressive organ.

Gideon held her gaze and pulsed gently in and out. "Do you want more, Alys?" he asked, his head almost dizzy with the effort of exercising restraint.

"Yes, Gideon," she said in a whisper. And then she flexed her pelvis and his iron control shattered.

Gideon slammed into her, pounding her with hard, deep thrusts. "Tell me," he rasped in between strokes. "Tell me when you're close."

She never answered because she was already there.

His restraint, already worn to threads, snapped and Gideon drove into her thrice more and then froze, emptying himself into her convulsing body.

He lost touch with consciousness while he gloried in his release, only slowly swimming back toward awareness.

His first thought when he looked down at their still joined bodies was that it had taken a lamentably short time to ejaculate in her. His second was that it was just as well he'd been so quick as she would already be sore tomorrow.

"Oh, Alys," he groaned, as he lifted himself up, removing his softening prick from her body before collapsing beside her, his muscles rubbery and skin slick from exertion.

"All right?" he asked her a few moments later, turning to look at her.

She nodded, never taking her gaze from the ceiling. "Yes, Gideon," she said in a low, but steady voice.

Gideon thought that would be all, but then she turned to him, the corner of her mouth pulled up on one side.

"It was more than all right. It was lovely."

Chapter Fourteen

Gideon drifted into sleep after collapsing beside her.

Alys had intended to rest for a moment and then leave, but she'd obviously fallen asleep because she woke with a start to find Gideon's arm around her naked waist.

They'd fallen asleep on top of the bedding but he must have pulled the blankets over them at some point. The fire had burned down to embers and the room was chilly. Two candles still guttered in their sockets on the nightstand and illuminated the bronze clock face: it was twenty-five minutes after three.

Gideon had pulled her so close that they were nose to nose and Alys had to move out from under his arm in tiny, painstaking increments, to keep from waking him. It took her several minutes until his arm slid off her. He muttered something and, for a moment, she thought she'd woken him. But he merely shifted slightly and resumed his deep breathing.

Instead of leaving, she studied him, her greedy eyes roaming his face and body in a way she would never be able to do when he was conscious and his knowing blue eyes were fixed on her.

She relaxed and examined him at her leisure, like a queen gloating over her jewels.

Up close he looked older, but no less magnificent. There were lines etched around his full lips—from that arrogant, intoxicating smile he flashed so often and easily—and deep creases radiating out from the corners of his glorious eyes. He behaved in such a youthful—childish would be more accurate—fashion that she often forgot he was closer to Sebastian's age than her own. It was a marvel, really, just how very different two men could be.

Sebastian had resembled what he was: a man who was no longer young, his body still fit from all his riding but becoming stout, his brown hair graying at the temples and thinning at the crown, the lines on his face had not been around his mouth, but on his forehead, from frowning.

Alys had seen other men bared from the waist before—farmers at the harvest, even Silber once, when she'd walked into the stables on a hot day and accidentally caught him with his shirt off. Of course, she'd run off rather than study him, as she was now studying Gideon.

He resembled one of the sculptures in the rose garden far more closely than he did those other men. From the tightly knitted V of his abdomen to his powerful chest and broad shoulders, every part of him was exquisite golden perfection.

His shapely lips were even fuller in sleep and his firm, angular jaw was the type that inspired sculptures and painters. His disheveled blond curls completed the image of an angel.

Looking at his godlike body in repose a person would never guess he was willful, selfish, vain, thoughtless, and arrogant to name only a few.

But Alys had also caught glimpses of another man: a man who could be gentle with an unconscious old lady, generous to the people who came seeking work from him, and kind to a foolish woman when she confessed the humiliating truth of why his house had no silver.

Alys bit her lip as she thought back over tonight. She should have guessed that Gideon knew she'd been watching him through the peep hole. He was the sort of man who would always be in control of his environment.

Control.

The word made her shiver and also made her sex—which was most definitely sore—ache with want.

Gideon Banks, Earl of Taunton, was a man of extremes; he was a man who would never do anything by halves. As a lover he'd been vigorous, stern, and demanding. But he'd also been passionate, generous, and considerate.

Alys didn't have much experience with the physical act of love, but she realized now just how little Sebastian had considered her needs or desires. He'd never wondered whether he hurt her or pleased her or disgusted her or frightened her. Sebastian had not considered her at all. She'd never been a real, feeling person with wants and needs, she'd just been a vessel to bear his child.

Oh, she didn't think he'd ever used her selfishly for his pleasure. Even though he'd spent inside her, Alys had always suspected—as inexperienced as she'd been—that he'd not taken any joy in the act. She had always been a chore for him.

Gideon, for all his domineering and arrogant ways had brought Alys to that almost agonizing state of bliss at least five times. Five. Times. And he'd withheld his own pleasure long enough to ensure she was satisfied. No, he was not entirely selfish.

As she studied his beautiful face, she knew she'd chosen an excellent teacher when it came to learning the pleasures of the body.

Alys also clearly recalled what he'd said earlier: he was not interested in love, fidelity, or marriage. As much as she'd told herself she didn't want to marry again, the truth was that she'd been enjoying not only the physical stimulation of living in the same house with him, but also the companionship. She'd only known him a week and already she'd told him more than she'd shared with Sebastian in over eight years.

So, yes, she *had* entertained the fantasy that perhaps something might grow between them.

Now she would make sure that fantasy never flourished.

Gideon murmured and turned onto his other side, facing away from her, and his action seemed prophetic to her.

He wanted her for physical pleasure, only. And when he no longer wanted her, he would discard her as easily as he'd done with the prostitutes he'd paid. This was not love and never would be. This was lust and sex.

Alys suspected she would have to remind herself of that fact frequently in the days—and nights—to come.

⊶ ♥ ⊷

Gideon was up before the cock crow.

He'd woken just before daybreak, momentarily disoriented and wondering why he was sleeping the wrong way on his bed. And then he recalled last night and glanced around, as if Alys might be lurking nearby.

He breathed a sigh of relief when he saw she was gone. It would already be awkward enough to see her today, the last thing he wanted was billing and cooing before first light.

162

He stared through the gray dawn at the ceiling as he remembered last night. Not surprisingly, the memory of her sweet body made him hard.

Gideon stroked his prick as he relived the evening in as much detail as he could recall, chuckling at her surprise when she'd discovered him in the not-so-secret passageway.

He experienced a pang of shame at what he'd done to her. She hadn't been a virgin, but she was a woman who'd been raised in a convent-like atmosphere. He couldn't help feeling he'd taken advantage of her.

Still, he'd given her multiple chances to leave—and yet she'd stayed.

But she didn't know what she was asking for, *did she? What if she becomes pregnant?*

His hand stopped pumping. Christ. He'd spent inside her.

"Bloody hell," he groaned, his delicious erection wilting.

But her husband bred her for years and she never became pregnant, he whined to the hectoring voice.

Ah, Gideon, I think we both know the reason for that.

"Fuck," he muttered, closing his eyes, as if that would make the truth disappear. Of course it had been the earl who'd been sterile; there was no point in trying to tell himself otherwise.

Gideon could not believe what an idiot he was.

It was only one bloody time! Surely she wouldn't become pregnant after one time? I can be more careful from now on. I needn't do anything . . . rash, not yet. I can wait a month or so, and if it turns out she's breeding, then—

You should marry her. Now.

"*What?*" Gideon yelped, scrambling upright.

"Did you call, my lord?" Jackson stood in the doorway of the dressing room.

Gideon dropped back onto the bed. "Don't you ever sleep?" he asked. Before the other man could answer he said, "I'm going for a ride, lay out my kit."

"Very good, sir."

Gideon stared at the ceiling. Marriage?

Just thinking the word drove a spike of fear through him. Fidelity? Boredom? Disappointment—not just his, but whoever he married.

163

Marriage: it was a state he'd always scoffed at. Why limit oneself to a single dish when life was an endless buffet?

Oh, he knew that most men of the wealthier classes did not remain faithful to their wives. Married men kept mistresses or went to whores in shocking numbers—he knew that. But at what cost? Tears and recriminations from one's spouse? Or, worse, frosty anger and disappointment that stared at you across the breakfast table for the rest of your life?

Marriage.

Gideon frowned. Actually, it wasn't as if the thought was *utterly* without merit, at least marriage to Alys. Because really, that's what he was talking about, wasn't it?

One fuck and you're already feeling guilty enough to offer marriage.

Gideon ignored the bitter, mocking observation. There were several very good reasons why such a union would be quite wise.

First, Alys already knew Foxrun and loved it. Second, she was of excellent blood to provide an heir for such an ancient name. Third, he'd already told her what he was prepared to give—pleasure, and only for as long as it amused him—and she'd accepted his terms. Fourth— well, he couldn't think of a fourth reason just now but he was sure there was one.

Anyhow, they could both get what they wanted: he an heir and a mistress for his grand houses, and Alys would get the security and prestige of her position and could continue living in a house she loved.

They already enjoyed each other's company and last night had proven they enjoyed each other's bodies. Once they'd quenched their desire for each other they could enjoy a comfortable marriage in which each of them would be free to live their lives however they chose— provided they were discrete about it, of course.

Because discretion is your strong suit, isn't it, Gideon.

Gideon gritted his teeth. *I can be discreet if need be.*

He ignored the echo of laughter in his head.

Yes, marriage could be a very good arrangement—most especially for Alys, who could enjoy the life she'd always lived in the country, only now she'd know she was secure and would never want for anything.

And Gideon could go on just the way *he* always had, free to pursue his pleasure, with the added benefit of having a wife to offer him the various comforts and conveniences of home—on those occasions that he decided he wanted to enjoy said comforts.

Gideon frowned. Would she view his *pleasures* differently if they were married? After all, she would be his wife, not his mistress.

Offer her marriage on your terms, or none at all. After all, you are the one who holds all the cards.

Gideon perked up. That was true, wasn't it? If she wanted what he had to offer, it would be on his bloody terms. He *did* hold all the cards!

Gideon would remember those words later.

Chapter Fifteen

It was the first time that breakfast was to be served in the breakfast room since Alys had come to Foxrun.

One entire wall of the small, sunny room was French windows and they'd leaked terribly over the years. When Gideon saw the state of the room it had been the first place he'd sent glaziers, plasterers, and painters to work. It was astounding what unlimited amounts of money could achieve in such a short time.

Although several sections of windows would still need to be replaced, the room no longer smelled musty and the doors had been repaired so they now opened onto the back terrace.

Alys was a bit nervous about what she would find in the breakfast room; today would be the first meal Gideon's chef prepared. She'd briefly met Mr. DuValle last night and had not been impressed.

He'd stormed into the kitchen like a conquering barbarian king, ignoring Cook as though she were his vanquished foe. And then he'd stalked around the vast, medieval room while frowning and muttering under his breath in French. Alys had to send Cook and her kitchen maids to bed early, telling them to return in the morning. She'd woken up first this morning with thoughts of the poor women.

That was a lie. She'd thought about them *after* thinking about Gideon for a good quarter of an hour.

Alys smelled breakfast when she was half-way down the hall from the room, and it was an intoxicating aroma. Her stomach grumbled as she opened the door, only to find Gideon serving himself at the buffet.

A sudden wave of shyness flooded her and she was considering backing out quietly, but he must have heard her and turned.

His lips curved into a slow, sensual smile that reduced her concentration to rubble. "Well, good morning, my dear. Please, sit and I will serve you." He turned to a new footman she'd not seen before. "Go bring fresh—" he broke off and glanced at Alys, "Tea? Coffee?"

"Coffee, please," Alys told the man.

Gideon waited until the door closed before saying, "I missed you this morning."

She frowned; had he believed she'd still be there when he woke up and—

He wagged an admonishing finger at her. "Look at you with your naughty mind. I meant I missed you in the stables." He made a vague gesture to his person, which is when she realized he was dressed in breeches and boots.

"Ah," she said.

"I believe Silber is finding me not as hopeless as he'd feared."

"I daresay he's seen worse."

He chuckled and clutched his heart. "Cruel beauty."

There was something about his casual, light-hearted levity that annoyed her. Hadn't last night meant anything to him? No, of course it hadn't.

She went to the sideboard but he shook his head. "Sit. I will get you a plate."

"It's all right, I can—"

He cocked his head at her.

Alys sighed. "Thank you."

His eyes narrowed slightly and the look arrowed directly to her core.

"I mean, yes, Gideon," she said, her voice irritatingly breathy.

He grinned. "*That's* better." He turned and resumed his business at the buffet.

Alys was grateful to be out from under his piercing, amused stare, her mind reeling. Why did obeying him set her body aflutter? She wasn't sure she wanted to consider that question here and now. It was a question for later, for the privacy of her own room.

Instead she studied his broad shoulders as he moved down the buffet. He'd never been a comfortable man to be around and now she felt twice as anxious after what they'd done mere hours earlier.

"It was lovely out just after dawn," he said, his back still toward her. "We rode all the way out to the Langston cottage."

The cottage in question was one that had been empty as long as Alys had lived at Foxrun. There were no longer any Langstons in the area, but the name had stuck.

"Oh? How is it coming along?

167

"Swimmingly. By the way, I now understand why you feel the way you do about Silber."

Alys's eyes bulged. "Er, I beg your pardon? I don't know what you mean?"

Like a predator that could sense prey, Gideon turned, his smile displaying white, even teeth. "Don't you?"

Alys stared. How could he possibly know what she'd fantasized about over the past few years, when the loneliness of her life had threatened to crush her?

He cocked his head, his brow wrinkled with concern. "Is aught amiss?"

"No, nothing." She licked her lips, which were as dry as dust. "I don't know what you mean," she repeated.

"I wonder what you *think* I meant, Alys." He chuckled at whatever he saw on her face and turned back to the buffet. "I just meant that Silber has a magnificent seat and is a very good instructor."

Alys sat in blessed silence until he turned again, this time with a full plate in his hand, and leaned across the table, setting it down before her, his eyes holding hers hostage the entire time. He smiled when she didn't respond and then turned back to the buffet.

"Even so," he continued, picking up another plate. "I want *you* to instruct me tomorrow. I should like you to be at the stables at . . . say, sixish?" He stilled, his posture expectant.

"Er . . . "

He let the silence drag for a long, uncomfortable moment and then turned again, not smiling. Instead, he fixed her with his heavy-lidded stare. "I thought we already discussed this matter and settled everything?" Alys's jaw dropped and he raised both eyebrows. "Was I mistaken?"

"But—"

"Yes?" His blue eyes glittered.

Her face was so hot she could not look at him. "All the time?" she asked in a squeaky, embarrassing tone, her sex thumping in a most distracting manner.

"Whenever I request something, yes."

Alys suddenly knew that her next answer would mean the difference between seeing him again tonight and sleeping alone.

"Yes, of course, Gideon."

"You will be dressed to ride astride." His lips curled. "I fancy seeing you in breeches."

"Yes, Gideon," she said in a voice that hardly wobbled.

"Very good." Smug satisfaction rolled off him in waves and Alys just *knew* he was aware of how his high-handed treatment left her wet and wanting. And he was enjoying it.

Alys watched as Gideon's long-fingered, strong hands poured more coffee, behaving as if the entire universe hadn't somehow shifted. Was it possible that he felt *none* of the things she was feeling? The idea was too dreadful to be born.

Not that it mattered *what* he was feeling. After all, what kind of woman became stimulated by such treatment—as if she were his . . . plaything? His *whore*.

Alys almost groaned at the thrill of pleasure that shot to her sex.

Something must be terribly wrong with her—it was just as her father had said all those years ago. Why would she—

The door opened and she looked up; it was the footman, followed by Mrs. Fanshawe.

Gideon stood and smiled, the expression so open and welcoming it took Alys's breath away: it was nothing like the way he looked at her.

"Hello, Nora, darling," he said, dropping a kiss on her cheek. "You're looking lovely."

She gave him an ironic smile but didn't answer, instead turning to Alys, her expression more genuine than when she'd greeted Gideon. Well, that was interesting.

"Good morning, my lady."

"Good morning, Mrs. Fanshawe."

"Sit," Gideon, ordered, sliding his heaped plate to the place setting beside his chair. "You have this, Nora, I've not yet touched it."

Mrs. Fanshawe glanced down at the pile of food and smiled. "Thank you, Gideon." She sat and picked up her napkin, shaking it out and saying to Alys. "I think I smelled this delicious food all the way up in our rooms, my lady."

"It's DuValle's eggs, nobody cooks eggs like the man," Gideon said above the clinking of cutlery.

Alys took a mouthful of the coddled eggs in question. "Mmmm," she moaned, before she could stop herself.

Gideon laughed.

Alys swallowed. "You're right, these are positively decadent. Mr. DuValle might actually be worth it."

Nora poured coffee from the pot the footman had just delivered. "I admit I was skeptical about the man when I heard about his tantrums, but then I ate dinner at Gideon's house and became a convert."

Gideon returned with another full plate and sat. "He *is* worth the fuss. And he shall settle down, eventually." He forked some eggs into his mouth and his eyelids fluttered. "I'm in eggstacy," he said once he'd swallowed.

Alys and Nora were groaning when the door opened and Mr. Chatham entered.

"Good morning, my lady, Mrs. Fanshawe," his stern mouth twitched slightly before he added, "my *lord.*"

"Stephen, what a treat," Gideon exclaimed ironically, pouring his quiet friend a cup of coffee. "I didn't think you ventured out in daylight."

The other man merely grunted and turned to the sideboard.

Gideon turned to Alys. "You will find Mr. Chatham's mode of communication is mainly composed of grunts. It's a sort of Morse Code. Over time you will learn to distinguish the nuances between them. That's if he doesn't ignore what you say entirely."

Mr. Chatham turned slowly, his hooded grey eyes even more uncomfortably direct in the light of day. "I'm sorry, did somebody say something?" he asked with a straight face.

Nora and Alys laughed, even Gideon smiled.

"Have you and Edward made any plans for today?" Gideon asked.

"Edward said something about going to a cider brewery not far away." Mr. Chatham answered, his speech slow and measured, as if he were counting the words he used.

Gideon groaned and turned to Mrs. Fanshawe. "Good God, Nora! Tell the man he is on holiday."

She shrugged. "It is what he enjoys doing."

"I'm sorry I told him about it," Gideon grumbled. He turned to Mr. Chatham. "And you encouraged him, I suppose?"

Mr. Chatham took a drink of the steaming liquid before turning slowly to Gideon. "Yes."

Gideon snorted with disgust and turned to Alys, lifting his hands. "You see what I have to deal with?"

Alys ignored him. "Will you be painting today?" she asked Mrs. Fanshawe.

"I'd love to—could you direct me to a pleasant spot? Or," she smiled, the expression transforming her rather stark features into something breathtaking. "Maybe you'd like to accompany me?"

"I'd love to," Alys said without hesitation.

"I must warn you that I'm rather tedious company when I'm painting."

Before Alys could respond Gideon said, "You should paint my portrait, Nora." He turned to Alys. "I'll need one to hang in the gallery, won't I?"

"Ah." Mrs. Fanshawe gave him a long, speculative look.

"What?" Gideon demanded when she didn't reply.

Mr. Chatham laughed, a low, velvety sound so unexpected everyone turned toward him.

"What's so funny?" Gideon asked him.

"You." The laconic man cut a piece of ham and raised it to his mouth, his eyebrows lifting with approval as he chewed.

Gideon looked from Alys to Mrs. Fanshawe. "Do you know why he laughed?"

For some reason his question made Mrs. Fanshawe laugh.

"Do *you* have any idea what's so funny?" he demanded of Alys.

Alys had no idea why they were laughing. But the expression on his face—confusion, embarrassment, and annoyance—was so unusual on his arrogant, gorgeous features that Alys couldn't help chuckling a little herself.

"*What?*" he demanded, sounding so wounded that all three of them just laughed harder.

They'd begun to recover—although it was hard to stop with Gideon stewing so noisily—when the door opened to admit Mr. Smith.

171

Smith glanced around at them, his gaze lingering on Gideon, whose arms were crossed, his expression mulish. "What did Gideon do now?"

Which just set them all off on another gale of silly laughter.

—◆—

"How the hell did I get stuck with you two?" Gideon demanded, looking from Fanshawe to Chatham.

"Just lucky, I guess," Chatham said.

He and Fanshawe chuckled like bloody schoolboys. They were currently sitting side-by-side pouring over a ledger as if it contained the mysteries of the universe rather than information about a cider operation.

Gideon slumped back in his chair, glaring at the two men's bowed heads. Look at them! Happy as bloody clams to spend a beautiful day in this room while Smith escorted Alys and Nora out to loll around on a blanket and eat delicacies prepared by *Gideon's* personal chef.

"Unbelievable."

"What's that?" Edward muttered, not even bothering to look up from the ledger.

Sometimes Gideon wanted to smash his business partners over the head with something heavy. They really were the most impervious collection of men he'd ever met. Well, Smith wasn't so bad, even *if* he insisted on behaving as if he knew the answer to everything. Not only that, but the man was *sneaky*. Just look how he'd managed to insinuate himself with two attractive, charming women while Gideon got stuck with a couple of boring, surly men.

If not for Smith's maneuvering, right now Gideon would be with Alys and Nora instead of *here* in this cramped, smelly office with these two—

"So, are you going to make an honest woman of Lady Taunton now that you've destroyed her reputation?" Edward asked.

Gideon's head whipped up. Edward was lounging in his chair, his massive arms crossed over his chest.

"What are you—"

"He's going to argue for a while, Edward," Chatham said, taking a drink of cider.

"Mmm-hmm," Edward nodded, his expression sage.

"You should just let him get all his blustering out before you waste any words on him," Chatham counseled.

"Uh-huh."

The two men stared at him as if he were some sort of unprepossessing laboratory experiment.

Gideon threw up his hands. "Fine. Say whatever it was Smith told you both to say."

"Did Smith tell you to say something?" Edward asked Chatham.

"No. You?" Chatham shook his head, his heavy, uncomfortable gray eyes never leaving Gideon.

Edward turned to Gideon. "You understand what people are thinking about you living in that house with the widow?"

"Since when do you care what people think? Aren't you the man whose divorce was in every newspaper in Britain for months?" Gideon sneered.

Rather than look angry at Gideon's rude tone—which is what he'd been hoping would happen, so they could drop the bloody topic of the widow Taunton, Edward nodded. "Yes, I *am* that man. Do you want to know what it feels like? Or would you rather learn from my mistakes?"

"Our co-habitation is unlikely to be on the front page of the *Times*," Gideon pointed out.

"True, but I'll wager it is on the mind of every person who lives in Taunton—or at least every person who resides on your land or works for you."

"So, all the people Lady Taunton will have to interact with, in other words," Chatham added, sipping his pint.

Gideon ground his teeth. "I don't want to talk about this."

"He doesn't want to talk about it," Edward said to Chatham, as if the man wasn't sitting a foot away.

"Ah."

Both men fixed Gideon with their brooding, uncomfortable stares.

It was going to be a long afternoon.

—❤—

The afternoon had been absolutely lovely. Mrs. Fanshawe—or Nora as she'd insisted Alys call her—was the sort of companion one couldn't help liking. She was both interest*ing* and interest*ed*.

Mr. Smith, once a person became accustomed to his sharp, hawkish looks and propensity for black—black leather buckskins, black riding coat, black linen, with impossibly glossy black boots—the man himself was warm, witty, and easy to converse with.

Alys had never seen anyone dress like him. He should have looked odd, but, somehow, he managed to appear very elegant.

They'd both been very interested about Alys and what her life was like at Foxrun. It had been an unusual pleasure to meet such fascinating people and discover she didn't bore them to tears. While they chatted, she noticed they dropped in comments about Gideon—minor bits of information that most people probably wouldn't notice. But as enrapt as she was by the gorgeous man, she latched onto any tidbit about him.

They'd made Gideon sound like a man who'd begun to embrace his new position in life and wished to become respectable. It didn't exactly fit with what she knew about him, but then, they were his friends, so they would know.

After a day spent by the lake, they'd come home and dined together. It was, she had to admit, the most enjoyable meal she'd ever had. Gideon's friends were clever, witty, and outrageous. She knew they were not the sort of people to ever be welcome at *ton* functions—not even Gideon, who was now a peer—and decided she liked them all the better for it.

But she had to admit that all through the day she'd thought of only one thing: tonight.

Thursby had *just* finished brushing and braiding her hair when there was a knock on the door.

"Who could *that* be?" Thursby demand, frowning at Alys in the mirror.

"Go see," Alys ordered, her voice remarkably level for the tumult occurring inside her. Surely it wasn't Gideon? He would know Thursby was still in with her—he wouldn't come to her when—

"It's his lordship's valet," her lips turned pruney, "Jackson. The earl wishes to see you in the library."

"Now?" she hoped Thursby would mistake the warble in her voice for annoyance rather than excitement.

"Yes, my lady."

Alys nodded and heaved an exaggerated sigh. "Very well."

Thursby's eyes widened. "Surely you're not—"

"What, Thursby? I'm not going to obey a request from the man who is paying for all this?" She waved a hand around her. "You may go," she said before the older woman could protest.

"But—"

Alys cut her a look similar to the one Gideon had given her last night and again at breakfast this morning.

Thursby heaved her own exaggerated sigh. "Very well."

Once her maid left Alys slumped back onto the bench in front of her vanity, staring at her reflection in the mirror. She was wearing the nicest of her nightgowns, but it was still just a plain white gown with a bit of openwork stitching at the neck. He'd said to come to her wearing only her dressing gown. Alys looked at the old, but perfectly serviceable, blue dressing gown and swallowed. Surely he didn't expect her to go all the way to the library naked beneath her dressing gown— especially not when there were people in the house?

No, that would be ridiculous.

She stood, straightened her collar, tightened her sash, and raised her chin.

There were candles in all the sconces, a luxury she'd never even imagined until barely a week ago.

Alys encountered nobody—not even a servant—on the hurried journey down the stairs and across two sections of house.

She hesitated outside the library door, smoothing her hair with both hands, as if it might have come loose in the short trip from her room.

"Coward," she whispered, laying her hand on the handle and pushing open the door. She hesitated on the threshold, frowning across the vast room. He wasn't at his desk, where he usually—

"Over here."

Alys startled and turned toward the sound.

He was lounging on one of the worn leather settees, wearing an outrageous peacock blue and gold robe of Chinese silk. He patted the cushion beside him. "Come here."

Alys's feet began moving before she gave them any permission. "Why are we meeting down here? What if somebody—"

"Shhh," he whispered, grinning up at her when she stood before him. "Nobody will bother us. Besides, that just adds excitement to

175

things, don't you think? Wondering and worrying about discovery?" He cocked his head. "Do you think you'd enjoy being watched?"

Her jaw dropped.

"Come, sit," he said again. He took her hands and pulled her down, not beside him, but onto his lap. "Yes, that's much better." Her bottom rested on his hard thighs—and that other hard part of him pressed against her hip.

He slid a hand around her head and pulled her close.

Alys didn't know why it was, but kissing was almost more erotic than the things he'd done to Lucy and Susan—whom she didn't recall him kissing. His tongue, warm and thrusting, explored her mouth as if it had every right to be there. Alys opened wider as he probed deeper, flicking and caressing her teeth, lips—and most shockingly—sucking her tongue.

"Come inside me," he whispered, "taste me."

Her tongue felt twice as big and clumsy, but she tentatively probed his parted lips.

He groaned, his arm tightening around her, his free hand rubbing her thighs in a very distracting manner while he opened wider for her, allowing her to explore.

"Mmmm," he hummed when she nipped his full lower lip, his fingers tracing the tight seam of her thighs. "What are you wearing beneath this robe, Alys? Is that a nightgown I feel?"

How could a whisper be so menacing? "I didn't think you'd want me to walk almost naked in the halls. What if—"

"Hush," he said, his eyelids heavy. "You've disobeyed me, Alys— and it's only our second night." He kissed up her jaw, his breath hot on her skin. "That means I'll have to punish you."

"P-Punish?" she said in a high, squeaky voice.

He chuckled. "Don't sound so frightened. I'll save it until later. But for now, pleasure first." He patted her thigh. "Stand up and strip for me."

She gulped but hastily stood.

He clasped his hands behind his head and lounged back, his body shifting sinuously to get comfortable. The movement caused his robe to open more, the loose sash doing a poor job of keeping it shut.

Alys's hands froze when the rich silk of his gown parted to expose his erection—which was thick, ruddy, and curved against his muscular abdomen.

He lazily stroked his chest, the movement causing muscles to shift and ripple all the way down his stomach, drawing her eyes back to that most fascinating part of him. His hand continued to caress, moving lower, lightly tracing the sculpted V of muscles that separated his compact hips— hips which had begun to subtly thrust.

"Alys?"

She looked up, her head thick and muzzy, just like it had felt the time she'd had three glasses of sherry—right before she'd thrown up.

"Why are you still clothed?" he asked, his hand sliding from his belly to the base of his stiff rod. He circled his fingers around his erection and pushed it forward, the ropey muscles in his forearm flexing as he squeezed himself. The action made him seem a foot long.

Moisture slid down her thighs as she fumbled with her sash and gaped.

He released the cruel hold with a sensual grunt, his fingers languidly caressing his length, his thumb sliding through the sticky pearl of liquid covering the tiny slit, spreading it over the flared crown.

Alys flung her dressing gown to the ground and then unbuttoned the four buttons on her nightgown. She pulled it over her head before she lost her nerve. She emerged from the cloud of fine muslin to find him staring at her body, his lips slightly parted as he continued to work himself.

His eyes made the slow journey from her feet up her legs, over her sex, her belly, lingering on her rapidly rising breasts. He smiled when his eyes met hers. "You're so beautiful, little one." He spread his thighs and shifted his body until his hips rested on the edge of the settee. "Come here and mount me."

Her body shook badly, but she managed to shuffle closer.

He chuckled as he looked up at her. "You'll find it hard to straddle me if you don't spread your legs. Come," he said, nudging her with one of his knees. "Open and get on top."

She was red-faced and breathless as she did as he directed. There was no way to do what he wanted without exposing herself, which is exactly what he wanted.

There'd been low lighting in his bedroom last night, but he must have lighted every candle in the library, and it was mortifyingly bright.

When she was kneeling with one knee on either side of his hips he nodded. "Good girl," he murmured, his hands absently caressing her legs. "Sit back on my knees, that's good—don't worry about how unladylike you are," he said, guessing her thoughts with alarming accuracy. "I want you this way—open to my eyes, my hands . . . my cock."

She shivered at the filthy word and he smiled. "Are you wet—aching?"

Alys swallowed and made that embarrassing gulping sound again. "Yes, Gideon."

His eyelids lowered and his hand moved toward her sex. Rather than part her with his fingers, he merely grazed the seam. "Such shy, pouty lips. I'll kiss them later," he promised, his finger probing her. Alys caught her breath and Gideon's smile turned feral and tight. "You *are* wet." He circled her aching peak, close, but not touching "And you're stiff—erect—for me." Alys flushed at his raw words and he chuckled. "Oh, does that embarrass you? Thinking of your tiny erection? It shouldn't—it's beautiful when it's all swollen and slick and eager. *You're* beautiful. I thought of you all day," he said, skimming from her pearl to her entrance and then sliding a finger deep inside her. "So tight. Clench for me, Alys." Her entire body jerked as she contracted around him.

He gave a husky laugh. "I like the way your cunt obeys my commands—like an obedient pet." His hand began to pump, slow and deep, his middle finger grazing something exquisite inside her. "I want to shove myself inside you but our fun would be over far too quickly. So let me pleasure you, first. Let's see how many times I can make my pet come."

It was his words as much as his actions that drove her toward the precipice with such dizzying speed. Any residual embarrassment at being so exposed slid away as he worked her with relentless, and increasing, intensity.

"Yes," he urged when she whimpered and shivered. "That's right—let it all out. Scream for me." His thumb pressed in the exact spot she needed and Alys indeed screamed.

The pleasure was exquisite, and his fingers never stopped, yet they avoided those parts of her that were too tender to touch. As she came down from the heights of physical ecstasy, he resumed his magical stroking.

"Mmm, my good girl," he praised. "You came so prettily; you're perfection. Now, I want you to do it again."

— ♥ —

Gideon held her in his arms, his cock straining upward, only inches from paradise. Good God but he loved giving her orgasms. He'd almost spent all over her belly more than once, only stopping himself by brutally constricting his cock.

He'd teetered on the brink at least four times, his balls full and ready to burst. He wanted to fuck her so bad he literally could taste it.

But he'd brought her here to talk.

Clearly he'd gotten off course, somehow.

The truth was that talking wasn't his strong suit when he came to women. Nor was thinking. He knew there was more than a grain of truth in all the abuse his business partners heaped on him when it came to his behavior around the opposite sex.

He was a smart man about machinery and could see everything so clearly. But when it came to humans—even himself—he just couldn't seem to make himself *concentrate*. It was far too easy to allow sensation, desire, and want to guide his behavior. But he had to do this—to talk to her, no matter how much it was scrambling his wits.

He watched as she came back from her orgasm, her expression going from dreamy and satisfied to aware and embarrassed.

"No, don't get off me just yet," he said when she began to stand.

Her face was as red as a glowing forge. Gideon pushed a strand of silky auburn hair behind her ear and then tilted her chin until she had to look at him. "Don't be ashamed," he said softly, his chest tightening when he saw the anxious frown on her plump lips. "You look beautiful when you orgasm."

She flinched at the word and he couldn't help smiling; she was adorable. She was sensuality in human form but she had the conscience of a nun.

"I want you to marry me."

Her eyes bulged. "*What?*"

179

He nodded, not put off by her reaction. "Yes, it's the best idea for both of us. I ejaculated in you last night—more than once. You could have a child growing inside you as we speak."

She shook her head. "But I never—"

"Don't," Gideon said. "I think we both know—along with everyone else in the area—that it was Taunton who couldn't put a child in your belly."

Her brow furrowed. "That still doesn't mean we must marry. Can't we wait until—"

"Until what? Until I slip up again and impregnate you?" Gideon held her chin when she would have looked away. "It will happen eventually, Alys. I'm a man and I'm at my weakest when I'm balls deep in a woman. Besides, I like coming inside you." His lips twitched. "Claiming you with my seed."

Her face tightened at his vulgar words and he thought she was about to chide him or argue with his logic.

"Look, darling," he said, "I'm not just proposing this because you might be pregnant."

"You're not?"

"No, I think marriage is an excellent idea for several reasons: you need security, I need a wife to run these big bloody houses that have fallen into my lap. If you have a child in the process," he shrugged. "So much the better."

"What if I don't get pregnant?"

"So then everything goes to some other ignorant bugger rather than my get. What does it matter after I'm dead?"

"It *does* matter. I *love* Foxrun and the people need a wise master—hundreds of people depend on the Earl of Foxrun."

"So marry me and you can be their mistress and ensure they get the best treatment possible." Gideon knew it was low of him to use this house, estate, and the people who depended on it to persuade her, but he'd never been opposed to underhanded dealings, why start having qualms now?

Her eyes flickered over his face.

"Speak," he said with a sigh, sitting back and crossing his arms. "Let's get everything out—*everything*. And you'll need to be direct with

me, darling, because I don't have an ounce of sensitivity in my body."
He smirked. "Well, except my cock. And my nipples."

She choked out a laugh, shaking her head.

"See, you'd have a husband who makes you come repeatedly *and*
occasionally laugh."

"Yes, there is that," she agreed, her face adorably flushed. "Would
it—would it be like when I was married to Sebastian? Would you leave
me here and come out and breed me every month?"

Gideon's eyebrows nearly shot off his head. "Good God no! You'd
have all the money you could spend—you can do anything, go
anywhere. If you want to live in London during the Season—or all year
long—it would be your decision."

She nodded, looking down at her clasped hands. "And what about
you?"

"What about me?" he asked, confused by the question.

"Where would you live?"

"Oh." He shrugged. "Here part of the time, I suppose. London
sometimes. I'll live where I like—the same way I always have."

"And you'll do whatever you like," she finished for him.

"Yes, exactly," he agreed, pleased she was so quick to catch on. This
was going remarkably well!

"Does that mean more, well, more whores?"

Ah-ha, so here it was!

"That's an excellent question. Here is your answer: I shall sleep
with whomever I want, Alys."

She nodded, not looking particularly surprised—that was good,
wasn't it?

"Can't you get diseases that way?"

"Ah," he said, relieved that was her concern. "You needn't worry.
I've been around a while, darling, I choose carefully to make sure that
sort of thing doesn't happen. I have woman examined by a physician
before I'm ever with one."

"I see." She hesitated and then said, "Would you bring them here?"

Gideon gave her a hard look. "Now listen here, Alys, I can see
where these questions are leading. We discussed this last night and you
said you had no expectations of me other than pleasure. If that isn't still
the case—if you think it would be different if we were married then

181

you need to tell me now. *Would* things change for you if we were to marry?"

"Wouldn't that change matters for you, Gideon?"

He frowned, utterly perplexed. "Why would it?" A sudden thought occurred to him. "You're still talking about other women, aren't you?" She gave a slight shrug, confirming his suspicions. "What are you trying to say, Alys? That you would expect me to be faithful?"

She smiled slightly. "No, I wouldn't expect that, Gideon."

Well, that was a bloody relief!

"That's good, Alys, because it is not a matter that is on the table for negotiation. Ever." He paused, and she nodded. "I already told you: I'm constitutionally incapable of being with only one person and I'd never want you to believe otherwise and be disappointed. I don't want to hurt you, Alys."

That was the God's honest truth.

"I understand, Gideon. It's just that, well, if we were to have children, I wouldn't be comfortable having that sort of woman around them."

Gideon blinked in surprise. "Ah, yes. Well, naturally, I wouldn't carry on like that around our children." He felt a strange tightness in his chest when he uttered those two words: our children. Children with Alys. It was his turn to swallow hard. Gideon smiled and took her hands. "I've had hundreds of lovers in my life, but you would be my only wife, Alys. I would respect you—your position—and I would behave with decorum." Well, he'd try to, anyway. "You would always be the most important woman in my life, regardless of how many others there might be."

She nodded slowly, digesting what he was saying. Good. She'd better make bloody sure she could live with him under those terms, because it would be too late to change her mind after they were married.

"And what about me?"

Gideon cocked his head. "I beg your pardon?"

"Shall I be allowed to take l-lovers?"

Gideon frowned at the question, surprise mingling with displeasure. "I'm not sure I'd be pleased to have our nest filled with cuckoos."

Her cheeks flushed and he could see she'd not considered that. Well, she was barely more than an innocent, wasn't she?

Gideon's heart softened—he'd need to keep her naivety in mind—and he slid his hands around her narrow waist and pulled her closer. "I'm well able to keep you satisfied, darling. And if you want variety and adventure," he shrugged. "I'm sure we can find some entertainment together." He kissed the base of her throat, where a pulse was fluttering rapidly. "I'm not jealous and I quite enjoy sharing. I daresay I'd enjoy watching you get pleasured by another man or woman." She jolted at his words and he licked her throat and bit her chin lightly, his cock throbbing harder. Perhaps they might do something like he'd done with Nora and Edward. He pressed his erection against her belly. "Do you like the sound of that, little one? Doing what I did with Lucy and Susan, but with you and another woman—or another man, if you like."

When she didn't answer he looked up

Alys was regarding him with a cool, serious expression that sent a frisson of worry up his spine. "What is it—is that not what you want?"

"I was just thinking."

"Hmm? Tell me," he said, stroking her from hips to breasts, leaning forward to kiss the hard tips, alternating between her nipples. "What were you thinking?" he asked, nipping her gently and making her gasp. "You needn't rush to make your decision—I want you to think this over very carefully. We can play in ways that won't risk pregnancy until you decide what you want. Take all the time you need, sweetheart. And if you'd rather not, I shan't be angry—although I'd be disappointed, of course, but—"

"I don't need any time." She arched under his hands like a cat being stroked.

Gideon smirked to himself as he tongued one dark pink nipple. He'd never had any doubt she'd marry him, but he'd thought it would take longer to persuade her to accept marriage on his terms—which was the *only* way that he would ever marry.

He released her nipple with a moist *pop* and smiled up at her. "Will you do me the honor of becoming my wife?"

"Yes, Gideon I will marry you."

183

Gideon chuckled. "Don't look so somber, darling." He squeezed her hips. "You've made me a happy man and I plan to make you a *very* happy woman." He returned to her nipples, speaking between kisses. "So what do we need to do? Doesn't the vicar have to hire a town crier or something like that?"

Her lips twitched up on one side. "I believe you are thinking of the banns, which must be called three times in a parish where one of us resides. But—" she chewed her lip. "I'd rather not make a big affair of it."

Gideon stopped his sucking and looked up, slightly affronted. "Why don't you want a *big affair*?"

"Well, it's not a real marriage—is it?"

Gideon frowned. "I don't know what you mean?" he asked, unable to keep the sharpness out of his tone.

"It's more of a business arrangement, isn't it? I mean, we don't love one another."

"Oh," he said in sudden comprehension.

"It seems rather farcical to have a big church wedding when we are really just entering a partnership."

Well, when she put it that way.

Gideon grunted. Why did he feel as if he were missing something?

"And I've already had a church wedding. I'd just as soon not go through it again."

She was right, and he knew it. Still, he didn't like to think he didn't have a *real* anything. He shrugged and forced a smile. "Fine, I suppose we can just get a whosy-whatsit."

"Special license?"

"Yes, that's it."

"Do I need to go to London with you?"

"I shouldn't think so. I'll ask Smith."

"Oh. Did he get married with a special license?"

"No. But he knows everything." He'd certainly known that Gideon was going to marry Alys, hadn't he? He snorted softly and pulled Alys toward him, thrusting his aching cock suggestively against her wet, hot crease.

"Now, my lovely little wife-to-be, I believe we have a little unfinished business. Let's pick up where we left off."

Chapter Sixteen

A lys stared up into the shadows, her hand resting on her mound. She was sore—an exquisite soreness that made her throb every time she thought about it.

Gideon had taken her only once, keeping her on his lap while teaching her how to *ride* him. He'd stared up at her, his blue eyes dark with lust, his full lips parted and smiling, so beautiful it made her heart ache.

"You see, my love," he'd gasped in between savage thrusts. "There is something to be said for riding astride. Now," his jaw hardened and his nostrils flared, "Ride me to a lather."

Alys had to admit she'd enjoyed the vantage point and being in control of their rhythm—at least to a degree. He'd not been a passive partner but had exhibited breathtaking strength as he'd thrust upward into her, every line and curve of his body hard and taut.

He'd made his pleasure obvious when he'd spent in her. "I love filling you with my seed," he'd snarled in her ear while he pumped inside her. "I going to fuck you every chance I get, little one. I won't be happy until you're swollen with my child."

Alys had climaxed when he'd said that, crying out and thrashing with abandon—just as he'd told her to do.

"I want you to scream the new roof off the house, Alys. Passion is nothing to be ashamed of and this is your house, if the servants don't like it they can bloody well plug their ears."

Lord, had this really been only their second night? Alys felt as if she'd been in his thrall all her life. And there was no denying she was captivated, pitifully so.

He'd fingered her to orgasm three times while loving—no, while *fucking*—her, and that wasn't counting the first time, before they'd had *the conversation*.

That's what it was, she thought as she reached between her swollen lips, sucking in a harsh breath when she touched her raw bud: it was fucking. They'd have a marriage with plenty of fucking—at least until he tired of her—but never any love.

To say she'd been surprised by his offer was an understatement. But it hadn't taken her long to see the wisdom of such a union, and not just because she might already be quickening. First and foremost, she was sure he'd asked her because he was lazy. Yes, lazy. Why put himself out when he could have Alys with no effort?

She wasn't vain, but she knew it wouldn't be a terrible hardship for him. After all, she was not uncomely. At almost twenty-six she was well past her prime, but she was not *too* terribly old, and she knew how to run this household and the people liked her. And then there was the fact she did what he told her to do: she was obedient. He could have whatever he wanted, do whatever he wanted, and she'd already agreed to accept it.

Thanks to growing up in her father's household and being married to Sebastian for eight years Alys was already pre-trained for the position of obedient wife. And not just her mind, but her body. She responded to Gideon's commands like a well-trained pet. He'd even called her his pet.

What man could complain about that?

Alys knew she should be angry at him—for his arrogance alone, not to mention his selfishness, his callousness, and a dozen other reprehensible behaviors—but any anger she felt was buried under heavy piles of lust. It was as if she'd been sleeping all these years and now she'd awakened with a vengeance. All she wanted, all the time, was *him*.

She told herself that she would enjoy it as long as it lasted and perhaps she'd even get a child or two out of the arrangement. Yes, he was doing this for his own selfish reasons, but there was no reason she couldn't benefit as well.

But she would need to be very, very careful because she'd already started falling in love with him—or at least falling in infatuation. How could she not? He was beautiful, clever, funny, a wonderful lover, and he wanted *her*. When was the last time anyone had wanted her? Had anyone? Certainly not Sebastian, who'd only wanted her money.

Alys would need to be vigilant and would need to remind herself daily that Gideon did not love her—never would. The moment she forgot that and wished for something more was the day he would destroy her.

—❤—

Gideon found Alys already waiting for him in the stables—as he'd ordered—the next morning. He heard her voice before he saw her— she was talking to Silber and the two of them were looking at something, their backs to him.

And what a fetching sight her backside was.

Gideon grinned and leaned in the doorway, appreciating the way the buckskins stretched across her plump arse. She had surprisingly long legs for such a small thing and his cock—never really completely dormant—jumped at the memory of last night's lovemaking.

Gideon had planned to keep her up all night, perhaps initiate her tight little arse into the pleasures it could give and receive. But he'd found the conversation more taxing than he'd expected and had only been able to take her once before he'd simply wanted to go to sleep.

That was an unprecedented reaction and he hadn't liked it. Luckily, he'd woken hard this morning so he knew that whatever had struck him last night had not been permanent.

Silber dropped into a crouch to look at something and Alys went toward a rack of blacksmithing tools and stood on tiptoe to find what she needed.

That was when Gideon caught the other man staring. The raw yearning and lust in his face was almost enough to drive Gideon to his knees. So, the gentle giant was not as perfect and moral as he seemed: he *wanted*—and what he wanted was another man's betrothed.

Gideon's lip twitched into a smile; poor Silber had it bad for his mistress. Right this moment Gideon knew the other man was, in his mind, bending her over, stripping off those tantalizing leathers, and mounting her from behind—just like the animals he so admired.

"Is this it, Mr. Silber?" Alys held up a tool and turned, but Silber's desire was already tucked safely behind his polite servant's mask.

"Aye, that'll do, my lady."

She started to walk back to him and noticed Gideon standing in the doorway. "Oh, Gideon, I didn't hear you. Have you been waiting long?"

Gideon looked into Silber's seemingly calm eyes and saw a flash of fear. He smiled at the other man as he strode toward him. "Just a little while," he said, stopping and looking down, enjoying having the big, strong man kneeling and at a disadvantage—his mouth so close to Gideon's cock.

Oh, yes. Gideon knew he was a bad man.

"Good morning, my lord. Just fixing the mistress's saddle—the stirrup seems to have cracked. I don't recall when I've seen that before."

Gideon's eyes never left Silber's face, which was ruddier than usual. He gave a bored shrug. "Throw it out and buy her another—buy her two."

Alys gasped softly. "Oh, but I don't need that. This one will be fine when—"

Gideon sighed. "Just do it, Silber. The next time I want to ride I don't want any excuses."

"Aye, my lord." Silber said, the notch between his eyes saying he'd not liked the way Gideon spoke to his lady.

That made Gideon smile; the man's loyalty to Alys amused, rather than irritated him.

"Come, Alys," he said, holding his hand out. "Since your saddle isn't useable we can go for a walk. You can show me all your secret places."

She flushed at the not so subtle innuendo in his words. "But I'm not dressed for walking."

"We are standing in the middle of fifty-two thousand acres that all belong to me. Anyone who doesn't like what you are wearing is free to leave."

She hesitated, but only for a fraction of a second as her eyes bounced between the still kneeling giant and her almost lord-and-master. "Yes, of course, Gideon. I would enjoy that."

─ ❤ ─

Alys was glad to escape the cool darkness of the stables. She didn't understand the odd undercurrents of tension between the two men and wondered if that was simply Gideon causing mischief. After all, he was a man who had to dominate all others.

Although he certainly didn't appear to dominate his friends, or, indeed, Nora. But then they were all wealthy and powerful like him.

Silber was a stable master—*Gideon's* servant. What could possibly be going on between them?

"I'm going back to town with the others when they leave," he said as she led him toward the vale, her favorite walk.

Alys stopped. "You are?"

He grinned and took her hands. "Look at you—worried I won't come back?" Before she could answer he leaned forward and gave her a smacking kiss on the mouth.

"Gideon," she gasped, looking back toward the house, which was still visible.

He threw his head back and laughed, sounding genuinely joyous. "Oh, my shy little darling. You must know I wanted you to wear those leathers so I could take them off you."

She gently disentangled herself, aware of the flicker of annoyance that passed over his face when she began to walk again. Gideon didn't like it if she pulled away. She tucked that thought away at the back of her mind.

That is a fine thing to be thinking before you're even married.

Alys knew it was shameful, but she had to find ways to survive the onslaught that was Gideon.

"How long shall you be away?" she asked.

He shrugged, the corners of his full, sensual mouth turned down, his expression sulky. "As long as I please."

Alys couldn't help laughing; he was so *childish.*

Yes, the willfulness of a child, but the power of a man.

The thought sobered her. "I only asked because I wanted to have your room ready for you."

He turned, suddenly smiling. "Oh, did you? Why, darling, how lovely." He looked pleased. "I shouldn't think longer than two weeks. Will that give you enough time?"

"Yes, for most of it."

"You should write a list of whatever you want in town and I shall fetch it for you." He paused, stopped, and then turned. "Really, though—why don't you come with me?"

Alys's first impulse was to throw herself into his arms. But the second thought in her mind was how awkward a visit to London—together—would be when they weren't yet married.

She looked into his glowing eyes and smiling face and chose her words carefully. "What a lovely offer, Gideon. But I really do want to have your chamber perfect for you."

His blue eyes clouded and his smile dimmed. But he didn't seem angry—only disappointed. "I appreciate your concern, sweetheart. Besides, there will be many other times."

Alys smiled, grateful he'd not taken her words the wrong way.

━ ❤ ━

The remainder of their guests' stay sped by far too quickly.

It was the last evening of their visit—they would all depart in the morning, Gideon along with them—and Alys had just taken leave of Nora. To Alys's extreme delight, Nora had asked if she could paint her portrait the third day of their stay.

Alys had been speechless.

"Not if you'd rather I didn't," Nora quickly said.

Alys shook her head. "Not at all! I mean, I should *love* it above all things. But—"

Nora's pale eyebrows arched. "But?"

"Perhaps you might do Gideon's first—he so wants to have one done."

Nora laughed. "I think it would be good for Gideon if he didn't get *everything* he wanted." She'd given Alys a warm smile. "After all, he's already got you, hasn't he? That seems like more good fortune than he deserves. I'm so pleased you two are to be married."

Alys had blushed, pleased by her kind words. But the next thing she'd said had left her feeling slightly anxious.

"I'm going to leave you our direction in London, Alys. And I want you to feel free to write me—about anything. All right?" She taken Alys's hands then and given them a squeeze. "You are a delightful woman and I'd like to keep in touch above and beyond the bond our men share."

Alys had nodded, too emotional to speak; it appeared she'd made her first friend.

She'd begun sitting for Nora that very day.

"Do you have enough sketches?" Alys had asked tonight after she'd sat for a few more, when Nora had been packing away her charcoals and sketch pad.

"Oh, yes, I always make more than enough. I'm eager to start painting you *right now*," she said with a laugh as she slung the leather satchel over her delicate shoulder. "Edward has been teasing me that I have that mad look in my eyes," she said, grinning at Alys in a way that warmed her through and through.

"Well, I'm just as eager to see it, Nora."

Alys had left Nora at the door to the suite that connected with her husband. She was headed to her room when the door to Mr. Chatham's room opened and his valet came out. But before the man—Alys believed his name was Leather—could shut the door Mr. Chatham opened it again. He smiled down at the smaller man, the expression one she'd not seen on his face before, and then murmured something while reaching out and caressing his valet's cheek. Like a *lover*.

Leather bowed his head, like an obedient valet would, turned, and left his master standing and staring after him.

Alys tried to blend into the wood paneling, but it was difficult to do when she was wearing a rose-pink gown. Just when she thought she might get away unobserved, Chatham swung toward her, his unnerving gray eyes widening with surprise.

"Hello, Mr. Chatham. I was just escorting Nora to her room," Alys babbled as Mr. Chatham's pale cheeks darkened.

His eyelids dropped to their usual half-mast and he gave her a formal—and forced—smile. "I'm sure she appreciated your assistance; it would be easy to become lost in this house." He bowed his head. "Good night, my lady."

The door closed behind him and Alys slumped against the hallway paneling.   Why,   how   very,   very   *odd*.

Chapter Seventeen

Two-and-a-half bloody weeks.

Gideon was pacing his railcar like an animal in a small cage. He'd stopped trying to fool himself—he was *eager* to get home. Home? When had he ever thought of a place by that name?

Mostly, though, he was eager to get back to Alys.

"Looks like our Lord Taunton has been caught in love's snare," Edward said after they'd finished their last meeting, just before Gideon left town.

"Go sod yourself," Gideon had muttered, staring at the blank notebook he'd brought with him—and then left with it, equally blank, as he always did—rather than look at his three partners with his flaming red face.

"Gideon's feeling *shy*," Chatham said, his low, usually monotonous voice brimming with amusement.

"When's the wedding, Gideon?" Smith asked in the same tone of voice he'd use on a small child he was afraid to frighten.

He'd snapped his notebook shut and surged to his feet. "A week after I return," he said, glaring at all three men and daring them to say one smart-arsed thing.

But they'd all just smirked. "Well, I think you're doing the right thing having a small ceremony. That's what Nora and I did," Edward said.

Gideon knew Edward's first wedding—to a marquess's daughter—had been at St. George's and huge—because he'd attended the stuffy, boring affair.

"Nora said to tell Alys that the portrait is coming right along." Edward gave one of his rare smiles. "I've seen it and it's one of her best."

Gideon forced down his jealousy. Nora hadn't let *him* come anywhere near it, even though Alys was to be *his* wife.

Edward and Chatham said their goodbyes but Smith lingered.

"You've chosen well, Gideon," he said, putting a hand on Gideon's shoulder. "I'm proud of you for making the right decision. I think she will make you very happy."

A shocking amount of emotion flooded his body at the other man's words, but he forced out a laugh. "Yes, well I'm not so sure about me making *her* happy."

Smith smiled. "She is young and has had a cruel start to life," he said, making Gideon wonder what the other man had unearthed about Alys—and he didn't doubt that Smith had been snooping about for a second. "Be good to her—*kind,*" he added as they walked together down the stairs to where their carriages waited.

Gideon had opened his mouth to say something caustic, but then a bolt of terror had struck him: he was to be married. *Married!*

Marriage was something he'd not for a second contemplated in his entire life until three weeks ago. He would be responsible for another human being—for *more* people if she was pregnant.

So, instead, he nodded. "Thank you, Smith."

And now he was mere hours away from Taunton.

"May I fetch you another drink, my lord?"

Jackson hovered in the doorway. "No, I'm fine. You say we brought all those—"

"Yes, my lord. We brought all the gifts you purchased for Lady Taunton."

Gideon's face heated again, just like a green lad gone-a-courtin'.

"Good, good," he said, turning his back to his servant, whom he'd swear had a glint in his eyes.

He flung himself into one of the overstuffed leather club chairs and stared out into the darkness.

Although he'd allowed for two weeks, he'd hoped only to be gone a week. But it had turned out that Beekman had loads of annoying business. And he'd had to schedule repairs for the falling down pile of bricks he'd inherited. And then there had been fetching the things Alys sent telegrams for on a daily basis.

His lips twitched at this last thought. He loved getting her telegrams because it was clear she'd never sent one before. She tried to use as few words as possible, and then ended up having to send another to clear up confusion. Gideon was glad, he adored getting messages from her.

The thought made him frown. He was acting like an idiot again.

He'd been doing it for almost three goddamned weeks.

First there had been his problems with sex.

He shook his head at the memory of going into the Birch Club a few nights after he'd been in town—already longer than he'd gone without having sex, or at least getting his cock sucked—in his life.

The owner of the brothel—which catered to clients with *fetishes*— had reserved a new woman for Gideon when she'd heard he was coming.

The whore had been exactly his sort: tallish, brunette, big hips, tiny waist, and large firm breasts with small nipples.

She'd had the pale-as-snow skin that marked so beautifully under a whip. And her lips were full—almost obscenely so—and had looked downright decadent wrapped around his shaft. Not only did she possess all the right equipment, but she knew how to use it.

She knelt for ages servicing him and he'd not been able to come. Finally, he'd had her turn off all the gaslights and start again. He'd imagined it was Alys and had come quicker than a fifteen-year-old aristocrat with his first housemaid.

He'd only gone out *four* times during the almost three weeks. Chatham, Fanshawe, and Smith had found that uproarious.

"Are you ill, Gideon?" Chatham asked in his annoying, slow drawl.

"I think he's come down with a chill," Edward said.

"We should tuck him in bed and get my cook to make one of her special draughts," Chatham responded.

And so on.

Honestly, going out to brothels had become a bloody chore. He was much happier fisting himself to visions of Alys riding him. Or making up new visions—imagining himself buried in her tight, virgin pucker. Yes, that was his favorite. He'd gone to his favorite shop—an unnamed business that catered to men with his peculiar tastes—and bought the damned place out, placing a few special orders while he was at it.

And then he'd taken those purchases a step further—he'd ordered a bed made for Taunton, a big, black, beast of a bed with metal rings sunk in all the right places.

HIS COUNTESS

So then he'd decide to buy a few more things. He'd sent three bloody train cars back, and that wasn't counting all the frippery he had shoved into the car this time.

His lips curved and his prick hardened at the thought of showing Alys all the things he'd bought for her. Things she would wear for his viewing pleasure.

He grunted and shifted his erection, wondering if he should relieve himself now—so he didn't make a fool of himself later—or let the anticipation build.

He decided on the latter, staring out the window and imagining exactly how he was going to use his cock on his wife-to-be's body.

❤

Thursby was crabby and taking her anger out on Alys's hair.

"Ow!" Alys said for the fourth or fifth time. "That hurts, Thursby."

The old woman just grunted. "It's what happens when you keep such heathen hours."

That made Alys laugh. "Oh, when I get ready for bed after the hour when *you* want me to is a heathenish time?"

Thursby met her eyes in the mirror, her lined face and tight, straight mouth almost gray; Alys knew the woman was hurting for her nightly gin. But Alys had kept her too busy tonight—putting the finishing touches on Gideon's room—to have her usual tipple.

Thursby's expression turned vindictive. "Aye, you laugh, my lady. You laugh now. You'll be suppin' sorrow with a long spoon."

Alys opened her mouth to say something sharp but then heard the sound of carriages in the front courtyard. She sat up straight, her heart pounding.

"Just *look* at you! You're like a bitch in heat, squatting to get—"

"Thursby!"

She could tell by the old woman's flushed face that she knew she'd gone too far.

"Sorry, m'lady." She continued her task in silence, brushing out Alys's waist-length hair until it shone. The entire time, Alys listened for the sound of his footsteps. It was two hours past his estimated arrival, so something must have happened to slow the train.

She chewed her lower lip and practiced tightening her inner muscles, using the trick Gideon had taught her before he'd left.

195

S.M. LaViolette

He'd given her a wicked look after teaching her the inner exercise, making her practice it in front of him, splayed naked on his bed, his face mere inches from her sex. "If you're a good girl and practice at least a half hour a day your sheath will get tighter—stay tighter. That will increase both our pleasure when I fuck you." He leered. "Especially mine. But the best part," he'd said, reaching down to massage her swollen, slick bud—her *clitoris,* he told her it was called—"You'll be able to make yourself come if you exercise enough."

He'd been right about that. She'd given herself at least a half-dozen orgasms that way. She wondered if she would really be tighter when he put himself inside her.

She swallowed hard at the thought, far too close to climaxing right now. She forced herself to stop tightening, even though it wouldn't take much to shove her toward bliss.

Alys yanked her thoughts away from her sex and watched Thursby, willing her to hurry up. When she put the brush down to braid her hair Alys stopped her. "No, leave it loose," she said, smiling as she heard Gideon's loud voice coming from out in the corridor.

Thursby frowned. "You should—"

The door to her room flew open without even a knock; Alys jumped up and Thursby yelped.

"What in—"

Gideon stood in the doorway, grinning ear to ear, his arms held out wide. "Hello, darling! Did you miss me?"

Alys began to run toward him when she noticed Jackson and other servants behind him, staring wide-eyed. So, she slowed down, stopping before throwing herself into his arms. Instead, giving him a chaste kiss on the cheek.

She could see he was disappointed.

He followed her anxious eyes and spun around. "Oh!" he said with a self-conscious laugh. "I forgot all about them. Well, get in here," he ordered stepping away from the doorway.

A veritable parade of servants bearing boxes marched into her room.

"Just put them all by the bed—yes, all around it."

"Gideon—why, what's all this?"

196

He smirked over at her. Gone was his boyish joy and in its place the hard, wicked lasciviousness that made her belly tighten. "Bridal gifts."

"But—but—"

He just grinned and they watched the presents pile up. When only Jackson remained, Gideon nodded to him. "I'll want you to shave me in a bit—go prepare my things." Jackson left without a word and Gideon turned to Thursby, his smirk growing.

"You, go to bed." When the older woman opened her mouth, he added. "Now."

Thursby stunned Alys by shuffling out of the room. But she did slam the door behind her.

No sooner had the door shut and Gideon swept her up into an embrace, kissing her while spinning her around and around, until she felt dizzy.

He put her down and grinned. "Did you miss me?"

Alys considered lying to him—for her own sanity—but couldn't take away his happiness yet again in such a short time. "I did," she admitted, having to bite her lower lip to keep from asking him the same question.

His blue eyes sparkled and his lips parted. He looked as if he were about to say something, and then thought better of it. Instead, he gestured to the pile of boxes.

"I want to watch you open these."

She laughed, breathless with delight. "*All* of them are for me?"

His nostrils flared and the look in his eyes made her inner muscles tighten with no help from her brain. "Well, some are for you—but really for me."

"Thank you, Gideon. I—I didn't get anything for you."

"Oh, bosh! You did up my chambers—I know you did because I ran all over London following your orders like a lackey."

Alys laughed and put her hands on her hot cheeks. "I'm sorry, was I terribly scattered? Did I drive you mad with all the requests?"

He slid an arm around her and jerked her into an embrace before crushing her mouth with his.

Oh, his kisses . . .

When he pulled away his eyelids were heavy. "You were perfect, my pet.   Just   perfect."

197

Chapter Eighteen

Gideon pounded the bed with a fist. "Get out here, Alys!"

He heard a giggle come from the open door between their rooms, where she was supposed to have changed into one of his *presents* while Jackson bathed and shaved him.

"Oh, I don't know Gideon—"

"Alys—" he warned.

"I'm coming, I'm coming."

When she entered his bedchamber she was wearing a dark purple silk dressing gown.

"Very pretty," he said. After all, he'd bought it for her. "Now take it off."

She swallowed, the sound audible across the room. His cock jumped at this innocent sign of nervousness.

Her hand shook when it went to pull the tie. It opened and the two flaps parted, exposing a strip of her body.

He felt as though he'd been kicked in the balls—but in a good way. "Fuck. Me."

"*Gideon!*" She glanced around the room, as if somebody might be in his bedchamber listening.

"Take it off. *Now.*" He was afraid he'd come all over himself before he could get near her.

She shrugged her shoulders and the dressing gown formed a purple puddle at her feet.

"Do-Do you like it?" She looked so *worried* that he wouldn't be pleased. Gideon couldn't recall that happening—a woman caring so much about what he thought. Didn't she know how beautiful—how wickedly seductive yet achingly pure she looked?

Tell her, you idiot.

But it was hard to breathe, not to mention speak. He made a *turn around* motion with one hand.

She complied.

When she faced him, he shook his head. "No, I don't like it." Her expression fell. "I bloody *love* it. Come here."

Her cheeks were flaming as she walked toward him wearing only a black leather corset. He loved such garments—but never as much as he had on Alys. She looked good enough to eat. And lick. And suck. His innocent little country wife, clear-eyed and pink-cheeked, and now she was a leather-clad temptress.

It's not taking long to pull her down to your level, is it?

Gideon frowned at the unwanted thought.

"What is it?" she asked, hesitating.

He smiled and shook his head, "You're just so lovely, it's making it difficult to think." That wasn't a lie, and it made her blush adorably.

His hands slid around her tiny waist and he groaned. "I love feeling you bound in leather."

He hadn't thought she could get any redder.

"Let's see if it excites you as much as me." He slid a hand between her thighs. "*Fuck!*" he yelled as loud as he possibly could, making her jump and squeak again.

"*Gideon!*"

"What?" he asked, sliding his finger through her slick wetness, stroking her tiny erection and glorying in the fact it was all for him.

"People will hear."

"Good, I want them to," he muttered, pushing his middle finger into her tight cunt. They both grunted.

"You've been practicing," he said, his finger pumping.

"You . . . noticed," she said softly, in between gasps.

Gideon dropped to his knees and roughly shoved her feet apart. "Hold your lips open for me. I'll need both my hands for what I'm going to do."

Her small fingers shook as she spread her auburn curls.

"My God you're gorgeous," he rasped. He sucked her clitoris into his mouth and massaged it with his tongue.

He made her come too damned fast. So, he did it again, and again. When she began to whimper and squirm, he reluctantly released her and removed the three fingers he managed to insinuate into her passage.

199

He stood and scooped her up in one motion, tossing her onto the bed.

She laughed as she bounced on a mattress that came from one of the syndicate's factories—it was stuffed with enough silk to make five hundred ballgowns and Gideon had ordered it made just for this bed. The cost of it would feed an entire village for a decade.

He smirked at the decadence of it—and at the woman lying sated on the dark blue silk cover. Nothing was too good for Alys to lay her delicious body on.

Gideon climbed on the bed and caged her with his arms and legs, gazing down at her.

She smiled drowsily up at him.

"You look well-fucked," he told her, being vulgar just so she'd blush.

She did. But he saw something hesitant in her smile.

"What is it?" he asked, a serpent of doubt coiling in his belly.

She swallowed hard, blushing even more, and shook her head.

"Tell me," he ordered sharply, not liking how anxious and powerless she was making him feel.

"It's just, well, I want to pleasure you."

He almost fainted from relief—and lust—as her words sent the little bit of blood remaining in the rest of his body to his cock. He grinned, pleased to be back in familiar territory: an area that included sex, his prick, and what he liked to do with it.

He pushed up onto his knees, smirking down at her, and took his shaft in his hand, languidly pumping what he knew to be a very respectable cock.

"Do you want to suck me?" he asked.

Her entire body shivered at his crude question and he could see it was hard for her to get enough breath with the tight corset on her. Next time, he'd lace it even tighter.

She nodded, the action jerky.

"Alys," he warned.

Her eyes flew open. "Oh, I mean yes, Gideon."

He smiled smugly and then grabbed a pillow from the bed and threw it on the floor before sliding off the high mattress. He turned to help her down. "Kneel on that."

She was pleasingly quick to obey. Gideon slid his feet apart just enough to put his crown at the level of her pouty lips.

"You see how excited you've made me?" He gave himself a pump, causing his slit to leak for her. "Tongue it, taste me," he ordered, holding his cock by the root, the action making it look even bigger, thicker.

She trembled as she leaned closer, opening her mouth.

"Take my hips with both hands. Good. Now, show me your tongue—yes, like that, stick it out and make a point. And then poke it into my little hole."

The tentative touch of her hot tongue ripped a groan from his chest.

"Christ! Yes," he snarled, shoving his hands into her hair and holding her skull immobile. It took every ounce of self-control not to start fucking her mouth like the beast he was.

Later for that.

He forced himself to calm down. "Do it again, yes, darling. Like that. Go ahead and lick me, get the feel and taste of me."

His head just about rolled off his shoulders; who knew that such an inexperienced mouth could feel so bloody amazing?

He opened his eyes, hungry to see her lips stretched around him. He grinned; she was sucking his fat head like it was a sweetie.

"The part below the crown is the most sensitive," he encouraged, shuddering when she immediately began to investigate. He allowed himself only the slightest pulsing of his hips, his fingers massaging her skull. "One day," he told her through clenched jaws. "I'm going to fuck your mouth as hard as I fuck your cunt."

Her groan went right up his cock to his balls and he almost came.

Gideon couldn't have that—not yet. He reached down and squeezed his root hard enough to slow the inevitable.

"See how much you can take into your mouth—Oh! Watch the teeth, kitten. Yes," he grunted as his sensitive head touched her palate. "Nice—very nice. Mmm, just like that. Such a good pet."

She was clumsy, but delightfully curious and watching himself slide in and out of her sweet mouth was better than the most skilled oral pleasure.

201

As he stared down, drinking in the sight of her, he knew he was behaving shamelessly; the entire house, and probably the village, knew what they were up to.

He should feel guilty about debauching Alys like this—as he'd always done with his mistresses or the other women he paid—but he simply could not stop himself. Being with her made everything else seem unimportant.

Besides, in a few days they'd be man and wife, so everyone could just go to hell.

Gideon smiled at the pleasant thought, realizing just in time that his naïve little lover had teased him to the brink of pleasure.

He moved back—or tried to—but she sucked harder, reluctant to let go of his prick.

Gideon laughed breathlessly. "That's enough for now, little one. Don't worry, I'll be giving you plenty of practice. But right now I need to be inside you."

—❤—

Alys had never felt so desirable in her entire life—she knew that meant she was a deviant. Wearing nothing but a leather corset, on her hands and knees while Gideon knelt behind her and licked her *there*.

"Such a pretty rose." His paused his licking and probing while whispering words of praise, his hands holding her open and exposed.

It was so very, very dirty. But it felt delicious.

And then he shoved his tongue into her and she cried out.

"Good girl," he said in a breathless voice, his fingers slipping between her thighs and teasing her clitoris until she was climaxing *again*.

He finally released her and she felt his hot, naked skin against the back of her thighs and her bottom.

He reached between their bodies and positioned his crown against her entrance. "I'm going to check and see if you've been exercising for me." He slammed into her without warning.

A mortifying animal moan slipped from her mouth; fortunately it was drown out by Gideon's crude grunts and words.

"So. Fucking. Tight." He punctuated each word with a brutal thrust.

He was wicked for saying such things and she was twice as wicked for loving his filthy mouth.

"You feel as delicious as you taste, my little pet." His hips pounded savagely as he held her with fingers that would leave bruises. "I'm *so* looking forward to filling your body with my spend," He said through clenched jaws. "I'll fill all your holes, darling," he whispered, the words so shocking Alys wasn't quite sure she'd heard him correctly.

"But not just yet, I think. First I want you to come for me."

Alys lost track of the number of times he made her climax with his hand, while his hips relentlessly drummed. She was about to go mad when he finally yelled her name, thrust himself deep, and spent, his body jerking violently as he filled her with warmth.

For a long moment, the only sounds were the pounding of her heart and their labored breathing. She was intensely aware of the place they were joined—to where Gideon's shaft filled her so perfectly, his spasms becoming increasingly weaker as he emptied himself. It was such an unspeakably intimate thing to take another person into one's body; Alys absolutely adored it. She absolutely adored *him*.

He lowered his body until he covered her completely. "Thank you for giving me such pleasure, little one." He kissed her cheek and then slid out of her, leaving her bereft. "Let's get you out of this," he murmured, his fingers going to the corset lacing.

Part of her never wanted to take it off, but that was impractical. Still, she wondered if he would look at her the same way—or want to be with her—when she was just plain Alys again.

But her worries were foolish. As soon as he'd freed her, he tossed the garment to the floor and pulled her down onto the sinfully soft mattress beside him, holding her tenderly: his front pressed against her back, one hand gently stroking the sensitive side of her breast.

"I can feel the marks the corset left on your skin." He sounded pleased—almost smug. "I like them," he whispered. "The next time I shall do the lacing myself and I will tie you even tighter." He kissed the top of her head. "Cruelly tight. Perhaps I might even restrain you— spread you open, keep you bound—hand and foot—to the bed and ready for my use. Would you like that?"

Alys's head buzzed. She opened her mouth but only a choked gurgle came out. For a moment she was worried she'd not be able to force out an answer.

But as stunned as her mind was, her sex immediately began to swell, her nipples tightened, and her womb ached: how did he do this to her?

"Hmmm?" He somehow managed to make a hum menacing.

"Yes, Gideon, I would."

He chuckled, and she heard his satisfaction beneath the soft sound.

He was right to sound satisfied, in a matter of only a few nights together he'd managed to train Alys's body to respond to his commands like a circus animal.

Her brain, however, was more confused than ever. She simply had no place to store so many new, bizarre, experiences and feelings. And he seemed capable of coming up with new—even more shocking— ideas and suggestions without any visible effort. Just who was this man?

What you should be asking is how long such a man could possibly be interested in an ignorant little country mouse like you?

Alys frowned at the nasty thought.

You're so naïve. Have you forgotten what he said to you? Have you forgotten what this means?

Perhaps it might be different between us if I were to have a child?

Mocking laughter echoed in her head.

Alys sighed. "Gideon?"

"Hmmm?"

"Could we . . . er, well talk a bit?"

His body, which had been warm, pliable, and relaxed behind her, stiffened and stilled.

Alys opened her mouth to ask him what was the matter, but he said, "What did you want to talk about, darling?" Gone was the warm languor of only seconds earlier. In its place was the brittle, jaded sophisticate she knew so well.

She hesitated, wishing she hadn't asked—wishing she'd not forgotten that their marriage was nothing more than a mutual convenience. "Nothing in particular," she said, hearing the defensiveness in her voice and annoyed by it. Why couldn't she ask him questions—she was to be his wife, not his servant or his slave.

Emboldened, she said, "I told you something about my past when we were in Bristol, but I don't know very much about you.

He heaved a sigh that shook the bed. "I suppose you're wanting to know about my less than auspicious beginnings."

She opened her mouth to deny it, but he plowed onward.

"My father was a drunk and a gambler—and not a good one. Oh— he was excellent when it came to getting drunk, but he was a terrible gambler. After my mother died, he drank even more and fought with my grandfather.

Grandfather wanted to keep me and my brother Lloyd—I was seven and he was twelve—but my father wanted to defy the old man more than he gave a bloody—well, that doesn't matter."

His voice had become rough, his accent subtly slipping.

He sucked in a breath and continued. "He kept us with him for a couple years, while he crawled deeper into the bottle. Right before he died, he dropped us both at an orphanage and workhouse. Lloyd was fourteen by then—almost a man grown, but he had no skills to sell, so he stayed with the intention of learning a trade." Gideon laughed and the sound was so bitter it made the hairs on her neck stand up.

"You'll enjoy this part, darling. My brother was what they call a *bad seed*. Let me give you an example of our childhood: I once scraped my knee and it was bleeding. Lloyd offered to put on a sticking plaster. Which he did, but only after rubbing salt into the bloody wound"

"Oh, Gideon!"

He ignored her breathy commiseration. "Once we were on our own, without even the pathetic protection of my father, Lloyd took great pleasure in rubbing salt into any situation and—" he hesitated, and then added, "Suffice it to say I was glad the day he ran away—or was chased, rather, since the bobbies had come to get him for knifing a man. Not long after, my grandfather found me. He found Lloyd, as well. By then Lloyd was in the Steel, waiting to do the hangman's waltz. He was fortunate enough to die of some jail fever and spare my poor grandfather the shame."

He'd been holding her until then, his grip increasingly tight as he'd related the gruesome tale.

"I'm sorry, darling," he said abruptly, pulling his warm body away. "I must have been crushing you horribly as I bored on about my wretched childhood."

She opened her mouth to protest, but she heard him yawn.

"I'm afraid I can barely keep my eyes open.

Alys felt the bed move and the room went dark after he snuffed out the single candle on his nightstand.

She waited for him to come back to her. But, after the bed shifted again, he stayed on his side of the mattress, and the sound of regular deep breathing soon filled the room.

Alys was covered by the thick luxurious blanket but was suddenly very cold.

—❤—

Gideon woke her just as dawn broke, taking her for the third time, this time face to face and slow and languid. He didn't speak, he just stared at her with his bottomless blue eyes, his jaw tight as he rode them both to an almost silent climax.

When it was over, he pulled out and rolled onto his back, his body sweaty and his chest rising and falling heavily. "Go put on one of those new riding habits and meet me in the stables in an hour," he ordered before rolling out of bed and striding across the room, his penis still tumescent, his sack of jewels—as he fondly called it—pendulous. He was so beautiful and unashamed. He stopped just before he went into his bathing chamber and turned, his muscular body stretching in a way that exhibited him in all his glory—from powerful thighs to tight hips and narrow waist, to broad, sculpted shoulders: he was breathtaking.

He met her hungry gaze and smiled. "I'm very pleased with my new chambers, Alys. You have exquisite taste and have done well, my dear. I look forward to enjoying many nights in that bed with you." He slipped into his bathing chamber and closed the door behind him.

She grinned like an idiot and then pushed herself out from beneath the covers, groaning at the soreness in her body.

It would be good to ride this morning; it had been several mornings since she'd gone.

He'd brought her back mountains of lovely gowns, hats, and dozens of other garments—some of which he'd not allowed her to see yet. But Alys was most eager to put on one of the habits—especially the one that was black leather breeches, a black coat, and a supple pair of black boots that hugged her calves as closely as a lover's hands.

Gideon had laughed when she'd said the outfit reminded her of Smith.

"It should do, it came from his tailor."

206

She got to her room before Thursby, thankfully, and was mostly dressed when the older woman drifted in.

"What is *that?*" she gasped.

"None of your concern," Alys said. "Will you put my hair up—I've brushed it already."

Amazingly, she was down in the stables ten minutes later without having to tolerate a lecture.

Silber grinned up from Nike, whose hoof he was examining; his eyes widened in a way that was worryingly gratifying.

"How did you know I'd be riding?" she asked.

"The master sent word—said I was to be ready for the two of you every morning." He chuckled. "Said he was tired of bein' humiliated in the saddle by me." He jerked his head toward the tack room. "Did you see what he brought you?"

She groaned. "Not more gifts."

Silber gave her a gentle smile. "I'm pleased he's spoilin' you, my lady. It's about time someone did."

Alys's face heated as his words as well as the knowing look in his eyes. She went into the tack room and found that Gideon was indeed spoiling her. Not one, but two new saddles.

"Do you like them?"

She turned to find the man responsible for all her happiness leaning against the door, looking like a god come to earth with the sun blazing behind him, turning his hair into molten gold. Alys did what she couldn't do last night and threw herself into his arms.

For one horrible moment he remained stiff—but then he chuckled and squeezed her. "I must have done something good, hmm?" he asked softly, and then kissed her head. "Let's ride."

—◆ ♥ ◆—

Two mornings later Gideon made sure to get down to the stables a few minutes before Alys.

"Mornin', my lord," Silber greeted him in the same, happy, thrilled-to-meet the day manner he always did.

"Morning, Silber."

"Am I to join you this morning, sir?" he asked.

"Not today. My lady has someplace special to take me this morning."

Silber smiled, genuinely pleased for Gideon. What a nice man. Gideon knew such a man should make him feel guilty for his shocking depravity, but it just made being depraved feel even more enjoyable.

"Also, I understand there are a few of Mr. Nixon's sheep that have sneaked through a break in the fence over by the northeast corner—not far from the big gate." He paused and then added. "I don't want to make a fuss about it—Nixon is hurting for extra hands. Would you mind handling it yourself? I know it's beneath you, but—"

"It would be a pleasure, my lord." Silber looked pleased that Gideon was so thoughtful. "Old Farmer Nixon is—well, I'm sure you know he's past it in many ways. It's kind of you to think of him. I'll take care of it with nobody the wiser. I'll head over at half-past ten, that should be enough time to take care of it."

Gideon smiled. "I knew I could count on you."

"You beat me down here, again!"

He turned to find Alys striding confidently toward them, swinging her whip in a relaxed, lazy way that as good as yelled she'd been properly pleasured this morning. Gideon cut a glance at Silber and saw the man smiled, his throat tightly corded as he took in Alys's slender, feminine figure in yet another manly riding habit, this one buff and navy.

They were soon on their way, riding their usual loop before heading toward the northeast corner. Gideon wanted to get there fifteen minutes before Silber.

"You seem almost fey, this morning, Gideon?"

He turned toward Alys, who was watching him with an affectionate look.

He grinned. "I'm looking forward to my daily riding reward."

As he'd intended, she blushed and rolled her eyes. "You know, some people might consider riding itself a reward."

Gideon laughed. "Not me." He allowed all his desire for her to show on his face. "I'm going to strip you naked, tie you to a tree, and spread your legs wide, exposing your beautiful body to the morning sun. The only thing I'll let you wear is your boots." He grinned. "And then I'm going to kneel between those delicious thighs and make you scream."

"The things you say." She shook her head and pursed her mouth, but he knew her looks by now, she wanted it every bit as much as he did.

— ❤ —

Alys couldn't believe she was even the same person. Two months ago, if somebody had told her she would allow a man to tie her to a tree naked she would have called the constable and had them hauled away to Bedlam.

But here she was, arms and legs spread wide, ropes restraining her wrists and ankles. And, yes, the only thing she wore were her boots.

Gideon stood back and admired his handiwork when he'd finished tying her. His eyes consuming her as he dragged the tip of his whip over her thighs, belly, breasts. The slightly menacing gesture made her shiver and he flicked the side of her breast with the crop. "Do you like that?" he asked, of course noticing the way her thighs had clenched— or at least tried to—at the feel of the whip. How did he know the things that would arouse her before she did? *How?*

"I think you do," he said, one side of his mouth pulling up in an evil smile as he flicked her harder and harder. "You have lovely legs, my dear." He struck the inside of one thigh hard enough to make her gasp. "So toned and supple—I suppose from all this riding." He struck her again, harder, on the other thigh. Her lips parted and her chest rose and fell faster.

He paused in front of her, rubbing her mound with the flat leather tip of his whip. "Perhaps I should leave you here for a while? Maybe invite some of the stable lads to come have a look?"

She gasped but bucked against her bonds—almost more aroused by his wicked words and cruel expression than she was by the feel of hard leather rubbing her swelling lips.

"What do you think Silber would say if he saw you like this?"

Pleasure rippled out from her tightly clenching sex. Alys only realized she was grunting and whimpering when he stepped closer and shoved a gloved finger between her folds.

"Did you just come, Alys?" he demanded roughly, pumping the finger inside her still-contracting sex. "I think you did." He flicked her sensitive bud and she cried out. "I think you love the thought of being watched, put on display." He lifted his hand, the black leather slick with her juices.

"So wet," he whispered, dragging his finger over her lower lip. "Suck it clean," he ordered.

She didn't hesitate to obey his shocking order, sucking his leather-sheathed finger into her mouth and working it the way he'd taught her to work his breeding organ.

"Do you like that I'm clothed—all the way down to my gloves—while you're naked and exposed?"

She shuddered and sucked harder.

He chuckled. "I'll take that as a yes." He pulled his finger out and stepped back, his crop resuming its distracting work. "I think tonight, to celebrate our impending nuptials I'm going to tie you to the bed and whip you properly before I mount you."

Alys made an embarrassing noise that caused her cheeks to flare.

He laughed wickedly. "Ah, your body tells me you'd like it." He dragged the rough crop over her hard nipple and she strained against her bonds.

"Please, Gideon."

"Please?" He cocked an eyebrow as he absently swatted the sensitive skin of her breasts, harder and harder. "Please what, darling?"

"Please. I want—"

He smiled like a cat that had eaten the canary. "What?" He smacked her mound and the stiff leather grazed her bud. "Do." *Smack.* "You." *Smack.* "Want?"

Each swat brought her closer to yet another climax.

Gideon dropped to his knees. "God, yes." He spread her with sheathed, impersonal fingers and sucked her into his mouth.

Alys arched against the rough trunk, not caring what debauched picture she made, or whether she scraped her back as she ground her sex against his eager, skillful tongue.

He laughed into her swollen folds and shoved a finger into her, thrusting with each suck.

Alys came again, already accustomed to the demands he made on her body: namely that she be forced to orgasm over and over and over before he took his own pleasure, which he sometimes liked to defer for hours.

She listened to the wet sounds of his hand pumping and forced her eyes open, needing to see him. His golden head bobbed, while his powerful arm worked her. The noises he made—moaning, sucking, animalistic grunting—were almost as pleasurable as the act, itself.

He brought her right to the edge, but this time he left her there, teetering.

She whimpered and pushed her hips toward him.

"Do you want it?" he growled in between licks.

"Yes, Gideon, please."

"Beg for it." He pulled away, staring up the length of her body with a maddening smirk on his slick, swollen lips, his hand languidly thrusting, his thumb nowhere near the source of her pleasure "Beg."

"Gideon, please—I want—"

"Yes?" he was grinning openly.

"I want to orgasm." The words were so soft that *she* could barely hear them.

He cupped his ear. "I beg your pardon?"

"I want to *come*," she hissed.

He gave a triumphant laugh, pleased to have driven her to vulgar language, and caught her sensitive bud between his lips.

As she began to unravel, something caught her sex-soaked attention. Alys's eyes widened, her brain not translating what they took in. Was it? No! It couldn't be—could it?

Oh, yes it could.

It was Silber.

He was staring at her, open mouthed, from only feet away.

Some part of her passion-befogged brain realized he must have come up from the small vale on the far side of the old stone wall. He stood where the wall met a broken-down section of fence.

He was holding a wooden box of tools in one hand, his huge body rigid, his eyes wide.

Even from this distance she saw his free hand come to rest over the big, long ridge pressed against his worn leather breeches.

So many sensations were assaulting her mind and body it was hard to think—hard to make her brain accept what her eyes saw: Silber was watching her. And he was aroused.

Something about his eyes on her made her orgasm even more powerful, her entire body straining with the force of it. She bucked and thrusted against her bonds, vaguely aware there would be marks, but not caring as she ground against Gideon's mouth.

Silber's huge frame shuddered and his brawny hand tightened over his placket, his body stiffening.

Alys knew—she *knew*—she'd made him climax without even touching him.

Instead of feeling ashamed of her behavior, her lips curled into a triumphant smile as she saw the way passion shook the big man's body.

She'd done that to him. And she wanted to do it again. And again.

Chapter Nineteen

Gideon was happy. Happier than he'd ever been in his life.

He looked down at the reason for his happiness. Alys was on her hands and knees, groaning with pleasure as his cock slid in and out of her tight little rosette. He'd taken a great deal of time to prepare her, opening her slowly, carefully. After seeing her body's response to the crop a few days earlier, he'd tied her to the bed earlier and made her come from the whip alone.

Her first flogging had been gradual and gentle—she was so new to such things—not even close to hard enough to raise any welts, just enough to warm her beautiful pale skin but not hurt her.

No, he didn't want to damage any part of her body.

They'd had a picnic in bed after, laughing over their tiny wedding ceremony, which had been interrupted suddenly when the vicar's basset hound went into labor beneath one of the church pews.

They'd begun the ceremony with only four guests—the vicar, his wife, Thursby and Jackson—and ended it with eleven.

They had been sipping champagne when his delicious wife had asked for her wedding present.

"Gideon—I want you to …"

"Yes?" he'd prodded, brimming with lust, excitement, and anticipation at what she wanted, and determined to make her vocalize it—preferably using vulgar words that would make her blush.

She swallowed hard. "I want you to take me back there."

He cocked his head. "Back there? You mean back in your chambers?"

She'd growled. "Quit tormenting me. You know what I want."

"I do—but I want you to say it. Say, *Gideon, I want you to fuck my arse.*"

It had taken a while to get her to say it, but it had been worth the wait.

Stretching and preparing her had been nearly as pleasurable as finally sliding into her delicious tightness.

Nearly.

"Am I hurting you?" he asked yet again. He was fucking her slowly, and with deep strokes, fingering her from time to time, unable to stop touching her responsive body.

"I'm *fine*," she gasped in between thrusts.

"How does it feel?" He loved hearing her talk about sex.

"Full—stretched so full." The last word was a groan. "So ... *good*."

Gideon grinned to himself at her lust-drenched tone and allowed her to enjoy her pleasure without torment while he relived the whipping again and again in his mind's eye.

He'd never had a woman who could come just from a whip. It made him insanely hard. Her pale skin was beautiful and marked so prettily. He'd wanted to keep her tied to the bed for the rest of their lives.

Her back passage tightened around him as he fingered another orgasm from her sweaty, shaking body. The sensation was exquisite yet painful on his aching cock. He wanted it again.

"I can't," she gasped when he began to stroke her again. "Not again."

"Just once more," he said. "See how I'm begging? Please. Come once more for me?"

She groaned, but dropped her head, her shoulders dipping but her bottom pushing toward him, the position deliciously submissive.

"My good, obedient girl," he murmured, stroking into her with his cock while he slowly brought her to orgasm.

When he felt the contractions coming, he fucked into her with vicious thrusts, until he could hold back no longer and drove himself deep, coming in wrenching jerks.

Mine! Mine! Mine! He crowed inside his head, glorying in his possession and marking her with each spasm of his cock until he was aching and empty.

After they'd both floated for a while, he pulled from her body with a reluctant groan and went about cleaning them both up with the cloths and hot water Jackson had delivered recently.

He collapsed beside her when he'd finished.

She took his hand. "Gideon?"

"Yes, darling?" he reached over and played with her nipples, pinching them to hardness.

She groaned. "I must be a harlot," she thrust her chest up to meet his fingers.

"I hope so."

"Are you sure you want the mother of your child to be a harlot?"

He laughed, and then stopped and spun onto his side. "Are you—" he stared, eyes wide. "Er, pregnant, I mean?"

She grinned up at him. "I'm not an expert, but I believe I am."

He gave a triumphant shout and then pushed up onto his hands and knees and crawled until his face was level with her belly.

He rubbed the soft swell reverently. "It doesn't feel any different." He licked her navel. "Or taste any different."

She laughed. "Not for some time, I think."

"How long?" he asked, rubbing, wanting to feel something *now*.

"I should think it happened that first night—so, just before you went to London. A little over a month ago."

He looked up at her. "We need to get you a physician, have you checked—regularly. To make sure you're healthy," he said when she gave him an amused look. His gaze dropped to the puffy lips that protected her sex. "Can I keep spending inside you?"

She blushed adorably. "I don't know—but I should think it wouldn't hurt."

"Maybe the baby won't like my seed making things all hot and sticky?"

She howled with laughter, which led to some wrestling, and then more stroking, and even a few more orgasms.

Later, as they both drifted off to sleep, he took her hand in his. "Thank you," he muttered sleepily.

"What for?"

"For making me happy."

♥

He'd spoken so softly that Alys wasn't sure she'd heard him correctly.

He seemed to fall asleep before he'd even stopped speaking.

But he *had* seemed happy—especially about the baby.

So was she.

Then why are you crying?
She touched her cheek: it was wet.
She had no idea why she was crying.
Liar.
Alys gritted her teeth, unwilling to allow such thoughts to ruin her wedding night.
These past few days had been the best of her life.
It did occur to her—often—that they never spoke of themselves, at least nothing serious. He was a diverting companion who could chatter amusingly on dozens of subjects, but never about Gideon Banks. He never left openings to ask personal questions.
I vow to ask him at least one personal question at the very next opportunity.
He was so reticent that it would be up to her. She would make an effort to ask him little things—just to get to know the man inside the glorious body.
He was so sweet, funny, sensual, and crude: she'd never met anyone like him. His emotions were so close to the surface. When he was happy, being around him was a euphoric feeling.
When he was petulant, his displeasure was crushing.
And when he was angry? Well, she'd not seen that side of him, yet, and hoped she never did.

—❤—

Gideon watched her eyes flutter open. "Hello, Lady Taunton," he said.
An instant of confusion cleared and she smiled. "Hello, Lord Taunton?"
They laughed softly.
She yawned, her cheeks coloring. "I'm sorry, how rude. What time is it?"
"We've only slept a few hours." Gideon absently stroked her naked flank. "Do you feel odd that you've married but your name didn't change?"
She nodded, her expression solemn. "Yes, it's quite upsetting, actually." She grinned at whatever she saw on his face—likely worry, because he was such a fatuous idiot.
"*Tsk, tsk.* Such talk will get you punished later, Lady Taunton," he retorted lightly to cover his moment of weakness.

216

"I should hope so." They both chuckled at her sweet attempt at wickedness. "Gideon?"

"Hmm?"

"You make me very happy."

The honest look in her eyes left him feeling utterly naked. What did one say to such a statement?

"May I ask you a few questions?"

His stomach tightened. Questions again.

Her brow had wrinkled at his hesitation.

"A few," he finally said. "But I have other things planned than talking."

"Tell me about your work—I don't understand what you do."

He felt weak with relief. Work, yes that was easy.

"It's hard to explain as the work changes so much with each acquisition. I suppose the clearest way to describe it is to say I fix things. For example, we bought three textile mills two years ago. Edward found the business, Chatham assessed its books, Smith—well, I'm not sure what Smith did, his part usually comes in later." He grimaced, not wanting to talk about Smith's murky practices. "My job is to look at the mechanics involved in each job and see how I can make the process operate more smoothly. So, with the textile mills, for example, I recommended improvements in our looms. One change I made was proprietary—which just means it is our special process." He wanted to tell her that he'd actually filed for a patent, but it didn't feel right to boast—an odd reaction as boasting was something he generally enjoyed.

"That sounds very. . . challenging."

"That's a good word for it. And it always changes, so I don't get bored." He gave her a wry smile. "I get bored easily."

She laughed. "I never would have suspected."

He opened his eyes in mock outrage. "*Lady Taunton*! Are you mocking your lord and master?"

Her nostrils flared slightly and the desire that sparked in her eyes made him thicken.

"I'm not finished with my questions, yet," she protested, feeling his shaft swell against her thigh.

"You'd better hurry and ask." He gave a few suggestive thrusts.

217

"Oh, when you put it that way." She gave him a mischievous grin, her hand sliding between their bodies, her fingers wrapping around his shaft.

"Oh, God, Alys. I love that." He shut his eyes, once again relieved that the bothersome questions were over.

⊸ ♥ ⊢

Gideon woke with a start, his eyes blinking as he looked through the gray light; it was morning.

He felt the bed beside him and encountered a small, soft body.

She groaned and muttered something in her sleep, turning toward him, molding to him. Gideon slid an arm around her waist without thinking pulling her closer. Immediately he was aware of how right she felt, how well she fit with him.

You idiot.

He frowned at the cold, mocking voice. Not for the first time did he wonder if it was entirely normal to have arguments with oneself—to insult oneself.

What do you want? he demanded when he sensed the presence wouldn't leave him alone until it had imparted whatever wisdom it needed to.

What are you doing, Gideon? Why are you pretending with her? Why are you encouraging her to believe you can set up house, have babies, and live in castles in the clouds? Aren't you the one who told her not to have such expectations? And yet here you are—giving the poor woman bad ideas—behaving like a love-stricken boy. You're not a one-woman, or even a twenty-woman man. Without variety and spice you'll simply expire from boredom.

Gideon ground his teeth at the words, some of which—admittedly—he may have thought himself, from time-to-time.

But that was before Alys and Foxrun.

Gideon startled at his pleading—he didn't sound fifteen, he sounded *five.*

So what if that's how I sound, he argued. He was here, with her and they'd made a child together. He *liked* Foxrun and he enjoyed getting to know the property as well as all the people who made their livelihood on it. Was it really so bad to want to stay here for a while and actually enjoy his good fortune rather than constantly be on the look out for

218

more, something new, the next business, the next mistress, the newest way in which he could titillate his jaded sensibilities?

As his last trip to London had proven, he was sick and tired of going to whorehouses and paying for bodies to use.

His arm tightened around Alys's sleeping fom. Why was it so bad to enjoy his life? Why?

You're whining, again, Gideon. It's bad because it's hardly fair to her, is it? Making her believe this will last? It will only become more difficult the longer you let this charade go on. The bald truth is that she'll be happier the sooner she knows what a shallow, self-centered, hedonistic prick you really are.

But—

Don't argue, Gideon. You know it's true. And if you think it's not true, the best way you can prove that you have even an ounce of goodness inside your pleasure-seeking body is to show her your true self now. Once she see's what you're really like, she'll run screaming. It's far less cruel to cut the cord now.

Gideon's heart was thudding in his chest and he felt like he couldn't inhale enough air even though he was gulping and gasping like a landed fish.

What do you mean, cut the cord?

He waited, stupidly, for an answer from his own brain, but the voice had gone—pissing off back into whatever dark hole it inhabited until it felt the need to pop up and destroy any chance at happiness.

Gideon bit the forearm that wasn't wrapped around Alys. He bit hard, his teeth breaking skin, the pain focusing his scattered wits until all he thought about was the agonizing sensation in his arm. Blood filled his mouth and yet his jaws still were clenched tight.

This is life—*this*: pain.

It was time to take control of matters and begin as he meant to go on.

His jaws loosened and he swallowed the metallic tang of blood.

The clarity was instant and astounding; his mind was as coldly focused as it had been the very first day he'd met the stranger lying beside him.

Foxrun was one of the many detours in his life, it was not his destination. Making the mistake of believing it was would make the pain in his arm feel like the merest pinprick.

Chapter Twenty

Alys woke in Gideon's big bed alone.

The clock on the mantle said it was almost eleven in the morning!

She wrapped a blanket around her body and was heading for her chambers when the door from the corridor opened.

"Ah, sleeping beauty has awakened." He strode toward her, looking unbearably handsome and rugged and sweaty in his boots, buckskins, and riding coat.

He kissed her hard on the mouth, plunging and invading, the smell of horse and leather and Gideon intoxicating.

Alys was reeling when he released her. "What are you doing out of bed? I gave strict instructions that you were not to be disturbed." His hands went to the blanket she was using to cover her nudity and he peeled it away, smiling with that insufferable smirk of possession when the blanket slid to the floor. "You know I don't like you to cover yourself when you're in my room, Alys. Please remember that in the future."

He turned and strode toward his dressing room, stopping in the doorway. "I want a bath and breakfast brought up," he said, shrugging out of his coat and tossing it to what could only be Jackson.

Alys squeaked and sprinted to the bed, diving beneath the covers. Was he mad? Making her parade naked in front of his manservant? What if Jackson had seen her? *Had* he seen her? After all, she'd woken naked and sprawled above the covers.

Her pelvis thumped at the thought of the stern-faced manservant seeing her naked, sleeping body. Alys hissed in a breath. What was wrong with her? Why would she like the thought of such a thing? What kind of woman liked to be looked at by her husband's valet?

The same sort who liked to be watched by her stable master ...

She felt the bed move. "Alys, darling? Are you in there?" his voice was heavy with amusement and something else—arousal? Had he *wanted* Jackson to see her?

Alys made her way slowly out from beneath the covers. "I didn't know Jackson was in here."

He shrugged, his hand going to her hair, his fingers sliding through it and his eyes tracking the progress. "It's my room and he is my valet."

"Yes, but surely you don't want him to see me."

His eyebrows shot up and his lips quirked. "Why shouldn't I want that?"

Alys sputtered. "Because I am your wife and he is your servant."

He chuckled. "Yes, that's true. But I *like* the thought of Jackson seeing you." His eyelids lowered and he leaned forward to capture her lower lip between his teeth, tugging hard enough to bring tears to her eyes before releasing her. "I *like* the thought of him becoming hard and wanting while he fantasizes about what it must be like to fuck your beautiful body. I like to think of him lying erect and leaking in his little valet cot, imagining his cock sliding between these perfect lips."

Alys felt woozy; she might have fainted had she not been laying down.

He stared down at her with hooded eyes, his smile tight. "I can see you *like* thinking about it, too. Your pulse is drumming a million miles a minute."

She swallowed. "Perhaps it's drumming because I'm angry."

He smirked. "Oh, Alys, you are utterly charming." He reached beneath the blanket, his hand sliding up her clenched thighs. "Open for me," he ordered sharply, smiling when her legs instantly parted. His warm, questing fingers slipped between her thighs and grazed the seam of her sex and he shoved two fingers right up into her body. Her *throbbing* body.

Alys whimpered and pushed her hips to meet him.

"Do you always get this wet and swollen when you are angry?" he growled in her ear, leaning closer, his arm moving in slow, deep thrusts. He bit her ear lobe and she jumped. "Never lie to me about what arouses you, Alys. Your fantasies are mine, all mine—they all belong to me. Now, open for your husband."

She spread wider to take him, her wanton body so greedy for the pleasure he could give that it didn't care how mortified her mind was.

"Say it," he demanded. "You're mine—you belong to me."

"I belong to you."

"That's right, pet." He worked her harder, his breathing ragged. "If I told you to go into my dressing room, drop to your knees, and suck Jackson off while I watched you'd do it without hesitation to please me, wouldn't you?"

His words set off a violent burst of lust deep inside her sex while her mind cried out against the vision his words created.

Yet again, her body triumphed.

Alys convulsed around his thrusting fingers, splintering into a million pieces of joy even as her brain recoiled from his depraved words.

"What's that?" he demanded as his thumb returned to her agonizingly sensitive bud and began stroking her toward another orgasm before the first was hardly over. "What was that?"

"Yes," she gasped. "Yes, Gideon, I would do anything for you. But, please, I can't—"

"You can come again and you will, Alys," he hissed. "You'll come for me as often as I wish and whenever I wish." And then he proceeded to demonstrate his mastery over her again and again.

—◆ ♥ ◆—

Gideon woke up when the light was just beginning to fade.

He yawned and stretched, his body sore from both the bruising ride he'd had as well as the rather strenuous afternoon he and Alys had spent in his bed. He'd been almost manic in his need to claim her.

And why is that, Gideon?

He clenched his jaw tight; he was never engaging with that bloody voice in his head, ever again.

The clock said ten to six. So, they'd literally fucked away seven hours. His lips twitched with pleasure at the thought.

Alys shifted in her sleep beside him and his lips began to curve into a smile. Oh what an afternoon they'd had. He grunted softly, his hand going to his rod, which was waking and eager for the night ahead. His smile turned to a grin as he stroked himself to hardness; he'd take her while she slept, fucking her to consciousness.

She'd been magnificent earlier—so responsive and eager, so *his*. It had been one of the most sensual days of his life. It had been—

A completely different memory slammed into him like a train and Gideon froze.

He swallowed convulsively, as if to dislodge a lump in his throat. But the lump only became larger.

Silber.

Snatches of the conversation he'd had with the strapping stable master came at him and Gideon flinched away from the memory of his ugliness. Because he *had* been at his worst.

Fear will do that to a man. The mocking voice laughed. *And I don't think there's ever been a man more frightened than you on the day after your wedding night, Gideon.*

"Christ," he whispered, wincing at the accusation but knowing it was true.

What the hell had he done? What had he been thinking to say the things he'd said to Silber?

It wasn't too late. He could send word to the man and end it before it even started. He still had several hours to call this off, to change his mind, to—

To what? Fall in love with your wife? You know as much about how to love as a pig knows about knitting.

The sneering voice was like a sharp slap across the face.

You deserve a real beating for your weak, idiotic thoughts, Gideon, the voice continued. *Wasn't it you who said you'd never pick her up on a white charger and carry her to a happily ever after? And yet here you are, a pathetic whimpering boy.*

Gideon stupidly squeezed his eyes shut, as if that would stop the voice.

This is who you are, Gideon. The sooner she understands that she is here to serve your needs, the better it will be for the both of you. You'll actually be doing her a kindness tonight. This way she'll not sit waiting for you like a devoted, loving wife. She'll be free to go on with her own life as you go on with yours.

You've done your work where she is concerned—she's with child and likely will bear you as many as you wish. That was the bargain you struck.

Tonight is a perfect time to begin your life. Not only will it set you free from expectations, it will set her free. Besides, the nasty little voice added gleefully, *you know she wants it—has wanted it for a long, long time. It's the perfect wedding gift.*

But what about Silber? The man he'd had to threaten and bribe?

He wants it as badly as she does, but he's too hidebound by pointless morality to admit it. Right now he's as hard as a bloody pike imagining tonight. He hates your guts, but don't fool yourself that he doesn't hate himself worse. He didn't have to agree to this—he's not an impoverished, skill-less vagabond. He's in demand and you know for a certainty he's turned away more than one offer from reputable horse breeders to stay and work at Foxrun. Well, now he can do some breeding of his own.

Gideon snorted bitterly at the ugly laughter that echoed in his mind.

He knew this other voice, which he liked to lock away and pretend to fight, was his true self. He was ugly and selfish and cruel. He was—

"Gideon?"

He turned at the sound of her sleepy voice, his smile already pasted on his face.

"Hallo, darling." He gave her a hard kiss to match the feeling in his heart.

"What time is it?" she asked through a yawn.

"It's after seven."

"Oh," she began to push up. "Have you rung to push back—"

"Hush, darling. I've taken care of it—you shall dine in your room tonight."

Her plump lips curled up at the corners. "We'll never leave our rooms at this rate, Gideon."

He chucked and shook his head, his heart thudding loudly in his ears at what he was about to do.

Somewhere deep inside himself a faint, tiny voice screamed for him to stop, before it was too late. Gideon slammed the door on the plea and kissed her again.

"I meant you'd dine in *your* room, pet. But I won't be joining you."

Chapter Twenty-One

Alys's smile faltered. "I don't understand. Why won't you be joining me?"

His beautiful mouth curved in a way that made her shiver. "Tonight I'm giving you your wedding gift."

Alys cocked her head. "But—"

He laid a finger across her lips. "Let me speak." He waited until she'd nodded and then continued. "You will go to your room soon. I've arranged for a bath to be sent up along with a light meal. After you've bathed and eaten I want you to put on the gown you'll find in a box on your bed. You'll find a bottle of fine red wine and will enjoy a glass while you wait for your present to arrive."

Alys frowned. "Gideon?"

"Yes, my love?" his expression was one of tolerant amusement.

"What is this—*what* will arrive?"

"I am going to fulfill your fantasy."

"But what—"

"Don't you remember what you told me that night—the night we explored all the peepholes together?"

Her eyes widened. They'd gone from room to room, looking in all the peepholes, each taking a turn and describing what they'd like to see on the other side.

It had been mortifying at first, but Gideon had plied her with champagne, until she'd admitted she'd like to see Silber—but not with her, with Lucy and Susan.

That had been a mistake because he'd eventually teased it all out of her and she'd had to admit that, yes, over the years, she'd had thoughts about him.

"You can't mean—" she couldn't make herself say the words.

"Silber?" He grinned.

She nodded shakily.

"Yes, of course that's what I mean—I'm giving him to you as a gift. Why? Was there some other fantasy you haven't told me, Alys?" He shook his head "Naughty, naughty. Don't worry, I'll get it out of you eventually."

Alys could only stare.

"Come now, is that any way to thank me for such a princely—or should I say earl-ly—gift?" He chuckled.

"This—you—I don't—"

He leaned forward to kiss her but she jerked back and he frowned, his beautiful face hardening. "I'm not pleased by your ingratitude, Alys. I'm giving you something you dreamed about for years—you *told* me as much. Instead of thanking me, you are behaving like a prude—like your old maid would react."

"I *am* your wife." The words came out wheezy and weak—her chest felt as if it were being crushed. Suddenly she needed to get away from him. She shoved back the blankets and threw her legs over the side.

His hand closed around her wrist, his grip like hot steel. "Where are you going?"

"Away from here—from *you.*" She tugged on her arm.

He raised his brows and tilted back his head, until he was looking down the length of his perfect nose. "I'm displeased that we're back to a subject I'd believed settled long ago. Yes, you *are* my wife. We both knew the terms of our marriage well before. Are you telling me you want to change them *now*, after?"

Alys glared up at him, furious at herself when she felt her lip trembling.

She was even more furious when the insidious thought of what he'd planned wormed its way into her treacherous body: Silber.

Alys swallowed and it came out a loud gulp. In a few hours she could have—

"If I were to reach between those sweet thighs of yours right now and insert a finger in your cunt I would feel the hot, strong pulse of want inside you." His pupils flared. "Already you're wondering about him—his length, his thickness—and imagining what he will feel like inside you. You're primed and ready for mounting just thinking about it. Can you deny it?"

226

Alys's chest was rising and falling as if she'd been running, but still she couldn't get enough air. "It doesn't *matter* what I think or feel. This man is your servant, Gideon, and he is loyal and kind. He would never agree to such a scandalous thing."

He gave a smug, amused laugh that made her want to slap him. "He already has, sweetheart. He'll call upon you at ten."

His words caused a contraction between her thighs that left her dizzy.

"Yes, I can see how you feel about that, little one."

Alys shook her head frantically, to deny him or herself or both? "Silber would never do such a thing—you must have threatened him with something?"

He laughed again. "Oh, sweetheart! What a sense of the absurd you have. Do you really believe that *any* man would need to be threatened into bedding you? Especially a man who has lusted after you for years?"

The reaction in her tight, tingling body made her feel physically ill, but no less aroused. "How could you do this—give me to some other man?"

He cocked his head. "Look at you," he teased. "You want it so badly and yet you hate yourself for it."

"Don't you care?"

"Care?"

"That you're giving me to another man?" the words wobbled and tears pressed against the back of her eyes.

"Oh, my pet. How sweet and young and innocent you are. And how much I'm going to enjoy taking that innocence from you, bit by bit." He brushed her chin with the back of his fingers, his gaze contemplative and amused. "Don't you understand? I'm not giving you to another man—I'm giving us an opportunity to explore our fantasies together. This will give us both a great deal of pleasure."

His lids dropped over his eyes and his nostrils flared; Alys knew he was aroused thinking of her with another man and his arousal sent a spike of lust straight to her sex.

Right then and there, Alys knew that she would do what he wanted. And she would do it even knowing it was the end of any chance of anything good or true or real ever growing between them.

She could see by the hard glint in his eyes that Gideon knew that, too. That he wanted to kill any possibility of them ever being anything more than mere business—or occasional sexual— partners.

If he truly valued her so little that he would give her to another man only a day after they'd married, then what was she fighting to protect?

Alys scrambled for the tattered shreds of her pride and summoned every bit of strength, giving him a smile she hoped was arch rather than miserable. "Very well, if you want to give me to another while you go enjoy your brandy in the library, so be it. I daresay I'll enjoy myself greatly," she added, cutting him a look of spite that went beyond bravado.

His eyes widened in surprise and Alys almost cheered: she'd scored a hit.

Then he threw back his head and laughed; big, deep belly laughter that sounded like a death knell. He looked at her through eyes that shone with amusement and she saw pity. "Oh, darling—I'll be enjoying a brandy, but not in the library." Gideon's perfect lips parted and he showed her his perfect white teeth.

Alys stared.

He yanked her close and kissed her hard on the mouth. "I can hardly wait, Alys." And then he released her and pushed back the blankets, climbing down from the tall bed, his erection jutting from his hips, hard and weeping, his expression one of triumph as he exhibited just what he thought about the evening ahead.

"Jackson!" he called out. "Where is my robe?"

Alys watched in stunned silence as his valet emerged from the dressing room and came to stand behind his master, helping Gideon into his dressing gown, behaving as if the mistress of the house wasn't sitting only a few feet away, naked.

The two men moved back toward the dressing room, conversing about which clothes Jackson should lay out, as if this were just like any other evening.

Alys couldn't move. He would come back—he would say *something*. Perhaps he was making a joke? Or perhaps it wasn't a joke but he wanted Alys to say she didn't want to go through with it?

Did she want to go through with it?

She tried to concentrate on the question—did she? Some part of her did, but not like this. Not to be given away like a toy he no longer wanted. Shouldn't she have some choice?

You can always say no.

She scowled at the unwanted thought. Of course she could, but that's not what she meant—

What do you mean? You want Silber, but don't want him because Gideon is giving him to you?

Every particle of her being shouted *No!* She wanted Gideon, no other man, just her husband.

You've fallen in love with him.

Alys felt her face crumple and struggled to control it. It was too much—she'd couldn't separate her body's wants from her heart—from how she felt for him. How could she have such incompatible desires?

The love she felt for him—because that is what it was, there was no denying it now—began to twist and distort as she struggled with the killing mix of pain and lust.

He *knew* how she felt about him—she'd seen that knowledge lurking behind the laughter. He knew that she'd naively fallen in love and he'd wanted to throw it back in her face as cruelly as possible.

He was a sick and twisted man with no heart.

He told you as much.

Alys flinched away from the thought, not caring if it might be true.

She forced herself to think about right *now*. She might not be able to stop these feelings she had for him, but she could do something about showing them.

She could not break in front of him. She could *not*.

Gideon returned to the bed holding the pale blue dressing gown she'd been so pleased to wear for him mere hours before. "Here you are, sweetheart." He held it up and waited patiently as she slid down from the bed, so anger-bound she moved jerkily.

"Thank you, Gideon," she murmured between stiff lips as he wrapped the soft silk around her body and kissed her neck.

He turned her to face him. "That's my girl." He smiled down at her. "I hope you enjoy your evening. I want you to come to me—after."

Fury coursed through every nerve.

"Of course." Alys smiled, stood up on her tiptoes, and kissed his cheek. And then she did the hardest thing she'd ever done in her life. "Thank you for my gift, Gideon."

His expression was arrested, surprised, and—was it possible?—displeased. But then he smiled, and Alys knew it had only been her imagination.

Chapter Twenty-Two

Gideon turned another page of the proposal he was not reading. Why he was pretending to work when what he was really doing was going slowly mad was beyond him. Nobody was watching what he was doing; he could run around the room naked with a feather duster shoved up his arse and nobody would see or care.

No, the only person who cared about him—who wanted to be around him— was currently up in her room waiting for another man.

He pulled out his watch; it was three minutes until ten o'clock.

He stared at the watch face, willing it to *do* or *say* something.

You know exactly what you'll do.

Gideon replaced the pages he'd been pretending to read on the pile and closed the leather portfolio. It was a proposal from Fanshawe about a company that manufactured yet another improved thresher built along the lines of Meikle's thresher. On a normal day Gideon could have flipped through the pages and made a decision within an hour. Tonight he'd been sitting here for two hours and couldn't have told Fanshawe even the simplest detail about the product.

His brain, so powerful and fast when it came to matters of machinery, was spinning wildly thanks to the interference of one small woman.

Gideon stood and snuffed out the candles. He'd decided against installing any gaslights—at least not in the library. He liked looking at the room with only flickering candles to illuminate it. It was somehow more majestic.

His feet were heavy as he headed up the stairs. There wasn't a soul about because he'd instructed his butler to see that every servant was in their quarters by nine.

What would these wholesome country folks think about their master if they knew about this? The thought shamed him—an emotion so rare for him that it had taken him some time to decipher it.

What kind of man gave his wife to another?

Gideon snorted as he strode down the hall that led to the secret panel. What the fuck did he care what these bumpkins thought? He doubted most of them got sucked off by their wives or took them anally, either. But did he want to do without those pleasures?

No.

So why should he curtail any of his other fancies or adventures?

Besides, Edward had invited Gideon to fuck Nora—in public.

The day after their wedding? Without even consulting her? Somehow I don't think so …

"Go sod yourself," he snarled. And then felt like a fool for shouting at himself in the middle of the corridor.

He found the panel latch quickly and pressed. The door opened with a soft click—he'd made sure Jackson had inspected and oiled and repaired all eight of the doors he'd found so far in the house.

Jackson had come earlier and lighted candles. It was also his duty to keep the passageways clean. Jackson being Jackson—which was to say meticulous to an almost frightening degree—he'd found a tall folding chair someplace. It must have been very old because he'd seen the valet replacing the leather slings that comprised the back and seat. It was cunningly made and folded into a compact, carry-ready package, the arms of the chair even forming a convenient handle. His valet—a man who possessed a breadth of knowledge almost as impressive as Smith's—said the chair was the sort used by coffer-makers. Gideon hadn't even known what the hell a *coffer* was.

But the chair was perfect.

A candle burned in each sconce beside the chair. Jackson had even provided a high side table equipped with a glass and a decanter. Gideon grimaced; why did that make him feel even more perverted? Why *not* enjoy a fine whiskey and be comfortable while watching another man fuck your wife?

He was a pig. A degenerate, disgusting pig.

Oh, Gideon! You say those things as if they are new discoveries—you know who you are. What you are. You've known for years.

Gideon thrust the voice away and was halfway back toward the panel door before he realized it. He stopped before he opened the panel and leaned against the rough stone wall, recalling the last time he'd been in this passageway: he'd been with Alys. Alys who'd been coming to spy on *him*.

What was sauce for the goose was sauce for the gander.

There's the ticket! Sit back, have a drink, and enjoy what will likely be a very pleasurable show.

He turned on his heel and marched back to the throne that awaited him. He poured a glass with only a slight tremor, took a deep drink, and then hoisted himself into the chair.

―❤―

Alys never really expected Silber to come.

The entire time she'd bathed, prepared her body, and dressed in the clothing her husband had selected for another man, she'd believed she'd be spending the evening alone.

"I don't understand, my lady?" Thursby said for at least the fifth time. "Why are you eating up here, alone? Did something happen? Did he do something untoward to you?" Her small, mean eyes creased with avid vindication. "I told you—"

"No, Thursby. Everything is fine. I just wanted to rest."

Thursby's lips thinned to nothingness. "It's not decent the way he kept you in his room all day. It's unseemly. A husband shouldn't—"

"You may go, Thursby," Alys said sharply. "I shan't need you again tonight."

Her maid's face puckered with hurt, but the truth was Alys only had so much strength left inside her. If Thursby kept poking and prodding she was likely to throw herself in the older woman's arms and sob everything out. And Thursby's bosom would be as kind and caring as a granite carving.

Thursby shook her head grimly. "Very well, my lady. Good night."

The door closed behind her and Alys dropped onto the chaise across from the fire. She'd poured a second glass of wine and it sat untouched on the side table. For a while she'd thought about becoming intoxicated—that would be one way to get through this evening.

But that was weak and pathetic.

Besides, this was her life now, she might as well learn to enjoy it. Gideon was right—she'd yearned for Silber physically for years. It didn't matter that her yearning had been nothing but a vague, romantic fantasy she'd considered on lonely nights. It didn't matter that she'd

233

only been able to think of Gideon almost since the first day he'd come to Foxrun. None of that mattered. She needed to do this to show him—because she could *feel* him watching—that he was no more important to her than she was to him. Let the marriage of convenience begin.

She laid back on the chaise, arranging her peignoir around her body. Alys hadn't been sure of what she'd find in the box. Instead of something leather and sinful, this was almost virginal. Almost. It was the color of fresh cream and there were yards and yards and yards of chiffon. When she stood, she appeared primly concealed. But when she lounged as she was right now, the shear fabric flowed over her body like the cream it resembled.

The dark triangle of her sex and her hard nipples were more naked than if she'd worn nothing. Oh, Gideon had a diabolical mind. While this garment would likely appeal to any man's carnal nature, she suspected it would just about derange a decent man like Silber. Yes, Gideon was a master when it came to such things.

She glanced up at the bed, at the spot where she knew the peep was hidden. He'd seen to everything, even the placement of her furniture. And he'd made sure she knew it.

Thursby had come to her during her bath, frowning with irritation and anger. "Why is his lordship's man moving furniture with one of the footmen in your bedchamber, my lady?"

Alys had been stunned by Gideon's audacity and then stunned that she was still so naïve. *Of course*, Gideon would arrange things to suit his pleasure. This entire evening was for his pleasure.

Ah, but that is a lie, Alys. This is the fantasy you shared with him—he didn't concoct it out of thin air.

Alys grimaced at the unwanted thought. So what? A fantasy was one thing, but decency was another. What would the world be like if everyone acted on every impulse?

Maybe you should run to him and cry—beg him to change his mind.

Alys bristled at the taunting. No, she was an adult woman and she would do this.

Because you want to, anyhow.

Yes! And what of it?

In fact, she hoped he was at the peep this moment, watching her prepare for another man.

The thought sent a frisson of heat to her sex, which was already slippery, even though she'd just had a bath. Her mind hated Gideon but her body adored him. The truth was—

A sharp knock on the door made her look up. Alys couldn't help smiling, Silber had decided not to timidly scratch like a house servant would. Well, she would not behave timidly, either.

"Come in."

Alys hadn't allowed herself to think far enough into this evening to wonder what he would look like in her bedchamber. After all, she'd not really believed he would come.

"Good evening, my lady." It was Silber, but it wasn't Silber. He was even larger in the civilized confines of her room. He was dressed the same as always: wool trousers, heavy-soled boots, a brown coat, plain gray waistcoat, and a handkerchief rather than a necktie around his thick neck. His prodigeous hands held his brown tweed cap. But his face was not the same, not even close.

"Good evening, Silber." Alys was proud of her steady tone. She shifted her legs and lowered her slippered feet to the floor, unreasonably gratified by the slight widening of his eyes and quickening in his breathing as she came around the settee toward him, not stopping until she stood in front of him. Their gazes locked. His eyes were the thing about him that was most different. They were not laughing and kind; they were hard, almost opaque. But as she stood this close to him, she saw flickers of emotion: confusion, hurt, and, yes, lust.

She took his hat from his hands, but his fingers clenched around it, the action seeming to jolt him out of his trance. "My lady, I—"

"Did his lordship threaten you to be here?" she asked softly.

His lips parted.

"Tell me the truth, please," she said before he could speak.

His lips—which she'd only ever seen smiling before—tightened for a moment, and then relaxed as he inhaled deeply, the action expanding his enormous chest before he sighed. "Of course he didn't, my lady." Heat warmed his darkening eyes. "You must know—" he broke off,

235

displaying nervousness for the first time when he turned his hat in his hands.

"I know this must be confusing and distressing to you," she told him, feeling no small amount of both those emotions herself. When he didn't demur, she continued, her voice shaking, "You may leave right now, Silber. You mustn't think—"

He took her fisted hand in his, the action so shockingly forward it froze her words. His gaze dropped to their hands and Alys's eyes followed.

What she saw was Silber's hand, familiar, huge, strong, kind. Her hand was completely engulfed by it.

"I'm not a cowardly man," he said, his head still bowed, his thumb lightly stroking her wrist. "But I'm finding it very difficult to look at you while I say this."

Alys swallowed hard but did not speak.

"I want you."

Her entire body tightened at the raw desire in his voice.

"I wanted you long before I saw you—and his lordship—out by the fence." She heard him swallow. "And after that—" he inhaled deeply and held it again. "Anyhow, I'd never seen or even imagined such a thing in my life. I'll probably go to hell for sayin' this," He looked up, his eyes dark, his kind face hard with suppressed passion, his heavy jaw taut. "But I wanted to be in his lordship's boots so bloody badly—" He gave a low, frustrated groan. "I want you so much it hurts, my lady. You are—" his eyes flickered over her face and body, his breath quickening. He swallowed and shook his head. "You're a dream—but I—well, I don't understand what *this*—" he gestured with a jerk of his chin to the room—the house—around them, "means. The same way I didn't understand why his lordship had me out in the exact field where he'd be doin'—well, where you'd be. Do *you* understand?" he asked, his voice pleading.

Alys gave him a tremulous smile and laid her other hand over his. "It is my fault, I'm afraid."

His brow furrowed.

"I said—well, I mentioned to his lordship that I'd thought about you." The last three words were the ghost of whisper.

His jaw flexed and his nostrils flared, his massive chest rising and falling fast. The effect she had on him made her feel ... powerful.

"I'd like to think we have been—*are still*—friends?" she asked, when he appeared to have gone mute.

He jerked a nod.

"His lordship is giving us tonight—only tonight."

She saw hope, lust, and fear war in his eyes, as if he were struggling with a concept that insisted on eluding him. Alys knew the feeling.

God only knew what he would say if she told him that his master was watching them.

She shivered at the thought. "I'll say this again, Silber: you don't have to stay if you would rather not. You'll not be punished for turning around and—"

He threw his hat to the side and his huge hands slid around her waist, jerking her hard against his immense body.

Alys stared up at his face, her heart pounding in her ears. His mask of pleasant subservience had slipped and beneath it was a man—a very aroused man.

"Do I feel like I want to leave?" he demanded harshly, holding her against a long, thick ridge that sent ripples of anticipation through her wanton body. His arm tightened and her spine curved, her head tilted at an uncomfortable angle to look up at him. "Do you *want* me to go, my lady? Because I'm rapidly passing the point when I'll be willing to leave."

Alys lifted her arm—the one not pinioned by his—and deliberately slid it around his hard, muscular neck, her fingers brushing the surprising softness of his gray-flecked hair.

He shivered at her touch. "I've thought about you—the way you were: bare, spread, bound—" He swallowed convulsively. "That image has haunted my waking and sleeping hours." His big body shuttered. "I never thought I was the sort of man—" he broke off and shook his head, clearly unable to continue.

Their eyes locked as she moved the arm that was trapped between them, sliding her hand around him, not stopping until her fingers rested on his buttock. He sucked in a harsh breath, his expanding chest crushing her.

237

Feeling this mammoth man quiver beneath her hands was one of the most erotic sensations she'd ever experienced. He was huge—he could crush her with one fist—and yet he quaked for *her*.

She gave him a smile that exposed every wicked thought and want she was feeling. "Did you like seeing your master use his whip on your mistress?" She lowered her voice to barely a whisper. "Did you imagine it was your hand that held the crop."

He gave a broken groan, his eyelids fluttering closed. "God have mercy," he muttered beneath his breath. He opened his eyes. "Please."

Alys thrilled at the need in the single word, she grabbed a rock-hard buttock with one hand and pulled on his neck with the other, drawing him close. "Kiss me."

Chapter Twenty-Three

Gideon's eyes were dry and sore but still he couldn't close them. Because every time he did, he saw the same thing: *them*.

He turned his head and stared at the clock: it was four in the morning. He didn't know whether the stable master was still with Alys, or not.

He told himself he didn't care, but the lie was pitifully unconvincing.

A dull, rusty blade had been twisting and digging in his chest for hours. When it first happened—right about the time when Alys peeled off James Silber's trousers, dropped to her knees in front of him, and commenced to pleasure his horse-sized cock—Gideon had believed he might be suffering a heart attack.

The pain had become intense enough to force tears from his eyes. But not so intense that he'd been able to tear his eye away from the peephole.

No, he'd watched every moment of Alys throating the other man. For his part, Silber had gazed down in wonder at his mistress as she'd taken every inch, her clever hands massaging his balls—just the way Gideon had taught her to do.

His touch on her head hadn't been violent and greedy—like Gideon's when he lost control and fucked her mouth—but reverent and gentle. He'd not even come inside her. No, that would have been too easy and quick.

Instead, Gideon had needed to watch as the two had fucked like ferrets over the course of the next few hours. For all he knew, they might still be at it.

He'd forced himself to stay and watch as the massive man had lifted his wife and then lowered her on his equally massive cock, impaling her slowly while he stood holding her. The strength he'd exhibited had been breathtaking. He'd held her with arms the size of bloody tree trunks, the muscles of his powerful thighs and arse flexing as he'd driven into her, holding her at the perfect angle to drive her to orgasm over and over and over.

He'd made himself watch as they collapsed against each other, curled up on the thick rug in front of the fireplace like a pair of ebullient puppies. He'd endured watching his wife laugh with the big man and feed him tidbits with her fingers.

He'd even managed to stay when Silber had rolled Alys onto her back, the two gazing into each other's eyes as Alys had deliberately allowed her knees to fall open, spreading for his eager mouth.

Gideon had pulled away from the peep at that point, not interested in the view of Silber's arse in the air, his heavy, pendulous sac and jutting cock hanging between his widespread knees as he feasted on Gideon's wife.

He'd realized then—after suffering chest pains for the better part of two hours—that he probably wasn't dying.

Although, to own the truth, death was preferable to what he was feeling: jealousy.

The snide voice in his head roared with amusement at that. *What drama! You should be on the stage, Gideon.*

Gideon ignored it.

At least he thought it must be jealousy. He'd ruled out every other unpleasant feeling and ended up with jealousy: an emotion that had never before desecrated his mind.

He'd never realized how wrong the wording was—he didn't *feel* jealous; he was *consumed* by it.

It was Gideon's worst fucking nightmare, perhaps even worse than losing all his money or never again being able to get an erection.

Not that his jealousy had killed his erection. No, unfortunately, his cock had experienced none of the jealousy and all the pleasure.

Which is why he'd only been able to stay away from the peep for no more than a minute before his prick had answered the clarion call of what was going on just a few feet away.

What he'd seen had caused explosions in his head that were likely to leave permanent damage. It wasn't something Gideon hadn't seen or done himself, dozens if not hundreds of times. It was just that Alys was doing this specifically for him.

Or perhaps *at* him would have been a better word.

She must have already orgasmed under Silber's mouth because the big man had picked her up again. He was holding her as if she weighed no more than a doll. Gideon was no weakling, but Silber was one of the strongest men he'd ever seen. His body was not the model of male perfection that Gideon's was. No, he was far too thick, his muscles huge, heavy slabs. But what he lacked in beauty he made up for in sheer power.

His big hands dwarfed Alys's bottom, and he held her easily while he lowered his mouth over hers and plundered her. The two kissed like lovers; Alys's arms were twined around Silber's bull neck, her hips gently bucking against Silber's washboard-hard midriff.

Gideon knew exactly what Silber was feeling—her hot, slippery sex rubbing against the thin, sensitive skin of his belly; he knew because she'd done the same with him.

His cock wept and throbbed, his balls so bloody tight he worried he might damage himself if he didn't get relief. But he couldn't; he wouldn't. His cock might force him to watch, but it could not force him to pleasure himself.

Instead he'd stared mutely, his stomach a violent, poisonous stew of jealousy, lust, yearning, and—yes, it was true—hatred. For *her.*

You forced it on her. She didn't want it, you knew that, the enemy that dwelled in his brain accused, no hint of irony that *it* had been the one encouraging him to do this.

That knowledge hadn't made it any better. If anything, it made it worse. *All this*—the agonizingly erotic scene he was being forced to witness—was *his* fault. This was turning out to be one of the worst nights in his life.

Beyond the peep, it was as if they'd heard him. Or at least as if Alys had. Because they broke off kissing and grinding and the next thing he knew, Silber gently set Alys down and then led her to the seat that faced the peep—the closest one, the chair Gideon had most specifically instructed Jackson to arrange. They held hands for a moment and then Silber lowered himself into the chair, his huge body filling it.

Alys turned her back to him and the stable master placed his monstrous hands around her slender waist and lifted her over his spread thighs. Alys opened her shapely legs and reached for his rod, her eyes not moving from the peephole as she guided the fat crown toward

241

her entrance—an opening Gideon knew to be exquisitely tight—and then took him into her body, inch by goddamned inch, her white teeth biting her lower lip and eyelids fluttering. She wore a rapturous expression as her body absorbed Silber's ridiculous organ, until she was stuffed full, her body utterly impaled.

Gideon's hand was nowhere near his cock when he came, splattering onto his waistcoat. His eyes flickered closed as his hips spasmed, powerful contractions wracking his body.

He wanted to crawl into his bed and forget every damned moment of the last few hours. But he didn't deserve escape, so he forced his eyes open and lashed himself with the bitterly erotic sight before him.

Alys sat still and full in Silber's lap, her hips shifting slightly to accommodate his size as she sighed and laid back against his chest, which was easily the breadth of a rugby pitch.

Gideon couldn't stop staring where their bodies were joined: her delicate pink lips stretched obscenely taut around his organ. Her face was a mask of ecstasy as she reclined, spread and speared by him—like a butterfly pinned by a punishing skewer. One of his hands caressed her shuddering breasts, big fingers teasing her nipples, while the other reached down to lazily rub her clitoris.

Gideon wiped a strand of drool from his chin, despising himself, but unable to look away.

Beyond the peep, Alys shuddered in the powerful arms of her lover, the orgasms Gideon had taught her to want—to need—washing over her again and again.

Silber's thick shaft pumped into her, impaling her with deep, slow thrusts as he fingered her to climax

She was beautiful—utterly gorgeous.

And you *threw her away, Gideon. Because that's what you've done; she'll hate you after what you've done.*

He'd physically pushed away then, not caring when the chair felt back, its wooden frame clattering loudly against the stone floor.

He had no memory of the journey back to his chambers, only of finding himself inside the door, his chest aching, as if he were being crushed.

That was how Jackson had found him, undressing him without speaking, not commenting on the fact his trousers were unbuttoned and his waistcoat ruined. His valet's face was as impassive as ever when he sponged the sweat and spunk from Gideon's body with a hot cloth and then put him in bed, tucking him in like a child of three rather than a man of thirty-eight.

He'd laid in the same position for hours, exhausted but unable to sleep, waiting for his wife to come to him, but knowing she would not.

Gideon had been behaving like a willful child since the moment he'd met her: selfish and impulsive and cruel. Not just with Alys, but for years—ever since his grandfather had found him at the orphanage and taken him home, ending the nightmare his bastard of a brother had plunged them both into.

But, no. He couldn't think about that now—not that there was ever a good time to remember those months of Hell.

Why dwell on the past when you've created a brand new Hell, here and now?

The enormity of the past weeks came crashing down with a violence that took his breath away. Alys was his wife—his *pregnant* wife. Right now his baby was growing inside her and he'd given her to another man, like an unwanted plaything. All because—No, he couldn't think about that.

All because what, Gideon? Come now, why did you do this? Because you are a frightened little boy?

Gideon thrust the blankets aside and pushed himself out of bed, stumbling when he forgot to use the ladder, righting himself without stopping his headlong charge toward the door that separated their chambers.

Some part of his mind wondered if it might be locked, but when he twisted the handle, it opened. He paused on the threshold, staring into the dimness, his breathing thunderous as his eyes landed on the big four-poster bed, desperately searching for recognizable shapes in the lumps of bedding.

"Alys?" he asked in a raw voice, bracing himself for her answer, or, worse, two voices. But nothing came.

He strode into the room, his skin prickling in the cooling morning air, making him recall he was naked. So what? This was his house and she was his bloody wife. He grabbed a fistful of bedding and yanked. There were only pillows and blankets. His relief was short-lived. Where the hell was she?

She's left you. Just like you wanted her to. Just like everyone does.

Gideon grabbed the drapes and yanked so hard the sound of tearing velvet filled the silence. Gray morning light illuminated the room, and he searched her dressing and bathing rooms: nothing.

He staggered back to the window and flung open the casements, gasping for air. What could have happened? Had she really—

A flicker of movement in the crepuscular dawn caught his attention. Two figures on horseback were thundering across the parkland toward the vale. They moved so closely with their mounts they might have been two creatures instead of four.

Even from this distance Gideon recognized his wife's small form. As for Silber, Gideon had never seen the man run his mount at such a breakneck gallop, but he knew the two would be perfectly matched for such a vigorous morning ride.

Yet another ride they can share.

He gritted his teeth and watched until they were tiny specks, the light just coming up over the horizon, his jaw becoming tighter and tighter, until they disappeared entirely.

Chapter Twenty-Four

"W here the *fuck* have you been?"

She yelped and jumped, pressing her palm flat over her wildly thrashing heart. "Gideon! You scared me half to death," she gasped, standing frozen in the doorway. "What are you doing in my room?"

He was sitting in the big leather armchair in her bedchamber, the same one she'd enjoyed so vigorously just last night. Her lips quirked at the thought. *How did you enjoy the performance, Gideon? Not so much, judging by your wild, furious eyes.*

His hands lay flat on the arms and he was regarding her with a tight, mocking smile. His eyes were moving over her body with an intensity that was unnerving, his gaze lingering on the front of her leather breeches before rising to her face. "Answer my question."

Alys's heart pounded at his tone, which was frightening in its utter lack of emotion. She flicked her top boots with her whip, aiming for a careless gesture and failing. "I've been out."

"Dressed like that?"

She shrugged. "As you see."

His jaw flexed as he stared at her, his gaze causing heat to spread through her body.

He took out his watch, the action deliberate. "It is five o'clock in the afternoon."

"Is it? How time flies when one is enjoying oneself." She dropped her crop onto the settee and began to pull off her long, gauntleted riding gloves. "You needn't worry, I'll be ready for dinner." Her gloves joined the crop and then she removed her top hat, shaking out her hair.

He stared, transfixed, as she caught up the heavy mass and gave it a quick twist before tossing it over her shoulder.

For some reason, he gave a mirthless chuckle. "That's not the point, my dear."

She placed her hand on her hip. "Oh? What *is* the point, Gideon?"

He was out of the chair and across the room in a flash. His hands closed over her shoulders and he drove her back against the wall.

Alys cried out at the impact, which was more surprising than painful.

"You will answer my question, Alys, or you will regret it." He spoke the words through an unpleasant smile.

Alys twitched her shoulders to shake away his hands, but they tightened hard enough to hurt. When she winced, Gideon just repeated. "Where were you?"

"I was with Silber."

His pupils shrank to specks and his fingers dug in harder. "Your gift was for last night, my dear. My employee was not intended to become a permanent fixture in your life."

"What do you care?"

His nostrils flared. "I think you've spent too much time with your *stable master* and have forgotten who your *real* master is."

"Trust me, Gideon, there is no danger of forgetting that."

"That's good, or I should have to remind you." He reached out to tuck a strand of hair behind her ear and Alys flinched away. He dropped his hand and frowned. "I'm starting to believe I gave you a gift you are not equipped to handle."

"I believe my equipment functioned quite well, thank you—both last night and this morning—several times, in fact."

His lips parted and his hand twitched; Alys thought he might strike her.

He gave a bitter laugh. "Very droll, darling. I meant mentally."

They stood locked in each other's gazes for what felt like forever, and then his mouth curved into the insufferable smile she hated. "You're quite correct about the performance you put on, my dear. And I must tell you I enjoyed it—every moment of it."

Alys's sex pulsed with hatred and arousal at the heat in his eyes; he was reliving last night as he stared at her, his desire for her pouring off his body in waves.

Good. She hoped he relived it until he went blind, because he would *never* get to experience any of it himself.

246

"Look at you—my little hellcat—bristling with anger and rebellion." He stroked her jaw with light fingers, not drawing back at her flinch this time. "I like your spirit, darling, it shall make breaking you to bridle all the more enjoyable." He chuckled, but the sound held no humor. "There is no point in trying to hide how wet I make you—just my touch—I can *smell* the arousal on you."

"I am aroused, but are you sure it is for you?"

He winced, as if she'd slapped him.

"I'm tired," she said, looking pointedly toward the clock. "I'd like to rest before dinner. Will you excuse me?"

His eyes were the deep, chilling blue of an iceberg. "Of course, my dear. I want you rested up for tonight. In fact, I shall have dinner and a bath sent to you again and will come to you afterward. I want you to wear the black lace for me tonight."

"I'm exhausted; I think I'll have an early night."

His fingers closed on her chin and turned her forcibly toward him. "The correct—indeed the *only*—response from you should be *yes, Gideon*. This should be your answer no matter *what* my request, but most especially when it pertains to our marriage bed and your presence in it."

Her palm itched to slap his face. Instead, she smiled sweetly and said, "*Yes, Gideon*."

He blinked and Alys could see her sudden compliance threw him off balance. She made a mental note of that.

His gaze flickered over her, as it to assure himself it really was his wife answering so obediently, and then he nodded. "Well," he said, releasing her and taking a step back. "That's very good, then." He appeared so lost for a moment that Alys's heart went out to him.

But then she recalled he wanted nothing to do with her heart.

"Will you arrange for my bath and dinner, Gideon?" she asked, careful to keep her tone neutral and respectful.

He nodded, still nonplussed. "Of course, my dear."

"Thank you," she said, moving toward her dressing room, where she pretended to busy herself with her coat until she heard the click of the door. She poked her head outside the room to make sure he'd really gone and then sagged against the wall.

Alys knew she should not defy him. Indeed, she was more than a little stunned at how much she'd already flouted his authority. She'd believed all defiance had been bred out of her as a girl—this sudden willfulness of character was surprising. And not a little gratifying.

But ultimately stupid and dangerous.

Her smile drained away.

Yes, defying him would be a mistake—she could see that by the half-mad glint in his eyes. She'd need to control herself and show him only a pleased and contented façade.

She'd given her future a great deal of thought after leaving Silber earlier in the day. Resisting Gideon only told him she cared.

The best way to get at him was to capitulate without any struggle. She would not resist him but neither would she welcome him—in *any* way. He'd discarded his right to her love and affection. Now he could live with the results of his actions.

Not that she believed the loss of her affection would hurt him. It wasn't as if he was angry that she'd made repeated love to another man or spent a very enjoyable day in his company. No, he was only peeved that she'd not come to him afterward, as he'd commanded her to do, to tell him all about it. He hadn't liked being disobeyed or excluded, that was all.

She snorted and pushed off the wall, unbuttoning the mannish riding coat he'd chosen for her—which she loved. She was sorely tempted to simply snatch up her gloves and hat and return to the stables. But that was unfair to Silber, especially after she'd already made it clear they could go no further.

Alys had waited until this afternoon, after they'd ridden all the way to a village several miles away, where she was not known. She'd spent a blissful hour enjoying a pint of cider and kidney pie with him in a quaint inn, pretending they were husband and wife out for an afternoon holiday. But the look in his eyes—one of mute yearning—had brought her to her senses. Her chance for happiness was gone, but it didn't have to be that way for him.

"Thank you," she said, not needing to explain. "I will never forget any of this."

"Nor will I." His instant and quiet acceptance of what her words meant had been almost as painful as her husband's utter disregard. But

248

as much as she'd enjoyed her brief fantasy with the kind, intelligent, and generous man, it had only served to demonstrate the vast gulf between mere sexual gratification and love. For good or for ill, she was in love with another man—an undeserving idiot, it turned out, but love was love.

Silber had been a wonderful lover and her body had rejoiced at his gentle mastery. But when the pleasure had ebbed away, it had left her hollow and hopeless. All the more so because the one man who could fill her heart did not care to.

"Do you want to seek a position elsewhere?" she'd asked, worried by his grim silence.

He'd inhaled deeply and then slowly exhaled, shaking his head. "I don't know where I'd go." He cut her one of his smiles—the sort he used to bestow so naturally but no longer came easily. "I'll not lie to you, it'll hurt to see you and not be able to touch you."

His words had given her a lump in her throat the size of a fist.

"But I knew what I was doing," he said, more to himself. "You're another man's wife—" He snorted softly and shook his head, his expression one of profound incomprehension. "I'll never understand your husband, my lady. *Never*," he repeated with frightening vehemence. He visibly restrained his anger, forcing a smile. "But I can't say that I'm not grateful for what he's gifted me. As much pain as I expect to experience, I would not have done things differently."

His admission just made her feel worse; this good man had become a pawn between her and Gideon, and he didn't deserve having his life toyed with so carelessly. But it was too late for regret on that score.

"You know you'll have all the help I can give if you want to leave. I would miss you, of course, but—"

He nodded, not needing her to complete the thought.

Alys sighed at the memory of his sadness and cast her coat onto the back of a chair and then sat down to wrestle with the brand new, snug fitting top boots. She'd just managed to remove the first one and was sitting back to catch her breath when the door opened.

"My lady!" Thursby stared at her as if she'd not seen her for a year rather than only yesterday evening. "Where *were* you today? Why did you leave this morning without ringing for me? What have you—"

"Help me with my boot, Thursby."

S.M. LaViolette

Her maid's jaw dropped, but whatever she saw on Alys's face made her swallow her mortification and turn and straddle her leg to help.

"His lordship sent for me and told me you would be dining in your room again." Her tone proclaimed clearly what she thought of that. She yanked off the boot and dropped it with a *thunk*. "I don't understand why—"

"Thursby."

Alys met the other woman's eyes. "That will be the last time you question me. About anything." Thursby's eyes immediately glassed over and Alys felt like an ogre. But her life would be difficult enough fighting her husband without having to fight Thursby every inch of the way. If the woman was agitated *now*, Alys couldn't imagine what she'd be like when Alys began her campaign against Gideon: the one that would drive him away from her forever. "Is that understood?" she asked the older woman.

Thursby swallowed and nodded, "Yes, of course my lady. I understand."

Alys smiled and stood. "Good. I value your service," she lied. "But I won't hesitate to discharge you if you insist on challenging me."

A tear trickled down Thursby's wrinkled face and it took a herculean effort to ignore it. Instead, Alys reminded herself of all the years her maid had spied and tattled on her to Sebastian. "Now, go see to my bath," she said gently.

"Very good, my lady."

She watched Thursby leave, her shoulders slumped: Alys knew exactly how she felt.

— ❤ —

Gideon was in no hurry to return to his wife's bedroom. He tried to tell himself it was not actual *fear* he was feeling, but a disinclination to bicker.

But that was a fucking lie.

"Christ!" he muttered, staring into his port, which—by the way—he despised but felt compelled to drink for some stupid reason. He pushed the untouched glass away and stood. He'd dismissed the servants after they'd cleared away the dishes. Already they were all staring at him as if he were a monster to be eating down here while his wife ate above,

250

alone. And how many of them knew about her bloody antics with Silber?

Just thinking the man's name caused a burning in his gut, as if he'd eaten a flaming coal.

He'd been a fool, but he had a solution for *that* problem and had already composed a letter to Silber and had a servant deliver it to the stables. His hung-like-a-mule stable master would not be an issue come sunset tomorrow.

Gideon smiled to himself, experiencing a sense of relief for the first time since he'd conceived of the stupid plan.

With Silber gone, he and Alys could go back to the way they'd been. There might come a day when he decided they needed other people to spice up their bed sport, but right now was not that time.

He had everything Alys needed and more.

He was grinning by the time he reached their floor, his hand going to his necktie and loosening it as he knocked briefly and then entered her room. And then froze.

Alys glanced up, saw him, and then smiled. The *foot*man who was kneeling at her feet—*touching* her feet—did not look nearly so pleased to see him.

Indeed, Andrew—one of the two men he'd hired on Smith's recommendation—leapt to his feet.

"What is going on here?" Gideon asked his wife through clenched teeth.

She gave him an exaggerated look of surprised innocence, but he saw the war-like glint in her eyes. "Going on? Why nothing. Andrew was just rubbing my feet, Gideon." She smiled charmingly from Gideon to the red-faced, miserable-looking footman.

Gideon exerted an iron-grip over his emotions to suppress the fury that threatened to lift the top off his head. "Thank you, Andrew, you may go."

The young footman set speed-records getting out of the room. Gideon, who'd stopped midway removing his tie, completed the job, tossing it onto the settee and taking the chair where she'd had such an enjoyable time with Silber last night.

"You are making a mistake, my dear," he told her, crossing one leg over the other in a pose of relaxation.

Her brow wrinkled and she tossed her thick froth of dark auburn curls over her shoulder in a manner that made him want to lick her entire body—no matter how angry he was with her.

"I'm confused, Gideon? I thought we were free to engage in whatever relations we chose. I cannot become pregnant with another's child, so why are you angry?"

"Angry?" he repeated, forcing out a chuckle that sounded . . . well, *forced*. "This is not angry, love—this is a trifle annoyed."

"But . . . why?"

He chewed the inside of his mouth as he stared at her.

Apologize, Gideon.

He flinched away from the idea as if it had sunk fangs into him.

He bloody well would *not* apologize.

No, he would not abase himself for her amusement—no matter how much he might deserve abasement for his foolish behavior yesterday.

What he *needed* to do was lay down the law—and quickly. "I cannot have you forcing your attentions on the servants and—"

"*Forcing myself?*" she screeched.

"Thanks to you, Andrew will have to find another position."

She jumped to her feet. "That is not *fair!*"

"Life isn't fair. Every servant you, er, *dally with* will get discharged."

She was breathing more violently than a horse at Ascot.

"I've decided our prior agreement will no longer suit me, Alys."

"What do you mean?" she asked shrilly.

"I don't know how to make it any clearer: I've changed my mind."

"But—but—you can't *do* that."

He gave her a slow, evil smile. "Oh, but I can."

"*Changed your mind how?*"

"Clearly you are not able to handle the freedom I granted you—at least not with proper discretion. Therefore, your privileges are revoked as of this moment."

"Privileges."

It wasn't really a question, but he decided to take the opportunity to clarify. "Yes, privileges. From now on, you will enjoy my bed—my embraces—and no other's." He knew it was wrong to enjoy her thunderous expression so much, but he did.

"And what about you?"

He opened his eyes wide and laid a hand on his chest. "Me?"

"Yes, *you*. Am I the only woman whose embraces and bed you will enjoy?"

He opened his mouth to say that hers was the only bed he *wanted* to enjoy, but some devil seized his tongue. "Darling, I'm a *man*. The same rules never apply." The obnoxious sentiment surprised even *him*. Where the *Hell* had that come from?

She leapt to her feet. "You *bastard!*"

Gideon stood. "I'm sorry you feel that way, but this is the way it will have to be." He paused and then added, "At least until I decide otherwise."

Her eyes narrowed and her nostrils flared; she resembled a fierce little animal. Perhaps some kind of cat or a—a— Well, he didn't know *what* kind of animal, but he suspected she would have quite a nasty bite or sting if he came near enough.

"So, let me make sure I *understand*. You can *fuck* anyone you want—"

It amused Gideon to see how she colored after uttering the vulgarity.

"But I can have *you* or nobody at all?"

He paused, as if considering her words, and then nodded. "Yes, that sums it up quite succinctly."

She crossed her arms and sneered. "Fine. Then I take nothing."

A startled sound—half snort, half laugh—broke out of him. But he was *not* feeling in the least bit amused.

Did your tender feelings get hurt, Gideon?

Not. Bloody. Likely.

He smirked at his wife in a way that visibly annoyed her. "Don't bite off your pretty little nose to spite your face, darling. We both know how much you enjoy *fucking*."

"Yes, that's true. So, it must tell you something that I am willing to forgo such pleasure if my only choice is *you*."

Gideon closed the gap between them in two strides, grabbed her shoulders, and crushed her mouth with his.

After her initial startled reaction, she went slack. So slack that he was surprised she was able to stand. He stabbed about in her mouth, stroking her tongue, sucking it, and she tolerated it. That was all she did: tolerate it. He released her and stepped back, so confused and furious and—and—well, he didn't know what the hell he felt!

"You don't want to play this game with me," he said in a low, threatening voice.

She lifted her eyebrows and gave him a look of cool loathing.

Gideon recoiled, another memory flashing through his mind's eye and slamming into him with the force of a fist.

He'd been eleven and the man giving him the disparaging look had appeared so wealthy to Gideon's young mind that he'd seemed like a king in his castle. A king with very frightening eyes and intrusive hands.

"Don't mind him, my lord," Lloyd—his bastard of a brother—had said with a nervous laugh. "He'll be good with a bit of persuasion."

Gideon swallowed the bile that rose in his throat at the memory of said *persuasion*. He wrenched his mind away from the ancient past and back to the *aristocrat* who was currently looking at him as if he were a steaming pile of manure: his *wife*.

He knew he should be accustomed to such disdainful looks by now, because no matter how rich or handsome he was—no matter how much he *resembled* a lord—he would always be an upstart tailor's grandson to these people. A drunken gambler's get. The brother of a procurer and pimp and murderer.

He took a step back, viciously pleased when her expression of distaste was joined by unease. She *should* be uneasy at her little declaration of hostilities.

"Very well," he said. "I'll not lay so much as a finger on you—I've never stooped to bedding unwilling bed partners."

"I sense a *but* in that statement," she said, her words inadvertently making him smile.

"Ah, you are such a clever girl, I'm sure you'll figure it all out with no help from me. I'm leaving for London in the morning."

Some emotion spasmed across her face, but he honestly couldn't tell if it was relief or disappointment it was gone so fast. What did it matter? She'd drawn battle lines and he would not stop until he had her full and utter surrender.

"When will you return?"

"I will return when I receive a letter from you begging me to come back to your bed."

A disbelieving laugh slipped from her mouth. "You are mad if you think I will *ever* write such a letter."

He shrugged. "We shall see."

"I shall be quite happy here without you, my lord."

"I can see you're already imagining how you will entertain yourself." He gave her a mock chiding look. "I'm going to help you, my dear."

"Help me do what?"

"Help you obey me. Here is what I will do to help: first, I will discharge your maid."

She sputtered. "What—why?"

He gave her his most annoying smile, the one that Chatham always said made him want to shoot Gideon. "I think we both know the answer to that, the woman is incompetent and needs to be pensioned off."

"But why *now?*"

For the first time Gideon heard fear in her voice and his stomach churned: *he* was the source of her fear; the realization left him feeling decidedly ill. He was not a bully by nature, at least he hadn't thought he was.

Then you are a fine actor, Gideon.

He opened his mouth to tell her this was foolish—to apologize for being a fool about Silber. That he would forgive her for what she'd just said to him. "Alys—"

"Never mind," she said, her face hard and cold. "I don't care. I'll be glad to get rid of her if it means you'll leave, too."

He shut his mouth with a snap, any feelings of conciliation crumbling. *Thank God,* he'd not actually begun to beg her.

Her eyes were like gray diamonds. "Now, is that all, my lord? You've taken my maid, perhaps you wish to take all my clothing so that I am confined to this room. Or perhaps you wish to chain me to the wall, naked, just to be sure I don't leave my cell."

Gideon sneered. "Don't give me ideas, darling."

"I hate you."

The words rocked him to his core because he saw the truth in her eyes.

255

'I don't care," he lied. "You may behave as dramatically as you wish. You're not confined to this room or to the house. You may go about your normal business—riding, visiting my tenants, continuing to work on *my* house using *my* money," he added pettishly. "The only thing that will change is that you will have an attendant at all times to ensure you don't proposition any of my employees."

She scowled. "You just said you were sending Thursby away. What are—"

"Jackson will attend you while I am away," he said surprising himself with the words, but careful not to show it.

Her jaw dropped. "*Jackson?*"

Gideon gave her another of his hateful smiles. "Yes, my dear, Jackson."

She gave a laugh tinged with hysteria. "And is Jackson to be my *maid?*"

"He'll do whatever I tell him to do."

"You would let your valet dress and undress your wife? You would let him *bathe* me?" She laughed again, but this time the sound was ugly. "He's not Silber, but I daresay he would do."

Gideon's jaw became so tight he swore he felt teeth cracking. It was all he could do not to grab her, put her over his knee, and give her the discipline he already knew she loved and craved.

But she doesn't want that from you anymore, does she, Gideon?

His mouth tightened at the thought. "You may employ all your wiles, my dear. Jackson will not have any difficulty resisting the likes of you. In fact, I'm willing to wager on his ability to ignore your lures."

She stared at him with loathing. "You are an *odious beast.*"

"I'm sorry you feel that way. In any event, you are lucky to get him. He is an excellent servant and will likely make you a far better maid than Thursby ever did. If it is any consolation to you, I would have fired her eventually as I don't want a sot around my child."

"Why are you doing this?" she asked, obviously forgetting she'd said she didn't care only a few moments earlier.

"You need to learn self-control, my dear." Gideon was astounded he could get that hypocritical statement out of his without suddenly catching fire. "Especially since you will soon be a mother. I would hate for reckless behavior like that you exhibited with Silber to jeopardize my unborn child."

Her hand was a blur, her blow hard enough to knock him back a step.

Gideon's fingers automatically went to his jaw and he moved it from side to side.

"How dare you?" she raged. "How *dare* you even intimate such a thing. This child is mine, as well. The fact you could think I would ever jeopardize my own child—or *any* child, for that matter—tells me you are singularly unsuited to be a father. Not surprising considering your appalling background."

Gideon grabbed her before he knew what he'd done.

She glared up at him, her eyes pulsing with hatred. Some part of his brain pointed out he was hurting her by gripping her so hard. But he didn't give a damn.

"It is prudent to keep in mind my low origins but unwise to throw them in my face, *my lady*. My sole interest in you at this point resides in the fact you are carrying *my* child. Don't push me too far."

She wrenched out of his grip. "I'm not some powerless, impoverished whore like the sort you usually consort with, my lord. My brother will give me shelter and oppose your vicious behavior. We shall see how your precious money protects you from the power of a *real* peer—one who can gather other powerful men to his cause."

"What an excellent idea, my dear. When you appear on his doorstep, you might ask him where the law falls when it comes to a man and his child—unborn, or not."

This time Gideon caught her hand before it made contact with his face.

"Once was more than enough. The next time, I'll hit you back."

She gasped, fear, disgust, and horror flickering across her face.

But she could not be more disgusted or horrified with him than he was, himself.

Tell her you don't mean it, some new, but faint, voice of reason begged. *Tell her you don't mean one word of what you've said. Tell her you want her, you care for her, and will cherish her if she will only give you another chance.*

Tell her you love her.

He flinched away from the thought; she'd throw his love back in his face the way she'd just done his body.

"I'll say goodbye to you *now*, my lord." She gave him a rigid curtsey and then turned toward her bathing chamber. "Send Jackson in, I'll want him to get me ready for bed." She slammed the door so hard Gideon felt it in the soles of his feet.

He   closed   his   eyes.   What   had   he   done?

Chapter Twenty-Five

Alys woke with a smile on her face, as she always did; she loved mornings.

But then reality descended on her like a huge boot, crushing all the joy and optimism and leaving her flat with despair.

She laid in her bed rather than get up. After all, why bother?

Alys grimaced at the defeatist thought. Why bother? Because she had a baby growing inside her. She smoothed a hand over her flat belly, wondering if there was more of a curve there than usual. Wondering when she would begin to show. She decided to go look in the mirror, one of her favorite pastimes of late. Perhaps today she would be able to see a difference.

She smiled at the thought and shoved back the blankets, lowering her feet to the floor.

And then dropping to her knees.

Moments later she'd emptied most of the contents of her stomach when a basin appeared before her.

Alys snatched it out of the masculine hands but said nothing. Even if she'd not seen his highly polished black shoes and the bottom of trousers that had been pressed with knife sharp creases, she would have known who it was. After all, nobody else in the house was allowed to attend her.

Gideon, it seemed, believed she was liable to mount any man—well, except Jackson—at the drop of a hat so he'd ensured that would never happen. If he couldn't have her, nobody would.

Jackson's feet disappeared and reappeared a moment later, perfectly timed to take away the fouled basin. Alys began to push herself to her feet when his strong, warm hands closed over her upper arms. She tried to slap him away, but he was implacable. He lifted her gently for all her squirming, his hands releasing her immediately when she was on her feet.

Alys glared up at him and then clutched a handful of her nightgown and wiped her mouth on it. If she'd hoped to elicit a reaction from him—*any reaction! Any!*—she was destined to be disappointed.

His hands went to the buttons of her soiled ni-ghtgown and he began to open them. Alys considered slapping him again, but it really made no difference; the man simply was not human.

He was her inhuman shadow. He was never rude or insolent or curious or anything. Well, that wasn't entirely true, Alys amused herself by making him hard, although even that activity was beginning to pall. So what if he had an erection that soaked the front of his proper black trousers? The man was as likely to act on his arousal as he was to run all the way to London on his hands.

And over the course of the past ten days she'd certainly *tried* to get him to act on it.

She stood like a child under his ministrations, cudgeling her brain for some reason to look forward to this day. She already knew that he'd come and dress her and take her out for fresh air and exercise—just like a pampered pet—if she tried to lay in bed. He would not hesitate to physically carry her, either—a fact she knew from mortifying personal experience.

He lifted the gown over her head, as usual not noticing by so much of a flicker of an eyelid that she was naked. He held out a robe and she slipped into it without making a fuss.

There was a light knock on the door and one of the footmen entered.

When she'd woken up that morning—the first day after Gideon sent everyone she knew or cared about away, including himself—she'd wondered how he could possibly believe Jackson could be her body servant without scandalizing every servant into quitting.

But she'd forgotten about the servants Gideon had brought down from London. These were the people chosen by his friend, Mr. Smith, who apparently behaved in such a way that he demanded complete discretion from all his employees.

After seven days of watching them—along with another three servants Gideon sent down after he'd returned to London—she'd come to believe they must have been trained in a whorehouse. *Nothing* phased them.

She sat on the settee and gestured for the servant to lay the tray down on the table in front of her.

She lifted the silver domes and couldn't help smiling. Yes, she was a prisoner, but no prisoner had ever been fed so well.

"Will that be all, my lady?"

She looked up at the handsome young man—the one she'd gotten to rub her feet that night, and whom Gideon hadn't discharged, after all. But he must have received a dressing down from somebody, because he now looked right through her, they all did.

"Yes, you may go."

She poured herself a cup of tea because Jackson wouldn't allow her to have coffee since Mrs. Tickle—who still haunted the house even though both she and her husband had been pensioned off—had told him it was not good for a woman who was breeding.

Indeed, Mrs. Tickle had a lot to answer for: no riding—it might damage the baby; be in bed by ten—the baby needed a lot of rest; eat plenty of eggs and milk and meat and fresh fruit—the baby needed a healthy diet. And on and on.

In Jackson, the older woman had found a remarkably receptive ear. Alys knew he wasn't solicitous of her because of *her,* but because those were Gideon's instructions. She was positive that if Gideon told Jackson to leap in front of a speeding train the valet would only hesitate long enough to thank him.

Alys put the annoying man from her mind and opened the newspaper. Even though Gideon was no longer here, the papers had continued to come. Alys was ridiculously grateful for this tenuous link to the outside world.

Oh, it wasn't as if she was a prisoner here, she could go to the village whenever she pleased, or even to Bristol—which she'd already done twice, and in great comfort since Gideon had sent back his private railcar for her use. She could go anywhere she wanted—and even places she didn't want to go.

Indeed, Jackson dragged her on far more excursions than she would have gone on if left to her own devices. Truth be told, other than her fury at Gideon and his high-handed beastliness, she quite enjoyed Jackson's company and having a companion to fetch, carry, and generally serve her every need as she paid her daily calls on the ever-increasing tenantry. He did all that and more, and without ever scolding or complaining, as Thursby had been prone to do.

While Gideon had essentially left her under house arrest, he'd not taken away any of her decision-making abilities when it came to Foxrun or its people—even when it came to finding occupants for the new cottages. Alys adored being able to manage the estate without interference.

If the people who lived in the area thought it odd that the mistress was constantly attended by a man who'd once been his lordship's valet, well, they chalked it up to the follies of the rich and powerful.

Alys knew Gideon's people were just grateful that his *follies* didn't include gaming dens and horses. The amount of money he was pouring into the property was lending him a godlike status. She shuddered to think about how it would go to his already big head.

Not that he'd be returning any time soon.

Not that she *wanted* him to return. Really, she'd be far happier with Jackson for the rest of her life, even if he was proving frustratingly immune to her sexual lures.

She smirked at the thought of all the teasing she did while munching on toast loaded with marmalade, a luxury she could not get enough of.

Alys poured another cup of tea and returned to the paper. There was nothing of any interest in the front section, which was usually the only part she cared to read, so she kept turning pages, loathe to get up and start the day.

She was midway through the society pages and rapidly losing interest when she saw it.

"N_____ W_____, who has just taken the lead role in a production at the C_____ Theater was seen on the arm of naughty industrialist G_____ B_____, the new and <u>newly married</u> E_____ of T_____. The two were spotted leaving the C_____ Restaurant in the early morning hours and last seen entering T_____ H_____ on Berkeley Square. It looks like one honeymoon is over, but another has just begun for the handsome E_____ of T_____ !"

Alys's head was so hot that her vision was red. She stared unseeingly at the paper, crushing it in her fists.

"My lady?" Jackson asked.

Alys barely heard him. Gideon was a—a—a—good God, she didn't know what a man like that was called—some sort of cur that was always out sniffing for a bitch. How *dare* he not only high-handedly change their arrangement, but then *flaunt* his liaison with some theater tart? Hadn't he been the one who—

A large warm hand landed on her shoulder and gave her a slight squeeze. "Are you ill, my lady?"

Alys wrenched her eyes away from the paper and looked up into Jackson's unreadable dark brown eyes.

She wordlessly handed him the wrinkled pages and slumped back against the settee, her eyes leaking tears without her permission.

Jackson held the paper at some distance to read it, the silver at his temples not the only sign of his age. He'd removed his coat and rolled back his sleeves, exposing powerful, broad hands and forearms with attractive ropes of muscle, dusted liberally with dark brown hair.

He found what she'd read and quickly scanned it, his face giving nothing away. He folded up the paper and put it aside. "Your bath is ready."

She closed her eyes and gave free rein to her tears, her sobs wracking her body. Jackson said nothing, but he pulled the sash on her robe, pushed it from her shoulders and scooped her naked body up like a child, his hands gentle but firm as he cradled her.

Alys buried her face in the serviceable black waistcoat that covered his hard chest. "I hate him so much," she said in a watery voice.

As ever, he remained silent, his biceps flexing beneath her head as he lowered her into the steamy tub.

She sniffed, suddenly exhausted by every single part of her wretched life. Gideon had left and it had taken him less than two weeks to find a woman and flaunt her to the world.

Jackson returned with a cloth and cake of soap and knelt beside the tub. Before he did, she saw the telltale evidence of his arousal, the tenting of his black wool trousers, his ridge long and thick. The imperturbable man had quite a respectable organ.

His hardness had the predictable effect on her body and she gave a watery chuckle.

This entire situation was something Gideon had arranged for his own perverse pleasure. She could imagine him, sitting in London— probably naked with a woman kneeling between his thighs, servicing him—and thinking about Alys here, being waited on by a virile man who took care of all her needs except one.

It would make him hard to think about her frustration—about her failed efforts to subvert his loyal servant. Yes, and he'd know how this twisted and sick arrangement would keep *her* in a state of semi-arousal.

How could she think that way? She was a perverted wanton who deserved all the punishment he dished out.

Alys glanced up at Jackson, who'd dipped the cloth in the water, soaped it, and was now proceeding to clean her. He began at her foot, and he was thorough, cleaning her between every toe. No part of her body was below his attention. Unfortunately, he would clean her swollen slit with as much interest as he did her neck or elbow. That didn't mean Alys was impervious to his ministrations. Quite the contrary; he drove her half-mad, and Alys was desperate to return the favor.

She slid her hand to the apex of her thighs, her eyes not leaving Jackson's face as he worked his way up her calf.

Alys's bud—her *clitoris*—was hard, slick, and at its most sensitive. It would take only a few flicks to bring herself to pleasure, but she didn't want it to be over so fast. Why hurry?

Instead, she shifted her hips and stroked down further, circling the entrance to her body, gently probing herself.

She'd not had a man inside her since that night with Silber.

Silber, who'd disappeared without a word the same day Gideon had left.

Alys had asked Jackson and every other servant about Silber's whereabouts, but nobody knew what had happened to the man.

Jackson had not stopped her from climbing the stairs to Silber's rooms that day: the day the only two lovers she'd ever had both disappeared.

She'd never been inside his home—not even during their one day together.

The furniture remained because it hadn't belonged to Silber, but there were no personal effects. Even so, the rooms smelled of him: of sweat and leather and horses and man.

Jackson had waited outside, allowing her privacy to cry. Something about his thoughtfulness had softened her attitude toward him. He was a servant, paid to do a job. He didn't hurt her or treat her cruelly. He wasn't even immoral with her, no matter how hard she'd tried to break his reserve.

No, he was not the villain. The real villain was her husband. It was all Gideon's fault.

Before Gideon had entered her life, she'd not believed the sexual act anything but an inconvenience. But now? It was all she could seem to think of. Perhaps it was being pregnant, although she was not even two months along. Indeed, she wasn't even showing signs of the child inside her. If the doctor Gideon insisted on sending out once every damned week hadn't told her it was true, she'd not believe she was pregnant.

But she was, and the mere thought of it had turned her into an insatiable wanton. She pleasured herself two or three times a day.

Alys moved her finger in lazy strokes, shoving away the voice in her head that howled at such disgusting behavior.

For the first time, her actions were having a visible effect on him; sweat was forming on his brow and a vein had begun to pound in his temple. Which is when she realized his jaw was clenched: he was struggling against his arousal.

She smiled, that slight sign of his silent suffering was all she needed to send a bolt of pleasure straight to her core. She didn't bother to hide either her swiftly stroking finger or her moan of pleasure.

Jackson's hands froze on her shoulder for only a second and she heard him swallow before he placidly continued his routine.

Alys didn't care what he did now. She'd already gotten what she needed from him: a reaction, no matter how tiny—a sign that he wanted her—even if he would never act on it.

Who knew why she cared? Maybe because it proved she was still a woman, even if Gideon had put her aside and was now making love to other, more beautiful and fascinating, women.

Not that Alys cared about that.

Nor did she care about how pitiful she was to be masturbating in front of a servant. No, it was simply enough that a virile, attractive man wanted her. She squeezed her eyes shut, imagined it was Jackson's finger between her thighs, and threw back her head, shaking and shuddering as she rode out a powerful climax.

265

Afterwards, she floated on a haze of pleasure, only vaguely aware of Jackson's hands as he passed the cloth between her thighs, cleaning her sensitive folds just as matter-of-factly as he cleaned the rest of her.

But later, when she was alone in her bed, she would think about him. He'd used a cloth to clean her, but there had been a moment, an instant, when she'd felt the lightest brush of the naked pad of his finger. It had been so fleeting that she wondered if she'd imagined it.

━ ♥ ━

Gideon received a letter from Jackson every day. The man wrote a lot like he talked, so the missives were brief and to the point: not exactly poetic but riveting all the same.

And then there was the letter he'd received today.

"My Lord Taunton:

Today my lady rose at the usual hour and took breakfast in her room. She ate two pieces of toast with marmalade, two coddled eggs, a sizeable slice of ham, an apple, and two cups of tea.

My lady became rather agitated by a reference to your lordship in the paper. She wept and expressed anger."

Gideon felt a little bad about that part. But the next sentence—infuriatingly terse—erased all other thoughts.

"During her bath she masturbated with her fingers to a successful conclusion."

"Bloody hell," Gideon groaned, his cock heavy and hard between his thighs—and this was the *fifth* time he'd read the letter in less than an hour.

The bedding beside him shifted. "My lord? Did you say something?"

"Go back to sleep," he ordered, stroking his prick as he imagined the sight of Alys masturbating in the presence of his staid valet.

"Christ," he muttered. Why did that make him so hard? What the hell was wrong with him?

He grinned. Who cared? He was truly hard for the first time in days—weeks! For the first time since he'd left the bitter little cat in her bedroom—after she'd rejected him.

He'd be jerking himself dry to this letter for days—weeks.

He returned to the brief message, not pausing his stroking.

"After her bath her ladyship expressed an interest in taking a walk. As the threat of rain was negligible, we set out not long after ten a.m.

Now that she is forbidden to ride, she's become a great walker."

Was Gideon a bad man to enjoy depriving her of that pleasure—a pleasure that likely made her think of her *lover*, his ex-stable master? Yes, he *was* a bad man. But he already knew that.

"She wished to visit, again, the cottage that had once been used by the old earl as a hunting box of sorts.

As you ordered, I had the box provisioned with her ladyship's favorite food."

Gideon squirmed at that sentence.

Look at you, his inner companion said with a laugh, *"still trying to buy your way into her affections.*

Fuck off, he told the voice—something he should tell it more often.

So, what if he wanted to make the little shack comfortable for her? Besides, it was all for the good of the child.

"The chaise longue you ordered for the cottage had been delivered so she was able to take a nap that lasted several hours.

When she woke, I gave her a second tea and we set off home sometime after three o'clock.

Her ladyship was tired upon reaching Foxrun but ate a bowl of soup, two slices of buttered bread, a leg of chicken, and a plum tart. She was asleep by nine o'clock.

Tomorrow she has expressed a wish to visit Mr. Hendrickson, the older gentleman who lives alone in one of his lordship's recently repaired cottages. She has said she will bring him apple jelly.

Respectfully,

E. E. Jackson"

Gideon lowered the letter, staring at it without seeing it. Instead, he was seeing her—not spread and stroking herself in the bath—although he'd certainly visualized that enough—but tramping through the woods—*his* woods. With his valet. And then having tea. With his valet.

And whose fault is that, Gideon?

Gideon was barely able to contain his fury—at *her*. If not for her bloody stubbornness, he could be there now, fucking her night and morn and tramping around with her distributing goddamned jars of jelly to *his* tenants.

Instead he was here, lying in bed with a woman whose name he didn't know and whose face he couldn't recall although he'd seen it a scant hour earlier.

"Dammit!" he snarled, wadding up the letter and hurling it across the room.

A head popped out of the dressing room. "Did you need something, my lord?"

Gideon frowned at Bedoes, the footman he'd been using as a valet since having the brilliantly stupid idea to leave Jackson with Alys, so that Jackson could effectively live out Gideon's bloody life.

"No," he snapped, but then changed his mind. "Yes. Fetch that piece of paper and bring it to me." He pointed at the crumpled letter.

Bedoes complied. "Anything else, sir?"

"See to it that coffee and toast and marmalade are delivered in a half hour." He glanced at the lump under the bedding, which he suspected was fully awake and aware. "Make that three-quarters of an hour." He might as well get some use from whomever it was before paying and sending her off. "And have a carriage waiting down below in an hour."

"Very good, my lord."

"Oh, and Bedoes?"

"Yes, my lord?"

"Once you've done that, I want you to tell Smithers to cancel the delivery of all newspapers to Foxrun. Effective immediately. Tell him to get his arse down to each place personally to ensure it gets done *today*."

"Very good, sir."

Gideon smirked. There. If Alys thought reading about his affairs was miserable, just wait until all she could do was *imagine* them.

He snorted. Well, hopefully her fertile imagination gave him a better time than what he'd really been experiencing these past ten, miserable days, which was too few bloody orgasms and those usually with his own fist.

The actress—yet another person whose name he simply could not recall even though it had been only a few days ago—had been a stunner. Not only that, but she'd been desperate to impress him, hoping to land herself a handsome townhouse all staffed with servants.

Ever since he'd turned off his mistresses every high-flyer in the city had set her sights on him.

Gideon might be arrogant, but he wasn't a complete idiot. He knew the only reason women like the haughty auburn-haired actress—her hair color was the merest coincidence—would behave like back-alley whores in his bed was because they knew his history of engaging and dismissing mistresses more often than most men changed their drawers.

They all believed—hoped—he was in the market for a new crop of mistresses, and Gideon did nothing to correct that assumption. Indeed, he'd had some of the most acrobatic and adventurious sex partners of his life this past week.

None of them could know that he'd never hire another mistress again; he was done with long-term liaisons with *any* woman.

Gideon opened the crumpled letter and smoothed it over his thighs, running his hands over it until it was as flat as it would get. He re-read the first part of the letter—*yet again*—and experienced the same results.

How was it that Jackson's few dry words could make him harder than the woman who was currently crawling her way toward him under the bedcovers?

Gideon tossed the letter onto his dressing table, closed his eyes, and laid back, his hand working his semi-hard shaft while his mind constructed the image he craved—the only way he could bring himself to climax since he'd met that *blasted* woman—his *wife*.

He imagined Alys in that bathtub, poor Jackson watching her while he was erect, his hard cock weeping and wanting. Gideon already knew what he'd write back to the man, and it made him smile. It also made him as hard as a bloody pike.

Hot breath and cool hands caressed his thighs, spreading him wider. "My lord? May I—"

"Yes, suck me. And no talking," he ordered, pumping furiously, as if that might keep the image he'd created from its dangerous wavering.

A slick mouth took him deep, the physical sensation exquisite.

For some reason, physical pleasure was no longer enough. He needed more. He needed Alys, floating in the water, her hand between her sweet thighs, her fingers stroking her pink, slippery slit and—

But phantom Alys's hand shimmered, broke, and dissipated like the curling smoke from the end of a cigar.

And then she was gone and Gideon knew there was no chance of getting her back.

—❤—

Alys knew that Gideon was responsible for the sudden curtailment of the papers. He would find it amusing to deprive her of all news of the outside world—of *him*—knowing it would drive her mad, and also make her wet, wondering what he was doing. And whom he was doing it with.

The end of the newspapers also confirmed what she already knew—that Jackson wrote to provide his master with information about her. What she'd *not* known before was just how minute and intimate those pieces of information were. So, Gideon knew she'd cried. Did Jackson disclose her masturbation? She was certain of it.

And why did thinking about the staid man writing that down in a letter—to her husband—make her inner muscles contract so hard that she'd had to slip a finger between her thighs to calm down her willful body?

Because there is something wrong with your head, the hectoring voice said.

Alys couldn't argue.

She'd learned that Jackson slept in the dressing room in Gideon's room. At first Alys thought that he'd only begun that practice when his master left for London. But on his fifth day she'd mentioned the arrangement and he'd confessed that he'd always slept in there.

"You were there on our wedding night," she said, not a question.

He'd bowed his head, no flush or twitch or change of expression to indicate he felt any shame. What a bastard Gideon was, fucking her with this man only feet away.

Why does that make your sex pulse so insistently?

Alys snorted at her stupid thought. "I want to see it," she told Jackson.

"Of course, my lady."

He'd opened the door and stood quietly to the side while Alys inspected the corner of the dressing room that he'd claimed for his own.

"You live like a dog." The words were cruel—as she'd meant them to be—but Jackson showed no response.

There was a small cot. Beside it a miniature night table with a traveling clock and one book.

"Great Expectations," he'd said before she had to ask. The fact that he liked Dickens made him more human. Slightly.

"My last husband's valet did not sleep in his dressing room," she observed as she left the dressing room, stopping in front of him.

"It is not the usual practice," he admitted in his toneless voice.

"How long have you been with his lordship?"

"Fifteen years."

That surprised her. Gideon was not a cruel master—at least not to his servants—but his mercurial behavior tended to drive many away, at least the staid ones. But Alys didn't think Jackson was just a servant. She had no idea what he was, really, but not just a servant.

Knowing that they shared a wall somehow made his presence feel more . . . intimate.

Four days after reading about Gideon's new lover in the paper she heard an unusual sound next door. It was late—almost midnight—and she'd been lying in the dark for hours, trying to sleep.

Jackson was draconian about her sleep—another thing she could thank Mrs. Tickle for—and came in every evening to put her to bed like a child. She'd tried rebelling and the result was just embarrassing. So now she allowed him to bring her a glass of milk, stoke her fire, and then snuff the candles.

Alys quite liked the quiet, private time. She would lie quietly and let her imagination run free. Predictably, her imagination—and her hand—ended up in the same place every night: between her thighs.

She'd been about to go there—for the second time that night—when she heard a sound from next door. She rose quietly, grimacing when the slats of her bed squeaked; would he hear that? She froze, waiting for the door to open. But it remained closed. She took up her dressing gown and tiptoed out of her room, thankful for the recent maintenance on all the doors since it left them soundless. It wasn't until she came to the panel that she realized she'd not brought a candle.

She hesitated. But she didn't want to go back. If she went back, common sense would kick in and she'd just climb into bed. She'd be fine; she been in the passageway often enough to feel her way.

Her fingers found the catch and opened the door. It was utterly dark inside and, for just an instant, she quailed.

"Don't be such a weakling," she whispered, stepping over the bottom section of wood panel and quietly closing the door behind her. She stood for moment, the sensation of such complete darkness making her feel almost weightless. She reached for the wall and used it to guide her way, shuffling slowly when she rounded the corner, careful not to kick over the stool.

Even before she put her eye to the peep she saw the faint light—he was in there—in the room, not the dressing room.

She climbed carefully onto the stool and pressed her eye to the small hole.

Alys gasped; her heart pounding in her ears, her body responding in now- familiar ways.

Jackson was in there, and he was not alone.

He was naked, and Lord but he stripped to advantage—but then she'd suspected he would, having been carried by him. He was not as big as Silber but he was broader and stouter than Gideon. Like the other two men he was muscular and hard and fit.

He was not on Gideon's bed, but on the rug in front of the fire, which cast a dull red glow over his body that made his skin look as if he'd been forged in the flames.

His profile was to her and he was on top of a female body, pumping into her with slow, powerful thrusts. He looked like Satan—or at least the way Alys imagined the devil would look if he mounted a mortal and took human pleasure: red, hard, and bestial.

Jackson was holding the woman's arms stretched taut over her head, her wrists clasped in one big hand. He was kissing her throat, her jaw, her face while every muscle in his formidable body bunched and stretched and flexed.

The woman arched her back off the floor in silent ecstasy, pushing small pert breasts up against his hard body. His thrusts became savage and she could see the woman's mouth was open, her profile one of pain or pleasure or both.

Alys squinted harder, her body shaking with want. Who *was* the woman? She looked like—

Jackson turned his head and stared straight at the peep and Alys gasped, wobbling badly on the stool, but clinging to the rough wall like a bat, unwilling or unable to look away.

That's when Alys knew that it was *her* Jackson was fucking—not this nameless, faceless woman. It was Alys he was pumping with such brutal, driving thrusts. He was taking her with all the violence she deserved for teasing him over and over and over, for making him hard and aching, with no hope of release.

His hips began to buck, his control visibly slipping as he drove into her with primitive force, the muscles of his torso, back and shoulders gloriously defined as he held her arms immobile. His jaw clenched in a grimace as he pounded into her so hard Alys swore she could feel it inside her own wet, swollen body.

He thrust deep and then froze, the powerful muscles of his buttocks clenching as he jerked into her. Alys knew what it would feel like—hot jets of his spend filling her, the contractions of his shaft throbbing against her sensitive sheath.

She shoved her hand between her thighs and grunted as her finger finished what Jackson had started. As she came, biting her lip hard to suppress her cries, Jackson's eyes opened, as if he *knew*. And then he did something she'd not believed possible: he smiled.

Chapter Twenty-Six

Rather than get easier with time, Gideon only wanted Alys more. And rather than soften toward her, his anger had intensified and become colder: Alys was a willful, stubborn little cat and he would bend her to his will and have her on her knees begging him if it was the last thing he did.

Unfortunately, it seemed that it might very well be the *last* thing he did, at this rate. It was five bloody weeks since he'd left and there'd been no change. Well, that wasn't quite true, there had been one: she'd stopped masturbating, at least in front of his servant.

At first that had made him both smug and hard—after all, he'd been the one who'd given her that one night of voyeuristic pleasure—a night he'd let her experience just so he could then deprive her of it.

If there was one thing in life he knew besides mathematics, it was sex. Pleasuring oneself in front of another is only satisfying to a certain point—especially if that somebody is less responsive than a marble statute.

But that night had both rewarded her behavior and given her hope. And then he'd taken it away.

He wanted her to know who controlled her life, even from hundreds of miles away. The punishment was twice as bad now that she knew what sexual satisfaction Gideon *could* give her—*even from afar*—if he so desired.

Yes, it was that simple. He wanted her to accept that she was *his*, completely and entirely. The sooner she realized it and apologized for her willful disobedience and cruel words the sooner they could go back to their lives the way they'd been before.

Well, almost the same life, although Gideon now knew he intensely disliked even having to *think* of Alys with other men—at least not if he wasn't there and actively involved.

He wasn't even sure if that was still acceptable. No, if she wanted a proper rogering, she could get it from *him*. There would be no taking of lovers—well, not for *her*. *That* scenario was now off the table, permanently.

Truth be told, he'd done bloody little tomcatting himself, now that he knew she wouldn't be reading about it with her morning tea. What was the point? It took so much effort and the sex had certainly ceased to be pleasurable.

It was easier to charm and make small talk with his fist, which was also better at bringing him off than the most skilled courtesan these days.

Gideon was just grateful that Alys would never know how miserable he was without her. Imagining her ever getting such an upper hand left him in a cold sweat.

Quit worrying; she'll never find out. How would she?

He smiled. Indeed, how would she? She'd see the logic of his demand. Eventually.

At first, Gideon had enjoyed himself immensely with each letter he'd received from Jackson recounting Alys's hopeful trips to the peephole. He'd reveled in Jackson's description of her dejection when she returned to her room, having found nothing. He'd been certain that robbing her of that pleasure would quickly bring her to heel.

But it hadn't.

Gideon had begun to feel like an arse as Jackson had described her increasing reserve and how she'd gone less and less to the peephole, until this past week, she'd not even gone once.

And then there was the letter he'd received this morning, the one describing how Jackson had found her yesterday.

It scared Gideon to admit how much the letter had shaken him. At first, he'd not known what to think—well, other than to feel gut-churningly jealous that Jackson got to spend even a second with the woman who consumed a good deal of Gideon's hours, both waking and sleeping.

Finally, after pacing half the day and getting nothing done, Gideon had folded up the disturbing letter and put it away. What he needed was something to take his mind off this nerve-wracking scenario, and he knew just the thing to do that.

━ ♥ ━

"Gideon Banks! You're an idiot and you are ruining both your and Alys's lives."

The words hit him like a spray of bullets and he turned to the source.

It was Nora Fanshaw—and she was yelling. He wouldn't have believed she was *capable* of yelling.

Edward and Nora had just been coming into the Birch Palace and Gideon was on his way out, and not alone.

Gideon forced his most charming smile on his face, as if he'd not heard what Nora had just said. "What a delightful surprise! Hello Nora, Edward."

Edward shook his head, his expression resigned. Nora, on the other hand, cast scathing looks at the very expensive pair of women on his arms.

"Oh, yes," Gideon said, as if only now recalling the voluptuous beauties cinched into identically scandalous black leather garments. "Let me introduce you to, er—" he bit his lip and looked down at one of the nearly identical beauties.

"We know each other," Nora snapped. "Myra, Ethel." She jerked a nod at the two women.

Gideon often forgot that Nora had once worked in a brothel in London.

He glanced down at the women on his arm. "Wait—I thought you said your names were—" Damn! He couldn't remember which one she was.

"Patience," the woman supplied.

"Grace," her sister added in a bored voice that told Gideon people must forget their names all the time.

"They aren't really sisters, Gideon," Nora told him with a look of disgust.

"I *know* that, Nora," Gideon lied, inwardly seething at having been duped by the duplicitous madam. He'd deal with her, later. But right now, there was Nora. He narrowed his eyes at her; why was she determined to ruin his harmless fantasy? His pleasure?

He forced himself to smirk at her. "I'd love to stay here and bicker with you, Nora," he lied, again, taking a step toward the foyer door.

276

"But *Patience*, *Grace*, and I were just leaving." He jerked a nod at Fanshawe.

Edward just kept shaking his head, his expression one of profound disappointment. But his wife never took her eyes off Gideon.

"What are you doing here?" she demanded.

Gideon recoiled at her harsh tone. "The same thing as you, I would imagine."

She scowled.

Gideon cut Edward a questioning look. But instead of calling his wife to heel, Edward just shrugged.

"You," she pointed at the two women in the rudest way. "Stay here." She turned to Gideon and said just as rudely. "*You* come with me."

Gideon was so aghast at her high-handed order—as if *she'd* been the one to pay for the not-real-twins—that he hardly noticed when she grabbed his hand and proceeded to drag him to the nearby cloak room, shove him inside, and shut the door.

Gideon's cock—always the optimist—began to harden. Maybe she wasn't going to rake him down after all but enact one of her erotic fantasies on his person—as she'd done on their only occasion at the Briar Palace—a night he relieved embarrassingly often. "I say, Nora, it's bloody nice to see you, too. But shouldn't we invite Edward in here wi—"

"Shut. Up." She actually *snarled* at him. Gideon took a step back.

"What are you *doing* here?" She'd stared at him in a way that shouldn't have been so menacing considering she must weigh all of six stone.

"What do you mean? I'm doing the same thing as you two." He'd laughed, but she hadn't laughed with him.

"Edward tells me you've been in town since only a few days after your wedding. Without Alys."

He was suddenly grateful that Nora had dragged him aside before she'd begun ripping up at him.

"I'm here on business—*earl* business, while the session is in."

"He says you don't even go back for visits."

Gideon squinted at his fingernails, hard to do in the dim light of the closet.

"What did you do, Gideon?"

His head jerked up at that. "Now why would you jump to the conclusion that it was me, Nora?"

She cut him a withering look.

"Fine," he said, holding up his hands, deliberating just how much to tell her.

"Gideon?" He heard her toe tapping.

"Give me a bloody minute to gather my thoughts!" He'd tell her just enough so that she'd not think him some sort of cruel, ogre husband. "I thought we'd agreed on the sort of marriage that both of us could enjoy."

"What kind of agreement?"

"Don't be obtuse, Nora. You know how I am. I told her I could never be faithful—or settle down. I wanted her to understand I wasn't husband material—at least not in the conventional sense." His face heated under her scathing glare. "What? I just wanted something like what you and Edward have."

"You're an even bigger idiot than I thought if you believe that is what we have, Gideon."

He bristled. "Well, you're here, aren't you?"

"Yes, we are. *Together.*"

Gideon opened his mouth, and then shut it. She had a point.

"Go on," she ordered.

"This wasn't a surprise to her, Nora. We'd discussed it thoroughly before our wedding. And then, the day after we were married—well, she lost her mind."

"*Alys* lost her mind?"

The tone she used told him all he needed to know about how much she believed that.

"Yes, she—well, she simply lost track of what we'd agreed upon."

"You mean she didn't like it when you loaded the house with whores and lost your head?"

"No, I don't mean that at all, actually." Gideon felt very much inclined to bloody well tell her just *who* it had been who'd lost *her* head. But he kept his private business to himself.

She crossed her arms. "Explain."

"What? No, I won't bloody explain!" He scowled at her. "My marriage is none of your affair."

He expected her to argue—to dress him down. Dammit, he'd *wanted* her to do it. After all, maybe she could find the end to the tangled ball of string that was now his life and somehow help unravel it.

But, instead, she merely shook her head, turned on her heel, opened the door, and left him there.

He followed her out of the closet just in time to see her striding up the stairs, Edward having to take long steps to keep up with her.

Gideon pulled his eyes away from them and looked at the two women; their faces instantly transforming from boredom to worshipful fascination. He suddenly realized that they actually looked nothing alike.

Dammit! He'd been looking forward to his first time with twins tonight and Nora had ruined it.

But he bloody well wouldn't let her.

"Come," he barked at the two women as he strode toward the foyer, the footman leaping to get the door for him.

His town carriage waited at the bottom of the steps and he vaguely registered the women's cooing as they climbed into the luxurious vehicle. It wasn't until they were both on the seat across from him that he realized they were dressed exactly like his seats: black leather on black leather.

Gideon smiled, his cock perking up at the fetching sight. And why not? He'd paid a fortune for these damned *twins*.

He unbuttoned his trousers, took out his soft prick, and pumped it until the crown glistened under the lamplight. "Let's play a game on our way home . . .."

Two hours later. . . .

Gideon was beginning to wonder if a man could die of boredom while having his cock sucked.

Patience, or perhaps Grace, had been working his rod for at least an hour. He was as hard as when he'd started, but his shaft was feeling raw. Perhaps he should just take a rest—let the poor girl whose jaws he'd been working rest as well. Perhaps he should just send them both home and go to bed.

What are you doing here, Gideon? Nora's question rang in his mind and sent a bolt of shock through his body, waking him from his stupor.

Goddammit! The woman was ruining his bloody evening. She'd planned this—guilting him into doing what she wanted.

Bollocks!

Gideon crooked a finger at his fellator's partner—her putative twin—who'd been masturbating herself for both their pleasure. "On your hands and knees, darling, it's your sister's turn for a bit of fun."

While the twin quickly complied, Gideon laid a hand on the tousled blonde head of the woman sucking his cock and detached her, he suspected to both their relief.

He smiled down at her puffy red lips. "That's enough for now, sweetheart. You get to relax for a while—yes, right there, in front of your sister. Spread your legs for her—that's a good girl." Gideon positioned himself behind the kneeling woman and took his alarmingly soft cock in his hand, irritated at having to pump himself to hardness. What the devil was the point of two expensive whores if a man had to stroke his own prick?

He looked down at the woman who was prone and was carefully moving her jaw from side to side. "Has your sister ever licked your cunt before," he asked in a purposely casual tone, the raunchy question making even him blush.

But the woman had heard it all and more in her twenty-or so years and merely smiled coyly and nodded.

"Tell me," he asked, pumping harder, but still softening, "Did you like it?"

"Yes, my lord."

Predictably, his cock jumped at the sound of *my lord.* Yes, he was pathetic. What of it? If he didn't come soon, he was going to lose his bloody mind. The entire point of this evening had been to clear the fog from his brain so he could *think.* But, instead, all he could hear was Nora Fucking Fanshawe's voice in his head.

"Put that pillow beneath your hips," he said harshly. "Yes, like that. Now spread those pretty legs wide for your sister and make your nipples hard for me."

The woman obeyed his orders, her lush body every man's dream, but one few men could afford.

Gideon reminded himself that not only could he afford *her* but he could also afford her non-sister.

As ever, the reminder of his wealth and power and status were enough to get him hard—or at least hard enough that he could finally enter the kneeling whore's body.

He slid all the way in and began fucking her faster than he normally would have done, just to maintain his erection. He locked eyes with the woman writhing on her back, being orally pleasured by a woman many men believed to be her sister.

It was the sort of taboo sexual act that he'd always reveled in, in the past. But now, he shivered, and not with pleasure. He was revolted—by everything. But most especially by himself. He was tired of pretending he was enjoying his debauchery. *Exhausted* by the effort.

And his cock was making his lack of interest evident.

Gideon stopped and closed his eyes: *enough.* Just. . . enough.

He could not bear this any longer—none of it.

What are you going to do, Gideon?

He had no earthly idea, but he could no longer do *this*.

Chapter Twenty-Seven

Alys sat on the wooden bench in her courtyard garden and stared down at the expensive, embossed envelope she held in her hands.

It was not—as she'd first hoped—a letter from Gideon. No, of course not.

It was from Nora Fanshawe.

Rather than open it, as a normal person would, she turned it around and around in her hands, thinking about what it might hold.

Yesterday had been Alys's birthday; it had also been the lowest day she could recall—certainly since the early days of her first marriage.

She'd wallowed in self-pity all day yesterday. She was over a quarter of a century old and nobody loved her.

She'd gone to bed early last night and cried herself to sleep after not a single person wished her a happy birthday. If she'd been honest with herself, rather than self-pitying, she would have recalled that nobody wished her a happy birthday because she'd not once celebrated her birthday since coming to Foxrun.

That first year, when she'd turned seventeen, Sebastian had been away on her birthday—an early sign of the way things would be. Her father had sent her a heavy, improving tome, and her brother had sent her nothing. That year had set the tone for birthdays: they were to be ignored.

This morning she woke before dawn broke, feeling lighter than she'd felt in weeks—months—even though her body certainly felt heavier.

But something had changed inside her; it was as if she'd washed away a barrier with all her crying.

She'd lain in bed this morning, staring into the gray light of dawn, and asked herself questions she should have asked months ago.

What was she doing with her life? Was this how she'd behave when her child came: morose and mooning? The thought of bringing a baby into such an atmosphere was enough to make her start crying all over again.

You love him.

She *did* love him—even after how horrid she knew he could be.

You miss him.

It was true; Alys missed him terribly.

One of you needs to take the first step. You know how to get him back.

That was also true. So, she'd gotten out of bed before Jackson came to wake her, wrapped her oldest, warmest dressing gown around her, and sat down at the secretary desk with pen and paper.

But the words wouldn't come.

The way to contentment—if not happiness—seemed to be a proverbial gordian knot.

That thought had given her pause. How had Alexander the Great solved the puzzle of the Gordian Knot? He'd cut it.

But your problem with Gideon can not be solved with a sword; not unless you stab him with one to keep him from his endless whoring.

The solution is meant to by symbolic, Alys told the mocking voice. What it meant was using the most direct approach to solve a problem.

But what *was* that method? Writing Gideon the letter, obviously. But that would be only be a temporary solution. If she wrote him, he would come—but he would wander away again.

You can't make him stay; you can't make him love you.

The thought was too much to bear so early in the day. So, she'd put down her pen, and went about her business—not in anguish, but feeling secure in the knowledge she'd know what to write when the time came—if the time came.

She worked in the garden beside her three new gardeners and Jackson, who never left her side although she'd stopped allowing him to bathe her or undress her. She still needed his help with her garments, but she'd stopped playing the games that had sustained her for so long. She didn't want Jackson, no matter how attractive she found him, and her teasing brought neither of them pleasure.

Since she'd stopped pestering him, they'd settled into a relationship like a contented, long-married couple. Or what she imagined that might be like.

They worked side-by-side until the day became too hot, and then had come inside for tea.

And found this letter waiting for her.

That had been hours ago. It was almost dusk now, and she'd decided she wanted to read it before darkness fell, while she could still draw some strength from the remaining daylight.

She ran her fingers lightly over the stark black writing. Nora Fanshawe's handwriting was like she spoke, without flourishes or pretension.

Alys sighed and opened the envelope.

Dear Alys:

I do hope you will forgive my unsolicited letter. You may recall when I visited I asked you to write, should you need a friend. You haven't written, and yet here I am—forcing my friendship upon you.

The portrait is almost finished and I am delighted with it. I haven't shown it to your husband because I don't believe he deserves it.

There, I've started already, and I'd meant to work up to the subject of Gideon slowly. But then he's not the sort of subject one approaches gradually, is he? He is the sort of man who burns twice as brightly as the rest of us, takes up more space than most people, and can suck the oxygen from the room. He is a beautiful, brilliant man who is deeply flawed.

But aren't we all?"

Alys smiled at that description of Gideon: it was certainly on point. She felt a twinge of jealousy that this woman likely knew her husband better than she ever would. But that feeling was drowned by the pure relief she experienced just knowing another human being understood the man who was not-so-slowly driving her mad.

'I've watched Gideon from afar these past months and Edward has told me more than enough about his behavior so that I know he is not happy. No, it's more than that. We are both agreed—as are Smith and Chatham—that he is profoundly miserable.

I won't mince words with you, Alys, because I sense you are the sort of woman who wouldn't want to be coddled."

"Thank you, Nora," she said, her eyes prickling with tears of gratitude.

"Gideon has tried to resume his old lifestyle. Yes, he's gone back to his old haunts, engaged prostitutes, and flaunted his amorous antics for the pleasure and profit of London's newspapermen."

This time the jealousy was stronger—more like a fist to her heart. It wasn't anything Alys didn't know, but reading it somehow made it more real and more painful.

"I suspect that information will cause you pain and I'm sorry to relate it. However, take heart; Gideon is not enjoying his amorous antics. Indeed, I would go so far as to say he is loathing them—and himself—but doesn't know what else to do.

'How can a thirty-eight year-old man be so stupid?' you ask."

Alys laughed out loud at that, almost able to hear Nora's dry voice.

"I can only assume you've heard of my past. If you haven't, you should know I spent several years working as a prostitute. I'm not ashamed of my life and it taught me more about human beings—especially men—than any sane woman should probably be forced to learn.

My relationship with Edward began in the worst of circumstances and played out for the entire country to read about. Our road to happiness was paved with the misery of several others—something I will regret as long as I live. It took us several years to find our way to each other. I'd hate to sit by and watch as you and Gideon let so much time slip away—especially when you have a child coming.

I'm not saying I have the power to fix your marriage—or Gideon. I'm saying I have advice, based on careful consideration, about the man you married.

He doesn't know how to love. No, that's not right. He's in love, or he loves you—I'm sure of it—but he doesn't know how to fit those feelings into what he knows. Love is like a piece of machinery that is too difficult for him to figure out—and that makes him scared.

I'd go so far as to say he is terrified. We don't expect our men to feel fear; they are so much bigger, stronger, and more powerful than we are in so many ways. I think they also don't expect it or have any mental faculties to manage such an emotion, which is why they behave like such idiots when they're confronted with powerful feelings like love.

He loves you, of that I'm sure. What does that mean for your future? Will he curb his self-destructive ways? I don't know—nobody can know, probably not even Gideon.

I see I've gone on long enough. What did I write to say?

Gideon loves you but does not know the way back, even though it is likely clear enough to everyone else.

If you love him, you may have to sacrifice some things—one of which might be your pride. That's rather easy for me to say because I've never had pride where Edward is concerned. Edward has always come before everything and anyone else—even my love of painting— but I know that is not the way for everyone.

Ask yourself what you need to make you happy, Alys. What do you need to make your child happy? And then make sure you get exactly that. I just thought you should have a clear picture of what matters look like from this vantage point, so that you are able to make an informed decision.

I hope you will forgive my unwanted and unforgivable intrusion. I told myself that the potential loss of your friendship was outweighed by the chance I might be able to help.

Yours, with respect,
Nora Fanshawe"

A tear fell on the page and meandered its way over the words, leaving a trail of blurred ink in its wake.

Alys folded the letter and went inside. This time, when she sat at her desk, the words flowed as easily as her tears.

━ ❤ ┝

It was still dark when a noise from the connecting door woke her. She sighed and turned onto her back, wiping the sleep from her eyes. It must be Jackson making more noise than usual in his small dressing room bower.

Alys hadn't finished the letter until just after one in the morning, but she felt oddly refreshed even after such a short sleep—and eager to face the day. She would walk her letter into town herself and post it.

She yawned hugely and glanced at the clock: it wasn't yet five, but she was wide awake. She pushed from the bed, smiling as she imagined Jackson's surprise when she rang for him before it was light.

She was slipping into her dressing gown when another noise came through the thick door—this one a loud thump: as if somebody had fallen.

Frowning, she tapped lightly on the door. When there was no answer, she pushed it open. The first thing she saw was Jackson's legs, splayed out on the floor in Gideon's room.

"Jackson!" she ran to him and dropped to her knees beside him. "Jackson?" He was fully dressed but his eyes were closed. The left side of his face rested on the floor and when she turned his head, she saw the ugly bruise and blood trickling from his temple.

She gave a muffled cry. "Jackson! What—"

"Hello again, my lady."

This time her cry was anything but muffled.

A man—the same brute who'd been here all those months ago and had taken all the silver—lay stretched out on Gideon's bed, his hands clasped behind his head.

Alys shot to her feet and began to back away. He just grinned, and when she collided with a big, hard body behind her, he began to laugh.

Chapter Twenty-Eight

"What kind of pervert reads something like this?"

Gideon's head jerked up just as Edward Fanshawe snatched away the journal Gideon had laid open before him.

"Give that back," he said, but without any real heat. He'd not been reading it, anyhow.

Edward squinted at it and read aloud, "A *Treatise on the Calculus of Finite Differences*." He cut Gideon a look of revulsion. "Good God."

Chatham stared at Gideon from his great height, his unnerving grey eyes glinting with something—humor?

"I didn't know he could read, did you, Fanshawe?" he delivered the insult employing the slow, almost ponderous voice that he used for everything he said.

Edward and Chatham had a laugh.

Smith, who'd been blocked by the two men's huge bodies, stepped around them and took the treatise from Edward and handed it back to Gideon, his expression . . . strange.

"It's Boole, isn't it?" Smith asked Gideon.

Gideon pulled his glare from the two guffawing men. "It's nice to see I'm not surrounded by unlettered savages."

That just made them laugh harder, and even Smith smiled as he lifted a hand and summoned the hovering waiter. "Bring us a bottle of our usual," he ordered, taking the seat beside Gideon.

It was their weekly meeting at Number 14. They used to hold it at eleven o'clock at night but had made it seven o'clock in deference to Edward, who was a staid married man who needed to be home for supper.

Gideon had been there since five o'clock because what the hell else did he have to do? Nothing—not since he'd suddenly taken up the lifestyle of a bloody monk two weeks ago. He shivered; he didn't even like *thinking* the horrible thought.

God forbid if the other three ever learned that he'd not been spending his nights whoring—but working, instead—the ribbing would be *endless*. As if spending every damned evening with his fist wasn't punishment, enough.

Chatham and Edward settled their satchels and persons in the big chairs that were always at the table for their over-sized bodies.

The room was a private one, only ever occupied by the four of them. The club manager thought they rented the small parlor from the owner, he didn't know that their syndicate actually owned everything, and that was the way they liked to keep it.

Chatham laid out his fussy implements, the man's accountant-brain so obsessed with order that Gideon guessed he'd probably counted and organized his pubic hairs.

"When is your last Session?" Smith asked him.

Gideon scowled. "Next week. And not too bloody soon, either." His seat in Lords, which he'd been looking forward to, had been tedious and had also served to illustrate just how big the gap was between Gideon and his fellow peers. He'd not believed his expectations—that he'd be welcomed into the club, if not with open arms, at least with some acknowledgement—had been particularly high, but the reality was that nobody even seemed to see him.

But he'd be damned if he'd let a bunch of toffee-nosed pricks keep him from attending to his duty. So, he'd gone before the Committee for Privileges on April 7th, received his seal of approval, so to speak, and had warmed the back benches over the past months.

August tenth would mark the beginning of the recess. However—unless some enterprising radical blew up Parliament—he'd have to go back and do it all over again sooner rather than later.

"Is there any chance you can introduce the—"

Gideon cut Edward off with a raised hand. "No. And don't ask me again. I'm not giving any bloody speeches. Maybe never, but certainly not this year. If you want to get your tariff issue taken care of, bribe a few of them—I can make you a list." There was no shortage of impoverished peers and more by the month.

Edward took his rude interruption with grace, which only made Gideon nervous: Edward always got what he wanted. He never gave in so easily. Well, it wasn't like he could force Gideon to give a bloody speech.

The meeting went quickly—*too* quickly in Gideon's opinion—and they were finished well before midnight.

Gideon picked up the three things he'd brought with him—mathematical treatises—and stood. "I'll see you all next week," he said as he gestured for the waiter to summon his carriage.

"What's this?"

Gideon stopped at the door and turned at the unusual sound of Chatham's voice—the man never spoke unless he had something cutting to say, or when somebody lit a fire beneath him.

"What?" Gideon demanded, in no mood for smart-arsery.

"Not going out tomcatting? No ambitious plans for the evening?" He raised his eyebrows in a way Gideon had never seen before. Since when did Chatham have a sense of humor? No matter how rudimentary.

"No, I'm going home—unless you're offering your mouth or arse up for my pleasure?"

All three men laughed and Chatham stood and smacked him on the back with a hand the size of a shovel. "That's more like our lad," he said in an exaggerated Yorkshire accent. "I was worried you might have taken ill."

"No, just tired."

"Want to stay for some cards?" This time it was Fanshawe.

Gideon looked from face to face to face. "What's going on?"

"Nothing nefarious," Smith said, his dark eyes unreadable. "We just noticed you weren't your usual self lately."

Gideon grunted.

"Perhaps losing all your money at cards might cheer you up?" Edward offered.

Gideon smiled, amused in spite of himself: the worst card player in the room was Edward Fanshawe.

"Thank you," he said. "Perhaps some other time."

He was just climbing into his carriage when Smith called out behind him. "Can you drop me at my house?"

Gideon cocked his head and smiled. "What? Did you lose all four of your carriages suddenly?"

"I wish to speak to you," Smith said, climbing into the open coach before him.

Gideon sighed. He knew what this was—they would have drawn straws over who got to talk to him, ignored the results, and then sent Smith, because Smith was the only one of their small group with any social skills.

Edward was too gruff and likely to start beating somebody to get their consent.

Chatham was too . . . well, too Chatham.

And Gideon had the sense of a toddler when it came to anything other than math, fucking, or machinery.

The carriage pulled away so smoothly it was hard to know they'd started moving.

"So, Gideon."

Gideon smiled. "So, Smith. Or should I call you Cornelius?"

Smith gave him the obligatory smile. "Let's talk about what you're going to do after the Session."

Gideon groaned.

"You need to go home."

Gideon bristled. "Oh, is that what I need to do, Father?"

"If you're going to behave like a child . . ." Smith threatened mildly.

"You don't know the first damned thing about it."

"Sure I do. You gifted your wife your stable master as a wedding present and then got all shirty when she had the audacity to enjoy her present."

Gideon gaped.

"I don't know why you look surprised, young lad, you know I know everything."

Gideon gritted his teeth and then took a deep breath and let it out slowly. No use getting into a further twist; Smith was right, he *did* know everything. Likely because he had people on the payroll in all of his business partner's houses. It didn't bear worrying about. As to the young lad comment, well, the man was pushing fifty, so he was due the respect seniority deserved.

He met Smith's unreadable dark eyes. "She doesn't want me in her bed."

Smith's brows rose.

"It's true. So I left. I told her that when she wanted to apologize for what she said she could send me a letter and ask for me back."

Smith, predictably, laughed.

"I'm glad I'm giving you entertainment as well as a free ride," he said sourly.

"I'm only laughing because I can't imagine saying anything *worse* to a woman. Has she written you?"

"Not a bloody word."

"Have you written her?"

Gideon recoiled. "Of course I haven't."

"What does the winner get?"

"The winner of *what*?"

"The bull-headed contest—is it a money? Or a medal of some sort?"

Gideon ground his teeth.

"You know this is foolish, Gideon." It wasn't a question. "You need to put aside your anger and hurt—"

"I am *not* hurt!"

"Fine, put aside your anger and annoyance, and go back to her. Talk about this. The last time I saw you two together you seemed happy. Surely that was not my imagination?"

Gideon scratched his head vigorously, as if it could stimulate thought. "I was beginning to think *I* had imagined it," he admitted gloomily.

"What do you want from her, Gideon? Why would you encourage such a woman as her to have sex with another man the day after you were married?"

"What do you mean *such a* woman?"

Smith tilted his head. "Come now, we both know the woman was as good as an innocent after eight years of marriage to Taunton." He snorted. "*I* probably fucked her husband more often than she did. But since you *did* insist on breeding her with your stable master, why didn't you want her to enjoy it? Was it some kind of punishment?"

"No! Of course not. It's not that—I wanted her to enjoy it, just not—"

"So much?"

He groaned and let his head fall back against the padded leather.

"You're jealous," Smith said.

Gideon groaned even louder "I know! And it's bloody awful."

Smith chuckled. "It *is* awful."

"You've been jealous?" he asked, hoping to turn the conversation to something less . . .well, about *him.*

"Of course."

"Of whom?"

"That hardly matters," he said, his abrupt answer shutting the door on further questions. "Do you think *she* is jealous of you?"

Gideon thought about the gossip in the paper. "I would guess so."

Smith shook his head in wonder. "You don't seem to find that particularly, er, distressing."

"Well, it's not—at least not to me. Probably not to her, either—or at least no more than a little bit. Women are always jealous, aren't they? They revel in it."

Smith laughed. "You really *are* an ass, aren't you?"

"What?"

"*You* don't like feeling jealous—do you really want her to suffer—even if it is only *a little*?"

"Of course not."

"Then *do* something about this mess."

"Like what?"

"What do you need *not* to be jealous?"

He frowned. "For her not to go fucking everything in pants, for a start—at least not if I'm not invited."

Smith smiled.

"Oh, no. No, no, no. You think that *I* should give up other women if she gives up other men?"

"You say that with such horror, my friend. It is the way of things in many cases, you know. Or at least most successful cases."

Gideon sputtered. "Would *you* ever give everything up for just one person."

Smith's jaw hardened slightly, as if he didn't care for the question. Good, let *him* see what it felt like to answer such things. "No, Gideon, I wouldn't limit myself to a single person. But then again, I'm not married, am I?"

"Look at Edward and Nora. They're married and don't limit themselves," Gideon pointed out triumphantly.

"Do they go off and have sex with other people?"

"They allow other people into their bedchamber—they bloody seek it out."

"With *each other.*"

Gideon blinked. "Are you saying that is what I might suggest to Alys?" he asked uncertainly.

"You might at least try asking it—wouldn't it be better than sitting alone in London?"

"I haven't been," he retorted. "I've been—"

Smith raised a hand. "Yes, yes, I know, you've been fucking every night—just on principle. And how has that been treating you?"

This conversation had a familiar ring to it and Gideon realized it was the same thing Smith had said all those weeks ago, during their conversation at Foxrun.

He took a deep breath and noisily let it out. "It's been bloody awful," he confessed. Something struck him suddenly. "Have you ever fucked and fucked and fucked and not been able to come?"

Smith frowned. "No."

"Oh." *Good God*—what was wrong with him? Was this some kind of—

"Gideon?"

"Hmmm?"

Smith smiled and leaned toward him. "Have you considered that you might be in love with her?"

Gideon opened his mouth to heatedly deny it, but then shut it again.

"It happens, Gideon," Smith said quietly, an odd undertone in his voice. "And when it does . . . well. It changes your life. Whether for good or for ill? That's up to you."

Gideon thought his head might explode if he had to listen to much more. Luckily the carriage began to slow.

He jerked open the door almost before it rolled to a stop. "Good night, Smith."

"Thank you for the ride, Gideon." Smith climbed from the carriage without putting down the steps.

Gideon began to close the door.

"Oh, one more thing."

Gideon sighed. "Yes?"

"Whatever you decide to do, don't wait too long." He smiled sadly. "Love doesn't wait forever."

Love doesn't wait forever.

The phrase rattled around in his head as noisily as a piece of shot in a tin can.

Gideon was shocked that he *wasn't* shocked by Smith's use of the word 'love.'

Have you finally stopped running from a four-letter word? the amused voice that lived to taunt him asked.

But Gideon was past the point of responding to taunts—from anyone, even himself.

It was love he'd felt the night of their wedding, and he'd spent months trying to avoid it. And months trying to ruin or destroy it.

These past few weeks—when he'd had only himself for company every night—he'd realized, perhaps too late, that women were not interchangeable machinery parts. It was disappointing that he'd recognized Nora's value—and had wanted the same for himself—but had not been able to recognize happiness when happiness had landed in his lap, with no effort needed to go out and find her.

The knife of fear that cut through him at that thought left him paralyzed. What if he'd already ruined any chance he had with Alys?

Are you going to run from that possibility, too, like a frightened child?

The door to his carriage opened and his footman put down the steps; Gideon hadn't even realized they'd stopped.

He had no recollection of walking the distance from the carriage to his library, but there he was. And so, he took a seat at the worn leather chair in front of the desk and opened the top drawer, which had already been stocked with stationary embossed for another Earl of Taunton when he'd moved in.

Gideon squeezed his eyes shut as he recalled the pitiful story Alys had told him about her husband and the way he'd treated her from the moment they'd married.

At the time, he'd believed his predecessor a cruel cad. And then he'd gone and treated the same woman even worse.

He did something he couldn't recall doing since he was a boy: he prayed.

He prayed that he'd not left it too late, that he'd not done irreparable damage, and that he would find the words to explain something he wasn't sure of, himself. He prayed that he deserved her.

And when he was finished, he picked up his pen and began to write.

Chapter Twenty-Nine

Gideon knew by just looking at Jackson's face that something was wrong.

"What is it?" he demanded as he strode toward his servant on the empty platform. He'd paid a great deal of money to have the syndicate's railcar brought up from London at such short notice and his car had been the only passenger car attached to the engine. At this time of night, the little railway station was as quiet as a graveyard.

"Jackson, what is going on?"

Jackson waited until the two servants he'd brought along had gone to fetch the bags.

"I'll tell you inside your coach, my lord."

Never had the other man disobeyed him in all the years he'd worked for him.

Gideon waited impatiently until they were inside the carriage, the door closed, and turned to his valet.

Jackson was holding out an envelope. It said only 'Gideon' on the front, and it had been opened. He glanced up.

"I apologize for reading it, sir, but I felt I needed—well, perhaps you might read it and I'll explain everything."

There was only one page. The signature leapt out at him like a wild animal: *Your brother, Lloyd.*

Gideon's vision blackened and he swayed, sliding off the seat.

"My lord?" Jackson's hand steadied him, his face anxious.

"I'm fine," he lied, pulling away and turning to face the horrific page in his hand.

"*Gideon:*

Well, well, well. It's been a while, hasn't it?"

Twenty-five fucking years by Gideon's reckoning: not nearly long enough.

"*I'm guessing you're not pleased to hear from me. Ah well, life can't be all beer and skittles—which it certainly seems to have been for* you, *my*" *fine young brother. I'll bet when that dried up old lawyer came to tell you about your title you were even happier than when you'd learned your poor older brother had died on a rotting hulk in the Thames.*

I'm curious, did you even think of me when you stepped into the very polished boots that should, by right, be mine?

"Not for an instant, you twisted bastard," he muttered.

I doubt it. You always were a self-centered little prick."

Gideon snorted. "Pot, meet kettle."

"Imagine my surprise when I heard about you only a few weeks ago— my brother, an earl. *You'll wonder why it took me so long?"*

That was the bloody truth; he would have thought that Lloyd would have sprinted to Taunton at the news.

"Well, I'm ashamed to say I was . . . well, let's just say indisposed."

In jail, in other words.

"When I was fortunate enough to come back among civilized folk, I learned my new employer had sent men to collect some money from the Earl of Taunton. I recalled that name—you'll be surprised to hear. Dear old Da, the fucking bastard, mentioned the earldom often when he was drunk. Before I shut him up, permanently."

Gideon's head whipped up and he looked at Jackson; his valet was staring out the window at nothing.

You'll wonder why I came and took your pretty countess this time, rather than just taking silver and plate and carpets."

"Jesus Christ," he whispered. This time Jackson met his eyes. "When?"

"Last night, sir. You must have just missed the telegram I sent—it would have passed you on the way."

"Is she hurt?"

Even in the dim lamplight of the carriage he could see Jackson's face darken. "I'm sorry my lord, but they knocked me out, first." His hand rose to his temple, which Gideon noticed had a huge goose egg, complete with bloody scab.

He turned back to the letter, swallowing repeatedly to keep from vomiting the contents of his nearly empty stomach.

"I don't want to have to work for Fast Eddie Morgan all the rest of my miserable life."

Even Gideon had heard of the violent criminal who was overlord of a good chunk of London.

> *"I didn't share our connection with my new employer—you can thank me for that when you see me—because I knew he'd bleed you dry and I'd not get a bloody penny. But don't worry, I'm not greedy."*

Gideon gave a bitter laugh.

> *"I want enough dosh to go away for good. I also want enough to send back with Eddie's thugs—to keep old Ed happy. So, here's what we're going to do: you'll give Eddie the £1300 he says the dead earl owed him. Once you've delivered that, I'll find a way to send them on their way. Then, you'll bring me my money, once I give the word.*
>
> *When I get that, you'll get your missus back and I'll disappear for good, this time. I think £10,000 will set me up all right and tight.*
>
> *Think of it this way, little brother, it's the least you owe me for taking everything that belongs to me.*
>
> *We know you're in London, so we're giving you until Tuesday to fetch the money. The instructions will be delivered to you just after dark on Tuesday. Give all your servants a holiday on Tuesday. Don't do anything stupid.*
>
> *Your brother,*
> *Lloyd"*

Gideon didn't want to meet his servant's eyes; he was afraid Jackson would see the secrets he'd spent so many years hiding—which Lloyd had magically made reappear in an instant.

He re-folded the letter and put it in his breast pocket. But when he did, he felt the letter he'd brought with him; the letter he'd wanted to hand-deliver to Alys, along with an apology. The letter he'd been afraid of sending without himself attached to plead his case.

He put Lloyd's letter in his overcoat pocket, not wanting it anywhere near his words to Alys.

Look at you—so romantic and caring. Now.

"I don't have the money here," he said. "But I'll get it." Today was Sunday, but first thing tomorrow he'd get it.

"There's one more thing, my lord."

"Good God, what else?"

"Young Jonathan—the new footman you hired?" Gideon nodded, amazed he could feel any sicker. "He's disappeared."

"You don't suspect—"

"No, sir. The lad wouldn't have anything to do with this. He must have seen something and—"

"And they've taken him, or—"

Jackson nodded grimly.

If they'd taken the boy, that was one thing. If they'd killed him—Gideon couldn't think about what that meant for Alys.

"We need to find out where they're holding my wife—before Tuesday bloody night."

For the first time he could remember, Jackson smiled. And it was not a pleasant smile.

"I have good reason to believe her captors are city dwellers."

"What do you mean?"

"I think I know where they are. They left a trail of destruction in their wake when they made their way to the hunting cottage."

The one he'd had provisioned and furnished for Alys. And now these animals had taken possession of it.

"They must have taken a wagon there and left a trail was impossible to miss."

Gideon wasn't surprised; if he didn't know how to ride, it was unlikely Lloyd—with so much of his life spent in jail—would have learned.

"One of the grooms asked me if it was for more deliveries to the cottage. It was lucky he came to me first, so I told him that a friend of yours had come to stay and wanted solitude—and that he should keep everyone clear of the cottage. I waited all day and went as soon as darkness fell." He gave Gideon a fierce smile. "My lady is alive—I saw her when one of the brutes accompanied her to the out-building."

Gideon gritted his teeth at the thought of the swine touching her.

"There are only three of them, my lord."

He met the other man's eyes. "You have a plan?"

Jackson had been in the army before he'd come to work for Gideon. Gideon had no idea what his valet had *done* in the army, but the man emanated danger the way other men exuded cologne or sweat.

Jackson's eyes narrowed to slits. "I have a plan, my lord."

Chapter Thirty

Jackson

Jackson watched his master closely.

He'd never seen the younger man so quiet and introspective. He'd become this way in the carriage from the station and had barely said a word all night. Now, as Jackson prepared to leave, the man appeared to be in a trance.

Jackson suspected he was ambivalent about what they had planned. That wasn't surprising as Lord Taunton had never been in the army or at war. If he had been, then he'd probably look at Jackson the way military men had done over the years when they'd learned about Jackson's specialty: with suspicion.

Career army snipers were on an even lower rung than spies. It was not, to the British way of thinking, sporting to kill one's adversary from a protected position over a half-mile away.

But those moral concerns evaporated like steam from a poorly lidded pot when Jackson's skills were the only ones that would do the job.

Gideon Banks was still a bit of a mystery to him, even after a decade and a half.

Take his recent behavior with his new wife—whom he clearly loved. Or at least it was clear to Jackson, if not to either Lord or Lady Taunton.

Jackson had done what Lord Taunton had told him to do these past months, hoping he might somehow heal the breech between the two stubborn lovers, but he feared he'd only made it worse.

He couldn't lie; he'd enjoyed waiting on such a lovely young woman—no matter how poorly that reflected on his character, or how being exposed to her body on a daily basis had caused him to behave like a fifteen-year-old in the privacy of his closet most nights.

As much as he'd appreciated being her body servant, he'd clung to the hope that all the reports of her masturbatory teasing would push *one* of them into doing what was necessary. He would have wagered—had he been a wagering man—that Lady Taunton, being the wiser of the two, would have come to her senses, first. He'd believed she'd eventually send a letter that would allow the brilliant, but insecure, man to come back to his wife without utterly losing face.

These past few weeks he'd noticed a change in her and believed she was finally considering what she wanted and how to get it, rather than how to triumph in a foolish game over her childish spouse. It was his belief that Lord Taunton would have received a letter before not much longer.

And then this had happened.

Jackson felt almost crushing guilt at moving so slowly the night he'd heard the noise in the earl's chambers. Instead of approaching with the care he should have, he assumed it was his mistress, roaming Lord Taunton's chambers as she'd done on more than one occasion.

He'd made a foolish assumption and now a young, innocent, and pregnant woman might pay for his clumsiness.

You won't let that happen.

No, he wouldn't.

He glanced at the longcase clock and saw it was almost time.

"I shall be leaving in a half-hour, my lord."

The earl looked up from his desk, where he'd been staring at something he'd been writing; Jackson hadn't seen his pen move in over a quarter of an hour.

He nodded his head, stood, and offered his hand—the first time ever. "Thank you, Jackson."

His face heated beneath the other man's grateful stare and he hoped to God the plan—*his* plan—worked.

"It is an honor, my lord."

After taking his leave, he went up to his lordship's dressing room, the small space he called home.

You live like a dog, Lady Taunton had said when she'd seen the corner of the dressing room he'd taken for himself.

Jackson couldn't disagree. But he also didn't care for large spaces after years of living in tents or caves or in any other inconspicuous location the army decided to place him.

Lord Taunton had been his very first master after leaving the army. Back then, the younger man had still been living from hand to mouth. Jackson had accepted the low-paying position on his new employer's confident promise of better wages and accommodations soon—and of excellent benefits to any man who stuck by him.

And he'd been true to his word. Jackson had stopped needing to work six or seven years ago thanks to his master's generous wages and clever reinvestment. The amount of money in his bank account was shocking. He could have stopped working years ago.

But then what would he do?

Once in his tiny room, he removed one of his only two pieces of luggage from the cupboard where he stored both his and his lordships bags.

He opened the case and sat down on the floor with his gun cleaning kit. The rifle, a Whitfield that Jackson had modified to his own specifications—he despised the Enfield that the British Army used—was already well-oiled and ready for use. But Jackson found the ritual of cleaning the gun soothing.

In the case, in a heavy felt pouch, was the Chance optical sight he'd paid half a year's army wages to purchase.

Jackson's hands worked without any attention from his mind. Instead, he considered the plan he'd devised with his employer.

If word of Lloyd Banks were to get out it would cause no end of agony for both Lord and Lady Taunton and the people who relied on them.

If they captured Banks and handed him over to the authorities it would provoke a circus that would destroy reputations. Banks was already wanted for three murders and had escaped the hangman's noose once already. He would hang, even without this current crime.

It was Jackson's opinion that the man should not leave the property alive.

It had taken some convincing on his part.

"Good God! *That's murder*," his employer had protested.

Jackson didn't want to tell him his true concern: that the group of thugs had already murdered poor young Jonathan—and would likely kill Lady Taunton once they had the money. They could not risk such exposure. They would leave no witnesses. In his rather expert opinion, it was a more than even exchange: the two thugs and a thrice-convicted murderer in exchange for the young boy they'd probably already killed and a pregnant woman.

Yes, it was murder, and Jackson was more than willing to take the killings onto his own conscience if his master could not.

After all, what were three more names added to what was already a very   long   list?

Chapter Thirty-One

Alys couldn't stop staring at the third man—the one she'd not met the last time—the one the other two criminals called Lloyd. He must have guessed what she almost said, because he'd given a slight shake of his head when she'd opened her mouth, eyes wide.

So Alys had kept the stunning observation to herself.

"I need to use the necessary," she said, directing her request toward the leader—Tom, his name was.

He and the other man—the *huge* brute called Bazzer—were eating from a selection of tins they'd found in the cupboards in the small kitchen, his cheeks stuffed.

"I'll take her," Lloyd said, sounding annoyed and resigned.

Tom nodded and then turned abruptly to wrestle the tinned plums away from Bazzer.

Lloyd grabbed her arm and frog-marched her out the cottage's back door. He didn't stop until he'd opened the door to the outhouse and shoved her inside. "You can talk to me through the door," he said in a low voice.

"Who *are* you?"

"I'm heartbroken—you mean my little brother didn't tell you about me? Well, I suppose I'll forgive him since he believed I was long dead."

"You look just like him," she blurted.

His laugh was bitter. "Well, an older rougher version."

Alys had to agree. A sudden, horrid, thought sprang into her head and she squeezed her eyes shut; *this criminal is* the new earl!

"Why are you doing this?" she asked him.

"Why do you think? Money, my lady."

"Gideon would give you money, you don't need to do this."

That made him laugh. "The only thing my brother would give me is a carriage ride to the nearest constable. And that, my dear sister, would be my death warrant. A death I've managed to avoid for over two decades. No, trust me—this way is best. You'll pay off old Tom and Bazzer in there and that will get Eddie off your back. And then Gid will pay me, and I'll disappear and leave my baby brother holding the prize."

Alys swallowed and asked the question that made her entire body quake. "They won't let me loose after I saw what they did to Jonathan."

The long pause told her more than anything else he'd said.

"Nonsense," he said, too late to be convincing. "They'll release you once they get the money—they're already wanted by the law, the boy's murder won't matter."

He must really think she was stupid; if the boy's murder didn't matter—why would hers?

"Come on, now, get out. They're not smart, but they're smart enough to know how long it takes a bird to have a piss."

Alys pushed open the door—a new, polished wooden door she knew Gideon had ordered when he'd re-fitted the entire cottage—and came face to face with her brother-in-law.

He grinned down at her, the action exposing two teeth missing on his upper left side. The rest of his mouth wasn't so pretty, either. Indeed, he looked like an older, rougher version of her husband—and a more dissipated, cast away one.

His nostrils flared as he stared down at her, his lips tightening. He opened his mouth, closed it, and then said, "You'll want to tell them you've got the pox when they come at you." He barked a laugh. "They might already have it themselves, so it might not stop them," he shrugged, and she saw the lack of humanity in his beautiful blue eyes—so much like Gideon's, "but it can't hurt to try."

"You could stop this—*now* and run with me."

His lips twisted into a sneer—for her, or him, she wasn't sure—and he grabbed her arm. "That's not in the cards, sweetheart. Now, come on, we can't stay out here mucking about."

—◆—

Gideon stared down at the brief note, which had been delivered only a few minutes ago: he was to deliver the money and had exactly an hour to do so.

He'd have to ride hard to reach the cottage in time, which is what he suspected the men had wanted—leaving him no time to gather help. Or so they thought.

As he rode out from the stables with a saddlebag full of money he thought about Jackson, whom he'd watched depart carrying a case that could only hold one thing.

He hadn't been surprised to learn his valet owned a sniper rifle, what surprised him is that he'd never seen it. After all, Jackson lived in his bloody dressing room.

You're self-absorbed, Gideon, that's why you never noticed.

Gideon didn't bother to argue as he carefully guided his horse through the dusk. That was the last thing he needed: to fall off his mount and break his bloody neck before he could deliver the money.

"They'll have the money delivered at night," Gideon had told Jackson. "Can you, er, well, can—"

"I can be accurate as long as I can site my target."

The other man's cool, calm words had made Gideon shiver. He supposed he should count himself fortunate he'd not annoyed Jackson at some point and woken up dead for it.

"They've chosen a full moon for a reason," Jackson had continued. "They'll want to be on their way—as your, er," he paused, clearly not wishing to mention Lloyd. "As the letter indicated," he finished.

Gideon liked the man even more for trying to avoid reminding him that it was partially *his* fault that his wife and child were currently being held by robbers. And murderers.

Gideon's hands jerked on the reins and the confused beast whickered and side-stepped.

"Shhh," he murmured. "It's all right." It *wasn't* all right, but he couldn't think about these men hurting Alys or he'd go stupidly barging into the cottage with guns blazing.

Thinking of guns made him pat the back of his heavy overcoat, where he'd tucked a pistol into his riding breeches. Jackson hadn't looked pleased by his decision but he'd not argued.

Gideon was no hand with a pistol—or any other type of gun—so he knew it would be all too easy to shoot off his own arse. Hopefully, he'd not need to use it.

S.M. LaViolette

He'd never ridden in the evening before and he was surprised how pleasant—and solitary—it felt. This was hardly a pleasure ride, but he was relieved to have a bit of time to gather himself on the almost forty-minute ride.

He tried not to think about how selfish, stupid, and hurtful he'd been, but it was impossible to avoid. The instant he'd learned Alys was in danger, it was as if someone had lighted a torch inside his head, illuminating parts of his mind he'd always avoided. He remembered a hundred things about her: how she laughed at his stupid quips, made sure he had what he wanted to eat, visited people on the estate who were lonely and alone, kept the estate and its people together through years of neglect. Most especially, how clear and honest her gaze had been whenever he looked into her eyes. He knew she'd fallen in love with him but had refused to even consider it. How had he been such a fool for so long?

Why did it take *this*—a threat to her life and to their child—to frighten some sense into him.

He just wanted her back. Her open, curious, clever, witty, loving ways and her beautiful, generous soul.

He wasn't so stupid as to think he'd be a perfect husband if he got her back safely, but the one thing he could promise was to keep his prick out of other women. Wasn't that the least he could do? Especially when he had a wife like Alys? He knew the other defects in his character—his selfishness, willfulness, and all-around ignorance when it came to other people—wouldn't be so easily remedied. But he believed Alys would be patient if he at least could give her his loyalty.

Please, God, just give me this chance—not for me, but for Alys and our child.

—◀ ❤ ▶—

Things had begun to go bad—or worse, rather—just around dusk, after the man Tom had come back from the village.

He'd slammed open the door, strode into the small kitchen, and struck Lloyd across the face so hard it had knocked him from his chair.

"When were you going to tell us, you weaseling bastard?" he shouted at the other man, who was lying on the kitchen floor, blood leaking from the side of his mouth. "And *don't* play stupid," Tom warned when Lloyd opened his mouth, probably to lie.

308

He turned, spat a bloody mouthful of phlegm on the beautiful wood floor and then pushed himself up into his chair.

"So, you know—now what? You want it all for yourself?"

Tom gave an ugly laugh.

"Wots all viss?" Bazzer asked in his almost unintelligible London accent.

"It seems old Lloyd here is really Lord Taunton." He cut Alys a dirty look. "Did you know?"

Lying seemed ill-conceived. "I guessed."

Tom snorted. "This calls for a whole new plan," he said, his eyes narrowing as he stared down at Lloyd. "I reckon it's just as well our fake lordship is on his way with the money—that way we can talk to him in person. I reckon Eddie'll want to talk to the both of youse," he said with an ugly smile.

Alys had already discerned that this Eddie person was some sort of criminal warlord, or whatever they called themselves.

Tom turned to Bazzer. "You go get the wagon ready to go."

Bazzer's jaw hung open. "But I fought you said—"

"Your job ain't to think. Just get it done!"

Bazzer left, taking the back door.

Tom kicked Lloyd's chair. "Get up, you."

The taller man stood slowly.

"You get up, too, my lady." Tom, secure in his power, pulled his eyes away from Lloyd only for a second to talk to Alys, but it was enough time for Lloyd to swing his elbow in a forceful arc. The bone hit Tom's jaw and Alys heard a sickening *crunch* just before Tom let out an animalistic howl and fell to his knees.

Alys, who'd already been on her feet, lurched for the door. She managed to yank it open—Tom had left it unlocked in his anger—but Lloyd caught her around the waist and pulled her back. She squirmed, but he turned her sharply, staring down at her, his hands on her thickened, uncorseted waist. She was wearing her old flannel nightgown and brocade dressing gown—which is how she'd been clothed when they'd taken her. She saw the comprehension dawn in his eyes.

"Well, well, well."

A flicker of movement behind him drew her gaze. "Look—"

A sharp crack pierced the near darkness and she screamed as Tom's head exploded, a red halo the only remains of his head.

Lloyd launched himself onto her, shoving her to the floor. Only at the last moment did she think to wrap her arms around her midriff and turn to the side as she slammed into unforgiving wood, covered only by a carpet.

Her head rang from the impact and her shoulder, which had taken the brunt of the fall, felt as if it had been torn from the socket.

Lloyd scrabbled, his legs thrashing and Alys realized he was trying to kick shut the door. She crawled away from him, hoping to keep him from closing the door on whoever was shooting—probably Gideon or somebody he'd brought in to help.

Lloyd caught her heel and held on tight, managing to toe the door shut even as another *crack* filled the air, sending chips of wooden door frame raining down on their heads.

"Dammit!" he hissed, abandoning the door and crawling to safety. "Go!" he ordered, shoving Alys ahead of him.

Tom's foot lay only an arm's length away; Alys saw the gun in his boot at the same time Lloyd must have because they both scrambled clumsily. Alys's hand slipped in something warm and wet and she slid to the side, losing precious time.

Lloyd's big hand closed over the gun butt and she felt the cold metal press against her temple.

"Stop. Now."

She quit squirming immediately.

He scrambled to his feet, holding the gun on her the entire time. "Get up."

Alys did as he ordered. "You do as I say and you might make it out of here alive," he said in a low, rough voice that sent shivers up and down her spine. "You understand?"

She nodded.

"Good. Now, stand in front of me. I'm going to put my arm around your throat and you'll precede me out the door. Understand?"

"Yes." She wasn't stupid; if anyone was to shoot, they'd shoot Alys first.

He raised the gun to her temple. "Now walk."

310

Gideon found the source of the moaning, it was a huge brute of a man who was missing most of one arm from the elbow down. He was lying not far from the little stable, crying piteously.

"Please, help me!" he wailed when he saw Gideon.

He assumed that Jackson had allowed him to live for a reason. Either that, or he wasn't as good a shot as Gideon had believed—which he found difficult to believe.

Gideon slid from his horse and tethered it with the other beast before turning to the man on the ground. He should have felt pity for him, but he was one of the bastards who'd taken Alys and it was all he could do not to kick his bloody stump. Instead, he crouched down beside the man as he pulled off his necktie.

"How many others?" Gideon growled.

"Just the three of us—me Tom and Lloyd, er, your bro—*ah!*" he howled like he was being murdered when Gideon wrapped the narrow cloth around his stump.

"Shut up," Gideon hissed, cinching the necktie tight. "Unless you want to bleed to—"

Another shot rang out, this one followed by a female scream.

Gideon almost fainted with relief: she was still alive and well enough to yell. He patted down his patient and removed an ancient pistol from his worn coat pocket, dropping it into his own.

"Keep your mouth shut if you want to live," he whispered, earning a violent nodding yes in return.

Still in a crouch that would keep him below the level of the windows he made his way to the house, flattening his back to the stone wall as he inched toward the front.

"I'm coming out now," Gideon's gut roiled at the sound of a voice he'd not heard in twenty-five years. "I've got the woman in front of me. If you shoot at me, she'll die first. Gideon? I know you're out here—come around to the front of the house *slowly*."

His heart both sped and plummeted—did he believe Gideon was the only one out here? He hoped to God that was the case. Stepping away from the wall, he slowly walked out to the front of the cottage.

Lloyd stood just outside the open doorway, his arm around Alys's midriff, his right hand holding a pistol to her head.

"Little brother!" Lloyd yelled, looking *happy* to see him.

He locked eyes with Alys, beyond stunned when she offered him a tremulous smile. Gideon stared into her with all the love he felt, hoping she saw at least a little of it in his eyes.

"Come around this way, Gideon," Lloyd called, turning slightly toward him.

"Lower the gun from her forehead," he ordered.

Lloyd laughed. "Very droll, little brother. *You* throw down your gun and I'll consider it."

Gideon tried to control his expression—fearing the leap of joy he felt would show on his face. If he complied too easily with Lloyd's request, he could ruin their only chance.

He shook his head. "No, you first."

Again, his brother laughed. "Look at you—standing up on your hind legs for a change." He lowered the gun, but only to Alys's stomach. All his humor slid from his face, leaving the cold, calculating bastard Gideon remembered. "Do it now or I kill the child and probably her, too."

Gideon reached for his coat pocket.

"No, use your left hand."

He sighed, but did as he was told, pulling out the gun he'd just taken off the big man.

"Throw it over here—to my feet."

Once he complied, Lloyd peered at it and then turned a nasty sneer at Gideon. "That gun belongs to that fathead Bazzer. Is he dead?" Lloyd shook his head. "Never mind, I don't care. Throw me your gun."

This time Gideon did as he was told.

The guns both lay at his feet, but Lloyd still held the pistol to her belly.

"Let her go—you can take me. You don't need to go back to your criminal employer, Lloyd—I'll give you all the money you asked for—and the rest of it, as well. Just let her go. You can hold me hostage until you get the money. Alys will see to it."

Lloyd laughed and shook his head. "Oh, my little Gideon—if you could see your face right now, you'd know that you have no intention of giving me money and letting me go: you want to kill me."

Gideon risked a look at Alys, whose expression told him he was doing a poor job of hiding his emotions.

312

This is your chance to <u>not</u> let her down, Gideon.

He seized his emotions with a killing grip and looked up at his brother. "Fine, then. What do we do next?"

"That's better," Lloyd said, his eyes nervously flickering about. "Where is Bazzer?"

"I left him out back." He shrugged. "Sorry about his arm."

Lloyd laughed. "You're quite the shot, aren't you—I'm lucky you didn't get me instead of poor Tom."

His brother had the instincts of a criminal and he saw the incomprehension before Gideon could mask it.

Fortunately for Gideon, his brother didn't think that a person was capable of loving anyone more than themself.

Lloyd lifted the gun from Alys's midriff and pointed it at Gideon's head.

He opened his mouth to yell, *"Now, Jackson!"* but his valet was already ahead of him.

There were two shots, and the second one hurt like hell.

Chapter Thirty-Two

Alys had never seen Gideon so quiet and pale. Even when she'd watched him sleeping—those few glorious nights they'd spent together—he'd not been so still.

But Jackson had assured her he would be fine.

Jackson.

Alys shuddered to think what she would have done without the valet's help after Gideon had been shot.

He'd come for her when she'd been covered in Lloyd's brains, too terrified to scream, kneeling beside Gideon with tears running down her face.

"It'll be all right, my lady," he murmured, laying a frightening looking rifle down beside him when he took her hand off Gideon's shoulder, pulling back the bloody clothing to see the wound. He lifted Gideon up a bit to examine his back. "It went through—that's good," he said, cutting her a quick glance before he stood and stripped off his necktie and then bound up Gideon's shoulder in a way that drastically stemmed the flow of blood.

"I'm going to fetch the wagon—you stay here with him."

Alys had nodded as she prayed—offering God anything he wanted if he'd just keep Gideon safe and alive.

She couldn't have said how much more time passed before the wagon rolled around, Jackson leading the cart horse, with two hacks tied to the hitch.

"I'll need a bit of help, my lady. Do you think you can lift his feet?"

"Yes, yes of course," she said, wiping away the tears and standing to help.

Gideon was taller than Jackson but not as heavy, which was lucky as it was all the two of them could do to lift him into the back of the wagon.

Once he was inside, Jackson helped her up beside him. "Will you sit back here with my lord while I drive?"

She nodded, unable to pull her eyes away from Gideon's face.
"I'll be back in a moment."

Alys never even heard him return or didn't notice when the wagon started rolling. Not until she smelled smoke did she look up, just in time to see the flames shooting out the front door of the cottage.

"Jackson!"

"I know, my lady," he said, clucking his tongue to get the horse moving faster. "It's the best I could do. The few trees beside it will burn, but the fire won't spread far—not with all this summer rain. I'll come back with some of the other servants as soon as I've dropped you and the master at Foxrun." He twisted in his seat to look at the conflagration, and then Alys. "It was the only way."

That had been hours ago, but Alys hadn't heard the men return yet. The entire house was awake and all the able-bodied servants had gone to help.

She stood and went to the window. She'd seen the blaze earlier, but it had dwindled until now all she saw was smoke against the moonlit sky; she was relieved to know Jackson had been correct.

"Alys?" the voice was hoarse, but recognizable all the same.

He'd turned his head toward her. "Are you—"

"I'm unhurt," she said, going back to the chair where she'd been keeping her vigil, suddenly shy of his brilliant blue gaze. "Are you in pain?"

He shrugged and then sucked in a harsh breath. "Not so bad, until I do that." He gave her a tired smile.

Alys stared into his beloved face, her mind on the letter she'd found propped on the pillow on her bed. It was as Nora had said: he loved her. He was just an idiot.

"Why are you smiling?" he asked with a quizzical look.

"I'm thinking about your letter."

"Ah." His blue eyes darted away, his cheeks darkening. And then they slid back to her. "Er, is it a good smile?"

Alys laughed, the sound slightly hysterical. "It is a very good smile." She lifted up the letter that she'd written to him but never had the chance to send. "I wrote you one, too."

His eyes lit up. "Oh? What does yours say?"

"It is remarkably similar to yours."

"Did you call yourself an idiot, too?" He chuckled and then winced.

"I did," she admitted, leaning forward and taking his big warm hand in hers. "Oh, Gideon—I'm—"

He squeezed her hand. "No, *I've* been such a fool."

"I wasn't going to say I was a fool."

His flush deepened. "Oh."

"I was going to say I'm so in love with you."

"Ah. That's far better than calling yourself an idiot."

She laughed, squeezing her eyes shut when tears began to flow.

"What's that for, darling?" he asked, concern throbbing in his voice.

She shook her head and opened her eyes. "I'm just so happy you're here with me. So very, very happy."

"I'd say you're a little mad to be happy about such a thing—but I'm too grateful to tempt fate." His expression became serious. "What happened to Lloyd?"

"They're all dead." She frowned. "They killed Jonathan when they were taking me out of the house. He tried to stop them—" she couldn't get out the rest of the words.

"Oh, darling," he said, looking as upset as she felt. He hesitated, and then said, "What did Jackson do with Lloyd and the other two?"

"I hope you shan't be too angry, but he set the cottage on fire with them inside."

"I'm not angry. We'll have to pass them off as criminals who'd been hiding out on my property."

"That was Jackson's thinking." Alys chewed her lower lip.

"What is it?"

"Your brother—will you tell me what happened?"

He took a deep breath, winced, and then gave a slight nod. "Our father left us at a workhouse when he could no longer afford to keep us." He gave a bitter laugh. "He knew my grandfather would take us, but the two men hated each other and he was the sort of father who put that first.

"Lloyd, who'd been pretty unbearable before, became even wilder and developed his criminal side." His hand tightened. "God, Alys, I was so glad when I heard he was dead—I know that's awful. But, if we'd taken him alive I would have driven him straight to the nearest constable."

316

"That's what he said to the other two." She cocked her head. "He said you hated him—why, Gideon? What happened?"

His expression shifted from fury to self-loathing. "He needed money to run his little criminal enterprise, so he sold me to the highest bidder."

Her jaw dropped.

"I was *twelve*, Alys. And he sold me over and over to any man who'd paid his price." He laughed bitterly. "Until I was too wild and hateful to be sold. I wasn't the only one Lloyd peddled—the workhouse was full of defenseless young boys. I know it's not my fault, but it took years not to despise myself for what he did. He was just evil all the way through." He cut her a grim glance. "I wish I'd been the one to pull the trigger and not Jackson, he doesn't deserve to have those burdens to bear."

Alys didn't tell him that she wished *she'd* been the one to shoot him. Besides threatening her life, she'd seen in his eyes that he would have shot her child to get away.

"Can you ever forgive me for bringing him here?"

"You weren't the one who brought him here—Sebastian was," she reminded him. "Beside, I'm glad you're here. I love you, Gideon; I love you a great deal."

"What did I ever do to deserve you?"

Alys smiled. "Let's hope you keep that thought in your head for a good long time."

"I mean it, Alys—I was an idiot and I am grateful that you are generous enough to give me this second chance. I l-love you and believe I have for quite some time. The night of our wedding I woke up in a cold sweat when I realized that I didn't want to continue on the way I'd been; I wanted *you*."

Alys brought his hand to her mouth and kissed it. "Why didn't you *say* something? Why did you—"

"Why did I give you to Silber on the day after our wedding?" He scowled. "I can't even say it without being seized by insane jealousy." He shook his head. "I don't know why I did such a thing."

Alys smiled. "I have to confess something—but I don't want you to get angry."

He already looked angry. "I don't know if I can promise that, but I need to start trying. What is it, Alys? Are you in love with Silber?"

His question surprised a laugh out of her. "Of course, not! I told you, I'm in love with *you*. But will you tell me where he is? I *do* worry."

He waved a hand dismissively and yelped. "Dammit," he hissed, and then visibly pushed away his pain. "He's managing one of the syndicate's breeding operations—that's *horse* breeding, darling, before you get too excited." His lips pulled up on one side, his smile naughty. "I've received several letters from him and he's as pleased as punch to be in charge of so much superlative horseflesh." He turned serious. "I'm sorry I sent him away," he chewed his lower lip. "I could bring him back, but—"

She shook her head emphatically. "No, no. Let him start anew—he deserves it. However," she felt her cheeks burn.

"Yes?" he gave her a quizzical look, and then smiled. "Why are you blushing, darling?"

Alys swallowed several times. "It's only right that I tell you I wasn't *entirely* angry about that night. I did rather enjoy myself—especially knowing you were watching."

His pupils flared. "Did you, now." It wasn't a question. He glanced down at his hips, which were covered with a blanket. Alys and Jackson had undressed him when they'd returned, meaning he wasn't wearing a stitch. She saw the blanket move.

"See what you've done to your poor patient, Lady Taunton?" he asked archly.

She laughed and released his hand, lifting both of hers to her burning cheeks. "It is difficult to believe I even think such thoughts—much less speak them out loud."

"I love that you do—and I demand that you tell me all your fantasies, Alys."

Her heart pounded at his words. "And you? Will you tell me yours?"

He looked surprised by her question. "My fantasies?" he gave a helpless sounding laugh, absently rubbing his erection with the heel of his hand. "I'm afraid I've been rather, er—"

"Debauched?" she asked, cocking one eyebrow.

He nodded, raising his hips to meet his hand and then gasping at the pain the movement caused.

Alys took his hand to save him from himself. "I want us to be debauched, together, Gideon. Do you—will you—"

But her wicked husband could read her like a book. "I only want to do things that please us both, Alys—whatever you desire."

His words sent her pulse racing. "Whatever?"

He nodded slowly, his eyes brimming with sin and promise. "Whatever." He hesitated and then added with a sheepish look, "But perhaps you might desire, er, less acrobatic activities for the next week. Or surely no longer than five or six days. I might even be able to—"

Alys laughed. "Oh, Gideon, I *do* love you." And then she embraced him with extreme gentleness. And if she made him scream, it was only a very little bit. And, after all, he *did* deserve it.

Epilogue

Gideon slowly stroked his cock—with his injured arm, since the doctor said it needed exercise—and stared through the peephole at the delicious show beyond.

At almost eighteen weeks pregnant, Alys was rounded and sensual in ways he'd never experienced before. A pregnant wife, he decided, was a fine addition to his life.

These past seventeen days, however, had been an experience he was not anxious to repeat.

Although her sexual drive was relentless, she'd not allowed Gideon to make love to her until the doctor approved him as being fit for exertion: that was today.

Luckily, she'd not excluded all the amusing activities two lovers could think up with their bodies, so he'd still managed to get in an orgasm or three every day. Still, he missed being inside her body, which he would be soon.

In the other room, the two were well into what he thought of as the first act of the evening.

When Alys had told him what she wanted, he'd been equal parts aroused and jealous. But, unlike with Silber, they'd discussed the matter fully, taking no action until both of them agreed.

That didn't mean he wasn't feeling a twinge or two of the green-eyed monster's claws, but he'd wanted to give Alys some time alone with Jackson.

As he watched them together, he realized what he was really jealous of was all the time they'd spent together these past months—without him.

During his convalescence he'd sat in the garden and enjoyed watching Alys order the gardeners—and Jackson—around as if she were the world's smallest general. The two shared an ease that made him think of people long acquainted, and he'd noticed they'd rarely even spoken most days.

Right now, they weren't doing much talking—well, Alys was doing some moaning, a few of which he could hear even through the peep.

Jackson had tied her hands over her head to one of the handy metal rings in the solid posts of Gideon's bed. He'd spread her feet, tying her ankles wide.

She was deliciously naked while Jackson had only stripped off his coat—although he *had* rolled up his sleeves, which is as relaxed as Gideon had ever seen the man. Based on the large wet spot on his trousers Jackson would be relaxing more before the evening was through.

Right now, he was applying a flail to Alys's back and doing so most effectively. Jackson had been paying close attention to Gideon, it seemed.

Or perhaps this is just another skill of his you didn't know about.

Yes, that was likely true. The man remained a mystery. Even his response to Alys's request had been baffling.

Gideon had summoned Jackson and watched with interest while Alys had stammered out her request. Or, at least she'd tried to. She'd ended up so red-faced and tongue-tied that she'd given him an irresistible beseeching look.

"What my wife is trying to say is that she wants to fuck you, Jackson."

Alys had squeaked, turned on Gideon, and smacked him in the shoulder, *hard.*

"Ow!"

"I would never say anything so vulgar," she forced through clenched jaws.

He'd grinned at her as he'd rubbed his arm.

Jackson had watched the interaction with the expression of a man tending children. Fractious children.

"It's true, Jackson, she'd never use such vulgar language. She said she wanted an evening with you. I'm to watch for the first part." He paused and then added with a rush of blood to his groin, "And then we are both to take her." His grin slid away. "But not the way Edward and I took Nora."

Lord! Letting *that* slip had been a mistake. Alys had kept him up until dawn that night, grilling him as effectively as the most hardened Queen's Counsel.

She had given Gideon a look promising punishment later and then turned to address the inscrutable servant. "I would like to spend an evening with you, Jackson—doing things *you* would like to do." She'd flushed charmingly. "To make up for being so bratty these past months."

Jackson had given his customary ghost of a smile. "Thank you, my lady, it would be an honor and a pleasure."

Gideon had snorted, earning chilly looks from both of them. "What?" he demanded. And then he'd frowned at Jackson. "I'll be there for part of the evening. Just thought you should know."

"You already said that, Gideon."

He narrowed his eyes at his wife.

"Understood, sir." Jackson hesitated, and then said. "I believe it is time I tender my resignation, my lord."

"*What?*" both he and Alys had shouted at once.

"Is this because of me asking you this?" Alys asked. Her eyes were glassy with unshed tears, telling Gideon just how attached she'd become to the other man. He'd gritted his teeth and bore the jealousy, letting it flow through him and out. After all, she loved *him*, not Jackson.

Jackson turned to Alys and, to everyone's surprise—including Jackson's he suspected—he took her hand in his much larger, gloved hand. "I very much look forward to our evening, my lady. I'm leaving because it is time to go." He glanced at Gideon. "His lordship has been very generous with his pay and he's also invested the considerable sum he paid me."

Gideon felt a flush of pleasure at the taciturn man's praise. "Indeed, Jackson, you are likely the wealthiest valet in England—and probably wealthier than most of the aristocracy." Gideon could tell by the tightness around the other man's eyes that retiring to live in luxury wasn't his real motivation for resigning. He suspected Jackson had grown to care about Alys more than would be comfortable for any of them. Especially him.

Alys being Alys, she threw her arms around the stunned valet, who'd turned an amusing shade of pink. "You must not disappear from our lives, Jackson, just because you are a wealthy, independent man. I'll want you to come to the christening."

Jackson mechanically patted her shoulder and cleared his throat. "Er, I would be delighted."

He'd glared at Gideon when he'd laughed.

But he wasn't glaring *now* Gideon noticed as he shoved his eyeball close enough to touch the peep.

"Bloody hell," he whispered.

Jackson had finished whipping Alys and was examining his handiwork with a smug smile on his usually impassive features. Leaving her tied, he pressed his clothed body against her back, his broad, muscular torso dwarfing her delicate frame.

The wool and cloth must have been rough because Alys shivered and caught her lower lip with her teeth, her eyes opening and fastening on the peep.

The little temptress *winked* at him!

The bolt of raw desire made Gideon pump himself faster; he'd not wanted to come before joining them, but he might not have a choice.

Jackson nudged his mistress's legs apart even wider and slid a hand between her thighs, the action closing Alys's eyes. His arm moved slowly and he lowered his mouth next to her ear, his erect cock pressed against the small of her back.

Gideon squinted; it almost looked as if he were saying something to Alys.

He smiled at the ridiculous thought; Jackson was as likely to whisper sweet nothings as he was to star in a pantomime.

—❤—

"You enjoyed tormenting me all these weeks, didn't you, my lady?" Jackson's voice was rough as his skilled, *ungloved*, finger slid inside her body. "You enjoyed sending me to bed with *this* every night," he ground his very substantial, clothed erection against her back. "The things I imagined in my little cot." He chuckled—a first as far as Alys knew. "Bathing you was the highpoint of my days, as I'm sure you surmised."

Actually, she hadn't thought any such thing, but she hardly wanted to interrupt this fascinating soliloquy just as it was getting started.

"I loved cleaning and tending to you, especially your delectable breasts." One hand slid over her ribcage and up to her breast, calloused fingers pulling hard on her tight nipples, alternating breasts until she writhed and whimpered.

His lips curved against the thin skin of her temple. "I especially adored caring for your exquisite *cunt*." Alys gulped at the sound of such a word on his cool, cultured tongue. "The entire time I was cleaning you with my cruelly gloved fingers I was imagining stroking you with my tongue." He grunted, his finger circling her aching core. "I dreamed of tasting you—I was tormented by those dreams, my lady." He pressed his thumb against the base of her clitoris and slid a finger into her body, pumping. "When you watched me from the peep—where the master is watching us now—I was imagining it was *you*." He added another finger, his thrusts hard and deep.

Alys whimpered.

"Yes, like that," he praised. "I imagined you making those same noises you made every time the master took you—but with *me*." He gave an evil chuckle when every muscle in her body contracted. "Yes, I heard—do you like thinking about me suffering as I listened and *wanted* and yearned for you so damned badly."

She smiled. "Yes, Jackson."

"Wicked, cruel mistress," he chided. His arm was moving faster now, his movements less controlled. "I know how responsive your body is—your beautiful, delectable, unparalleled body," the last part was barely a sigh, and the raw need she heard sent the waves of pleasure rippling out from her sex.

"Yesssss," he hissed. "Come for me, this time, my lady. Only for me."

She groaned as he shoved her toward the edge. "It's for you, Elliot. Only for you."

His body jolted against hers and she knew the use of his name had surprised—and pleased—him, although he didn't speak.

He removed his hands from her and released her wrists. He turned her body and looked down into her eyes, his own as dark as the sky on a moonless night. "Tell me how you want me, mistress?"

Alys sank to her knees.

"Oh, God." It was somewhere between a groan and a whisper and it almost sent her spiraling into another climax.

Alys's hands shook as she unfastened his damp placket. His fingers—powerful, rough-skinned yet so very gentle, carded into her unbound hair. She shoved down his trousers and drawers in a rush, sucking in a breath when she freed him.

"Oh, my." Her words drew a low chuckle from the man attached to the remarkably thick organ. He was not so long as Gideon, or all around enormous as Silber, but he was beautifully wrought and heavy with want.

The little slit wept for her and she took his crown into her mouth and licked him clean.

His groan sent a shiver through them both. "Suck it," he growled. "And look at me while you service me."

Alys shuddered at his rough command, her thighs wet with desire as she took him deep, as Gideon had taught her to do.

"Yes," he praised, his finger stroking the stretched skin of her lips, his hips gently pumping. "Soon I'm going to give the master the sign . . . *Alys*, but before I do, I want you to know there is no other woman like you. You are perfect in every way." His eyes told her what his lips held back and Alys wished, for that moment at least, that she could love him the way he deserved. "I am very fond of his lordship," he said with a faint smile, his hips beginning to move. "I hope you shall both be good to each other." And then looked up and nodded in the direction of the peep.

-→ ♥ ←-

Some Hours Later . . .

Gideon stroked Alys's rounded belly while she lay sprawled above the covers, her skin the passion-mottled color of a well-satisfied woman.

"Darling?" he asked.

"Yes, Gideon?" she replied, her voice that of a person nearly drifting off to sleep.

"I think Jackson might be in love with you."

Her eyes opened, and her smile was sad.

"What do you think?" he asked, when it was clear she wouldn't answer.

She took his hand and brought it to her mouth, kissing his palm. "I think I'm in love with you, Gideon. You and only you."

Her words were like a balm to his raw, wanting soul. Was it bad—weak—to need her so much?

He drew the covers over both their bodies and then reached to the nightstand to snuff out the candle before he kissed her in the darkness and lay down beside her.

Perhaps it *was* weak to love her so deeply. But if that was weakness, he decided as he wrapped his body around her far smaller one, then Gideon was satisfied to be the weakest man in Britain.

About the Author

SM LaViolette has been a criminal prosecutor, college history teacher, B&B operator, dock worker, ice cream manufacturer, reader for the blind, motel maid, and bounty hunter.

Okay, so the part about being a bounty hunter is a lie.

SM does, however, know how to hypnotize a Dungeness crab, sew her own Regency Era clothing, knit a frog hat, juggle, rebuild a 1959 American Rambler, and gain control of Asia (and hold on to it) in the game of RISK.

S.M. also writes under the name Minerva Spencer

Made in the USA
Middletown, DE
10 July 2021

43913902R00198